SUNBLIND

Rachelle -

Enjoy!

Michael

Books by Michael Griffo

The Archangel Academy
UNNATURAL
UNWELCOME
UNAFRAID

The Darkborn Legacy
MOONGLOW
SUNBLIND

Published by Kensington Publishing Corporation

SUNBLIND

THE DARKBORN LEGACY

MICHAEL GRIFFO

KENSINGTON PUBLISHING CORP.
www.kensingtonbooks.com

K TEEN BOOKS are published by

Kensington Publishing Corp.
119 West 40th Street
New York, NY 10018

All Kensington titles, imprints, and distributed lines are available at special quantity discounts for bulk purchases for sales promotion, premiums, fund-raising, and educational or institutional use.

Special book excerpts or customized printings can also be created to fit specific needs. For details, write or phone the office of the Kensington Special Sales Manager: Kensington Publishing Corp., 119 West 40th Street, New York, NY 10018. Attn. Special Sales Department. Phone: 1-800-221-2647.

Kensington and the K logo Reg. U.S. Pat. & TM Off.
K Teen is a trademark of Kensington Publishing Corp.

ISBN-13: 978-0-7582-8074-9
ISBN-10: 0-7582-8074-2
First Kensington Trade Paperback Printing: September 2013

eISBN-13: 978-0-7582-8075-6
eISBN-10: 0-7582-8075-0
First Kensington Trade Paperback Printing: September 2013

10 9 8 7 6 5 4 3 2 1

Printed in the United States of America

For Heather and Kirsten—
Mother, daughter, groupies.

Acknowledgments

As always, I must say a big "thank you" to my agent, Evan Marshall, and to my editor, John Scognamiglio—it's hard to believe this is our seventh journey together!

Special thanks to the Kensington copy editors for keeping me on the grammatical "straight and narrow," and the art department for, once again, creating a gorgeous cover.

Part 1

The morning comes, the moonglow fades
Replaced by what the night forbade.

A ruthless light that reveals the worst
Of what I am—
A blessed curse.

Part 1

Prologue

Which came first, the wolf or the girl?

That's the question I've started to ask myself these past few months, especially in the moments right before I transform. Right before my blood turns to fire inside my veins and starts to burn my arms. Just as my legs break and my knees point in the wrong direction, just as I see my skin disappear underneath a cloak of red fur. It should be an easy question to answer. The girl came first, and sixteen years later the wolf showed up. But that's not really the truth. The wolf was conceived long before the girl was born, long before the girl's father even thought of having a child. So doesn't that make the girl an afterthought? Doesn't that put her in second place behind the wolf? A subset instead of the whole package, or even some kind of weird descendant of the wolf spirit? I thought it was an easy question, but the more I think about it, I realize it isn't. And now, quite frankly, I don't care. Because right now I'm hungry.

Saliva drips from my mouth like thick water oozing out of a leaky faucet. A low, constant growl drones out of me like metal scraping against stone. There's a dull ache in my empty stomach that needs to be filled, and it needs to be filled now.

I'm trying to control the hunger, keep it from consuming me so I can still be in control, so I can remain languid, but ready to strike. My razor-sharp teeth are exposed and my blue-gray eyes alert, but my soft, red fur ripples in the warm breeze, and my body sways gently with every step I take. Could be out for a stroll, could be out for a hunt, no one can tell. But one thing is clear: Underneath the silver glow of the full moon my body looks nothing like that of the girl I was and everything like the thing I've become. A wolf. A wolf that desperately needs to feed.

The problem is, at this very moment, I'm the one who's being hunted.

Behind me are sounds, sounds that shouldn't be heard at this time of night and definitely not in the middle of the woods. These aren't sounds from nature; they're human. Well, part human, because the sounds I hear are coming from one very sick and demented and vengeful woman.

Luba.

When I whip my head around, keeping my snout low to the ground, I can see her right in front of me. I can see her wrinkled face, the skin so pale and thin it looks like it could be peeled away, and her jet-black hair, long and straight, as lifeless as her eyes.

I can hear her laughing, her voice rough and childish and foul, echoing all around me. Instead of dying out the farther it gets from its source, her laughter grows louder until it shatters the peaceful quiet of the night. It's a sound that makes me ill.

There she is. She's standing before me, her body emaciated, her white hospital gown lifting in the wind to expose bony, scarred knees, her spindly fingers pressed against her chapped lips that form a gruesome smile. I can feel my heart beat faster; I can feel my empty stomach churn, because when I look at Luba, it's like looking in the mirror. We're completely different, and yet we're the same. We both violate the laws of nature. We're both creatures that do not belong in the world. We're wrong, we shouldn't exist, and yet here we are.

Or are we?

I blink my eyes and Luba's gone. Twisting my head to the left and the right, I scour the darkness, but can't find her. Is she hiding? Was she ever here in the first place? Have I started to hallucinate?! Maybe. Who knows? She's not in front of me; she never was. I must have imagined her presence. But she is close by. I know that because I can smell her.

Her anger fills my nostrils like the smell of dead flesh baking in the sun. I follow my instinct and start to move away from the smell, because her anger is stronger than ever before, and now it's mixed with another emotion that I never expected I'd sense from her—fear.

Why is Luba afraid of *me*? She's never been afraid before; she's always been confident and vicious and proud. What's changed to make her become fearful? I wish I could waste time trying to figure that out, but I can't, because anger mixed with fear is a dangerous combination that makes people do crazy things. And when that mixture of emotions lies within the heart of someone as evil as Luba, dangerous can quickly become deadly.

My slow gait turns into a run, and I make sure to avoid breaking twigs with my paws or overturning rocks. I need to be quiet; I need to remain undetected. I jump over a small puddle filled with rainwater and have to swerve quickly to the right to avoid disrupting a small pyramid of crushed beer cans. The litter is evidence that humans have been here, which means I can never assume the woods are safe. Crouching, I crawl under a spray of low-hanging branches, their mass of leaves tickling my fur as I pass through, and come out to stand on the edge of a clearing. A wide, flat expanse of lush, green grass decorated with wildflowers in colors that brighten the night—yellow and pink and orange—colors that turn the earth into a galaxy of vibrant stars. It's a beautiful sight. But one that offers no protection.

How wonderful would it be to lie in this field for a moment, let the coolness pierce through my fur and put out the fire I can feel raging inside of me? But even just a moment is too long to hesitate, to let down my guard. Even just a moment will surely get me killed, especially when Luba's right behind me.

But why is she hunting me? And why does her hatred for me now contain fear? I look up, and it's almost as if the full moon is pulsating, trying to communicate with me in some sort of intergalactic Morse code, telling me to use my natural instinct to make sense of a situation that doesn't seem to contain logic. I force myself to hold still, to not breathe, to do nothing but accept the full moon's message. It's a complete waste of time! All I can feel is the painful ache that's returned to my stomach. And then all I smell is blood.

The stench is so glorious I open my mouth to howl, to announce to whomever or whatever is bleeding that I'm coming to feed, but my howl turns into silence. The wolf wants to cry; the girl is cautious. Even though the wolf wants to make a sound, the girl knows that it will only help Luba discover the location of her prey. It's the perfect illustration of how the wolf and the girl have learned to coexist.

The other thing I've learned is that if I ignore the hunger, there are consequences. The violence and aggression and primal urges I feel as a wolf spill over into my human form after the transformation reverses itself if I don't indulge in wolfen hunger when the feeling overcomes me like it's doing right now. So while I can hear and smell and sense Luba is approaching, and I know I should keep running, I can't. The hunger pains have become more intense, as if a sharp-edged claw is burrowing through my skin from the inside out. I have no choice; I must feed.

And only a few feet away is my meal.

A mound of fur and blood. A family of rabbits all huddled together, clinging to one another as if they're sleeping and trying to keep warm. Except this family is dead and lifeless and bloody. Such a beautiful sight.

A string of saliva drips from one fang and is lifted into the air by my hot, anxious breath. The unmoving bodies are pulling me closer to them as if they're magnets and I'm a piece of steel. I am unable to resist, powerless to do anything else but take one step toward the bloody mound and then another and another. When I'm a foot away, I regain some self-control and begin to circle the carcasses, just so I can look at the heavenly display from all sides, my long tongue dripping wet and gliding over my teeth. Halfway around I can wait no longer. The hell with Luba! Right now quenching my hunger is more important than guaranteeing my survival.

I lunge forward, but instead of burying my teeth into flesh and bone and blood, I crash into something hard and fall back. I look up, and separating me from my meal is a yellow wall. No, not a real wall, but a huge block made up of what looks like golden marble. Furious, I ram my body into it again, my front paws colliding into the barrier with all my might, only to careen back again, my left side slamming into the ground.

Dazed, I shake my head, strings of spit whipping into my snout and my eyes. What the hell is going on?! I turn toward the glowing wall, and my lips form a sneer as a growl escapes from my body. The wall starts to glow with a yellow light, growing brighter by the second, and I try to keep my eyes open, try to see what's creating this display, but the light is blinding. For a few moments darkness replaces the light, as if they're joined together, and I can't see a thing. I'm consumed by blackness, utterly alone and utterly afraid.

Until Jess appears.

The yellow wall melts into a thin vertical line that hangs in the air, slicing into the dark night, and then bursts open like a fireworks display, shooting sparks into the sky that twinkle and fall and combine to create something unimaginable—an Amaterasu Omikami, a legendary Japanese sun goddess. Or simply the new person that Jess has become. The supernatural being that she became after I killed her. And now I want to kill her again.

What the hell are you doing?!

"Saving your life," Jess replies to my silent cry.

By interrupting my meal?! By making me go crazy with hunger?!

Ignoring my unspoken comments, Jess flicks her wrist, and a piece of sunshine flies into the air. I watch it twist and turn and hover for a second over the dead rabbit family until it falls on top of them, dousing them in golden light so they look as if they're bathing in honey. The light is immediately extinguished when I hear a loud crash that makes me jump back. The rabbits were huddled together not because they had been sleeping when they were killed; they were arranged that way so they could conceal a bear trap.

Oh my God, you really did save my life!

Floating several inches above the ground, Jess smiles at me. "I'd say you'll have to do the same for me one day, but it's a little late for that."

Involuntarily I bow my head and scrape the dirt with my front paw. I know Jess doesn't blame me for her death, but still, I am the reason she's dead. I tug at the earth one more time, sending clumps of dirt into the air. My stomach hurts, my head hurts, and now my heart hurts. Enough! I don't have time for this; I don't have time for reflection; I have to focus on the matter at hand—someone has gone to a lot of trouble to try and lure me to my death, and that someone has got to be Luba.

But why? She has amazing powers of her own; she doesn't need to resort to something so basic. Unless, of course, she wants to make it look like it was an accident and not the result of some sick, demonic intervention. Get rid of me and keep her secret safe. Yes, that's got to be it!

"Wrong."

I'm not sure what's more annoying—being contradicted or seeing Jess's smirk.

I'm not wrong. This is a trap!

Sitting cross-legged, but still several inches above the ground, Jess smiles at me. She extends her arm to touch my fur, which I know she loves to play with, but I'm not in the mood to be caressed so I flinch, which only makes Jess roll her eyes at me. Now we're even; we're both annoyed with each other.

"Yes, it is a trap," Jess relents. "But no, Luba wasn't the one who set it."

It takes a second for the reality of Jess's statement to sink in.

If Luba didn't set the trap, that means she has help; she isn't working alone.

"Well . . . kind of," Jess replies cryptically.

Once again I'm reminded that in Jess's current superior state she is still limited, and she can't tell me everything that she knows. She's bound to a different set of rules that even she doesn't completely understand. But I've learned that you don't have to uncover the answer to something to know the truth. I may not know who's working with Luba, but I do know that if Jess hadn't intervened, I'd be dead right now, split into two separate pieces by that bear trap.

Thank you.

"Don't thank me yet," Jess says, gazing behind me. "Luba isn't your only enemy."

What?!

I turn around, and I don't see anything, but the noises I heard earlier are back, and they're getting louder. I have no idea what's going on, but now I'm the one who's afraid.

"People are scared, Dom," Jess explains. "And when people are scared, they act all jerktastic."

I want Jess to tell me more. I want her to explain what she means, but there's no time left; the sounds are getting louder with every second. I'm about to find out just who my enemy is.

"The trap is right up here!"

Barnaby!!

The voice is unmistakable; it belongs to my brother. I am frozen in my spot; the only thing I can do is take a deep breath. The smell I thought belonged to Luba is my brother's, and it's the ripe mixture of anger and hatred and fear. He's the one who's hunting me; he's the one who set this trap; he's the one who wants me dead. The air around my throat seems to want to strangle me. Luba doesn't want to kill me; my brother does.

"Get behind me!"

Lost in my own thoughts, I can't respond to Jess's command.

"Seriously, Dominy, do I have to do everything myself?!"

Jess disappears into the night, and I'm left alone. Suddenly the air is cold, but it's not actually the air; it's me. It's like the opposite of when I transform; my blood has turned to ice and has stopped flowing through my veins. In the distance I can see shadows approaching and then a light. My brother is at the front of a group, holding a torch like the leader of some modern-day witch hunt. Except the witch is a wolf and the wolf is me. I want to run; I want to get as far away as I possibly can, find somewhere safe to hide, but I can't. And anyway, where can I go when so many people are hunting for me?

Maybe this is my destiny: to die at my brother's hand like my father was supposed to die by mine. But I'm not ready to die! I'm not ready to give up! Thankfully, Jess agrees with me.

Just as Barnaby comes into plain sight, Jess appears in front of me and spreads her arms. From her fingertips a wall of flames erupts, and the sun goddess is replaced by the beginning of a forest fire. The flames spread out several feet on both sides of me and then curve inward as they start to form a circle. In a matter of seconds I'm going to be surrounded by hot, raging fire. Instinctively, I want to break free before I'm burned to death, and my paws start to dig at the ground, a high-pitched whimper joining the chorus of crackling flames. Only two feet remain open behind me; if I don't move now I'm going to be engulfed, and there won't be any escape. Crouching low to the earth, I position my body to leap forward, but before I can fly into the air, Jess's voice slams into my ears.

Trust me!

The two separate ends of the line of flame connect and a circular wall is created; there's no longer any way to escape unless I want to be burned alive. But wait.... Why can't I feel any heat? Because the flames aren't threatening to me. They're not even flames at all; they're an illusion! Once again, Jess is saving my life. And confusing my brother and his fellow witch-hunters stuck on the other side of the wall.

"It's a fire!"

But that isn't my brother's voice; it's Louis's! Why in the world is he helping my brother hunt me down? Or hunting this animal that they think is terrorizing the town? He's the chief of police, not a vigilante! Could this be the only way he could think of to avenge the death of his best friend, my father? Could they have figured out that the killings are all connected to the full moon? It doesn't matter; what matters is that if they find me, they won't know it's me. They'll think they've found the wild animal that needs to be killed, its dead body put on display to show the rest of the town that the horror has finally come to an end. Louis won't know that what he's looking at, what he wants to kill, is Mason Robineau's daughter, the girl he's agreed to raise as his own child. He'll only think he's looking at a murderer that needs to be put to death.

The voices are louder now and pull me from my thoughts, which are completely useless anyway. I don't recognize who is shouting; it could be a neighbor, a teacher, anyone who's known me my entire life. But whoever they are, they're just as startled by the sudden, unexpected fire and just as angry that it has interrupted their outing. Once again, if it weren't for Jess, I'd probably be dead.

"Go back to town and get Tourtelot!" Louis screams.

I know that name. Nathan Tourtelot is the fire chief.

"Tell him there's a fire," Louis commands. "He's got to put it out before it gets out of control."

Louis's voice is different from the others. Yes, it contains a hint of fear, but close behind the fear is the air of authority. After years of sitting back, following my father's command, and acting as if he didn't have a decisive bone in his body, Louis has started to go through his own transformation. He's becoming a leader. Which means, to me anyway, that he's very much like Luba. Another nemesis I need to be wary of.

But I can't help feeling that he's also like my father. Protective and strong and courageous. All he's trying to do is keep his family and his town safe, which is exactly what my father tried to do his entire life. Wherever my father is, I know that he's proud of his friend. He may, however, feel a bit differently about his son.

"Look!" Barnaby cries.

Taking a step back, I lower my snout, thinking that this in some way will shield me from my brother's stare. But I have nothing to worry about; Jess's flames are impenetrable. And besides, he's not looking at me; he's found something else even more interesting.

"The trap is shut!" he tells the crowd. "The thing was here!"

Thing?! The word fills me with rage, and if I weren't being held prisoner by Jess's flames, I don't think I'd be able to restrain myself; I'd reveal myself to my brother and Louis and the entire town, show them I'm not a thing! I'm a *werewolf!* It isn't something I chose to be; it isn't something I ever imagined I'd become; but it's what I am! But then I realize with heartbreaking clarity that even if Barnaby and the others knew what I was, knew what I have been forced to become, it might not change their minds. They might not be able to separate the wolf from the girl, and they might still want me dead.

"We have to split up," Louis orders. "Half of you go that way; the rest follow me."

I have no idea which directions they're heading into, but I can hear them leave, not retreating, but moving closer to what they hope will be victory. When the flames around me recede, I don't have to look up; I know that we're alone. My enemies have gone, and it's just Jess and me.

"Tonight's special-effects display was brought to you by the letter O for Omikami," Jess explains. "Just something I've been working on for a while to, you know, test the limits of my skill set."

I nod my head in gratitude, too exhausted and shocked and confused to respond.

"We're very much the same, you and I," she adds.

Looking at her splendid beauty, I have no idea what she's talking about.

"We're both works in progress," she says, one hand running its fingers through my fur. "We're both finding our places in this world and in our new selves."

Impatiently, I nod my head. Not because I don't agree with Jess or want to hear what she has to say, but because the hunger has returned. Licking my lips, I walk toward the dead rabbits, unable to contain my joy.

"And that, Dominysan, is my cue to leave," Jess says. "I love you, but I cannot watch you eat. It is beyond gross."

Before I can say good-bye, Jess disappears, taking her sunshine with her and leaving me alone in the glow of the moon. The truth, however, is that I'm never alone. I'm never just me. For the rest of my life I'm destined to have a companion, a connection. Like darkness and light, like the sun and the moon, the wolf and the girl will never be separated.

So which came first, the wolf or the girl?

It doesn't really matter, because it looks like they're both here to stay.

Chapter 1

The first day of school. A time to reconnect with friends you haven't seen all summer long, a time to ponder which new clubs and sports you should join, a time to promise yourself that this is the year you'll finally get that 4.0 GPA. For me, it's a time to figure out which one of my fellow classmates wants me dead.

Munching on a trans-fat-free French fry that tastes more like imported cardboard than France's most delicious import, I scour the lunchroom, looking like an eyewitness trying to pick out a criminal in a lineup through a one-way window in a police station. My stare is focused, yet indifferent. Who could be the guilty party? Could it be Rayna Delgado? She's always been jealous of my red hair. Once in eighth grade she dyed her own black hair to match mine and turned out looking like Ronald McDonald's younger, but way uglier, sister. Luckily for her it was a few days before Halloween, so the whole school thought she was getting a jump start on the festivities. I knew better.

It could also be The Dandruff King himself, Danny Klausman, if he somehow found out that I'm the one who dubbed him The Dandruff King. I can't imagine he would interpret that nickname as a term of endearment. Either of them could have been part of last night's witch hunt, but it could have been anyone at school for that matter. Since I was hidden by Jess's wall of flames, I couldn't see who obtained a membership. Other than Barnaby and Louis, whose voices I recognized, I have no idea who the town vigilantes are. Scratch that! A third member just sauntered into the lunchroom—Jody Buell. He's my brother's best friend and Siammate—I call him that because he and my brother are joined at the hip. If Barnaby was playing teenage avenger, guaranteed that Jody was his superhero sidekick.

Incredible how one night can change everything. Yesterday, most of these kids were my friends; today I look at them with a much more cynical eye. I mean, I know that high school can sometimes be a battleground, with everyone jockeying for the top spot, but I never got caught in the crossfire. I'm not the prettiest or the most popular or the smartest, but at Weeping Water High School—Two W to us locals—I'm way closer to the top spot in each category than to the bottom. Translation: I've never had to work that hard to be liked by my fellow classmates or, honestly, most of my teachers. It doesn't hurt that my father was the chief of police and since his death I've effectively been ordained an orphan, because having a mother who's in a coma doesn't really qualify as having a full-time mom. So I'm used to being respected and pitied; being loathed and wished dead is a totally new experience for me.

The fact that people want the wolf—or whatever they think is turning our town into the setting for some new horror movie—dead, and not me—Dominy—doesn't soften the blow either, because like I said it's getting increasingly harder to separate the two. It isn't like in the beginning when I couldn't remember anything from when I was a wolf after I transformed back, when the lives of the wolf and the girl were skew lines. Now our lives intersect. I remember most everything; some memories are clearer than others, but mainly the transformations are mentally seamless. So if they want the wolf dead, I can't help but take it personally and feel as if they want me dead too.

Unable to shake the bothersome thought from my head, I look around the cafeteria again to examine who my potential enemies could be. Who was carrying a torch last night with my brother? They all look like they're more interested in their franks 'n' beans or their conversations, but I know better. I know that behind those faces, whether they're filled with acne or animation or apathy, there exist Lubaphiles. They may not even realize that they're part of Psycho Squaw's army; they may never have heard of the crazy witch, but they're doing her bidding all the same. And how ironic is it that her two right-hand men appear to be my brother and my guardian? I guess that should be her right- and left-hand men? Doesn't matter. Without her even formulating a strategy, my adversary is closing in on me.

Because Jess is right; people act jerktastically when they're scared. I just have to make sure their fear doesn't get me killed. And one of the best ways to thwart an enemy's plan is to make sure he knows his plan is no longer secret. So I need to tell him. Or at least tell his daughter.

"I know your father is trying to kill me," I announce before Arla even places her tray on the lunch table.

Her reaction is as smooth as her complexion. Obviously, being my friend and now my sort-of stepsister has taught Arla to expect the unexpected and to take outlandish comments in stride.

"I thought his meatloaf the other night was really good," she replies, sitting down across from me. "The chipotle in the gravy gave it some kick."

"I'm not talking about his meatloaf, which *was* really good, by the way," I say. "I'm talking about the vigilante crusade he was on last night."

Her forehead crinkles like one of my French fries. "Sister-friend," she says. "I have no idea what your mouth is yakking on about."

I stare at Arla and try hard not to laugh. It's not that I find our conversation hilarious, but considering she's wearing a 1950s-style Junior Miss platinum blond wig in honor of the fact that we are now in our junior year and at the same time adopting a tone of voice that is more appropriate to one of those 1970s blaxploitation films, she's quite funny. Yup, the more I get to know Arla, the more I realize she's filled with contradictions. Just like me.

"Clearly your dad's learned how to be clandestine," I suggest.

"Unlike you," Arla replies, scooping up a spoonful of beans.

"What do you mean?" I ask.

"You put my father, kill, and clandestine all into the same conversation," she states. "Not exactly subtle."

I take a deep breath, because I realize what I'm about to say is less bizarre than it is a tad-bit accusatory. "Well, I'm, um, pretty sure your dad is the lead operative in a clandestine plot to rid Weeping Water of its first-ever serial killer," I speed-say. "A.k.a. me."

As I fill Arla in on last night's events, she slowly pays more attention to me than to her food, a clear sign that her father's and my brother's late-night antics are news to her.

"That's a twisted way for them to bond," she offers.

"I wish it were more twisted than it appears, but it isn't," I explain. "They both share the same goal—to avenge my father's death."

Five streaks of blue cotton candy whip through the air. They're Arla's fingernails—the same color as her headband—as she waves her hand in the air as if to swipe away the unspoken thought that hovers between us. Grumbling, she responds, "But you didn't kill your dad."

"They don't know that," I reply, trying hard to keep my voice quiet and not shout my innocence to the world. "They think there's a serial-killing animal on the loose."

"We've been through this before, Dominy. You are not a serial killer!" Arla protests a bit too loudly for my comfort zone.

"Could we please use our inside voices?" I ask. "Considering we are inside."

"Sorry," she says, holding up her hand so the cotton candy blue is replaced with the dark caramel of her skin. "But that comment is ridiculous, redundant, and regressive. You're a victim too."

It's nice to hear that Arla doesn't think I'm a candidate for *America's Most Wanted*, but it also rings false. She knows exactly what I am and what I've done, and it's bad enough that I have to hide from the world; I don't want to feel that I have to hide from my friends.

"Arla, come on," I start. "I may not be like that guy, who killed kids while wearing a clown suit, but I *have* killed, and come to think of it I have my own disguise so, okay, maybe me and clown face aren't siblings, but we're kind of distant cousins."

She whips off her plastic headband so fiercely, I almost think that Arla is going to use it as a deadly weapon, but she's merely readjusting her accessory. She isn't, however, readjusting her conviction.

"The guy in the clown suit and every other serial killer you want to bring up committed premeditated murder," Arla says, sounding very much like the daughter of the new chief of police. "You, on the other hand, acted while under meditation."

I committed murder while practicing yoga? "I'm not following you."

"You were under a spell," she clarifies. "When you killed Jess and that vagrant, you weren't in control of yourself;

Luba and the wolf spirit were. There is absolutely no way that you can be categorized as a serial killer or a killer of any kind."

Tell that to the torch-bearing group who almost captured me last night. "My ears hear what you're saying," I reply, "But . . ."

"Keep your buts out of it," Arla interrupts. "You know I'm right. You are not a killer, because you were not born to kill."

Automatically, I tilt my head, and my nose points downward, toward the floor. It's a peculiar move, a reflex, and it reminds me of how the wolf responds when it's in an uncomfortable situation. I don't want to get all philosophical, because more than ever I only want to grab hold of simple, tangible concepts, but Arla's comment has triggered something that's a bit more complicated.

If the wolf did indeed come first, which I'm beginning to think is a possibility, doesn't that mean that I *was* born to kill? That's what wolves do, isn't it? Sometimes they kill out of a necessity to feed, but sometimes they do it maliciously, out of an innate desire to be violent.

"Honestly, Arla," I whisper, my voice soft so maybe I won't hear my own words. "I'm thinking that maybe I was."

I can tell by how quickly Arla replies that she responds by reflex too. She has an innate desire to protect her friend.

"Dom, that isn't true!" she protests. "You weren't born as a result of Luba's curse; you were born in spite of it."

But I wasn't born alone.

"I was also born with the wolf as my invisible twin," I remind her. "Since the moment I was conceived, the wolf has been living inside of me, so doesn't that mean I was destined to kill?"

This time when Arla opens her mouth reflex falters, no words follow the motion. Which makes sense, because how could they? What could she possibly say when we both know

I'm right? I can see her embarrassment; I can practically cut it with the flimsy plastic knife I'm holding. Arla isn't moving, but she's struggling; she wants to say something to contradict the truth she can't conceal in her eyes, but she's not a natural-born liar like I'm a natural-born killer, so she remains silent.

Feeling bad, I turn away. I stare at the new "back to school" posters that line the walls of the cafeteria. *Play Hard, Work Harder. Two W's Are Better Than One—Get A Study Partner.* And my personal favorite, because it makes education fashionable: *School Spirit Is The New Black.* My preoccupation with the school's new in-house marketing campaign gives Arla enough time to collect herself so she can rack her brains and think of a better topic of conversation. Turns out she doesn't have to. Archie speaks for her.

"Love the wig, Arla," he exclaims. "Hate the face, Dom."

Forcing a smile that will hopefully brighten my expression, I look up from the table and into Archie's concerned face. Over the summer, Archie cut his hair really short and discovered some hair gel called Brylcreem that pre-metrosexuals used in the fifties. For the time being he's parting his hair on the left side and combing it over and back, so there's a little wave on top that makes his white hair look like a snowdrift. When he sits down next to Arla, I get the feeling that the two of them are getting ready to go to a sock hop.

"Sorry, Archie," I say. "Arla and I went a little emo for a momo."

His violet eyes stare at me like two beautiful flowers, soft and delicate, but firmly rooted in the ground. "Any chance your convo was about last night's skirmish?"

"You heard!" Arla and I shout at the same time.

Archie pauses not because he's taken aback, but because he just shoved half a hot dog into his mouth. Mid-chew, he replies, "It hasn't gone viral yet, but I overheard Jody Buell bragging about his exploits to the rifle squad."

"I knew he was involved!" I shout, ignoring my own inside-voice mandate.

"He does realize their rifles can't carry ammo, right?" Archie asks. "'Cause it sounded like he was trying to recruit new members to join his posse."

"Who cares if he recruits the entire ROTC," Arla adds. "Only silver bullets can hurt Dom; regular bullets bounce right off."

"Hmm, someone's been brushing up on her knowledge of mythical creatures," I say.

"Wikipedia does devote several pages to werewolves," Arla admits, proving me right.

But when Archie speaks, it's evident that he's a more astute student in the study of all things werewolf.

"Miss Robineau?" Mr. Angevene begins. "How were the townspeople chasing you if you were snuggled up all snuggly in your cage?"

I was wondering how long it was going to take before I got busted.

"Oh my God, Dom!" Arla shouts, then forces her voice to lapse into a whisper. "Why weren't you in your cage last night? Why were you out gallivanting all throughout town? And why is a smart girl like me missing these important bits of information?"

"Because you're spending too much time in hair and makeup," Archie jokes. "And searching Wikipedia when you should be paying attention to the wolf living under your own roof who's gallivanting all around town."

I focus on my lunch even though it's suddenly become thoroughly unappetizing. "Gallivanting is really an unfair assessment," I mumble. "It was more like a reconnaissance."

Archie's violet eyes retain their beauty, but they lose a little bit of their sympathy. "You don't even know what reconnaissance means," he accuses.

"I do too!"

"Define?" Archie challenges.

Suddenly I'm twelve years old again, and I'm in front of Miss Kelleher's class, and I have to explain the difference between *i.e.* and *e.g.* I say to Archie what I finally said to Miss Kelleher. "May I be dismissed because I really have to pee?"

"Cross your legs," Archie answers back, which, ironically, is the exact same thing Miss Kelleher told me.

Ignoring both of us, Arla backtracks. "Dom, what were you doing out of your cage?" she asks. "I thought that nonsense with Luba unlocking it had stopped?"

There's no way I can tell them the truth; they won't understand. Involuntarily, my mind races back to my past again, and I decide to give Arla the same answer I gave Miss Kelleher. The only difference is that back then it was the truth, now it's a lie. "I don't know."

Archie, for one, isn't buying it. "I thought you said you now remember everything about your transformations?"

"*Most* everything," I say confidently, because I'm finally speaking the truth. "Not every tiny, micro-cific detail about the entire night."

Then I do something I don't like to do, something that doesn't make me feel proud, but I concoct yet another lie. This time, it's one that plays upon their sympathies.

"Barnaby probably confided in Luba about what he and Louis were going to do," I start. "And she seized the opportunity to make the night a victory for them by unlocking my cage again."

This does the trick; I can see it in their eyes. They feel bad, ashamed for verbally attacking me when just last night my brother, Arla's father, and their band of merry avengers were hoping to attack me physically. My, um, *fabrication* of last night's events has served its purpose: Arla and Archie think I'm telling the truth, so they're embarrassed when I'm the one who should be ashamed.

"Kind of gives new meaning to the word *awkward*,"

Archie says, now playing with his food instead of eating it. "What with your new sister's father trying to kill you."

"My dad isn't trying to kill Dominy," Arla objects. "Per se."

"Is that French?" Archie asks.

This time Arla doesn't ignore Archie's comment, only his tone. "Yes, it means that my father wouldn't be spearheading the witch hunt if he knew the witch was Dominy."

"Dominy is definitely not a witch."

Three heads snap in the same direction, and we see Nadine standing at the end of the lunch table looking like a very perturbed hall monitor. Draped over her de rigueur Two W polo, she's wearing a pink cardigan sweater that's held together by a jeweled clasp in shimmering sapphire. I'm a little surprised by Nadine's choice of accessory since a) her sweater is pushing the school wardrobe policy, b) normally she's a by-the-books kind of girl, not an envelope pusher, and most important, c) she's not a fashion trendsetter. Maybe it's simply that everybody got the memo that the first day of school was Retro Day except me.

That's not the only surprise. Even though the decibel level in the cafeteria is at an all-time high, since everyone is catching up with the exciting things they did on their summer vacations, we were speaking in really low whispers in case someone decided to listen in to our conversation. Obviously we need to take a remedial class in Whispering: 101 to fine-tune our skills, since Nadine had no problem overhearing us. And by the way she's glaring at us, it's obvious, though unreasonable, that she doesn't like what she's heard.

Sitting in the seat next to Archie, Nadine is gripping her lunch tray tightly, and I can hear her white sneakers squeak underneath the table. I'm not sure if she's nervous or if she has that weird restless-leg syndrome disease that I personally thought was a *Saturday Night Live* skit when I first saw the commercial. Or more likely, having to deal with my affliction on top of all the nutcases she has to work with at The Retreat is finally getting to her.

"Dominy isn't a witch; she's a werewolf," Nadine explains unnecessarily. "There is a huge difference."

"And thank God for that!" Arla exclaims. "Witches are evil."

Slowly, Nadine turns to look at Arla as if she's getting ready to tell off a guy who's just made a pass at her even though I don't think Nadine has had any experience in that department.

"Does the name Glinda the good witch ring a bell?" Nadine asks, in a smug, patronizing voice.

Pointing a forkful of chocolate cake in Nadine's direction, Archie is still playing with his food, but this time it's because he's excited, not embarrassed. "I *j'adore* Glinda!" he cries, trying to sound as French as Arla. "I mean how can you not *j'adore* someone who travels by bubble?!"

My friend's got a point that I can't argue with, but my other friend wants to take her point and burst Archie's bubble.

"Glinda is just as evil as the Wicked Witch of the West and every other spell-casting, hook-nosed, demon-worshipping witch in real life and on the printed page!" Arla sermonizes. "In fact she's worse!"

Judging by the ominous way Nadine is now glaring at Arla, she clearly finds Arla's hypothesis incomprehensible. I would be alarmed if Archie didn't share Nadine's opinion.

"How is Glinda worse?!" Archie asks, chocolate cake spewing out of his mouth. "She's Glinda . . . the *good!* It's right there in her name."

"Wrong!" Arla cries. "She should be Glinda the apathetic and passive aggressive."

I have no idea what Arla is talking about, but I'm grateful that Witchgate has steered the conversation away from Cagegate.

"Arla, you're very pretty," Nadine says, even more condescendingly than before. "But you sound like an idiot."

Dumb move, Nadine. Arla's a fashionista and an athlete, but first and foremost she's a straight A student and prides herself on being intelligent. She doesn't mind if someone questions her wig choice, but she gets very defensive when anyone questions her thought process.

"Are you going to sit there and tell me that Glinda's modus operandi wasn't to have Dorothy do her bidding and kill the Wicked Witch of the West for her?" Arla asks.

The question is both so insightful and so absurd that none of us can respond or rebut.

"Glinda could have told Dorothy to click her heels three times and go home upon Kansas Girl's arrival in Oz, despite her claims that such an easy resolution would've been met with disbelief," Arla rants. "But noooooo, Glinda instructed her to follow the yellow brick road, which she knew would lead Dorothy to the faux wizard, who she knew would ask Dorothy and her cronies to bring back the witch's broom, which they could only do if they killed her." Arla stops only because she has to catch her breath.

"I hope you're satisfied!" Archie cries again. "You've totally ruined it for me. Now I can see right through Glinda's bubble."

"And what you can see, Archibald," Arla replies, "is that all witches are evil."

"And werewolves aren't?"

Nadine's question is very simple, but also very severe. Not to mention direct and cruel and honest, which, I'm learning, is *Nadine's* modus operandi. Where Arla and Archie try to sugarcoat my situation, Nadine sprinkles salt into the wound. Just a pinch, but just enough. She may not always say what I want to hear, but she always says things that I need to hear.

"Yes, Nadine, they are," I answer.

"No, they aren't!" Arla and Archie reply a second later in my defense.

"No, she's right, werewolves are evil." I add, "*If* they don't learn to control their instincts."

Arla and Archie appear to be surprised by my comment; Nadine is intrigued.

"And you're learning to control yours?" she asks.

I don't even have to look at their faces to know that Archie and Arla are shocked and consider Nadine's question and tone unacceptable and harsh. I find it a relief. How wonderful to have found someone who, like Jess, will always speak the truth. Someone who will always confront me so I can confront my own reality. Without getting too sentimental, her arrival in my life is a godsend.

"I am, Nadine," I admit. "I'm not all the way there yet, don't know if I'll ever be able to control such primal urges, but I'm getting better at being the stronger one in this inter-species relationship."

When Nadine smiles, her face softens and her body relaxes. Maybe it's an East Coast thing, but she really is high-strung and always takes longer to calm down than the rest of us. Too bad, because when she lets down her guard she's pretty. Even if she's still pretty blunt.

"So nothing against your father, Arla," Nadine starts, "but how in the world did he even figure out that last night was a good night for hunting?"

"That's something else I missed!" Arla shouts, pounding her fist on the lunch table. "Maybe I'm not as smart as I think I am?"

"No, maybe your dad isn't as non-smart as we all think he is," I say. "He probably did his detective thing, connected the dots, and realized all the killings took place on nights when there was a full moon."

One cotton-candy-colored fingernail moves back and forth in the air. "That doesn't make sense," Arla remarks.

"Sure it does," Archie continues. "Your dad is Creole, so

he not only has a lot of mixed races in his blood, he's got superstition too."

Shaking her head and scrunching up her face, Arla isn't buying Archie's logic either. "My father is Creole in the kitchen, but he's no Sherlock on the clock," she starts. "I really don't think this is something he would've deduced on his own."

"But he's desperate to solve the murders," I say.

I feel a hand on mine; it's Arla's. When she continues speaking, her voice is as soft as her touch.

"With your dad being one of the victims, my father is too close to the situation to think clearly," she whisper-states. "Plus, he wants to solve this case so badly he wouldn't act on such a bizarre clue on his own for fear of being ridiculed. No, someone else must have convinced him that the full moon holds the key."

So who is Louis's confidante? Who is his very own Iago? Before I can suggest my brother as a prime candidate, I feel a gentle breeze, like someone blowing warm air across my earlobe. It's a wonderful feeling, soft, like the flutter of a butterfly's wings.

I look up, and the good feeling is crushed, replaced with the icy sensation of dread, because standing in the archway to the cafeteria is Napoleon. When he sees me staring at him, he turns and flutters away. He might have fled, but the dreadful feeling remains.

Chapter 2

Just like a wolf I control my primitive urges and keep silent. I don't throw Napoleon's name into the suspect bin for group discussion. I keep my suspicions to myself. But very quickly I regret my decision. A wolf may be a very patient animal; a sixteen-year-old girl not so much.

Two class periods later I'm standing in the gym wearing the standard Two W gym uniform—white T-shirt with the words Weeping Water spelled out in navy lettering and navy shorts with white piping—finding it difficult to maintain both my fashion sense and my composure. I can't do anything about my lame wardrobe, but I have got to get Nadine's attention to ask her if she thinks her brother could be Louis's informant. The problem is Miss Rolenski takes gym class very seriously, and even though it's day one of the new school year, she's already starting to prepare us for some recently implemented state-wide athletic test we have to take before the end of the semester. I guess government officials have given up trying to improve our minds and have shifted their focus onto our bodies.

She's split up the class into several groups that are supposed to be random, but were clearly organized by physical abilities. Of course Miss Ro has put me in Group A. I'm not complaining; it's just that I can't help feeling like a fraud. I've never been as naturally gifted as Arla when it comes to sports, but as a side effect of my transformations, my athletic prowess has increased dramatically. So my inclusion in this top group is a bit of a hollow victory, sort of like winning a gold medal at the Olympics because you're steroidal. Earned or not, there isn't anything I can do about my current top-tier placement without drawing extra attention to myself. Anyway, my problem isn't with Miss Ro; it's with Nadine.

Most days, Nadine shows up to gym class with a pass from Nurse Nelson allowing her to skip gym due to some undisclosed medical reason or she gets to leave school early to volunteer at The Retreat. She's one of those girls who spends more time in the bleachers during gym class than actually participating in an activity, and she has not given Miss Ro any reason to think she has mastered eye-hand coordination. The one day I need Nadine to sit on the sidelines so I can have easy access to her, she's decided to actively participate.

As expected, Miss Ro has put her in Group C, the group of the physically unfit, which is super annoying, because now Nadine and I are separated by an entire group of mediocre B-level athletes, so there's no way I can speak with her. If only Nadine considered physical skills as important as a superior intellect, if only the state didn't feel it necessary to give us yet another test to pass, and if only I hadn't tried to be Miss Congeniality and had asked Nadine about her brother when I had the chance, then I wouldn't be so pissed off.

But sometimes wolf-like patience has its benefits and opportunity falls right into your lap. Or right next to you.

After blowing on her whistle louder than necessary, Miss Ro makes the three groups form a circle around the circumference of the gym. Defying all tenets of popularity and mathematical logic, Group A winds up standing right next to Group C. It's royally unheard of, but the stars align so the Two W starlets are right next to the losers, which is exactly what I need so I can finally talk to Nadine and ask her the question that's been burning a hole in my brain since lunchtime.

Meandering to the left end of Group A, I try to catch Nadine's gaze, but she must have decided to turn over a new leaf this year, because she appears to be truly interested in physical fitness. She has to pick today of all days to pay attention to Miss Ro?! She's not looking at me, and if I didn't know better I'd say she was deliberately ignoring me. Maybe she's actually embarrassed to be in GOT-PU, the Group of the Physically Unfit, not that she knows that's what we A-listers call it. Then again she is really smart; she might have figured it out on her own.

Shaking my head I try to clear my thoughts, rid myself of my internal monologue so I can concentrate on getting Nadine to work her way over to the right side of her group, so we'll be next to each other. Leave it to The Hog to save the day.

Standing in the middle of the middle group, Gwenevere Schültzenhoggen, known to the student population as The Hog, raises her hand in the middle of Miss Ro's speech about how we need to fight obesity before obesity makes us unfit to fight. First of all, who raises their hand in gym class? Second of all, since The Hog is almost as broad as she is tall, she just has to breathe to be noticed; hand-raising is superfluous. But her father is German and her mother is Korean, so she's had a very strict upbringing; adhering to rules is in her blood.

"Miss Rolenski?"

"Yes, Gwenevere," Miss Ro replies, unable to hide her displeasure at being interrupted.

"What kind of a test is this going to be?" The Hog asks. "Qualitative or quantitative?"

"Says Quasimodo!"

Ouch! That's even more brutal than The Hog. Leave it to Rayna Delgado to make me see the error of my ways. Don't get me wrong. I don't like Rayna; she really is a superbitch, and she's made me see that I'm not that far behind. Gwen—as the girl formerly known as The Hog will henceforth be dubbed—cannot help that she inherited her father's strong, brawny, and unfortunately unfeminine German DNA. She's a good kid, and even though she's 5'11", she's got the confidence to wear high heels. For that reason alone she should have my support, and if I didn't have my own problem to solve I would come to Gwen's defense, but luckily Miss Ro is already lecturing Rayna about mutual respect, female-to-female support, and the fact that Rayna should work better at covering up her neck pimples before she makes fun of someone else.

While the rest of the class is laughing and joining in the impromptu and unorthodox girl-power assembly, I make my move.

"Nadine!" I power-whisper.

How can Nadine possibly be more interested in Gwen's plight than mine? I don't care if she doesn't know that I have a plight; she's supposed to be my friend, and friends come before the downtrodden.

"Naaaa-diiiiiiine!"

Still nothing! All she's doing is staring daggers at Rayna, who's freaking out because she swears her neck was pimple-free at the start of class and now it looks like a Jackson Pollock painting if, of course, the man only used red paint. I'd feel sorry for her if I wasn't so determined. I pull a barrette out of my hair—placed there this morning because I'm having an extra-frizzy hair day—aim, toss, and hit my target. Grabbing her shoulder, Nadine finally turns in my direction, wearing an expression that can only be described as one big scowl.

"Come here!" I order.

Bounding over to the far end of Group C, Nadine won't let

go of her shoulder. She's acting like she's pressing down on a gunshot wound. Seriously, the girl is weak; she should know what it feels like to have every limb break and then point in the opposite direction. That's pain.

"What did you do that for?" she whines.

"I was trying to get your attention, and you only had eyes for Rayna," I snipe.

For a second Nadine's eyes cloud over as if she didn't hear me properly or as if she did hear me and hates me for what I've said. Repeating the statement silently to myself, I realize she might have gotten the impression that I think she's kind of hot for Rayna, which she might not consider a compliment. The noise quotient around me is starting to dissipate since Miss Ro, as usual, is taking control of the situation, which means my time is running out. I hear a very loud voice reverberate inside of my skull, and its tone is not pleasant: *Ask your question, Dominy!*

"Have you told your brother everything that's been going on with me?" I blurt out.

Nadine recoils, so she looks like I've just dumped a bucket of piping hot water on top of her head and she's melting into the gym floor.

"What?!" she replies.

Evasive! I remember my father telling me that the number one sign that someone is guilty is when they're evasive, when they respond to your question with a question and try not to answer you directly. Nadine has fallen right into that category.

"Have you told Napoleon about the curse?"

I can't be any more direct than that. And neither can Nadine.

"Absolutely not!" she replies, clearly insulted by my lack of faith in her principles and our friendship. "How could you even ask me such a thing?"

Thanks, Dad! Now I feel like an ingrate. After everything

Nadine's done for me, this is how I repay her. With an allegation.

"I'm sorry, Nay, I really am," I plead. "It's just that, well, like we said, it's a stretch to think Arla's dad figured out the connection between the killings and the full moon on his own, so he must have had help reaching that conclusion."

Instead of clutching her shoulder, Nadine is now crossing her arms in front of her chest. Different gesture, but same result; she's protecting herself.

"And you just assumed that I betrayed your confidence and told my brother?" she asks. "That I shared with him everything that I promised to keep secret."

"Well, right when we were talking about it at lunch . . ." I stop myself. What am I going to say? I felt a butterfly whizz by my ear and then saw Napoleon? That would make me sound ludicrous. So of course I say something that makes me sound doubly ludicrous.

"You know what they say about twins," I start. "Sometimes they're psychic."

Nadine doesn't smile, but her features soften. She drops her arms to her sides and shakes her head. I can tell that she thinks I'm crazy, but at least she understands where I'm coming from. I'm grasping at straws and not questioning her friendship or her honor.

"Napoleon cannot read my mind," Nadine asserts. "And I—thank the stars above—cannot read his. Can you imagine the thoughts running around that creepy little head of his?"

Actually, I can. I have a brother, and I know how creepy they can be. And how dangerous.

"It was my brother then," I manage to get out. "Barnaby must have told Louis about the connection to the full moon."

Leaning in toward me, Nadine whispers. Her tone is a curious mixture of conspiratorial and condescending and compassionate. "Dom, it doesn't matter who told Louis," she informs me. "Someone was bound to figure it out sooner or later."

She's right. It's no use pointing a finger; the finger's already been pointed. But I still want to know whose hand the finger belongs to. I was convinced that it was Napoleon, but I can't prove it. He appears to be wearing several gloves to protect his identity.

"Nap and I have never had a psychic connection. He's always been a bit closed off, not just to me, but to everyone," she confides. "Lately, though, I don't know, he's been weirder than usual."

I'm about to ask her to explain herself, to define *weirder*, but I'm too preoccupied watching the silver mist that's starting to outline her body. It's just as entrancing as the first time I saw it, but as Nadine chatters on the mist begins to change. It's no longer intangible like fog; it's more like liquid metal, thick and shiny and touchable. Clasping my hands behind my back, I compel myself not to reach out and run my fingers through the silvery body stocking that's now undulating and rippling all around Nadine's body. I don't know if I can see this phenomenon as another byproduct of the transformation or if I'm somehow looking through wolf eyes, but either way it's fascinating. Watching this incredible sight is hypnotic, and I have to shut my eyes tight to break free from the trance. When I reopen them Nadine's silver outline is gone, and I can finally hear her voice again.

"Nap's been moody and just plain unmanageable," she finishes.

That's a peculiar word. I've described Barnaby as lots of things, but never unmanageable. Then again twins do have a different type of sibling relationship, so why not a different vocabulary? I'm the big sister, so I'm usually Madame Bossy Pants, but Nadine is pretty much Napoleon's equal, so maybe she yearns for more control? Or not.

"That's what my mother says," she corrects herself. "She calls Napoleon unmanageable."

"And what does she call you, Miss Jaffe?"

During our whispered conversation Miss Ro has worked herself to our side of the circle. Standing in front of us, hands on her hips, she doesn't look happy as she waits for an answer. She looks even less happy when Nadine finally responds. In a way that makes me drop my jaw, and poor Gwen Schültzenhoggen drop the ten-pound medicine ball she was about to throw on her foot.

"The better one."

For the rest of the day all I can think about is the bee and the butterfly. The imagery just won't leave my mind, and it's not pretty images of two insects buzzing and flapping whose only joint goal is to sniff flowers and collect pollen; the imagery is violent. Buzzing is more like dive-bombing and flapping resembles flying for your life. Could my sermon at Jess's funeral really be coming to life? Does the bee really want the butterfly dead? I'm not sure, but it actually makes me trust the bee more, because she isn't hiding; she isn't concealing her true nature. She is what she is. Which means the butterfly is a stool pigeon.

"It has to be Nap," I declare.

"Do you have evidence?" Caleb asks.

Why can't my boyfriend just agree with me?!

"Not a shred," Archie adds.

"Then I'm with Archie, Domgirl," Caleb says. "Just 'cause your gut thinks it's Nap, doesn't mean your gut is right."

And why must he always agree with his best friend?

I grabbed Caleb and Archie as they were on their way to football practice, thinking I would be able to convince them that Nap cannot be trusted, that he's the missing link that has led Louis and my brother on this dangerous path that may wind up getting me killed. But now, standing underneath the bleachers, doused in a jumble of shadow and afternoon sunlight, they're offering logic and pessimism and contradiction instead of sympathy and kudos and acceptance. It is not what I want or expect from these two. Especially Archie.

"Lift the needle, Dom," he says. "You sound like a broken record."

I have reason to be stuck in my groove! "Ever since Nap came to town he's been lying!" I proclaim. "The way he acted at Jess's funeral is all the proof I need."

"That isn't proof," Archie rebuts. "Just your point of view."

And just what point is Archie trying to make?

"I get why Domgirl is blaming Napoleon. She's looking for an explanation," Caleb states. "But, Winter, dude, why are *you* defending him?"

Finally! At least I'm not the only one perplexed as to why Archie has become a Napoleonic advocate.

"I'm not *defending* him, just trying to make y'all see reason," Archie declares. "I'll let up if you can tell me what his motivation would be."

"Sometimes people don't need motivation to do stupid things; sometimes it's just their nature," I say.

"Like choosing not to spend the night in your cage?" Caleb asks.

Newsflash: A fast-beating heart can actually be heard. I can hear my heart pounding so fast in my chest I can't believe no one is commenting on it. They're probably not commenting on it because Caleb is waiting for me to speak and Archie is trying to figure out what his question means. It doesn't take him long to figure out the truth.

"You lied to me!"

"Sorry," I mutter sheepishly.

"I can't believe you lied, Dom!" Archie squeals, his voice

sounding nothing like the voice of a testosterone-fueled football player, which is what he is. "You told us you were in your cage and Luba unlocked it again."

"I never said those exact words," I say.

"Inferred! You *inferred* that you went into your cage and then Luba used her magical squawbilities to unlock it," Archie shouts, his voice still incredibly high-pitched, but now he sounds like the incredibly betrayed friend that he is. "Why didn't you just admit the truth?"

He has to ask why?

"If I had told you guys that I deliberately chose not to go into the cage, you would've flipped out!" I shout back. "You would've disregarded our need for silence, and the entire cafeteria would've heard everything. I couldn't take that chance."

"And why didn't you tell me last night when I dropped you off?" Caleb asks.

His voice is a stark contrast to our yelling. It's quiet and contains even more hurt and betrayal than Archie's yelling could ever convey.

The details aren't necessary, but I need a diversion, a simple task, so I explain to Archie that last night, Caleb dropped me off at the abandoned barn on his Uncle Luke's property off Route 75. The land is isolated, uninhabited, and for sale, which is why Caleb felt it was the ideal solution and the ideal location for my transformation. Caleb set up the cage inside the barn because he knew that it would keep me safe, but I had other plans.

I told him to leave before the transformation because I couldn't bear to have him see me leave my human form again. That was the truth. My lie came when I promised him that I would go into the cage, toss the key far enough away so I couldn't get to it, and see him in the morning when he came to let me out. He even bought two plucked and beheaded chickens at the butcher over in Pawnee City so I could feed.

Now if that doesn't describe the perfect boyfriend, I don't know what does. And how do I repay perfection? With a broken promise.

"I'm sorry, Caleb," I say. "I couldn't do it. I couldn't go into that cage again."

And how does my hurt boyfriend repay his lying girlfriend? With empathy.

"I understand," he replies.

I know his words are meant to console me, to heal me, but they only serve to humiliate me. My body flinches involuntarily, like a hot poker was pressed onto my stomach. I stare at Caleb's feet because I'm not worthy of looking into his eyes. I open my mouth to speak, but my voice betrays me, unable to find the right words to respond to Caleb's kindness. My silence prompts Archie to ask the question I'm too ashamed to utter.

"You *understand?*"

Smiling, Caleb leans back against a metal pole, his hands clasped behind him to reveal that the armpits of his practice jersey are stained with tiny circles of sweat, the only imperfection on an otherwise perfect body. He looks like he's resting, taking in the slivers of September sun that are shining through the bleacher seats overhead, instead of contemplating his girlfriend's considerably reckless actions. Once again he surprises me.

"Sure it's dangerous," he starts, "But in the long run it's the best thing you can do if you want to fully control this wolf spirit and be the more powerful of the two."

He really does understand. Too bad Archie doesn't.

"And while you're trying to maintain control, more people could wind up hurt or killed," he says, his voice mixed with fear and anger, just like the voices I heard last night. For a split second I think that maybe Archie was one of the hunters, but no, that's ridiculous. He's acting strangely, nervous and not his typical carefree self, but he would never join the crusade to hunt me down. I'm unsure about a lot of things, but not that.

"Don't you see, Dom," Archie continues, "Even if you can control the wolf, you can't control this town. What if you got caught last night? What would've happened then?!"

I would've been killed or maimed so I could've been captured, and when the sun returned this nightmare would have been over. For me anyway. Not for the two faces staring at me. The hot poker pushes all the way through my body and emerges out the other side as I suddenly realize that their nightmare is never going to end. They're always going to worry about me and do whatever they possibly can to protect me. This curse is like a restless octopus whose tentacles keep stretching out, destroying everything they touch.

The air around me is as thick as the silver mist that won't leave Nadine alone. I can't breathe very well, and it only gets worse the more I look into Caleb's and Archie's eyes. These two have become my family, and I'm terrified to think that my actions and this curse will destroy them just like they destroyed my father.

How quickly things change. A few minutes ago I thought I wanted their support, but right now I want to be as far away from them as I possibly can be.

As I run across the football field I hear them shout my name behind me. I stumble and almost fall to the hard, hateful earth below me, but I force myself to stay upright and strong and focused so I can keep running.

With every stride one thought becomes more and more evident: There's no place in this world I can run to that will keep the two of them safe.

Chapter 3

She's staring at me.

I don't have to turn to the left; I don't have to look up. I could be blind, and I'd still know that her eyes are on me, peering through my skin to see what's inside of me, to see if there's anything left worth looking at. It doesn't matter that her eyes are wooden and lifeless; The Weeping Lady can see me. She can see who I am, she can see what I am, and that's why she knows I'm nothing but trouble. But despite that she can't look away because she feels a connection. Hanging in limbo, residing in two different worlds at once, she knows the two of us are very much the same.

Curiosity wins out, and I whip my head around, certain that there's going to be a real woman standing next to the tree, her skin the color and texture of bark. Or the tree itself is going to be flesh and blood. Just another everyday miracle in our little freak-magnet town.

But I'm wrong.

The Weeping Lady isn't a real lady, nor is she really weeping, but she is staring at me. It's kind of amazing actually. Her eyes are in the same position they're always in, the way they've looked every day I've passed by here, every day for decades from what I've been told, but right now they look as if they're fixated on my face.

"Why don't you take a picture?!" I shout. "It lasts longer!"

The Weeping Lady remains stuck in the oak tree and doesn't break free of the bark shackles and jump to the ground to confront me for being rude and disrespectful. Really? Is that what I expected would happen? I'm overcome by the absurdity of my thoughts, and I hear a loud gigglaugh pierce the quiet. It's been a while since I've heard that sound, so I don't do anything to stifle it; I let it expand and grow until it dies a natural death. I've missed that sound.

Standing in front one of the town's prized obscurities I feel good even though the sun is so strong I can feel beads of sweat form on my upper lip and on my forehead and slip down the hollow curve of my spine. My body wants to get out of the sun, wants to hide from the glare; my mind is at peace, so it wins out and I don't move.

Slowly, The Weeping Lady changes, not by her own choice or by my will power but due to the sunlight. Circles of hazy light surround her face so it looks like gauze is being wrapped round and round her, making pieces of her face disappear. The blazing light lengthens to envelop her body in an attempt to consume and devour and annihilate her. She is fighting for her life, and all I can do is watch.

I refuse to give in to the harsh sunlight and blink despite the puddles of tears that are starting to form in my eye sockets. They collect as much fluid as they can, and soon the tears overflow and trickle down the sides of my face. I'm not crying, but bearing witness.

Still my vision is totally blurred, and I can feel my eyes trying to shut. I hear a voice inside of me. I have no idea who it belongs to—my mother, Jess, the wolf—but it's telling me to keep my eyes open, to keep looking, to keep staring into the sun. I join the voice and tell myself that I can do this; I'm stronger and better and more determined.

And then there's nothing but darkness.

It only lasts for an instant, but it's long enough to offer confirmation to me that I lost. I blinked. I gave in to the harshness of the sun; I gave in to the forces outside of me and ignored the spirit living within. The Weeping Lady is back to normal; nothing about her has changed. Her metamorphosis was nothing more than an illusion; I'm nothing more than a girl who's lost her way.

Well, it's time to get back on track.

The Retreat looks exactly the same. Boring brick exterior, institutionalized black, gray, and red interior, overall uninviting atmosphere. Its main receptionist, however, has undergone a transformation. Essie looks like she spent a month at a spa or underwent instachange by going on one of those reality TV shows where they make you over from head to toe by performing sixteen different cosmetic surgeries on your body in one weekend. Whatever she's done, Essie looks beyond great.

"Essie! What gives?!" I shout, ignoring the signs that forbid exclamations of any kind. "You look awesome!"

Smiling like one of the celebrities in her magazines, Essie does a full-swivel in her chair. "You like?"

"No," I reply. "I do not like."

Swiveling comes to an abrupt stop. As does Essie's smile. "You don't?"

"No, Essie!" I squeal. "I love!"

Her mousy brown-gray hair is no longer mousy brown or gray; it's the color of mouth-watering dark chocolate and cut in a super flattering bob. Hair parted on the right, her bangs swing over and curve around her eye while the other side is tucked behind her ear. Her makeup is soft and shimmery and sexy in that "I could easily be a grandmother, but I've still got some life left in me" sort of way. I'm shocked. I knew she was looking for a solution for the mid-to-late-life crisis she was going through, but I had no idea the result was going to be so physically dramatic.

"Seriously, Es, you look absolutely mag-tastic!" I gush. "I'm surprised Lars Svenson hasn't unleashed the paparazzi to get a photo of you for the cover of the *Three W!*"

Essie has no idea that I'm not one-hundred percent serious.

"Oh, Dominy," she blushes. "No one wants to see my face on the cover of the *Weekly.*"

Grabbing Essie's hands, I tell her, "You then and you now are the most incredible before and after I've ever seen."

Blushing an even deeper shade of red, Essie squeezes my hands tighter. "You really think so?"

Well, not really. I am the Queen of the Before and After, but Essie is a super-close second.

"Absolutely!" I white-lie.

"It's all thanks to my new boyfriend," Essie shares.

For a second I think that she's white-lying too. Until she blushes yet a deeper shade of red, so it looks like she has a third-degree sunburn. Essie's way too old to have a boyfriend, isn't she? Then again, maybe she isn't as old as I thought and she only looked ancient because she let herself go and kept her face buried in magazines that only show glamorous people, so she looked even worse by comparison. I guess at some point watching life was no longer satisfying and Essie decided to live. I have to be honest, it's a bit weird to think about Essie on a date with some guy, flirting and making small talk, all the while wondering if the guy is going to kiss her good night, but I'm happy for her. As long as she keeps all the details of her romancecapades to herself.

Of course the moment that thought pops into my mind, I

simply have to know who she's been having romancecapades with.

"'Fess up, Essie," I demand. "Who's your new fella?"

All the red from her cheeks fades and is replaced by a pale gray. I know that color well; it's the color of fear.

"I-I'd rather not s-say," she stutters.

Why would something that should bring Essie joy make her afraid? Could I be misjudging her or could she just be acting coy so I make an even bigger fuss and drag the information out of her? Unsure, I don't do anything. I don't say a word; I don't agree with her, I don't try to coax her to offer a name; I remain silent. Which is exactly what Essie does. Obviously she meant what she said. But why?

Could she be making the whole thing up? Could this boyfriend be an invention? No, if she did that she'd ramble on about him, give me an exact physical description, and tell me all sorts of personal details I would rather not hear. That's what people do when they lie; they go overboard, fill in the blanks with a non-erasable marker to make it look like they're telling the truth when all it does is make them look like a liar. Nope, Essie's no liar; she's got a boyfriend, but a secret one.

Could she be dating a married man? Or someone very well-known in the community? Or both?! Then again maybe their relationship is in the early stages and she's adopting the new mother approach—not announcing she's pregnant until the first trimester is over just in case complications develop and she miscarries. Essie is smartsie. She probably wants to keep her boyfriend's name secret until she's a bit more certain he's going to turn into something more long lasting than just a boyfriend. I can't blame her. She's waited a long time for some happiness after her first husband died; why not be cautiously optimistic?

"I'll let you off the hook, Essie," I say, adopting a magnanimous tone to my voice. "But when you're ready to announce his name to the world, I want to be the first one to know."

A wave of relief crests over Essie's face, and her color rushes back. "Deal."

Grabbing the index card that has the number 19 written on it in sparkly gold marker, I feel sorry for giving Essie a hard time. Of all people, I should understand the importance and necessity of keeping secrets. Before the door to my mother's room closes behind me, I realize that Essie and I aren't the only ones who have something to hide.

"I'm going to make everything right again, I promise."

I've never heard such heartfelt devotion in my brother's voice.

"Barnaby?"

More furious than startled at being interrupted, my brother looks up at me, unsuccessfully trying to turn a grimace into a smirk. He's also unsuccessful at letting go of my mother's hand before I witness the connection, so, much to his credit, he holds on to the hand I haven't seen him touch in over ten years.

I should be happy to see my brother sitting next to my mother's bed, holding her hand, talking to her, but instead I'm filled with the notion that I've stumbled upon something I wasn't meant to see. Instead of being thankful that he's finally come around and accepted the fact that our mother isn't to blame for lapsing into this coma of unknown causes, I'm scared. I know that whatever he was whispering to my mother had something to do with me.

What did he say? He's going to make everything right again. What exactly does that mean? And why am I so afraid to ask him about it? I'm his older sister; I'm the one who he should be afraid of, not the other way around. Why am I complicating things? Be like the wolf, I remind myself; be simple and straightforward and strong.

"What do you mean you're 'going to make everything right again'?" I ask.

Yup, sometimes the wolf knows best.

"None of your business," Barnaby replies.

And sometimes he's totally off the mark. Time for the girl to take over.

"Come on, fill me in," I whine. "You're supposed to tell your big sister everything."

I can tell by looking into his eyes that Barnaby wants to confide in me. No matter how angry he's ever gotten with me, and through the years he's gotten pretty mad, he's never allowed his anger to consume him. There's always been a light in his eyes, a flicker of hope, reassurance that through all the screaming and name-calling and fist-fights we'll still be close. I see it now; I see the spark; it's like a bright light that's connecting his heart to mine. But just as quickly the spark is lost. I don't know if it's extinguished or if it's been replaced by something else. All I know is that, for the time being anyway, Barnaby is lost to me, and no amount of begging or cajoling or pressuring is going to get him to tell me what his cryptic remark really means. Just like with Essie, I accept defeat.

"Fine, don't tell me," I say. "See if I care."

"It's just between me and Mom," he says.

Now I really do feel awkward, as if I interrupted nothing more than a private mother-son moment. Barnaby's hand hasn't let go of my mother's since I walked into the room, and it's clear by the way that he's holding her that this isn't the first time they've touched. His grasp isn't tentative or suffocating, it's relaxed and gentle, as if he's done this hundreds of times before. Witch hunts by night, bedside vigils by day. What other secrets is my brother hiding?

"Well, it's nice to see you and Mom together like this," I say. "I know it always makes me feel good when I sit with her."

Whatever connection we shared is destroyed.

Abruptly Barnaby drops my mother's hand, and it falls limply by her side. "Then I'll give you two some privacy."

We both feel the electric shock when I touch Barnaby's shoulder. All I wanted to do was tell him that he didn't have to leave, and all I did was give him another reason to not want to stay.

"You don't have to go," I urge.

"Yes, I do," my brother replies. "I've . . . I've said all I needed to say."

The sound of the door closing after my brother leaves the room is heartbreaking. When I turn around and see my mother staring at me I want to rejoice. She's looking at me with the same intensity as The Weeping Lady, except her eyes are alive and open and loving.

"Mom!"

There's no response, but that's fine because her eyes stay open; they don't close; they don't retreat. Best thing is that they don't make me think that I'm hallucinating, trying to conjure up more miracles and magic. This is beyond a marvelous spectacle; this is validation that my mother is still fighting whatever force is keeping her locked away from this world, and I just know that she's closer than ever to finding her way back to us.

"Oh, Mom, can you see me?" I plead.

Kneeling next to her bed, I clasp her hand and press it against my cheek. Her skin is so warm and her eyes are so bright, part of me thinks she's going to yawn and stretch and jump out of bed eager to reclaim her life. But the smarter, more realistic part of me knows better. This is not a beginning, but it is a sign that I know my father had something to do with.

Guaranteed my father has been speaking with God or an angel or Jess, telling them that since he was taken from his children, our mother needs to come back. It's only fair. I feel like a little girl again, convinced my father is the strongest man in the world. Holding my mother's hand, I know that my father is still protecting me, that he's still in my life and he's still determined to help me deal with this curse.

Luba has other ideas.

I didn't notice the smell right away, but now it's overpowering. Similar to my mother's favorite perfume, Guerlinade, it's a mixture of lilac and powder, but there's another scent added to the mix, something I can't distinguish. But the more I breathe in, the more I feel like I'm going to choke.

As if I'm ripping off a day-old Band-Aid, I throw back the blanket and see what's making that awful smell. In her right hand, my mother is holding a bouquet of moonflowers; she looks like a bride taking a nap before her wedding ceremony. My first instinct is that Luba put them there, that she snuck in before my brother arrived and placed them underneath the covers. But then I remember the first rule of deduction: The simple answer is most always the correct one. The solution to a mystery is usually so obvious, it's often overlooked. Taking a deep breath of the toxic fragrance I inhale the truth: The flowers were my brother's gift.

A son bringing his mother flowers is a beautiful gesture, no cause for alarm. Then why do I feel frightened? Why do I feel as if this is even worse than my brother's carrying a torch and leading a group of fanatic townspeople in search of a would-be serial killer? Once again the answer isn't difficult or convoluted or elusive. It's worse because this action, this simple gift, links my brother to the enemy.

There's no way it's a coincidence that my brother chose to give my mother the same kind of flowers Luba gave her. He has no way of knowing that he's under that evil witch's influence, that she's using him like she used me as a way to get revenge against my father for an accident. An accident!! One that happened when my father was just a boy!

I gasp for breath, not because the smell of the moonflowers

becomes even more poisonous, but because I think my father has just tried to speak to me. Not with words, but with a memory. When he was a teenager, roughly the same age Barnaby is right now, he made a mistake that set into motion this curse and this horror that we're all living through.

What if Barnaby is about to make a mistake of his own? What if his friendship with Luba is more than that, what if it's more like an allegiance? Could Luba have armed Barnaby with enough information for him to think that I'm the enemy and not her, so he would consciously choose sides? It's a horrifying possibility, but a possibility all the same.

I may not be able to destroy Luba, but I can destroy her connection to my brother. Reaching out I grab the revolting flowers and crumble them in my hand so they resemble a mound of white petals that were ripped from a vine.

Take that, you psycho!

I toss the mangled mess into the garbage and look back at my mother. Her eyes are shut tight again; her beautiful blue-gray eyes are no longer looking at me. Perhaps she didn't want to see what I'm seeing right now, that the moonflowers are defying nature and blooming back to life in the garbage can. It's an all-too-obvious sign that Luba's power and her connection to my brother cannot be so easily severed.

As I stand underneath the shower, the hot spray of water envelops and cradles and revitalizes me because I know that I don't have to fight Luba alone. I have allies. Really? Then why do I have to press my forehead and my palms against the cold tiles to stop my body from shaking? If I have so many allies on my side why do I feel so alone?

My palms contract and my fingernails claw at the wet, slippery tiles. I feel like a fly desperately trying to climb its way out of a spiderweb, but for every step it takes closer to freedom, it takes two steps back toward defeat. We're both lost causes. Just as my friends have rallied around me and re-fused to abandon me, my family has done just the opposite. My father is dead, my mother's in a coma, and my brother has chosen to believe that I'm his enemy. Whether they've made their choices consciously or involuntarily, the result is the same; they've left me to fend for myself.

Out of the shower, I dry myself as quickly as possible. The towel smells different, more fragrant, like lavender I think. I don't like it. It's nothing at all like the smell that used to cling to our towels when my father did the laundry. I wrap the towel around me and try to remember what my laundry used to smell like. After a moment the memory comes back to me, the smell of too much bleach—my father was never good at doing laundry—but it's as if the memory is being held at a distance, slightly out of reach, so it's hard for me to get a firm hold on it, and I wonder how long it'll take me to forget most of the things I took for granted while my father was alive.

Thankfully the mirrors are steamed up so I don't have to look at my body, but as I gather my clothes the fog starts to lift, and I can see my partial reflection. I force myself to look at the pale skin, then the long red hair, and finally the blue-gray eyes that stare back at me. I can see the girl completely now, and contrary to my griping she isn't alone. But it isn't the wolf I see standing next to her; it's her brother who's joined her, standing behind her with a gun.

"What the . . . !?"

Whipping around I expect to see Barnaby pointing a gun at my face, but he's not there. The bathroom is empty; there's nothing in front of me but the wall and the towel rack. That can't be. I saw him! Heart pounding, I wipe away the rest of the steam that's still clutching at the mirror, and I'm the only person in the reflection. Maniacally, I slide back the shower curtain to reveal more emptiness.

Get a hold of yourself, Dominy! This is insanity!

Gripping the side of the sink, I breathe deeply several times. I avoid my gaze and focus on the pale blue porcelain until I can trust my body to move without shaking. When I enter my bedroom, I don't scream. I wasn't hallucinating; I was just having a premonition.

Barnaby is sitting on my bed pointing a gun at me.

Chapter 4

I should be frightened, but I'm not.

Maybe it's because I know that there's a very slim chance that Barnaby's gun is loaded with silver bullets, the only type that can do any permanent damage to me if, of course, the folklore and the information I've gleaned from Wikipedia and at Lycanthropy.com, are true.

According to legend (and the larger-than-I-expected online lycanthrophite community), it takes a very specific type of ammo to take me down. And if my brother shoots I may be wounded, but since there's no full moon tonight, there's no risk that my other self will emerge while I'm in the emergency room doing my best imitation of my mother.

But wait! Am I only immune to regular bullets when I'm a wolf? Will they harm me when I'm not in wolf form? Another philosophical question emerges: Is a werewolf always a werewolf even when the werewolf isn't a wolf? I have no idea, but I feel the formidable wolf-strength push underneath my skin, and I feel way more invincible than vulnerable. A good way to find out how I'd be affected by a regular-strength bullet would be to provoke Barnaby and get him so pissed off that he actually pulls the trigger. I have a feeling that won't be a very difficult task.

"What the hell are you doing with that thing?" I ask.

"Aiming it at you," he replies.

"Why?"

"Because that's what you do with a gun, isn't it?" he asks rhetorically. "Point it at people."

"For starters," I respond defiantly.

Looking at my brother, I notice that his feet are planted squarely on the floor; he's grown a few inches since last year. His gym shorts reveal that his legs are muscular, well-developed from track practice, and they're covered with spotty patches of brown hair, a thick cluster around his shins and calves, much thinner around his thighs. His arms and upper body are still on the skinny side, and he needs two hands to hold the gun. That, however, could be more for effect than necessity. The overall impression is that he's aged. I'm not sure if it happened overnight or if there's been a steady growth that I've ignored, but my brother looks older than I last remember.

And yet regardless of what he's holding in his hands, he's still my little brother.

"So you gonna do something with that thing other than point it at me?"

As usual when a bully is confronted, a bully wavers. The gun lowers just enough in the air to convince me that Barnaby has absolutely no intention of using it the way that its maker intended. Gone is the cocky attitude, and in its place is confused apprehension. It's like I can hear his thoughts rolling in his mind, like a huge, heavy wheel that a weakling is trying to push. Clunk, clunk, clunk, until the momentum clicks and the wheel starts to roll, and I realize with more than a mild amount of surprise that my brother is no longer a weakling. That's when Barnaby pulls the trigger.

Despite my steely determination to be aloof, I flinch. Not a quick flinch that I can hide as a shiver, but a full-on, body shake so violent I have to clutch my towel so it doesn't fall to the ground and give my brother a free show.

After I stop shaking and am satisfied that my private parts are still covered, I realize that either my skin is human Kevlar or Barnaby's gun isn't loaded. His laughter proves it's the latter.

"Gotcha!"

He falls back on my bed squealing, the weight of the gun making his outstretched arm bend so he looks like some underage assassin who finds his career oh-so-hilarious. Right now I find my brother oh-so-repulsive.

While Barnaby is reveling in his self-staged amusement, I do what a big sister—as well as a big, bad wolf—was born to do: I take control of the situation.

Lightning quick, I grab the gun from his wiggling grip. When he finally notices the piece is missing, he's still laughing so hard that his protestations aren't filled with any of the anger I know he was aiming for.

"Give that back!" he shouts childishly.

"Make me," I reply, sounding equally as childish.

Barnaby lunges forward to reclaim his prize, but I have supernatural speed on my side, so I step out of the way and turn around just as Barnaby slams into the sliding closet door, the impact ripping it from its hinges. His cries of pain are muffled by the sounds of the door falling and crashing onto his back. His bawling combined with my gigglaughs create a raucous sound, so it's no wonder within seconds Louis is standing in the doorway.

"Dominy!" he screams. "What the hell are you doing?"

Just like Barnaby moments earlier, I can't stop laughing even though the situation calls for a serious face. Guess inappropriateness runs in our family. And you can't get much more inappropriate than I appear to be right now, dripping wet hair, wearing only a towel, brandishing a gun, standing over my brother who can't move because a closet door is weighing down his back. I understand how Louis could interpret the situation as being my fault. But he's wrong.

"This isn't my fault!" I cry.

"Put that gun down!" Louis cries back, doing a great job of sounding fatherly. "Now!"

"Who's got a gun?"

Arla's not yet in my bedroom, but she must have heard the commotion and is en route. When she takes in the situation, she has a different take on it than her father.

"What happened to the closet?" she screams.

"Just came off its little rollie things," I assure her. "We can get it back up in a jiffy."

Quickly, though, her concern escalates to match her father's.

"Is that Barnaby?"

"Will you get up!?" I demand.

If Louis and Arla weren't in the room, Barnaby would've jumped up immediately and started punching me. I know this for a fact because this scenario has happened before, when we were living in our old house. Without the gun of course. The last time my brother was knocked to the ground by a closet door, he was upright within twenty seconds, ready to do battle with me. Now that he has an audience, he's milking it.

"Can somebody help me, please?" he asks, trying to make his voice sound fearful and fragile and frightened. None of which I know he is.

"Oh come on!" I hear myself shout. "It's a closet door! It's hollow! It's not like the front door which, you know, would be really . . . *really* . . . you know, heavy."

By the time I finish my sentence, my tirade has become quite tepid, and I can see myself the way Louis and Arla must see me, like some crazy girl who showers with a weapon.

Waving said weapon in the air, I announce, "This isn't mine."

Wrapping his fingers around my wrist like a vise, Louis

points the gun toward the ceiling and quickly wrenches it from my hand. Once again I'm reminded that despite his lackadaisical nature, he really is a trained cop.

"I know it isn't," he says, examining the firearm. "It's Barnaby's."

A trained cop with insane detective skills.

"How do you know that?" I ask, very curious and very impressed.

"Because I gave it to him."

And now I'm very scared.

Just how irresponsible can he be? First allowing Barnaby to join the witch brigade and now arming him with a weapon to kill the witch. Is this what my father had in mind when he put our lives in this man's hands? Did my father have any idea that this man would work overtime to destroy our future?

"It was your father's, and I wanted Barnaby to have it as a memento," Louis explains.

Finally vertical, Barnaby doesn't ask for his gun back; he doesn't demand it be returned to its rightful owner. He silently basks in the joy of feeling superior, knowing that Louis and Arla think I'm the one who violated a beautiful memory.

Think again.

"He was pointing that memento at me," I say.

"What?!" Louis screams.

His usually quiet voice is so unexpectedly loud that it literally makes me and Barnaby jump. Arla, obviously used to her father's sudden outbursts, doesn't move. She remains leaning against the doorjamb, arms crossed, head tilted, with the smallest of smirks on her lips. Even though I'd look horrible in a black pageboy wig, I so want to trade places with her right now.

"I didn't give you this gun so you could wave it around and scare people!" Louis starts, waving the gun around and kind of scaring most of the people in the room. "I gave it to you so you could remember your father! Do you understand the difference?!"

I'm sure that Barnaby does know the difference, but since his face has turned ghostly white, I'm also sure that he doesn't have the ability to respond to Louis's question beyond a non-verbal head nod. Nonverbal communication, however, will not satisfy Louis at the moment.

"Answer me!!"

"Y-yes," Barnaby stutters. "I . . . I'm sorry. I didn't mean to scare anybody."

Breathing deeply through his nose, Louis examines my brother for a few seconds in an attempt, I think, to determine if he's telling the truth and if he's truly sorry for his actions. I could put Louis's mind at ease and tell him that Barnaby is being honest; he's not trying to pull a fast one. Barnaby only stutters when he's contrite. Physically, he may be changing, but emotionally he's still the baby of the family. No matter how much our family has changed.

"I-I thought it would be f-funny," Barnaby continues. "Guess I was being st-stupid."

"*Very* stupid!" Louis shouts.

After he paces restlessly for a few seconds, Louis's demeanor softens. He kneels down in front of my brother and holds the gun in both of his hands like it's an offering in church.

"Your grandpa gave this gun to your father when he graduated from the police academy," Louis whispers, his voice rough. "He said, 'Those guns they give ya won't protect ya; ya gotta have one from your family.' "

Louis doesn't have to say another word. He doesn't have to lecture Barnaby about gun etiquette or why it's beyond wrong to point a gun at your sister, or anyone for that matter, as a joke. He does inform my brother that he wants him to put the gun back in its box and leave it there; it's a for-show gun, nothing more.

Nodding his head Barnaby agrees and then adds, "I knew there weren't any bullets in it."

When Louis laughs I know that this reminds him of my father too.

"None of Mason's guns had any bullets in them," he says. "He must've emptied them all. I know he didn't run around town with a gun he couldn't shoot if he needed to."

Arla's smirk disappears into a look that can only be described as "uh-oh," which, in turn, disappears when I catch her eyes. We both know that her father's offhanded comment is correct, but there's no reason to fill him and Barnaby in on that secret as well. Let them think that my father was like every other policeman in the world and carried a loaded gun; no need to tell them that his guns were bullet-free because once upon a time he had made a pact with God.

"Like he would ever do that," I say sarcastically.

Sarcasm, once again, does its trick. It calms the situation and diverts Louis from the truth he unwittingly stumbled upon and toward the reality he wishes he hadn't seen.

"And there's, um, no reason for you to walk around the house like that," he says, pointing a finger at me, but keeping his eyes focused on the carpet.

Clutching my towel, I make a mental note to bring my clothes into the bathroom from now on so I can change before exiting into shared territory. Even though I'm totally covered and wearing more than I would at the pool, I guess the fact that I'm naked underneath the plush cotton is making Louis a wee bit uncomfortable. I decide to give the guy some slack and apologize.

"Sorry, Mr. Bergeron," I say.

"That's okay," he mutters, busying himself with lifting the closet door and jamming it back into its correct position with one easy push.

Before he heads out into the hallway where he doesn't have to deal with guns or half-naked teenagers, he turns back around. A glutton for punishment?

"And I told you I'm not Mr. Bergeron anymore," he declares. "I'm Louis."

As he waves at the three of us, his smile can barely contain the joy and the sorrow that's filling up his heart. He'll never replace my father—he, more than any of us, knows that—but he really is a good man. And after he leaves Barnaby takes one step closer to making me wish I were an only child.

"Nice to see that your scars are almost all healed," he hisses.

Involuntarily, I cover the faint remnants of my wounds with my hand.

He takes another step closer to me, and I can feel the gun in his hand rest against my thigh. "You know, the scars you got the night Jess was killed," he whispers.

After Barnaby closes the door, I wonder if Arla heard him. I wonder if she knows how complex he's becoming. When she speaks, I realize she didn't hear him.

"That's sweet," she says, flopping onto my bed. "My dad's really enjoying having a son."

And my brother is really enjoying taunting me.

What exactly does he know? Has Luba filled him in on our secret? Has Barnaby told Louis what he knows? These are the questions that are racking my brain so I don't hear anything Arla's chattering on about. Through the window the moonglow is so bright it looks like sunlight, and it illuminates Arla's face. Her bronzed skin shimmers in the light, and she looks beautiful, until she takes off her wig and I can see her entire face. The light glistens on her scar, the scar that runs diagonally from the outside of her left eye down toward her cheek, the scar that I gave her when I wasn't in control of my body.

I stare at the scar and marvel at how close she came to losing her eye, how close I came to blinding my friend. Even though I can't remember it, I can't remember slashing the air with my paw and connecting with her flesh, I'm still responsible. And no matter what everyone says, they all know it.

Unable to look at the product of my actions any longer, I announce, "I think I'm going to turn in. Been a long day."

I don't know if Arla agrees with me, but thankfully she doesn't argue. Alone, I try to focus on the shapes that the moonlight creates, but my mind is buzzing with thoughts, so I close my eyes tight, try to force my brain to be quiet. Forget about the friend I mauled, forget that I'm living in the house of the man who wants me dead, forget that he's working with my brother to achieve the same goal. Good, Dominy, focus on all the really positive things in your life.

After what seems like hours, I finally drift off to sleep. Just as I do I remind myself that things can't possibly get any worse. When I wake up in the morning, I have proof that I'm wrong.

"Morning," Arla chirps. "I tried to wake you, but you changed from Little Red Riding Hood into Sleeping Beauty overnight."

"What are you doing?" I croak.

"Didn't think you'd mind if I used your mascara," she explains. "I ran out."

Arla's fully dressed and putting on the last touches of makeup at my vanity table. Today is Wig-free Wednesday, so without a special hair feature, she's taking some extra time putting on eye shadow and lipstick and picking out just the right accessories. My vision is still blurry because I'm not fully awake, but I can see as she puts her makeup on that she never touches the scar around her eye. She doesn't try to conceal it; it's part of who she is. She doesn't need the world's admiration to know that she's beautiful and amazing and confident. As groggy as I am, I know that's advice I should file away and use for myself. Who knew I'd need to use it so soon?

My cell phone vibrates angrily on the nightstand.

"That is like the fourth text you've gotten, missie, and it's just after seven," Arla announces.

Grabbing my cell phone, I force myself out of bed. "It's Caleb," I say.

"Who else would it be so early in the morning, but Prince Caleb?" Arla replies. "Do these work?"

Arla spins around on her chair and flicks an earring with her finger. It's a modified chandelier, a long silver chain that ends in a ball of hot pink mesh, the color being a few shades bolder than her lipstick and clashing perfectly with her light-blue eye shadow. I totally approve of her look; I totally disapprove of Caleb's text.

"The prince is breaking another date with me!" I shout, now fully awake and pacing the floor.

Squeezing her left hand into a silver cuff bracelet, Arla grimaces. I'm not sure if it's because she's hurting herself in the name of fashion or if she's indicating her support in the name of friendship. Turns out to be neither. The cop's daughter is getting ready to cross-examine.

"What's his excuse?" she asks.

"He has to study," I say, as if that's a valid excuse.

"For what?"

"That stupid, idiotic advanced math class he's taking!" I reply, holding up the cell phone so Arla can read his text, which she can't because as I'm holding it up I'm also waving it around.

Multitasking, Arla checks herself out in the mirror and is as pleased with her look as she is with her interpretation of the facts.

"Caleb's stupid, idiotic advanced math class is probably

going to get him a scholarship to Big Red or some other college he can't otherwise afford," she lays out. "So if I were his girlfriend, instead of his girlfriend's pseudo-stepsister, I'd text him back and ask him if I could help him study."

I hate rational thinking this early in the morning!

"I can't do that," I reply.

"Why not?"

"Because I've already sent him a text," I reply, my voice a little bit less forceful.

Without asking, Arla grabs the phone out of my hand to read my text. She responds in much the same way I envision Caleb responding now that I've had half a minute to calm down.

"Seriously?!" she exclaims. "You typed that message and then hit Send?"

I think for a moment, wondering if there's any way I can reply with anything else but the truth. There isn't.

"Yes."

"Do you want this house to be full of single ladies?" she asks. "'Cuz that's where we're headed if you don't rectify this situation ASAP, and I mean rectify with a capital B because you need to *beg* Caleb to forgive you." Pausing for effect, Arla puts her hands on her hips. "Do I make myself clear, Miss Robineau?"

Justifiably chastised I reply, "Yes, Miss Bergeron, you've made yourself very clear."

"Good!" she declares. "Now shower up and make sure you accessorize because you're going to need all the help you can get."

Actually I'm about to get more help than I deserve.

"I'll write a draft of your apology while you're in the shower," Arla announces. "We can edit on the bus."

By the time I see Caleb in the hallway before homeroom I have my and Arla's apology memorized.

"Caleb, I'm sorry," I start.

He's not smiling, but he doesn't look spellbindingly angry. Until he speaks.

"For calling me, and I quote, 'a disrespectful d-bag a-hole who treats his girlfriend like a piece of garbage,' end quote?"

Did I really text that? Geez Louise, that sounds even worse when spoken out loud. I'm about to tell Caleb that I wasn't even out of bed yet and I overreacted when I remember Arla's instructions: unbutton an extra button. Unfortunately, our school-sanctioned polo only has two buttons, not a lot of room to be sexy and seductive. Luckily, Arla's instructions were twofold. The second part was to tell the truth.

"I'm a jerk," I say. When he doesn't protest, I continue. "Last night Barnaby and I got into a fight, he had a gun, Arla's father got mad 'cause I was only wearing a towel, and I didn't get any sleep last night, and then I saw your text, and I flipped out. Can you forgive me?"

"Your brother has a gun?" he asks, his eyes bugging out.

That's his takeaway!

"Can we table that explanation for now and concentrate on forgiving me?" I ask.

He leans his head forward and a few stray blond curls hang in the air, like little stars. After a second he smiles, but it's a little bit different from the smile I'm used to seeing. Something's changed. It's not a big thing, I know he's not breaking up with me, but there's a change nonetheless.

"You don't need forgiveness," he replies. "But . . ."

"But there's a but?"

His smile fades completely, and now I definitely know there's a change.

"You can't freak out like this all the time, Dominy," he declares. "You know how I feel about you. I can't do anything more to convince you I'm not just crushing on you or trying to get into your pants."

Okay, a little crass, but I get the point. What am I thinking? My text put the *ass* in *crass!*

"Remember this is my senior year," he adds. "I have to prepare for my future."

And there it is. The perfect boyfriend is planning the perfect escape. Not that I can blame him; this town is a dead end. So is a relationship with me. There's nothing and no one for him here, so it only makes sense that he's laying the groundwork for a quick getaway.

"I understand," I say, even though I don't want to.

"Thank you," he replies.

"And I'm sorry," I add, because I am.

I was wrong. My family members aren't the only ones who have abandoned me. My boyfriend is planning to do the same thing.

Chapter 5

Star light, star bright, first star I see tonight. Wish I may, wish I might, have the wish I wish tonight.

I love that poem. It's filled with childhood memories of my father and me sitting together in the backyard swing, looking up at the night sky. It's filled with hope that the magic of the stars can be all yours just by wishing really, really hard. The only problem is it isn't nighttime and there are no stars hovering on the ceiling of my Algebra II classroom. Which, if you ask me, is one algebra too many.

But I am reminded of a constellation because speckled against his navy Two W polo shirt—a new alternative to the standard white version—Danny Klausman's dandruff looks like a galaxy. Let's call it Galaxy DK for short. If you look at it and accept it for what it is, it's hygienically disgusting. Honestly, I cannot believe that after all these years someone hasn't shoved a bottle of Head & Shoulders shampoo in Danny's locker, but on second thought it's really a good thing that no one has. Sure, it would result in Danny's having dandruff-free hair, but it would also mean we would have one less thing to mock.

When I squint my eyes, the unhealthy collection of flakes turns into something quite beautiful. Each speck is unique and geometrically interesting, like stars look in the sky. Much more fascinating than listening to Mr. Takamoto describe the principle of inequalities. I learned about this mathematical bore-fest in Algebra I. I hated it then, and I hate it now, but the rest of my class is inexplicably interested in what Mr. Takamoto has to say.

"Excuse me, Dice," Gwen says, after Mr. Takamoto acknowledges her raised hand. "If 'a' is greater than 'b' and 'c' is negative, then 'ac' will be less than 'bc,' is that right?"

"Last I checked it was," he replies, tossing a piece of chalk into the air from one palm to the other.

Mr. Takamoto is part of a new team of teachers who have invaded Two W this year. Due to the drastic financial cuts to the federal and state educational systems, blah, blah, *blaaah,* blah, blah, we witnessed an exodus of teachers last year who either retired or decided to give a job in corporate America a try. As a result, we not only have to learn new information this year, but new personalities as well. So far, Mr. Takamoto's got a good one. He even allows students to call him Mr. Dice or sometimes just Dice without the "mister," because Dice is short for his real name, Daisuke. His relaxed nature is one of the reasons he commands attention from his students.

But can he compete with a supernova?

As the fireball descends into class from out of nowhere, I'm about to scream, but quickly realize I'm the only one seeing this spectacle. And when the room is suddenly filled with a blinding yellow light, I know why. A supernova hasn't landed, only Jess.

"Je...!"

Luckily, I catch myself and turn the first part of Jess's name that I shouted out loud into a sneeze. Based upon the number of "bless you"s and "gesundheit"s that my sound receives, it was obviously a success. I mumble a "thank you," ignore Danny Klausman's dirty look because he thinks I sneezed on his back—as if my germs and snot are going to make the bacterial mess on his back any worse?!—and watch Jess materialize.

"How ya doin', Dom?" Jess asks.

She's hovering in the air with her legs crossed in some kind of awkward yoga pose, in the middle of the aisle between Gwen and me. By now I know that no one else can see her, but I still get nervous when she pays a visit in public.

"Don't worry," Jess replies, reading my mind. "I've experimented before in crowded places like the supermarket and the boys' locker room, and like I said no human being can see me."

I'm utterly shocked. *"Jessalynn Rosalie Wyatt!"*

And totally curious.

"Did you see Caleb naked?" I silently ask.

As she raises her right hand, specks of sunshine shoot into the air like golden raindrops. "I turned my head the second he took his shorts off," Jess answers.

I so don't believe her, but what's done is done, and what does it matter anyway? Even if she did see my boyfriend's full monty, it's not like she can act upon it. Could she? Can she have goddessex? Why am I thinking about Jess and Caleb having sex when he and I haven't even had sex yet? Why am I thinking about sex at all when I should be focusing on trying to find out what Jess is doing here so I can get her to leave?

"You don't want me hanging around?" she asks, definitely insulted.

Trying to appear as if I'm paying attention to the algebraic formula Edgar Sullivan is writing on the chalkboard under Dice's microscopic scrutiny, I mentally convey my concerns to my best friend.

"I love when you're around, you know that," I say. *"But I have to pay attention."*

"Since when do you like math?"

"I don't like math," I rebut. *"That's why I have to pay attention."*

"Life is too short, Dom, to pay attention to stuff you don't like," Jess sermonizes. "How happy and proud am I that I daydreamed through most of biology? I mean, really, corporeal substances and functions don't matter to me anymore."

I sigh so loudly Gwen looks in my direction, thinking I'm trying to get her attention. Sorry to disappoint you, Gwen, but I'm just trying to deal with the Amaterasu Omikami in the room.

"Deal with me!"

"Sorry!"

"Miss Robineau?" Mr. Dice asks. "Did you say something?"

Thanks a lot, Jess! This is why I don't want her barging into class like a sunburst, hovering in midair, and trying to have a telepathic conversation with me! There's only one end result when that happens, which is that I get into trouble.

"Dominy," Dice continues. "I asked you a question."

Time to play dumb. Literally.

"I'm sorry," I say meekly. "I just don't understand Edgar's formula."

"Well, it really isn't Edgar's formula," he explains. "Though he has made it his own with the addition of this extra plus sign."

Erasing the extraneous plus sign, Dice surrounds the "ab" with parentheses. He looks at me with his arms out to the side in the classic "voilà" stance, as if this simple change will make the formula on the chalkboard decipherable.

"Sorry," I repeat. "Still don't get."

Dice looks through Jess to stare at me as if he's trying to

determine if I could be so arithmetically challenged and quickly comes to the same conclusion as most of my previous math teachers: I can. He then announces that he's going to take us through the steps of the associative property one more time. When he turns his back to us to erase all evidence of what I incorrectly assumed to be Edgar Sullivan's personal equation, I turn my attention back to Jess.

"Now do you understand why your presence makes me nervous?" I ask.

"You're just nervous because your new teacher's kinda hot," Jess gushes.

Ignoring the little pellets of golden sunlight that are cascading down from her fingertips, I close my eyes, hoping that this action will get Jess to realize she really needs to leave me alone so I don't have to spend the entire night relearning what I should be learning right now. When I open my eyes, I see that I've failed. Jess is way too interested in Two W's newest academician.

"I know that I'm predisposed to thinking your new teacher is attractive because we're both Japanese," Jess says, continuing on quickly before I can remind her for about the seventeen-thousandth time that she is only an honorary Japanese citizen. "But seriously he is adorable. Look at his butt!"

"I am not going to look at Mr. Dice's butt!"

I swear my heart literally stops beating for about ten seconds until I am absolutely certain I did not scream that statement out loud. I love Jess, but seriously, right now I think I'd rather face Louis, Barnaby, and their horde of vigilantes fully armed with machine guns filled with silver bullets than have to spend another second fake-talking to Jess. She doesn't even know the havoc she's causing.

"I can tell by his lack of an accent that he's been abso-thoroughly de-Japanized, but since he's educated, being a teacher and all, he may know about our heritage," Jess rambles on. "I'm sure he'd be very interested to know that there's a real live Amaterasu Omikami in his classroom."

Since *I* can hardly believe that there's an Amaterasu Omikami in class, I doubt very much that my teacher is going to accept that fact. He barely accepts the fact that I say I understand what an associative property is when he finishes scribbling on the blackboard and asks me if I comprehend.

"Oh now I get it!" I squeal in the most unconvincing voice ever that even makes Gwen snicker.

I glare at her, and she immediately shuts up, and Dice proves that he's as cool as Jess thinks he looks by not calling me on my obvious fib. He does give me Teacher Eye for a few seconds, that look that silently conveys that the teacher knows that the student doesn't know what the teacher wants the student to know, but the teacher knows that the student will not acquire the required knowledge through further interrogation. It's an educational win-win; the student isn't unduly embarrassed, and the teacher doesn't have to waste time re-explaining a basic theory that should be easily understood. Unfortunately, now that Jess is not part of any educational institution, she's forgotten that sometimes it's necessary to move on from a concept.

"I'm so glad that we can communicate silently and that we're eternally connected," Jess states. "You being my murderer and all."

Terrific! I'm stupid *and* a murderer. There isn't an ounce of malice in Jess's voice. She understands and accepts that I personally didn't kill her; I was being used in Luba's psychotic vendetta against my father. But the word still stings. It's a reminder that I'll be eternally connected to Jess's death as more than just a witness or a mourner. I'm the reason she's dead.

I don't say a word in reply or protest, but Jess, being my best friend, can still gauge my emotions even if we're in separate metaphysical worlds.

"Dominysan, I'm sorry. It's just a fact," she says. "Please don't take it personally."

Don't take it personally?! How the ef can I not take it personally? That's the most ludicrous thing I've ever heard anyone say.

A glimpse of the clock above the door reveals that there are still fifteen minutes of class, way too long an amount of time to spend trying to half-listen to today's lecture and half-ignore Jess's quips and comments and veiled jabs. I have to put an end to this.

"Jess, I love you, but you need to go," I say, all assertive and adult-like.

"I can't," she replies, all petulant and childlike.

"You have to!" I silently cry. *"You're being disruptive and, honestly, keeping up this charade is really exhausting."*

"But I came for a reason," she finally admits. "I have something to tell you."

"Then tell me!"

"It's about the twins."

The twins? Jess has to tell me something about Nadine and Napoleon that's apparently important enough to pay me an unscheduled visit, and she's been wasting time goo-gooing over my teacher's butt?! Don't goddesses possess self-control and occupy themselves with existential conundrums and other vitally important things? Since when do they float in and out of classrooms just to say hi?

"I have manners, Dom!" Jess yells so loud little golden cloud puffs shoot out of her mouth. "I am not going to suddenly appear and announce that you can only trust one of the twins because the other one is dipped in pure evil and then poof, disappear again, go on my merry way, and leave you to ponder the ramifications of my statement."

What did she say?

"Correction," she adds. "I really do have to let you ponder

the ramifications on your own because of the whole limita-
tion thing. I can supply you with information, I can gently
nudge you in the right direction so you can combat the negative forces that are multiplying all around you, but I can't tell
you everything so that the scales tip and you have an unfair
advantage."

That is a lot of information that I'll dwell on later. Right
now I want to zero in on the comment about the twins.
"What do you mean I can only trust one of the twins?"

"That's correct. That's what I said."

I give Jess a bit of a pause, but she clearly doesn't understand that she needs to complete her statement.

"Which one?!"

Adopting a shocked expression that borders on outrage,
Jess almost flips over right onto the floor at Gwen's feet.
How can she be shocked? Can she be so inhuman as to not
think that her comment is going to arouse my curiosity, pique
my suspicion, and lead me to ask for specific clarification? I
mean there are only two twins. Just give me a name!

"I absolutely cannot," she says grandly. "Nor can I give
you a gender or an age, since, you know, one twin is always
technically older."

Infuriating! Absolutely infuriating! And also very scary. If
Jess felt the need to make a surprise visit, risk being seen no
matter how many times she's practiced her mumbo jumbo in
a crowded space, just to tell me this one fact that her superi-
ors—whoever or whatever they may be—have allowed her to
share, this has to be really mega-important.

"Actually I can say one more thing," Jess adds.

"What is it?!"

"The evil twin is super skilled in the art of deceit," she
says. "Oh and he or she has vowed to, you know, destroy
your life and stuff."

Oh my God! When I silently speak that phrase, I translate

it into Japanese so Jess will fully understand my freak out. *"Nanite koto!"*

So I was right about the twins all along. They are different, and they do play a role in my life. Perhaps a much larger role than I ever imagined. But according to Jess these twins are on opposing sides, one good, one evil. But which one is which?

"Jess, please, you have to give me a hint," I beg.

Miraculously the sunlight fades from Jess's body, and all that's left is the girl that I remember. The change only lasts for an instant, but it brings back such cherished memories that I feel tears sting my eyes. Jess may be this immortal entity, but underneath all the sunshine and wonder, she's still my best friend. Death hasn't changed anything. Except that now Jess can't tell me everything that's on her mind.

"Sorry, Dom," Jess says, resuming her golden goddess appearance. "I've said everything I can."

I nod my head. I'm not happy, but I understand. I feel Jess's hand brush against my cheek and watch her disappear, her sundrops mingling in with the dandruff galaxy that's still visible on Danny's back.

Pondering the question about which twin I can trust, I suddenly zero in on three dandruff flakes that are lined up perfectly in one horizontal line. I've seen that before in the sky, but somewhere else too. Yes! Jess's diary. Caleb said it was Orion's constellation. The same star cluster as is in the tattoos Nadine and Napoleon have on their hips. Somehow the twins are connected to Orion. And thanks to Jess I now know that one of those connections is made up of pure evil. But which one?

When the bell rings signaling the end of class, I'm not worried about writing down Dice's homework assignment; I'm not worried about the pop quiz he's threatening to give us this week; I'm not even worried that if I maintain this study ethic I'm bound to get my first failing grade in my entire life.

The only thing I'm concerned about is finding out which twin I can trust.

Slamming my textbook shut I feel my body shiver as if deep inside of me the wolf is trembling. And I know exactly why: We have to unlock the latest mystery and quickly.

Our lives depend upon it.

Chapter 6

Weirdness doesn't always begin with a capital W.

Transforming into a werewolf, yes, that's *weird* capitalized, no doubt about it. But there are other times that can still be classified as weird that don't scream at the same decibel level of weirdness. Like earlier, when I bit into one of The Worm's mother's brownies in honor of our special half day thanks to some off-site teacher meeting, the brownie was stale. Stale! Beverly Worman's brownies are never stale; they're always nothing less than scrumdillyumptuous. Again, weird. Or like just now when I snuck into the choir room to avoid bumping into my boyfriend and my best friend on their way to football practice. Also weird.

Why would I do such a thing? Why would I want to avoid Caleb and Archie, especially when I could use their help in deciphering Jess's cryptic message? Is it because they've been acting strangely lately? Because I've been acting strangely around them lately? Or because I don't want to introduce any more strangeness into their lives? Lots of questions; not a lot of answers.

If it's because they've become Mr. and Mr. Strange, how can I blame them? I've turned their world into an episode of

Stephen King's Most Bizarre Happenings in the History of the World. And I have to admit, they haven't been acting that odd. I just get the sense that the novelty of my affliction is starting to wear off.

I know that Caleb and Archie have both sworn to have my back for as long as I'm cursed, but I don't want to keep bringing them down with my drama. I want to make sure they're fresh and invigorated and excited to do battle on my behalf whenever the time comes for us to fight. Right now, however, is the time for a detour. So I've decided to leave my little soldiers alone and let them do battle on the football field, while I hide out among choir robes, choral risers, and music stands. I definitely got the bad end of the deal though, because I hate to sing.

"Oh my gosh, Dominy!" Gwen squeals. "Are you joining show choir?"

"No," I reply.

"Jazz choir?!" Gwen squeals again.

"No."

"Madrigal choir?!" Gwen squeals for a third time with remarkably the same amount of excitement in her voice as she had the first time.

"Sorry, Gwen," I start, amazed that I never knew how many types of choirs Two W had before. "I'm not here to join any type of choir or to do singing of any kind."

Gwen's face contorts into the same expression of horror and disbelief and fury that Jess's used to whenever I expressed my disinterest in becoming a member of Broadway Bound, the drama club she was the president of.

"Then what are you doing here?" she demands.

"I just needed a safe haven for a few minutes," I confess.

It's the perfect reminder that honesty is not always the best policy. Gwen interprets my need for a safe haven as the simultaneous need for a friendly ear and a sympathetic shoulder. I don't need either; I just really need some quiet. But now that Gwen thinks I'm some sort of emotional basket case or a girl with a deep dark secret, she wants to be my bestie.

While Gwen is babbling on about how important it is to open up to people and not keep problems and secrets and morbid thoughts quiet, I silently formulate a plan of escape. I don't want to hurt Gwen's feelings, especially now that I've vowed never to call her The Hog again. I don't want to dismiss her kindness, and I definitely don't want to come off as evasive so she IM's Miss Martinez, our guidance counselor, with an anonymous tip that I'm in need of a special one-on-one session. I don't want to do any of that, but I don't want to listen to her jabber on any longer either.

"You have been exactly what I needed, Gwen!" I shout, mimicking her squealy sounds.

"Me?"

Gwen might be a good singer, but she's a horrible actress, and she's unable to make her voice sound as humble as she intended.

"Yes, you!" I add.

"What did I do?" she asks. "I mean, I don't even know what your problem is or why you needed a time-out."

Sometimes you don't have to scramble to think of something to say; it just spills out of your mouth naturally. Maybe because the truth is more powerful than any fib.

"I just needed to hear somebody else's voice for a little bit so I could turn off my own."

The smallest sopranoesque note pops out of Gwen's mouth. "And I did that for you?"

Before I can reply, Gwen's arms fly around me and wrap me in what can only be described as a very intense bear hug that threatens to suffocate me and sends the books I'm holding falling to the floor. A few kids scramble into the room, presumably songbirds like Gwen hurrying into rehearsal, and either they are so excited because they're going to get to sing in a few minutes or super hugging is a common occurrence at choir practice, because no one raises an eyebrow at our embrace. My eyebrows, however, practically fly off of my face when Mr. Dice bursts into the room.

"Dominy," he says. "Jess never mentioned that you like to sing."

What did he say?!

"You never mentioned that you like to sing," he repeats.

Okay, that makes a little more sense. Less sense than the math teacher also being a choir instructor, but more sense than his mentioning Jess's name.

"I don't," I reply, picking up my books from the floor.

"Are you sure you don't want to give it a try?" he asks. "Finding your voice can be very liberating."

The only way I'm going to feel liberated is if I can get out of this room. Suddenly the walls feel as if they're inching closer toward me every second. Gwen's hulking body contact, Mr. Dice's sudden appearance, me thinking I heard Jess's name—all signs that I have overstayed my welcome. Guess it serves me right for trying to duck out of the way instead of just ramming into the oncoming traffic of my boyfriend and best friend. That's the last time I do that.

"I think if I freed my voice you'd all want to lock it back up," I joke. "My father used to say I couldn't carry a tune if someone gave me the handle."

The way Mr. Dice looks at me and the hush that comes over the choir room is startling, because it takes a few seconds for me to understand that I'm the cause. I crossed the line into Taboo Land by mentioning my father's name, effectively reminding everyone in earshot that I've been legally orphaned. And since everyone in this room aspires to tap into his or her sensitive side, they're even more affected by my comment than if I were surrounded by the more analytical minds that make up the debate team.

"Sorry, I didn't mean to put a bummer on the music fest before the music even begins," I mutter.

This time Mr. Dice's expression is startling, but in a positive, uplifting way.

"Never apologize for remembering something or someone who brings you joy," he says, his features softening into a kind smile.

Too bad I have absolutely no musical talent whatsoever, because I think this room would be a comforting place to spend some after-school quiet time.

On my way home the good energy stays with me, clinging to me like a crocheted poncho, light and flowing and warm. Sometimes it's necessary to take a detour to get back on track, and standing next to The Weeping Lady I know I'm exactly where I'm supposed to be. Looking up I can see that The Lady is in full bloom. Her body is covered with thick leaves; most are a deep green, but some have already started to turn yellow and that interesting shade in between that I'm not sure really has a name other than the not-so-original yellow-green. Regardless, the cluster of colors is vibrant, and it makes her look beautiful and sad and alone, the way she'll always look to me. It's an image that has become a source of calmness to me. Today, it's also a source of camouflage.

Off in the distance, somewhere beyond the rows of tall, majestic-looking trees that serve as the unofficial entrance to Robin's Park, I can hear two people talking thanks to my ESP—enhanced sensory proficiency. The fact that I can hear people speak who I can't see has become normal to me. What's odd is the fact that voices are coming from inside the park, a place that Louis has urged residents to steer clear of until the serial killer can be captured. Odder still, these voices are making me afraid.

How is that possible? I'm the one the town is supposed to be afraid of. I'm the reason there are witch hunts and curfews and no trespassing signs. And yet the sound of these voices, soft and muffled and unidentifiable, is actually making my knees buckle and my heart race. So much for latching on to good energy.

Impulsively, I straddle the huge oak tree and scramble up The Weeping Lady's body. My fingers act as claws, digging into the trunk, ripping pieces of bark off during my ascent, pulling me higher and higher until I'm face-to-face with the woman I've come to consider a friend. Her wooden eyes are staring back at me, and I know that she will do her best to protect me from the voices that are getting louder. I'm not sure what's more disconcerting: the fact that I can communicate with a tree-woman or the idea that I need protection.

When I recognize the voices, I know it's the latter.

The faces are still just shadowy outlines that I can barely see from within the combination of branches and foliage, but the voices are familiar. They belong to Nadine and Napoleon.

What are they doing coming out of Robin's Park? They got out of school the same time I did; there's no way they could have passed me, gotten all the way into the park, and then turned around. I did dally a little bit while I was trying to remain unseen, but it was hardly that long. Plus, it doesn't make sense that they would be in a part of town that's strictly off-limits. Sure, Nadine knows that it's okay to wander through the area, but Napoleon doesn't. Why would she arouse his suspicions by bringing him along for an after-school nature hike? And even if she did, Napoleon has never appeared to be a risk taker like Archie; it doesn't make sense that he would do something that's so completely against the rules. Unless Nadine for some reason convinced him to follow her into the park? Maybe she has a much stronger hold on her brother than anyone suspects.

I position myself so I'm straddling The Weeping Lady, my body pressed right into hers, and I'm reminded of Gwen. Maybe our embrace was a foreshadowing to this event? Maybe I'm just losing my mind? Maybe I should concentrate on not being seen so I don't cause the twins to stop talking?

The closer they get, the easier it is for me to eavesdrop, because they're speaking so loudly it's obvious they're not trying to hide from anyone. But when their conversation becomes clearer and I can finally understand every word they're saying, I realize that they're not having a friendly chat; they're having a fight.

"It's time that you man up, Nap," Nadine hisses at her brother.

"Stop talking to me like I'm a child," Napoleon replies.

"Start acting like an adult and I'll speak to you like one!" she screams. "You need to make choices."

"I have."

"The right ones, Nap!" she replies, hurling her words at him like daggers. "You have to start making the right choices!"

"Right for who? Me?" he asks. "Or everybody else in our family?"

My grip is so tight I expect The Weeping Lady to shriek in pain. The tips of my fingers are white, and I loosen my hold slightly just so I don't accidentally break off a branch and reveal my hiding place to the bickering siblings below. They're still about two hundred yards away, but they're walking in this direction, so in no time at all they'll be passing right underneath me.

"We're all in this together, Nap," Nadine answers. "You know that."

At some point I stop listening to their words, because even though I hear them clearly, I have no idea what they're talking about. However, I am learning a great deal by listening to the tones of their voices.

It's come as no surprise that Nadine is the louder one, the angrier one, the one who seems to be steering the conversation. In their twinlationship it's clear that she's the dominant force, the one with the more aggressive personality. Napoleon has always been the follower. I don't know if he's technically younger or if Nadine, being a girl, is just more authoritative, but Nap definitely takes a backseat to his sister. Until he decides the ride is better up front.

"The only thing I know, Nadine," he replies, "is that somewhere along the way you appointed yourself the boss of us all."

While Nadine's voice is brittle and loud and shrill, Napoleon's is quiet. But within that softer sound lies some unexpected strength. Their roles have become reversed; the butterfly's wings are made of steel, and the bee's stinger is easily bent.

Stopping in her tracks directly beneath me, Nadine makes her brother turn around to face her. I don't know if his words shocked her so much that she can't move or if she's adopting some strategy to make Nap have to react to her sudden actions. Either way she appears to be unsettled.

"A long time ago I made a choice," she says, trying hard to keep her voice even. "A choice to control my fate and not be a pawn in someone else's game."

Now when Napoleon's voice echoes throughout the empty land and into the air, it sounds different. Because it's the sound of laughter.

"You really think you're in control?" Napoleon asks when his laughter finally subsides. "You're being used just like I am."

Nadine's lips form a smile, but there is no indication whatsoever that she's going to laugh. It's the creepiest, most malicious-looking smile I've ever seen. I press my thighs and ankles closer to the trunk of the tree and tighten my grip so I don't slip. There is no way that I want these two to see me. I have got to keep my presence hidden because I know—somehow—that they'd rather kill me than let me live if they discovered I overheard their argument.

"I'm not being used because I've chosen what side I want to be on!" Nadine rails at her brother. "Now you've got to do the same thing!"

For the first time Napoleon raises his voice, and it's as unexpected as thunder on a beautiful summer day.

"I *have* made a choice!"

Breathing deeply, Nadine takes a step closer to her brother. "And whose side are you on?"

Not backing down at all, Nap moves into his sister. It's like he's suddenly found courage because he doesn't think he has an audience.

"Mine."

I can tell that it's the wrong answer even if Napoleon can't.

Without saying another word, he turns and starts to walk away, letting his fingers graze against the trunk of the tree. He peels off a piece of bark and flicks it into the air. If he looks up to watch it fly he'll look right into my eyes, so I melt even closer into the body of The Weeping Lady, wishing that I could somehow burrow inside of the tree to completely disappear so Napoleon won't see me. But before he's taken a handful of steps I can tell that he's about to be distracted.

Instead of answering verbally, Nadine chooses to respond physically, although I'm not sure if she has any control over her reaction.

Slowly the silver mist emerges from her body like an extra set of twisted limbs, but instead of shrouding her, instead of insulating her from the rest of the world like it has before, this time it serves as a way for her to connect.

The pieces of the mist begin to grow and lengthen and conjoin until they resemble a silver snake floating above Nadine's head, then into the sky, and then toward Napoleon. Slithering in the air, determined and focused and relentless, the silver streak moves with one apparent goal in sight: to capture her brother. I look at Nadine's face, and she looks just as determined; her eyes are unblinking and filled with hatred. She may not be controlling this thing that's been released from her body, but she knows exactly where it's headed and exactly what its intentions are, and she isn't doing anything to stop it. This is why I was afraid; this is why Jess told me I can only trust one of the twins. Nadine wants to make her brother pay for what he said.

Blithely walking through the open field, his hands in his jeans pockets, Nap looks like he doesn't have a care in the world. I think I might even hear him whistling, but my own heart is pounding so fiercely I can't be sure. I don't even notice the sound of my own gasp until a split second after it's released into the air.

Like the connected twins they are, Nadine and Napoleon both look up at the tree at the same time. They heard me, and it's only a matter of time before they see me. I cling to the tree even tighter and hold my breath as if that lame action is going to make any difference. I wasn't in control of my body or my emotions or my voice, and I've let myself be exposed! If Nadine is going to let some otherworldly silver mist attack her brother, what the hell is she going to let it do to me?

Why isn't anything happening? Why isn't the mist encircling the tree, wiggling its way up, in, and through the cavalcade of twisted branches to find the source of the sound? Why isn't it wrapping itself around my body and flinging me to the ground? The answer comes from a source that is both expected and unexpected at the same time: The Weeping Lady.

Looking beyond my own fear I see that I'm entirely covered by leaves. It's as if the tree has grown more robust and fertile in seconds. Above me, underneath me, on all sides are thick leaves that have left me completely hidden from any spectators, even those who suspect there's something very close by worth seeing.

Thankfully, I'm now in more control of my reactions, because when I turn to the left I see that The Weeping Lady has opened her eyes. Two wooden eyes that look as if they were carved and not created are staring right at me. Bending her head slightly she leans close to my ear, and I hear her speak.

"Be quiet and listen."

Her voice is like a rustle of the wind, and I'm not sure if she's truly spoken out loud or if her voice has somehow penetrated me, flown through me telepathically like Jess's. I don't waste time trying to figure it out; instead I obey her command.

Ever so slowly a few of the leaves separate, by less than an inch, but enough to give me a view of what's happening below me. It's not what I had expected to see.

My gasp must have interrupted their fight, because Nadine's silver mist isn't moving; it's hovering in the air like a metallic airborne puddle. It's only when I see what Napoleon's doing that I understand what's going on.

Nap's hand is raised in the air, and the same mist is seeping out of his palm, moving toward Nadine's silver source, making it retreat back toward its home base. I don't know if this is the first time Nap's ever done such a thing or if he's just more powerful since he's a guy, but Nadine isn't doing anything to fight back; she's standing rigid, and her skin has a deathly pallor. Even without my enhanced vision I can tell that she's terribly frightened.

Part of me wants to jump down and help the one twin that I instinctively know I can trust, but it's as if The Weeping Lady can read my mind, and I feel pieces of twine wrap themselves around my wrists and my ankles. I'm not going anywhere. And just as well, because when I hear Nap scream, I know I'm being kept safe.

"DO NOT PUSH ME!"

His voice is like the cry of someone who's been bullied his entire life and has finally decided to stand up for himself. But the way Nadine's body shudders, the way she clutches at the air for support, tells me that this isn't the first time Napoleon has reacted this way, despite the quiet, meek demeanor he's put forth ever since he came to town.

These two are very complicated creatures who have their own very special powers. I should feel relief that I'm not the only mutant in town, but the only thing I feel is scared. Yes, I've figured out that Nadine is the twin I can trust, but I've also found out that Nadine's mother is right—Napoleon seems to be totally unmanageable.

And that also means he's totally dangerous.

Chapter 7

I need my boyfriend.

I know that very recently I went out of my way to avoid him, but it's a girl's prerogative to change her mind. Even if that girl's only part girl. That's why I've decided to pay Caleb an unexpected visit.

Luckily Louis was called into the station to handle some for-chief-of-police-eyes-only business, so I was able to leave the house after dinner without having to sneak out and defy the town-wide curfew for anyone under twenty-one. Caleb only lives a few blocks from Arla's house, which I guess is now my house, but based on previous experience Louis would have either refused to let me go outside or demanded that he drive me there and pick me up when I was ready to go home.

As it turns out had Louis been my chaperone he wouldn't have had to wait very long at all for the return trip, because it appears that my boyfriend isn't up for any visitors.

"Hey, Domgirl," he says, coming out onto the front porch and nervously closing the door behind him. "It's, uh, not really a good time."

Excuse me? I know it isn't proper dating etiquette to show

up unannounced, but it's not like we just started our relationship. We've been going out with each other for over a
year. And Caleb knows everything about me. I obviously
don't know all there is to know about him.

"It's my parents," he confesses.

"What's wrong?" I ask. "Everything okay?"

"Oh yeah, of course," he says, then quickly adds. "Well,
no, not really. They're kind of in the middle of a big fight."

I know I should feel bad about this. I know I should say
something sweet and consoling and girlfriendesque, but all I can
think of is how lucky Caleb is to have both his parents around
so they can fight. How I wish my father was alive and my
mother conscious so they could have a rip-roaring, knockdown,
drag-out fight. I never witnessed the two of them fighting, but
that's because my mother slipped into her coma before my sixth
birthday. I'm sure the two of them had plenty of arguments,
both big and small, while they were dating and in the early
days of their marriage, the biggest fight probably being when
my mother found out that I was cursed and it was entirely
my father's fault. But I think I can speak for both of them
when I say that they would give anything to be able to have
one more fight, even if it meant that their kids would have a
front-row seat.

The screaming, the name-calling, even the cursing would
be better than silence. Loud, angry voices filling up the entire
house, spilling underneath my closed bedroom door to remind me that my parents are human and that they love each
other enough to fight passionately. I'd love to hear their
voices now. Which reminds me: Why can't I hear Caleb's parents?

Shouldn't people who are in the middle of a fight be yelling
at each other? Or at least doing that too-loud-whisper thing
that is even louder than a normal speaking voice? Besides,
shouldn't a girl who has super hearing be able to hear them
even with the front door closed?

"Caleb, are you sure they're fighting?" I ask. "I can't hear a thing."

Scrunching up his face, Caleb looks at me like I'm deaf, which he knows is so not the truth, and opens the door just a crack to peek in.

"Must be taking a break. They've been going at it for the past hour," he says, turning back to me. "Something about my mother's latest shopping spree. You know how she gets."

I do. His mother loves her shoes. And her clothes. And then her jewelry. After that I think comes her family, and I really do believe she loves them in that order. For the entire time we've been dating, I don't think I've ever seen her in the same outfit twice, even though Mr. Bettany lost his bigwig job as head of the Weeping Water Animal Protection Center when it shut down and was forced to take a pay cut when he started working as one of three assistants over at the center in Lincoln. Mrs. Bettany only works part-time at a law firm. Not really enough income to maintain such an ever-changing wardrobe, but every woman has her priorities. I may not officially be a woman, but I also have my priorities, and right now my number one priority is to have some private time with my boyfriend. My boyfriend, however, has other ideas.

"I'll see you tomorrow," Caleb says rather dismissively.

"Well, um, okay," I reply rather stupidly.

Before I can ask Caleb if he'd like to meet up before school tomorrow morning for a quick chat or maybe a make-out session, he closes the door right in my face. Okay, it's not like he slammed it or anything to make some dramatic statement, but he walked back into his house and quickly closed the door without saying good night or giving me a kiss.

Walking down the front steps, I try not to dwell on how much I already miss his sweet smile. I try not to read too much into the situation and make the situation all about me. *Not everything is about you, Dominy!* His parents are fighting. He's upset that they might get a divorce, and then he'll have to live with his mother in a trailer park in Omaha and sleep on a pull-out couch because his mother will want to use his bedroom as a closet for all her clothes, shoes, and accessories. He's worried that this fight could lead to his family's financial ruin, his not being able to go to college, that this could be the beginning of the end of his future, and all I'm thinking about is how I didn't get kissed good night.

No kiss, but I think I just got stung.

"What the hell?!"

I feel a sharp pain in my arm and slap myself. Lifting up the sleeve on my T-shirt I expect to see a bug bite, a mound of red flesh filled with some insect venom, but underneath the light on their front porch I see nothing, just my skin. I could've sworn I just got stung by a bee. When I look up I could swear that I see Nadine looking down at me.

Involuntarily I shake my head, which distorts my vision, and by the time I look up again and have a clear view of Caleb's window, all I see are his navy blue curtains. No Nadine, no shadowy figure, no nothing.

It's been almost a week since I heard the twins argue, but obviously I'm still thinking about them, so when I thought I got stung by a bee, I immediately got a mental picture of Nadine, because to me Nadine will always be a bee. That's got to be it. There's no way that Caleb would be in his bedroom with Nadine at this time of night. No way at all.

I don't even make it to the curb before turning back around, my eyes peering up and zeroing in on Caleb's window. Still nothing. I don't even see him through the curtains. Not that I have x-ray vision. I mean I can see farther than most normal people, but I'm not Superman's long-lost relative; I can't see through objects. I also don't see things that aren't there.

Whenever I've thought I was hallucinating, like with my brother in the bathroom, it turns out I was having a premonition. This time shouldn't be any different. Maybe it wasn't

Nadine up in his bedroom, but I definitely saw a girl looking at me, which means Caleb was lying to me. Which means I'm not going to get any sleep tonight until I confront my boyfriend and find out the truth.

My finger is about to press the buzzer on the front door when I stop myself and channel my inner Charlie's Angel. Instead, I twist the doorknob and am not terribly surprised to find that the door is unlocked. Aha! Caleb was in such a rush to get rid of me and get back to the slut in his bedroom that he didn't even remember to lock his front door.

Now I don't feel so bad for trying to trick him or catch him in the act. If he's that stupid to leave the door unlocked so I could waltz right into his house unnoticed, he deserves to be caught. When Mr. Bettany enters the living room wearing his pajamas and holding two empty plates, I'm the one who feels trapped.

"Dominy," he says, surprised, but smiling. "I didn't know you were coming over."

Thinking quickly I lie. "I forgot my algebra book, and I have homework."

"Do you want me to call Caleb for you?" he asks.

"That's all right. I sent him a text; he's expecting me," I lie once more.

Did Mr. Bettany just give me a weird look? Does he not believe me? Or does he not believe that his son would let me come over when he's shacking up with another girl in his bedroom? Or is he just embarrassed that I caught him in his pajamas?

"We were just having some dessert," he says, lifting the plates into the air. "Mrs. Bettany's apple pie. It's so delicious you don't even need the à la mode part."

How can a couple fight with their mouths full of pie?

"You guys were having dessert?" I repeat, knowing that I sound like a moron.

"Perfect way to end the day," he replies, "Homemade

dessert while watching an old Meg Ryan movie. Reminds Mrs. Bettany of when we were dating."

Did Caleb's father just blush in front of me?! If this wasn't absolute proof that Caleb was lying to me about his parents having a fight, I would be sort of grossed out by the TMI factor. But I'm too mad to be grossed out. All I want is to get upstairs and rip my boyfriend's blond hair out of his head. Strand by strand!

"That's so sweet," I say instead. "But I have to get my book so I can get home and do my homework."

"You didn't walk over here alone, did you?" he asks, shifting gears from romantic husband to concerned father figure.

"No, I borrowed Louis's car."

What's one more lie? I've said so many lately, I'm starting to lose count. When I push open Caleb's bedroom door, however, I realize this is the first time he's ever lied to me. When I see Nadine sitting next to him on his bed, I realize that I picked the wrong twin to trust. When I feel the tears start to well up in my eyes, I realize this was the stupidest thing I've ever done in my life. Have I not learned that the truth is usually painful, and that's why it needs to remain hidden?

"I'm sorry," I hear myself mutter.

And I am. I wish I were back home watching TV with Arla or trying to mend my torn relationship with Barnaby, letting him know that despite everything that's happened to us and despite everything that he suspects, I will always be his older sister and I will always look out for him. I want him to know that the only thing you can count on in this world is family. Because you definitely can't count on boyfriends!

"I'm sorry," I repeat. "I didn't realize you were busy."

Turning quickly I start to leave the room, a huge collection of emotions exploding inside of me. Anger, hurt, disappointment, sadness, all these things are ricocheting inside my head and my heart, making me wish I was still the ignorant girlfriend. My life has been so crazy lately, the one true constant has been Caleb. I always thought that his feelings for me were stronger than mine were for him, but maybe I was wrong? What I feel for him may not be undying love, but I love being his girlfriend and more than that I love knowing that he wants to be my boyfriend. I guess all of that's over now.

"Dominy, wait!" Caleb cries.

I feel his hand on my arm, and it isn't me who reacts; it's the wolf. Roughly, I shake his hand off of me, and I swear I hear myself growl. Now that I'm free I don't want to move, and I just stand there with my back to him and Nadine, standing in the doorway afraid to make a move, when out of nowhere I hear my mother's voice, soft, but powerful inside my head.

Remember, Dominy, you are blessed.

Thankfully I understand exactly what she means this time. My life may not be perfect, no one's is, but I've been blessed with a few things that my mother handed down to me: self-respect and inner strength. Those words get tossed around a lot, and people often ignore them or take them for granted, but they shouldn't, because when a situation like this arises you need to be ready to grab hold of them. Like I am right now.

Turning around to face my boyfriend and his new girlfriend, I smile, which has the desired effect, because I can tell from both their expressions they weren't expecting this. They were expecting a face filled with tears or contorted into a wolfen rage, but I'm better than that. And I'm better than both of them.

"That's all right, Caleb. If you'd rather go out with Nadine, that's fine with me; I wouldn't want to stand in your way," I say quite calmly. "I just wish you would've given me a heads-up."

Just as I'm about to unfasten the faux-diamond necklace

he gave me last Christmas, Caleb and Nadine both start shouting at the same time.

"We are not on a date!"

Isn't that sweet? They're so in sync that they're lying simultaneously.

"Then why are you both sitting on your bed, Caleb?" I ask. "And why did you lie to me to get me out of your house?"

"Because I'm tutoring Nadine in math," Caleb explains. "And she didn't want anyone to know."

"But I never meant for you not to tell Dominy!" Nadine adds. "I mean Dom's your girlfriend; you shouldn't be keeping secrets from her."

"No, you shouldn't, Caleb," I say, unable to resist.

"Dom, I'm really sorry," Nadine says, grabbing my hand. "I assumed Caleb told you and you were keeping it a secret so no one would find out I'm not as smart as I pretend to be."

Shrugging my shoulders, I reply, "Caleb didn't tell me nuthin'."

Nadine and I both look at Caleb at the same time expecting an answer. Since the odds are unevenly matched, two against one, Caleb's mouth opens, but he doesn't say anything for a few seconds. Then he starts to ramble.

"I didn't think you wanted me to say anything, Nadine! You said not to tell anyone, so I didn't. And, Domgirl, you can't possibly think I would cheat on you ... especially with Nadine!"

Now it's my and Nadine's turn to be in sync, and we cry out at the same time, shocked by his rudeness. "Caleb! That's a terrible thing to say!"

"You know what I mean!" Caleb cries back in exasperation, trying to defend himself. "We're all friends. Well, except you and me, Domgirl; we're more than friends."

Yes, we are. And Nadine has proven that she's much more

than a friend as well, even if for a fleeting moment I thought she was total B.S., as in boyfriend stealer.

"I'm sorry, Nadine," I say.

"No, I'm the one who's sorry!" she says, quickly gathering her books. "I feel like a fool."

Now it's my turn to grab her hands and look her in the eye.

"You have absolutely nothing to feel foolish about," I tell her. "You suck a little at math. Trust me, there is no way you can suck worse than me."

"True that," Caleb agrees.

My boyfriend so needs a refresher course in the art of subtlety.

"Dominy was a lot dumber than you are when I first started tutoring her," he continues. "She couldn't even grasp mathematical concepts. At least you get that; it's just that you sometimes get lost in the execution."

Nadine and I stare at Caleb dumbfounded, and after a few seconds we look at each other and crack up laughing. Gigglaughs and deep-throated chuckles fill up the room.

"You're lucky he's so cute, Dom," Nadine whispers in my ear as we hug.

"Don't I know it," I reply. "And don't worry, your secret's safe with me."

The embrace feels good, and I know that I've chosen the right twin to trust. After Nadine leaves and I've taken my rightful place on Caleb's bed, I see that my choice might not have unanimous support.

"I don't trust her," Caleb announces.

"What?!"

I don't realize how volatile my reaction is until I see Caleb rubbing the palm of his hand. I must've slapped it away when he was trying to run his fingers through my hair, which he loves to do right before he starts kissing me. Maybe I can't always contain my primitive strength.

"She's a lot more trustworthy than you are!" I exclaim.

"Seriously?" Caleb asks, seriously offended.

"Caleb, you lied to me!" I remind him. "You told me your parents were practically ready to file for divorce just to get me out of the house so I wouldn't catch you tutoring Nadine. How many other times have you lied to me?"

"Only a few," Caleb admits.

Gotta give the guy points for being honest.

"So this is why you've been breaking dates with me!" I shout, jumping off the bed. "So you could cozy up to Nadine!"

"Yes!" Caleb replies. "To get information from her."

This is a perfect example that someone who is book smart doesn't always have common sense.

"That's not how tutoring works, Caleb!" I scream. "The tutor gives the information, not the tutee!"

"Well, the tutee cannot be trusted!"

The absurdity of our words and our conversation finally hits us both, and now we start laughing. The sound is different than when I was laughing with Nadine; it actually sounds prettier—my gigglaughs mixed in with Caleb's high-pitched snorts. I cling to my boyfriend's arms and feel the muscles underneath his shirt, focusing on how smooth and hard he feels. I wish I could rip his shirt off and see his chiseled body, see a little more than I've ever seen before, but it isn't the right time for action; it's time for explanation.

We sit on his bedroom floor, Caleb behind me, his arms and legs draped over mine. He explains that he overheard Nadine talking to Danny Klausman one day, complaining about a C she got on an algebra quiz. Caleb took it as the perfect opportunity to offer his services as her private tutor in order to get closer to her to find out if there was any truth to the stuff Jess wrote about Nadine in her diary. I'm pretty impressed with his initiative, but I've already decided that Jess was just writing that Negative Nadine stuff because she was jealous of her. To take it a step further, Jess probably knew that her relationship with Napoleon was doomed from the start, but didn't want to admit it even in the privacy of her own diary, so she took out her frustration on the one twin she could.

When Caleb leans his head against mine, I can smell the super-strong smell of the shampoo from the Two W gym in his hair, like disinfectant mixed with only a hint of citrus. Yucklean. Right now, however, I think it smells heavenly. I'm so lost in Caleb's arms and hair smell that I almost forget to tell him about Jess's latest visit.

"She showed up right in the middle of Dice's class?" he asks.

"Practically gave me a heart attack," I reply. "I'm not sure if I'll ever get used to her doing stuff like that. Or the things she says."

I explain to Caleb what Jess told me, that I can only trust one of the twins, and Caleb nods his head furiously in agreement.

"She's right!" he exclaims.

"Exactly."

We might agree that only one of the Jaffe twins can be trusted, but we can't agree upon which one. Because the moment I say Nadine, Caleb says Napoleon.

Chapter 8

"Nadine!"

"Napoleon!"

Over a week later Caleb and I still can't agree, so it's time to bring it up to the two other members of the Wolf Pack for a confab. Since the fate of one of the charter members is going to be discussed, we couldn't talk in the cafeteria; we had to pick a more isolated rendezvous spot where we could speak without fear of being overheard and a place where Nadine wouldn't expect to find us. That's why, instead of crowding around a lunch table, the four of us are cramped into a large closet off of the band room where they keep extra instruments.

I saw this place when I ducked into the choir room, and Archie confirmed that this entire section is soundproof. So even if Nadine or Napoleon is suddenly overcome with the need to explore his or her hidden musical talents and enters the main band room, they won't overhear us talking about them. It allows us to speak freely behind our friends' backs.

Sitting next to a tuba that makes me feel incredibly svelte, I inform Arla and Archie about Jess's visit and her message, and then dive into my pitch.

"We all know that Jess's diary is mainly a work of fiction,"

I say. "It's her interpretation of the life around her and from her point of view, which was influenced by her, um, well, by her jealousies."

"She did have a wild imagination," Archie interjects.

"Yes, she did," I agree. "She loved to exaggerate, and I'm sure each one of us could spend the next hour citing examples of Jess's embellishments. So just because she put those same fancy phrases on paper doesn't make them true."

Twirling her long blond ponytail around with her index finger, Arla asks, "So that's why you think Jess's anti-Nadine entries don't contain any fact. They're just manifestations of her true negative feelings toward Napoleon, because she knew down deep that he never wanted to become Mr. Jessalynn Wyatt?"

"Exactly," I say.

Tossing back her ponytail, she asks another question. "That's a pretty big stretch, don't you think?"

"Yes, it is," Archie says.

The space is so small that when Caleb, who's sitting on the opposite side from me, stretches his legs out in front of him our toes touch. "And that's why that theory is wrong."

Maybe if I use my newfound strength I could push really hard and send Caleb barreling through the cushioned wall and into the choir room next door? I don't want to hurt him, but I need to convince Arla and Archie that I'm right. In order to do that, however, I have to convince them that Jess would make up stories even if she thought she would be the only one to read them.

"My theory isn't wrong," I correct. "It's the only plausible explanation."

"So explain," Archie commands.

It might be the tight quarters, but I'm getting an antagonistic vibe from Archie. He hasn't really said much, but his whole attitude is confrontational. It's a bit off-putting, considering he knows how often Jess would make things up about people when she was alive and how she loved to create drama when it wasn't there.

"Regardless of how Nap felt for Jess," I explain, "she was completely in love with him, so she couldn't see him for the person he really is."

"And what type of person is he?" Archie asks.

Okay, now I'm certain Archie is being confrontational, because he couldn't look at me when he asked that question. He spit it out while he was pulling out the little spit thing on the trumpet he's holding in his hands, acting as if he's more interested in the instrument than in what I'm about to say.

"In his mother's own words, he's unmanageable," I convey.

"Why don't you use your own words, Dom?" Archie demands.

This time when I turn to my left to look at Archie, he's looking right at me, and I'm the one who immediately shifts focus. I lock eyes with Caleb first and then Arla across the room, and the three of us are all surprised; we all share the same thought, the same common denominator: Why is Archie so pro-Nap all of a sudden?

"In my own words?" I repeat. "Nap's dangerous."

Even though Caleb disagrees with me, he keeps silent to see how Archie will respond. Our friend doesn't disappoint.

"Methinks you're jumping to conclusions," he says. "And methinks your conclusions are the wrong ones."

Archie is still twiddling the trumpet mouthpiece in his hands, but at least now he's looking at me; he's not avoiding my gaze. He really believes what he's saying. I can accept disagreement from my boyfriend, but not from my best friend.

"Archie! Why are you sticking up for him?" I ask. "Nap treated Jess horribly. He's a loner and hardly talks to anyone. Look at everything Nadine's done to help me; she's a charter member of the Wolf Pack. It's obvious that Nap's the twin Jess was warning me about."

Instead of Archie responding, Caleb does. He folds his legs underneath him to create space between us literally and figuratively.

"I'm with Archie on this one," he says. "No offense, ladies, but girls know how to play the game; they know how to scheme and plot and say one thing, but really mean another."

"It's called using our feminine wiles," Arla helps.

"Thanks, Arla," Caleb says. "That's exactly what Nadine's been doing this whole time."

I will admit that generally girls play more mind games than guys, mainly because physically we're not as strong—well, maybe I am, oh and Gwen too. But generally speaking, we girls have more brains than brawn, so we have to rely on our minds when battling against the opposite sex. Sometimes we take a detour, venture into the dark side, and use our brains for nefarious deeds like manipulating boyfriends and parents and teachers, but most of the time it's a harmless, though effective, method of getting our own way. What Caleb's talking about is different.

Caleb's suggesting that Nadine is on a par with some KGB, double agent, super spy. All this time she's been helping me, acting like my friend, when her motives have been nothing but unpure. I can't accept that. If I've learned nothing else through this journey so far it's that my gut instinct is reliable, and right now it's telling me that Caleb has no idea what he's talking about. I wish I had a nicer way of conveying my thoughts, but I don't.

"Caleb, you have no idea what you're talking about."

"Domgirl, you're just upset because you didn't see it for yourself," he replies. "Nadine has been playing you; she's been playing all of us. We've all suspected it, and now that we have proof . . ."

"What proof?" Arla asks.

"Jess's visit," Caleb replies.

"That's not proof," I remind him. "She never mentioned Nadine's name."

"She made a cross-dimensional visit to offer a clue," he says, his arms flailing at his sides so wildly that Arla has to duck out of the way or else risk getting bashed. "She's got to know that you've read her diary; she's just hoping that you'll connect the dots."

"Do you really think she knows we peeked in her diary?" Arla gasps. "I feel so uncool!"

The only thing that's uncool is that I have to defend Nadine's friendship and loyalty and integrity by admitting that her brother is a letch.

"Napoleon made a play for me at Jess's repast, right in her own bedroom!" I confess.

"Give me that tuba, Dom," Arla says. "I may need something to throw up in."

"You never told me this," Caleb adds.

"Because it never happened!" Archie shouts.

What the hell is going on with him? "You walked in on us! Had you shown up a few seconds later, you would've caught Nap in the act of trying to get into my pants."

For a second I think Archie is going to chuck the brass mouthpiece at my face. "He was not trying to get into your pants, Dom!"

Our voices are starting to bounce off the walls and echo so loudly that I'm surprised no one has flung open the door to find out why so much noise is coming from a soundproof room.

"Yes, he was!" I cry. "He's always trying to get into my pants!"

"That's a lie!" Archie shouts even louder.

"No, it isn't!"

"He doesn't want to get into your pants, Dom," Archie says, "because he's already gotten into mine!"

It's like the end of a rousing symphony to which no one applauds. Siss, boom, bang, silence.

"Napoleon's gay?" I shriek-ask.

"Napoleon's my boyfriend," Archie replies.

"What?!"

I don't know what's more shocking, the fact that Napoleon's gay or that he's Archie's boyfriend. No, wait, I totally know! The first part is shocking, but the latter part is just plain disturbing. Of all the available gay guys at Two W, Archie has to pick the twinemy?

"Ahhhh!!! That is BNE!" Arla squeals. "Best news ever!!"

Really? I mean really, Arla? Am I the only one who understands the ramifications of Archie's poor choice for a bf?

"No way!" Caleb shouts.

Okay, maybe I'm not the only one.

"Way," Archie replies. "Since August 2nd; that's our anniversary."

Arla squeals again. "I have to start shopping for a two-month anniversary gift for you guys."

It's obvious by the scowl on Caleb's face that he will not be joining Arla at the mall. But what's the reason for his scowl? He doesn't share my opinion about Nap's being the bad twin, so Archie's announcement shouldn't make him angry. Unless my boyfriend is a closet homophobe, which would be impossible; I mean if that were true, how could he be Archie's best friend. Oh no! No, no, no, no, no! If Caleb isn't a closet homophobe, maybe he's a closet *case?!*

"Caleb," I say. "Are you ..." I can hardly say the word. "Jealous?"

"No, I am not *jealous!*" Caleb shouts. "That's absurd!"

Whew, that was a close one. Well, if he isn't jealous, what's his problem?

"I'm thrilled for Arch," Caleb admits. "But I'm also pissed off."

"Why?" the three of us ask at the same time.

"You've had a boyfriend for almost two months, and I'm just finding out about it now?"

There it is. Caleb isn't upset that he lost Archie to another guy; he's upset that Archie didn't fill him in.

"I'm sorry, Bells, but not everybody is as out and proud as I am," Archie declares. "Nap didn't want me to tell anybody, not until he gets more comfortable with the whole gay thing."

"Well, we're all comfortable with the whole gay thing," Caleb announces. "So Nap is just going to have to deal with it."

"What about you, Dom," Archie asks. "Are you going to be able to deal with it?"

I have to make a decision, am I going to be a wolf or a girl? Do I grind my fangs, relentlessly pursue my objective, and continue to try and convince everyone that Napoleon is not to be trusted? Or do I embrace my inner girlie-girl and howl with delight that Archie's found happiness? I'm conflicted, but I ultimately make the choice that I know will make my friend happy, even if I'm not fully certain that it's the right choice to make. What helps is when I look into Archie's eyes and see his staring back at me. The eyes that I've grown up with and, hopefully, the eyes that I'll see for decades to come.

"I'm very happy for you, Archie," I say, holding him tight. Not tight enough to make him forget my doubts though.

"But not happy that I'm with Napoleon," he replies.

It's a wonderful feeling not being able to pull one over on your friends, even if it means you have to squirm a little.

"Well, why don't you arrange a meeting for us and the Napster so we can all get to know him better," I suggest.

For the rest of the day, Caleb, Arla, and I exert so much peer pressure onto Archie that he has no choice but to arrange a surprise meeting after school. Somehow Nadine didn't notice what was going on nor did she catch our whispering and note-passing during class, so when I saw her right before last period I almost blew the whole undercover operation to uncover Archie's paramour.

"Hey, Dom, are we still getting together after school?" she asked me.

If it weren't for Rayna's bumping into me and jostling my books, I would've slipped and told Nadine to meet us on the stage, which was where Archie told us to meet him after school, but the physical interruption gave me a moment to collect my thoughts. Once again, Nadine was not being invited to a Wolf Pack gathering.

"I'm sorry, Nay. I can't today," I lied.

Either it wasn't a very good lie or I was just feeling guilty for choosing a side that Nadine wasn't on, but my palms started to get sweaty. It's an incredibly gross feeling, and there's absolutely nothing you can do to stop it except maybe tell the truth and reverse the process. But in this instance I couldn't tell the truth, because Archie told us one of the main reasons Nap wanted to keep his same-sex relationship secret was because his opposite-sex twin would freak out.

Personally, I don't believe that's true. Nadine has never once said anything nasty to or about Archie or the gay population as a whole, and her mother was even cool to Archie when he made a gay comment in her presence. However, I imagine that Napoleon is frightened to take his first step out into the world wearing a huge gay sign on his head, and he automatically thinks that everyone, including his family, is going to hate him and want nothing to do with him. I've heard and read stories of it happening to kids before. In fact there was this kid a few years ahead of me at Two W, Michael Howard, who was gay and had to deal with lots of bullying, so it's a real issue. Nap will just have to find out that it's a nonissue for Nadine on his own timetable. There's no way I'm going to speed up the process because I can't keep my mouth shut.

"I have to get home right after school and help Barnaby with some project," I said. "I think I'm making the solar system out of Styrofoam, which isn't the best way to spend the afternoon, but I need to bond with my brother."

Nadine clutched her books a bit tighter to her chest. "Is he still acting out since your father's death?"

A flicker of silver light shined over Nadine's body for a second, less than that, but long enough for me to witness it. Did Nadine will the light to remain within her body? If so, it's the first time that I realized she may have control over this silver shadow, just like Napoleon obviously has control over the light that's within him.

"Let's just say it's been a difficult time for him," I replied.

"Of course it has," she said. "But it would be even more difficult if he knew why his father died."

The silence that followed Nadine's comment was interrupted only by the clicking of her pen. Two quick clicks, then a pause, then two more. I waited for Nadine to continue clicking, but she stopped. Once again an interruption offered me a moment of clarity. I knew it was time for me to stop talking about my brother and my father and how death is now their only connection.

"Maybe we can meet tomorrow," I said. "I don't have cheerleading practice."

Nadine smiled just as the bell rang, and we both had to sprint or risk being late for class. I whipped past her and ran off to my World History II class, but just as I turned the corner I saw Nadine staring at me. Her lips were moving like she was talking to herself, and the silver mist slowly started to rise above her head. I was transfixed as the mist began to move down the hallway toward me. I don't know what would've happened if the wolf hadn't taken control of my body and ran the rest of the way to class. I sat in my seat just as Mr. Lamatina entered the room. I wasn't late, but definitely was puzzled.

Now after school, I'm even more puzzled because I'm standing in between Arla and Caleb behind some scenery on the stage. The curtain is drawn, so even though I can hear voices in the theater, our presence will remain secret. Unlike Archie and Napoleon's relationship.

Archie is sitting in the half-built convertible Corvette that is being constructed for the upcoming production of *Grease*—the PG version with all the dirty words and references cut out, of course, and starring a boy and a girl Danny and Sandy and not the all-male version that's about to take place.

Just as I hear footsteps, Arla nudges her elbow into my stomach, and we both peer through a tiny crack in the wooden flat we're standing behind to see Napoleon nervously climb into the car and sit next to Archie. They start whispering to one another, and Arla and Caleb look at me, expecting me to interpret what they're saying, but it's a private whispersation so I tune them out. I wouldn't want someone listening in to my intimate conversations with Caleb. But my boyfriend's so determined to hear what's going on that he presses his ear closer to the flat so hard that I'm afraid it's going to topple over. But very quickly there's nothing to hear except for the sound of kissing.

All wolf instinct is gone, and the girl has taken over completely. Arla and I clutch each other and we press our free hands against our mouths so we don't scream in sheer delight when we see Archie and Napoleon start to make out. Caleb isn't so quick to conceal his comments.

"Dude! You really are gay!"

The shock of hearing Caleb's voice causes Napoleon to jump out of the fake Corvette and fall right onto his head. I fight the urge to call Nurse Nelson because it looks like Nap might be suffering from a heart attack. He's gasping for breath and sweating, but he doesn't need my help; he's got Archie.

With one deft movement, Archie grabs Nap under his

armpits and lifts him off the ground. He's not going to die, but he's still in shock.

"What the hell is going on?!" Nap screams, clutching his heart.

"I'm sorry, Nap," Archie starts, "but they didn't believe me when I told them you were my boyfriend, so I thought it would be best to show them."

"We believed you," Arla and I say at the same time.

"Caleb was the only doubter," I add.

Napoleon should be starting to look better, but instead he looks worse. His skin is losing all its color, and he's actually holding onto the convertible for support. Maybe we do need a nurse.

"Are you okay, Nap?" I ask.

"This stays among us, okay?"

More of a command than a question, but it's his personal life, so it's totally his decision that it should remain contained to a small group. We all assure him that we're not going to say a word about what we just witnessed or start singing "Nap and Archie sitting in a tree." Except for those times when we know no one is within earshot so we can tease the lovebirds, because that's what friends do.

"Thank you, Dominy," Nap replies. "I appreciate it."

I don't know if I misjudged him or if I'm just a sucker for a happy ending, but despite my promise I want everyone to know the good news.

"Jess is going to be so happy about this!" I beam, tears starting to gather in my eyes.

I can only blame my faux pas on the fact that I'm ecstatic that Archie has found a boyfriend. Even if that boyfriend is the twin I thought Jess was trying to get me to mistrust. I'll focus on that later; right now I have to focus on correcting my tongue-slip.

"Full disclosure," I begin. "I talk to Jess all the time, and I know that she can hear me."

Listen hard enough and you can hear Caleb, Archie, and Arla sigh in relief. I'm not sure if Nap believes I really can speak with Jess or if he thinks I'm just speaking metaphorically, but he buys my explanation.

"When you speak with her again, please let her know that I never meant to deceive her," he says sincerely. "I was just trying to be, you know, *normal* and date a girl, and Archie's made me realize I was already normal."

Now I'm crying. And so is Arla. Even Caleb looks moved by Napoleon's comment. So moved that he gives the guy one of those multipart fist-bump, high five, handshake things.

"Welcome to the family, Nap," he says.

"Don't worry, Bells," Archie says. "You'll always be my special guy."

Whispering into my ear Arla asks, "You know what this means, right?"

"That you are officially the fifth wheel," I joke.

She doesn't laugh. Have I gone too far? I didn't think she cared about not having a boyfriend, but maybe I'm wrong.

"No," she whispers. "If this is the reason Napoleon's always been the strange twin, now that his secret's out we can trust him."

Damn! This also means my gut instinct has to do a 180.

"So the twin we absolutely cannot trust," I say, "is Nadine."

Chapter 9

I barely notice the transformation this time.

It's still painful and grotesque and terrifying, but the sensation is nothing in comparison to what I felt upon learning the truth about Nadine only a few days ago. The girl who has become a confidante to me, the girl who I was beginning to feel could be a Jessurrogate, who I thought could become a lifelong friend, is nothing but a fraud. I don't understand how Nadine's duped all of us, and I definitely have no idea why she's done it, but I know that she is my enemy. And if she's an enemy to Dominy, then she's even more of an enemy to the wolf.

Before the full moon rose above the horizon and started to glow in the night sky as it's doing now, casting a purplish haze like a bruise over the world, I decided that I was going to roam free tonight, regardless of the risks. Caleb fought me on it, bitterly, but I wouldn't listen to him. Now that I have another enemy lurking out there and not just Luba, Caleb flip-flopped and changed his mind, thinking that it would be safer if I spent the night in my cage in the uninhabited barn on his Uncle Luke's property. But I wouldn't give in. Finally, he accepted my decision because deep down, he knows that the rules have changed.

We might not know exactly what or who Nadine is, but we do know that she isn't what she pretends to be. And although she's been doing her best to act like our ally for the past year, she's just the opposite. We have to be on guard; we have to be ready to fight back. And it's kind of hard to fight back if I'm stuck in a cage.

That's why I find myself within the belly of Robin's Park, uncaged and free, swallowing the last bits of a deer that I killed because he was too scared and I was too determined to have an early feast. Licking my lips I wash away the last traces of blood and flesh from my lips. Now that I don't fight the hunger, now that I understand the wolf needs to be nourished as much as the girl, my meals taste so much better. Once the hunger and thirst have been quenched, once my wolf appetite is satiated, I can embrace the spirit living inside of me and enjoy the part of me that normally stays hidden. I lift my snout toward the dark violet sky and open my mouth; the sound of my howl is clear and loud and unafraid. If someone hears it, so be it. I'm not in the mood to hide.

In this part of the park the trees are farther apart from each other. The land isn't open and flat like it is near the low hills, the area known as Dry Land, but it's also not densely wooded. Still, I could find a hiding place if I wanted to; I could become part of the landscape until the dawn. But remaining invisible isn't on the agenda for tonight; tonight I want answers. At the thought of this my body twitches, a shudder that rustles my fur so it looks like it's gotten caught in a breeze. There's an ache deep within my body, in the place where girl meets wolf, like the physical manifestation of a premonition. Yes, tonight will be different.

The third time I walk in a circle I stop myself. I didn't even realize I was absentmindedly tracing and retracing my steps, but when I look down I see that I've created a circle in the dirt. A circle that is now drenched in a pool of moonlight. Nothing is a coincidence, and everything happens for a reason. Standing inside the makeshift circle, I look up and let the moonglow spill all over me. A smile sneaks slowly across my face, because I know that the moon is shining on me like a spotlight; it's drawing me out, drawing me closer to someone who's patiently waiting for me. Let them think that I don't know; let them think that I'm not prepared; let them think that I'm easy prey.

A low, guttural growl seeps out of my mouth; I don't even know I'm making any noise until half a minute later when I hear the sound join the wind. As a wolf my body seems to understand things before my mind. I find that I react physically before I can mentally assess a situation. It's something that I fought at first, but now that I'm more familiar with these restraints, now that I'm learning to trust this other part of me more fully, I let the wolf lead, and I willingly follow. Even if it leads me into danger.

I feel Luba's presence as easily as I can smell the rotting flesh of the deer. She's nearby; she's waiting; she's smiling because she thinks she's going to be victorious. She's also thinking that tonight is going to be special. It is, but not in the way that she imagines.

Giving in to the wolf spirit, I feel my body weave in and out of trees, in and out of the moonlight, and walk toward the scent of evil. Suddenly my body stops, and I feel myself crouch low to the ground. My head is almost flat on the dirt, camouflaged by a bulky spray of long, thick leaves from a large bush. The early autumn chill has made some of the leaves turn color, so the bush is a collection of reds and oranges and yellows mixed in with the vibrant greens and my fur isn't immediately recognizable. It looks as if I've taken another form, just like evil has.

Nadine is standing alone, her silver mist forming curlicues all around her, making her look like a metal statue of Medusa. Keeping my body still, I scour the land with my eyes, searching for Luba, but she's nowhere to be found. I could've sworn I sensed that witch, but it must've been Nadine's scent. My sense of smell must have gotten confused, or different types of sin simply smell the same.

Fighting the innate desire to spring forward and pounce on Nadine, tear her limbs from their sockets, I dig my paws into the earth and allow the coolness to squash the fever building inside of me. But when Nadine's companion comes into view, the fever threatens to overtake me. When I see Barnaby I actually think I can feel my blood boiling.

What is he doing with her?! What is she trying to do to him?!

Slowly the silver tendrils start to float into the air, stopping to hover over Barnaby's head. The preternatural force seems to be invisible to the human eye, because he's not moving. He is, however, speaking, and I can hear every word of their conversation.

"I don't know what you mean," Barnaby says. "What are you talking about?"

His voice is soft and not angry and contemptuous like it is when he speaks to me. I don't know if this is his normal voice or if Nadine has somehow enchanted him. She clearly has powers. I just haven't figured out what they are yet or their origin.

"You have to choose sides, Barnaby," Nadine replies. "And it shouldn't be that difficult a choice to make; there are only two."

The silver mist now looks like a river floating in the air, whisking against Barnaby's ears and his arms and his heart. Whether or not Barnaby can feel it, he's doing nothing to get away from it. He's standing completely still as if he's paralyzed.

"But why?" he asks. "Why do I have to make a choice?"

When Nadine speaks, her voice is no longer friendly or sweet; it's the vile, disgusting voice that she reserves for use when she's speaking with her brother.

"Because every boy has to make a choice if he wants to become a man," Nadine spits. "And the time for you to make your choice is now."

I can hear growls escape my lips; a constant rumbling from my soul into the air. If it had wings it would race into the night and wrap itself around Nadine to silence her, to keep her away from Barnaby, to kill her.

"But why now?" Barnaby asks.

His voice sounds as young and unsure and confused as it did in the first few days after my father died.

"I told you, Barnaby; there's good in this town, and there's evil," Nadine starts. "Which side do you want to be on?"

Before Barnaby can answer, the silver mist dives to the ground with such force it looks like it's going to pierce the ground and burrow a hole until it disappears. But at the last second it veers to the right and begins to wrap itself around my brother. Round and round and round it whips, moving up his stationary body, not touching his skin or clothing, but hugging so tightly that if Barnaby moves an inch in any direction, if he lifts his arm or shifts his leg he'll collide with the unnatural fog. When he speaks I can tell that even though the silver mist isn't touching him, it's controlling him.

"I want to be on your side," he declares.

It's not his announcement that convinces me Nadine is controlling his mind, but his voice. He doesn't sound like my brother; he sounds like a zombie, a robot, a voice that has had all the life sucked out of it. He sounds dead.

"You chose right, Barnaby," Nadine whispers. "And now it's time to reap your reward."

Nadine takes a step back and slowly raises both her hands.

As she does the silver mist rises above the ground, taking with it Barnaby who is trapped within its tendrils. She can control this force; she has the same power as her brother.

Barnaby makes no move to resist or maintain his balance or prevent himself from levitating in the air; he accepts the movement almost as if he was expecting it. If Nadine can do this to him, what else can she do? No, I'm not going to wait around to find out. I've seen enough!

The howl is so loud and powerful and filled with rage that it startles even me. It startles Nadine so much that she drops her hands and as a result loses control of my brother. Barnaby falls to the ground with such an impact that a cloud of dust rises and comingles with the silver mist; earth and unearth join together as one. For a moment he doesn't move, and I'm afraid that the crash or my wolf cry or the sudden release from Nadine's power was too much of a shock and he's been seriously injured, but it's just the opposite. He's free.

"What am I doing here?" he asks. Then he looks up at Nadine staring down at him through a silver cloud. "Nadine? Is that you?"

Her lips form a smile, but like before when she was fighting with Napoleon, her eyes do not join in.

"Of course it's me, Barnaby," she seethes. "Don't you remember? You asked me to take a walk with you."

Upright, Barnaby slaps his thighs to get rid of the dirt that's clinging to him. Next he waves his hand violently in the air. Maybe he can see her silver extensions; maybe he's trying to swipe them away before they latch onto him.

"No, I didn't!" he screams. "You followed me!"

What?! She was stalking my brother. Why?!

"You said you wanted to show me something," he says. "And that's all I remember. Everything's blank after that."

With desperation etched on her face, Nadine moves closer to Barnaby, which makes him take a few steps backward.

"Stay away from me!"

"Oh you don't mean that, Barnaby," she replies, trying very hard, but failing, to sound sexy.

"Yes, I do!" he screams. "Stay back!"

This time when confronted, Nadine doesn't shrink like she did when Napoleon fought back. Now she shows her true colors and unleashes an even greater power.

As she lifts her arms overhead, bolts of silver light rip out of her hands and lunge for Barnaby. He may not be a supernatural creature, but he has incredible speed, and just as the light tries to grab hold of his legs, he turns and runs, making sure to push into the ground with his left foot to spray Nadine with a shower of dirt.

"Get back here!" she roars.

Ignoring her, Barnaby runs off into the inner depths of the park. The second I see Nadine sprint after my brother, I spring forward. There's no way she's going to get close to him again. Not while I'm around, not tonight.

Just as Barnaby fades into a bevy of thick-trunked trees, I run into the clearing. Shocked, Nadine loses her footing and stumbles forward, falling onto the ground. When she looks up, the first thing she sees is my fangs.

Her nails clutch at the ground and disappear into the dirt as she tries to prevent herself from shaking in my presence. She isn't successful. The skin on either side of my snout rises to show off more of my pure white fangs, chiseled to a point like a series of ivory knives. My red fur is thick and standing straight up, bending only slightly whenever the wind picks up, and my paws are restless, unable to stay put for more than a few seconds. Nadine and I both know that I desperately want to attack.

"Dominy," Nadine says softly, her voice shaking a bit, "I know you can hear me."

My howl in response doesn't deny or agree.

Crawling backward, Nadine looks pathetic and scared and weak. She is such easy prey. All I have to do is lunge forward, let my paws fly through the air, and extend my legs so my nails can rip through her flesh. Tear the skin off of her cheeks and her arms and destroy that silver mist as well. Maybe the mist is like her lifeline—if I tear that to shreds, it'll destroy her too. Worth a try.

"Dominy, no!"

This time I'm the one who's startled. I heard the voice, but I didn't see Nadine's lips move. She's just staring at me with a look of fear in her eyes. No, wait, she's not staring at me; she's looking behind me. Whipping my head around, I understand why. Who wouldn't be afraid to see Luba, looking like a corpse, floating six inches above the ground, with her arms outstretched and clawing at the air?

Nadine screams something, but I don't hear it because my howl is too loud. Suddenly there's too much going on, Nadine, Barnaby, Luba, all my enemies together, everyone who wants to hurt me in one place. It's too much! I knew tonight was going to be different; I knew something unexpected was going to happen, but I didn't expect so much. I didn't expect to be torn between attacking Nadine and destroying Luba.

I can feel the violence and anger and confusion erupting within me, and I can't control them all. The wolf and I are no longer working together; it's trying to take over, and I'm fighting. I don't want to lose myself within the beast. I want to be part of the destruction of my two enemies.

"Leave now!" Luba bellows.

Her voice is so loud some of the branches on the trees shake as if a strong wind erupted out of stagnant air and took them all by surprise. The branches may have bowed in Luba's presence, but not Nadine. I don't know what game she's playing now, but her initial fear has given way to a crazy confidence. She's not afraid; she looks defiant, as if she's possibly a match for Psycho Squaw. Nadine may have skills; she may even be a master of black magic, I don't know. But I do know that Luba has had lots more years of practice.

"I SAID GO!"

Raising three fingers on her left hand is all Luba needs to do to send Nadine flying backward, barely missing a low hanging branch. My eyes are fixed on her; I want to see if she can fight Luba's power; I want to see just how strong this girl or this witch or this creature is. Turns out, not very.

About two hundred yards away, Nadine falls to the ground as if someone had been holding her up by the scruff of her neck and just decided to let go. I swing my head around and see that Luba's arms are now by her sides. It was her; she manipulated Nadine and made her fall as easily as she made her fly through the air.

I hear Nadine scamper away before I see her flee. Good, go. Tomorrow I'll deal with you. Tomorrow we'll have to make some decisions, but right now I have to figure out what to do with Luba.

Now that my focus is entirely upon her, I realize that she really does look like she's a few breaths away from death. Her skin is paler than before and just hanging off of her bony frame. Her hair is no longer the color of ebony, but more like black-tinged snow, and her eyes are glassy. She's still unnaturally powerful, but something's wrong with her; something doesn't look right. Perhaps it's simply that she's old and evil does have an expiration date.

"Dominy," she taunts. "How does it feel to wander the earth without your father?"

A series of growls heave out of my mouth, and I swipe at the air with a restless paw. My actions hardly scare Luba. In fact, they only make her laugh and send streams of hot, rancid breath in my direction. She's truly foul, inside and out.

"You stupid fool!" she cries, her feet descending onto the ground. "Haven't you learned you cannot defeat me?"

She starts to walk toward me, but I stand my ground. I will not let her intimidate me. I will not let her curse me again.

"Haven't you learned that you will never win?" she says, this time in a voice dripping with contempt. "Haven't you learned that one day you will die because I decided it should be so?"

No, I haven't. And I'm not the only one who has not learned that lesson.

We're both surprised when the bullet pierces my skin. The blood that starts to stain my fur is a much darker shade of red than I ever expected. I fall to my side and look up just in time to see Barnaby raise the gun with both his hands and pull the trigger for a second time.

Chapter 10

I wish it could always be just the four of us.

I forgot how wonderful it feels to nuzzle against Daddy's fur. It's like stepping into the comfort of a shadow on a hot, summer day, a brief escape from the relentless heat. His fur feels cool against the top of my head, and behind me I can feel my mother's chest breathing out and in and out and in, a steady rhythm, a message from mother to child that one will always be close to the other. I may not always see her, but I can turn around and she'll be right there waiting to comfort me, like an easy breath.

That's how I feel right now—easy and comforted and protected. We're a huddled mass, my brother and I in the center with my parents on either side. Looking at us, it's hard to tell we're four separate wolves; we look like one large, alpha male, his fur a patchwork of colors. The center is split—one side is red, the other brown, spreading out to the near-black of my father and on the opposite side, the pure white of my mother. Conjoined, one color to the next, our bodies swirl together to create something new, something connected, something that can never be broken.

But then the world begins to tremble.

I don't remember when the shaking started, but I remember being woken up. It felt like the ground underneath me was pushing up, trying to stand like a two-legged creature stretching its body after a long slumber. My parents were already awake, crouched low, their fur no longer flat and smooth, but thick and rigid. Turning from my father to my mother, I can see that they are ready and aware and determined to protect us. They just don't know what they need to protect us from.

The earth screams underneath our paws. A deep, sorrowful wail as if it can no longer contain all the pain within its soul, as if it needs to uncage it, thrust it into the world so it can be shared. But the sky above wants no part of the ugliness; it remains a soft blue, the color of the pretty birds that sing in the trees and wake us in the morning. So it falls upon us to carry the weight of the newly freed pain.

I lurch forward and crash into my father's shoulder, certain that the only reason I could stumble so violently is because my brother pushed me. Why is he playing games when our parents look so serious? When I turn around I see that he's not near me; he's several feet away, pressed so close to my mother he's almost underneath her belly. No, I lost my balance because the ground I'm standing on has broken apart.

My father's snout presses into my side and pushes me back, not away from him, but away from the part of the earth that's starting to splinter apart, starting to separate into several smaller chunks. The ground suddenly resembles a leaf that's streaked with veins. And it's starting to become just as fragile.

The tip of my father's wet nose tickles my fur. I concentrate on that wonderful feeling so I can ignore the sounds erupting all around me. I close my eyes, and the noise grows louder, which I can't believe is possible, and the blackness only serves to strengthen my hearing, so it sounds like the whole world has gone mad with fear. I open my eyes, and it's clear that things are only getting worse.

Far below the earth a sound begins. It's a low growl, the kind that I've heard come out of my father's mouth when a bear or another wolf has threatened our den. As it rises closer to the surface, the sound grows in intensity. Terrified, my brother and I mirror each other and press our shaking bodies closer to our parents. Try as they might there's no way they can protect us from the ear-splitting scream that rips through the ground and slaughters the air.

Louder and louder and louder the howling grows, each extended note destroying another part of the ground around us. There's a crackle to my left, and I see a small rip burrow through the dirt as easily as a beaver tunneling through mud. Before I can catch my breath the land next to me is turned into three islands that seconds ago were one flat plain. A boom to my right announces a fallen tree; a whimper behind me alerts me as to my brother's location; the soul-scalding cries from other animals remind me that my family isn't alone in this horror. It's not just our world that's being destroyed by some unseen phantom, some cruel bully, but there aren't enough of us to fight back. We're powerless to stop him until he grows tired of his game.

I recognize my mother's howl, but in the confusion surrounding me I can't find her. She was right behind me with my brother, but now there are only rocks and dust clouds where they stood. Looking up into my father's eyes, I can see that he's scouring the land, but he can't find them either; there's no recognition in his eyes, no hope, only panic. He bares his fangs, and the howl that he releases is louder, stronger, commanding my mother to respond, defying the world around him to keep them separated. Silent, he waits for her reply, but none comes.

He lifts his paws impatiently from the ground, his body jutting forward as if he's preparing to run, but he has no idea where to go; there's nothing around us but chaos. My ear is pressed against his side, and I can feel his heart beating wildly. I try to tune out all the other sounds so all I can hear is the life thumping within his chest, because I know amidst the savage destruction taking place around me, if that sound continues, I'll be safe. Keep beating, keep beating!

I lose the connection for a few seconds, but only because my father howls again so ferociously that his body jostles mine and we separate. Despite the command in his voice, my mother doesn't return his cry. I push my paws into the dirt, secure my footing, and once again feel my father's fur connecting with mine, but the link doesn't last very long. The ground shakes under my feet, briefly, but so violently that it sends me crashing into the jagged rocks and the uprooted earth. I'm dazed, my vision blurs, and the sounds begin to fade. Everything seems to be coming to an end. And then there's silence.

The explosions and clatter and roars linger only as memories, a reminder that peace can and always will be interrupted. By the world below, by an unseen bully, and even by a father.

A sound emerges from my father's throat. It's a horrifying wail I've only heard once before, when another wolf, who used to be in our pack, found the bodies of his children ripped open, lying motionless near the banks of the river. By the time I shake the stones off of me, rid myself of the debris that's collected on my body and stand up, my father is silent once again and merely staring off into the distance. I look at him, and I'm desperate for him to look at me and nuzzle his snout against my cheek so I'll know that everything's okay, but he doesn't move; he doesn't glance at me. His eyes are soft and wet and unmoving, focused on some image in the distance. I turn to see what he's staring at and immediately wish that I could block out the vision, erase it from my mind, but I can't. This is my reality.

About a hundred yards away, on a separate piece of broken land, my mother is lying on the ground, not moving, her body twisted unnaturally. Next to her, my brother keeps trying to stand up, but each attempt ends with him falling back onto the ground. The bloodstain on his forehead is growing larger, spreading across his head and down the front of his face, covering his eyes. So eager the blood is to travel; so anxious it is to have its freedom.

After a few seconds, a few minutes maybe, I'm not sure, his shaking legs give out, and he collapses onto my mother. She doesn't move when his body hits hers; she merely acts as a cushion. But by the way my brother's body folds into my mother's soft fur and by the way he closes his eyes, slowly and surely, I can tell that he's grateful that she has not left him.

Desperate to escape the terror closing in on me, I lean into my father, and I feel that the beating of his heart has slowed down; it's normal, familiar. But that's the only thing familiar to me right now; the rest of the world around me is wearing a disguise. It's foreign to me. And about to change yet again.

Grumbling loudly, the stones and dirt and ground under and all around me tremble once more; they're not yet done with their attack. My legs wobble as I search for steady footing, and just as I find my balance, my father falls forward and his head pushes into me, toppling me over and sending me careening toward an opening in the earth. Clutching the dirt, I dig my nails in deep, determined to stop myself from rolling. Just as my hind paws reach the edge, the shaking stops, and the earth's movement subsides.

The relief I feel at not falling into the black abyss only inches away is fleeting and soon replaced with terror. The parts of my father's body that are visible, his back legs and his head, are twitching; the rest is covered by a massive tree, its thick roots swaying in the breeze like fingers, wiggling and stretching and trying to grab hold of something, anything that feels right and secure and recognizable. Looking around at this unknown landscape, I feel like the roots of this fallen tree, except that I know I'll never see anything that looks familiar again.

I rush to my father's side. He doesn't see me right away, and so his expression is unguarded. Pain and terror and anguish flit about the surface of his face. When he sees me staring at him, he immediately tries to hide the truth and replace it with the kindness I've always known. Stupidly I push my paws against the tree, thinking I can somehow lift it, as if my small, insignificant body could challenge something so majestic. My paws fail, so I lean into the trunk with my forehead. My father's eyes beam with pride; it doesn't matter that I'll never succeed; it matters that I tried. It matters that my instinct is to protect my family, to protect my blood no matter what the odds, no matter what the chances are of winning.

A few seconds after he dies, I feel his spirit move through me like a gentle rush of wind, and whatever pain I was feeling has disappeared, whatever wounds I might have suffered instantly heal. Even after his death my father is still protecting me, still showing me, by example, how to live.

Looking beyond the cracks in the earth, over at my brother lying on top of my mother's unmoving body, I know that I will protect him the way my father protected me. I can see his tiny stomach moving slightly with each tired breath, so I know he's not dead. He's hurt and frightened and confused, but he's still alive. Which means there's still a chance I can save him.

My eyes flick open, but see only darkness. It takes a few seconds for the dream to slip from my mind, not disappear entirely, but make room for reality to take over. Shadows form, enough for me to see two pairs of feet standing in front of me. When the voices follow, I shut my eyes tight. I don't need to see in order to know exactly who's speaking.

"This is what killed my father!"

The flicker of triumph in Barnaby's voice is quickly over-powered by his rage. When he kicks me hard in the stomach, I have to smother my cry to keep it buried in my throat so he thinks that I'm dead.

"Go get the others so you can revel in your victory!"

He doesn't immediately respond to Luba's order.

"Show them how a son's vengeance is undaunted!" she tempts.

Cocky and proud, he takes the bait.

"Stay with this thing, Luba!" Barnaby demands. "I'll come back with Louis, and we'll drag it to the center of town for everyone to see!"

Barnaby's footsteps pound jubilantly into the ground as he races back to town. His joy can be felt in each stride. He's killed the killer; he's avenged his father's death. At least that's what he thinks.

"Get up."

Luba's voice is like fire. Soft with a slight crackle, but within the depths of her sound there lies urgency, as if the fire can erupt, become wild and out of control in an instant. Despite the dull pain that's begun to take over my entire body, I try to obey her command.

On the third attempt, I'm able to roll over onto my stomach, so I'm no longer on my side, but it's even harder to push myself into an upright position. My front paws seem to be collecting most of my strength, so I push into the dirt with them, but my back legs shake uncontrollably when I try to stand, and I fall back onto the ground. The next time I try, my belly gets a few more inches off the ground, but the result is the same: my back legs are too weak, and I can't fully support myself, so once again I fall.

Craning my neck to the right I see why I'm having so much trouble. The second bullet from Barnaby's gun hit me right over my hind leg. There's no way I'll be able to stand; there's no way I'll be able to escape to safety before Barnaby returns. Without lifting my head, I look up and see Luba standing over me. She's smiling, because she's come to the same conclusion.

"Are you deaf as well as stupid?" she asks. "I said get up!"

You think I want to lie here until my brother comes back?! You think I want to make it easy for them?!

"*That's exactly what I think,*" Luba says, her voice filled with pure disgust.

I'm about to respond when I'm gripped with an even stronger fear of being captured and killed and put on display so all of Weeping Water can witness the death of their serial killer, the wolf that at dawn will transform back into the girl they all thought they knew. What's even more frightening is that Luba can speak to me telepathically. She and I are connected the same way I'm connected to Jess. That can't be! That can't be right! But somehow it is.

"*Fool, I created you!*" Luba hisses. "*I can hear your words, I can hear your thoughts, and if I choose, you can hear mine.*"

She looks at me like an outraged teacher, furious that her student is turning into a disappointment.

"*I will tell you for the last time to get up!*" she cries, her silent voice echoing in my brain. "*It wasn't a silver bullet. It's knocked your breath from you, but not your life.*"

She's right. Looking back at my leg, I don't see any more blood seeping from the wound. The bullet might have struck me, it might be causing me intense pain, but it doesn't have the power to kill me.

With renewed purpose and an increasing sense of urgency, I push into the ground once more, and, although it's a struggle, I finally heave myself into a standing position. I can't hold the position for very long though before my back legs begin to shake. As I lean forward, relying on my front legs to take the brunt of my weight, I feel a sensation on my hind leg, like pricks, tiny needles jutting into my skin. Wincing, I whip my head around and am once again amazed by the ungodly sight.

Luba is saving my life.

She is arched forward. Her long, straggly black hair hangs limp in the air and shields her face from my view, and even though I can't see her mouth move, I can hear her voice. She's speaking out loud now, but the words are hard to decipher, because the words are coming quickly and the sound is like a growl, born from the center of her throat, not latched to her heart or her mind, but from some borrowed place.

While she speaks her hands hover over my leg, her long, bony fingers undulating and retracting as if pushing and pulling energy into my body. At least I found the source of the prickly sensation, but what is she saying? And why in the world is she helping me?

My silent questions are interrupted when I see her body start to levitate off the ground. I've seen Jess perform this trick before, but when she does it it's a graceful move, a gift, a golden spray of light floating effortlessly. Luba's different. Her body is being pulled up off the ground almost against its will by some darker force; her feet are flexed downward as if her toes are desperately trying to make contact with a surface that isn't made of air. All she's wearing are black slippers and a long, gray-tinged white dress, so I can see the blue veins in the tops of her feet and her ankles press against the thin veneer of her flesh. Her body seems to be fighting against this profane movement. Or maybe the action is just exhausting her.

I can hear some words now because she's speaking more slowly, not because she wants to, I don't think, but because she's gasping for breath. *Stars, three, undo, beseech.* Other words surround them, drip from her lips, fall onto the gash on my skin, but I can't make them out. It doesn't matter, because suddenly I can't hear anything except my own howl.

The prickling on my flesh is replaced with intense pain, as if Luba's hands are no longer inches above my body, but burrowing deep within me, fiddling around my insides to find the bullet my brother shot into my body and rip it out of me. Instead of moving quickly, her hands loiter where they shouldn't be, linger inside of me, and I can feel Luba's poison.

"GET! OUT!!"

I don't know if my cry causes Luba to relinquish her hold on me, or if my thrashing body makes it harder to hold me, or if she simply finished her task, but finally the pain is gone. Completely. I look behind me and see that the wound is healed. There is no gaping hole; it's as if I had never been assaulted. And Luba looks as if she never had the strength to levitate.

She staggers slightly, so I only see a glimpse of her face, and she's ghostly pale. The only color is coming from the shadows in the folds of her wrinkles. For someone with such immense power, she looks like she's going to faint.

Despite her obvious frailty, once she sees me glowering at her, her entire façade changes. Her back stiffens, her body becomes grounded, she raises her left arm toward me, and her eyes take on that sinister combination of revenge and impish glee I've grown accustomed to. Her thumb and pinky touch, so only three fingers are pointed at me as her lips part to form an eerie smile.

"It's too soon for our game to end," she seethes. "And when it is time, I will be the one to end it."

That's why she saved me. That's why she used her magic to heal my wounds so I could escape before Barnaby returned with his entourage. She wasn't trying to protect me from the wrath of a bloodthirsty gang; she was saving me so her own thirst for vengeance could be quenched at a later date.

When I hear the ground shake almost as violently as it did in my dream, I know the time has come for me to take advantage of this reprieve. Even if it was offered to me under the most duplicitous and selfish terms imaginable.

Fully recovered, I start to bound off into the woods when Luba's voice stops me. "Aren't you going to thank me, Dominy?"

She speaks her question out loud and deliberately uses my name to remind me that she created me and she could expose me at any moment. Barnaby, Louis, and their gang aren't close enough to have overheard her; they can't even see us clearly yet. But her comment is just another warning shot, with the potential to do even more damage than Barnaby's gun.

I snarl at Luba as viciously as I possibly can, and although she remains silent I can hear her laughter in my head. It's demonic and torturous and damaging, and I need to get far away from it or risk being permanently contaminated. But not far enough that I can't hear what takes place next.

Several hundred yards away, I crouch in between two thick, overgrown bushes. My red fur blends in with the russets and deep oranges among the leaves, so I'm camouflaged from view.

"Where is it?!"

Barnaby's voice is so loud it reaches my ears with the intensity of an unexpected explosion.

"Luba, what happened?!"

Using my enhanced vision I can see an older man help Luba up off the ground. She must have positioned herself to look like the wolf attacked her. I bet she even gave herself some wounds to make it look that much more believable.

"I don't know," she says, her voice shaky and fragile. "One second it was lying there, and the next it . . . it leapt up and attacked me."

The commotion Luba's lie creates is too raucous and too angry, so I can't make out the voices or the words. Luba's next comment, however, silences everyone.

"It's as if the thing can't die."

Her voice is barely a whisper, the perfect concoction of fear and wisdom, and it's all that's needed to make the bounty hunters shriek and gasp and vow to find me once and for all. Find the thing that defies logic, the thing that supersedes nature, the thing that begs to be destroyed.

Expertly I zero in on one conversation amidst the din of voices.

"Barnaby, I vow to find your father's killer," Louis says, his voice exuding strength and order. "But if you ever take matters into your own hands again and leave my house with a loaded gun, I will whip you within an inch of your life."

Good. That's what Barnaby needs, direction and reprimand and love. Everything that my father once gave him and everything that I'm clearly incapable of offering him.

"I told you before that I gave you that gun to remember your father," Louis adds. "Not to avenge his death! You leave that to me."

Barnaby's resistance is as thick as the crowd. I can see his body tense, I can almost feel it, and I know he wants to break free from Louis's grip and search the woods for the wolf, but our new guardian is holding him squarely by the shoulders. Louis is not letting Barnaby go so he can try and find me, so he can continue to play hunter, so he can kill. Good for Louis; he's making it impossible for Barnaby to do anything but remain the confused teenager that he is.

"You promise you'll do everything you can to capture that thing that killed my dad?" Barnaby asks.

Louis doesn't hesitate or flinch. He replies immediately. "Yes."

Barnaby's reply is just as immediate. He throws his arms around Louis, grateful for a confidante, but relieved to have found an heir. Clinging to Louis, Barnaby sinks into him. It's clear that he's tired of fighting.

Until Luba catches his eye.

As he looks at the witch, Barnaby's body changes. It's as if his spirit and compassion and soul are sucked out and replaced with venom. First Nadine and now Luba! But this time it's not a silver light that is trying to destroy my brother, but a filthy black-colored venom that only Luba can control. And this time Barnaby doesn't have the willpower to resist.

Unseen by anyone else in the darkness, Luba lifts her fingers to her mouth and smiles victoriously. A heartbeat later, Barnaby joins in and smiles too. A smile that I believe seals his fate.

Chapter 11

This can only be a very bad sign.

When I woke up this morning, I did what I do on the first day of every month; I checked the lunar calendar. I had been keeping a year-long chart, but peering that far into the future got to be depressing with a capital Mega, so a few months ago I stopped doing that and adopted a new tactic. Now I only check the moon on a month-by-month basis.

When I first made that decision, I took my father's green metal box filled with the calendar he made for me and the rest of his werewolf memorabilia, added my old Two W Timberwolf banner to the collection, and shoved it in the back of my closet. Way back. Who needs to be constantly reminded of what I already know: that one day out of every month I will transform into something grotesque and primitive and yes, even exquisite. It doesn't matter if I know which day that will be a year in advance or just a month; the outcome is going to be the same.

But this morning when I checked I realized this month would be different. November's full moon will fall on the 29th. My birthday. Also, the anniversary of the first day I was cursed. And the day Jess died. If that's not a bad omen, I don't know what is.

All during school I tried to convince myself that it was nothing more than a coincidence, but I've learned that there are no coincidences. Plus, there were signs to the contrary everywhere I looked.

First period somebody pulled the fire alarm, so we all had to stand outside in the cold without our jackets until Principal Dumbleavy was convinced of what the students knew immediately—that it was a false alarm. Rumor has it that a group of pothead seniors paid The Worm fifty bucks to pull the alarm to get them out of having to take an English exam. Memo to potheads: Smoke less; read more.

Later on Mr. Dice gave us one of his pop quizzes in algebra. Testament to his popularity: None of the kids groaned; in fact, many of them got excited to prove to Two W's favorite new teacher that they were absorbing what he's been teaching. I tried to fight the excitement, but quickly joined in. I mean why not? It isn't every day that I get to fail a test.

Things got worse at lunch when they served meatloaf surprise. The surprise being that it tasted nothing at all like meatloaf or like any meat that I've ever tasted. Even if I had been in wolf mode I would've spit it out. After that Miss Ro declared November to be Dodge Ball Month, which will undoubtedly be abruptly called off when Gwen channels her German-Korean heritage and fights fairly, but brutally, and breaks someone's arm. And finally the day ended with Mr. Lamatina telling us in graphic detail why the Vietnam War was so unpopular.

The bad feeling that I woke up with has been maintained. And it's about to get worse.

"Dominy," Louis calls out to me. "Can I . . . um, see you in the kitchen?"

Sitting on the living room couch between Caleb and Arla,

I momentarily ignore his question to finish writing out a history homework answer. The Vietnam War ended on April 30, 1975. I sense that another war is about to erupt.

This can't be good. Even B.T.C. (Before The Curse), whenever my dad wanted to have a private conversation with me, it always meant I was in trouble. Since becoming a member of the Bergeron clan, I've been able to avoid a one-on-one with Louis. Not that he hasn't asserted his authority, casually letting Barnaby and I know that it's his house and therefore his rules, but that's been the extent of our very important tête-à-têtes. Which is understandable because as far as he knows I haven't broken any of his house rules. And I've made sure not to wander the hallway clad only in a bath towel any longer, but maybe he's found out about my late-night sneak outs? From where I'm sitting I catch Louis in the kitchen glance over at me, then at Caleb, and then back to me. Oh my God! Could he think that I've been sneaking out to hook up with Caleb?

"Of course," I say, continuing to scribble in my notebook. I try to keep my expression neutral, like Switzerland, a country that did nothing to help end the Vietnam War by the way, but when Arla speaks I know I wasn't successful.

"Is something wrong, Daddy?"

Arla knows I know I'm in big trouble, because she's pulled out the D word. Every daughter has tools to thwart a tirade or scolding from her father; the most efficient is to call him Daddy. It unnerves them and reminds them that they are not about to yell at the teenager who is aggravating them, but at the little girl who used to consider her father the most amazing man in the world. I'm not sure if I should be thankful that Arla's stepped in or scared silly that she's felt the need to.

Louis looks equally confused.

"Um, no, nothing's wrong," he stammers. "It's just that . . ."

"Just what?" Arla questions.

She really is pulling out all the tricks now. Interrupting a nervous and/or angry parent is another excellent way to take control of the situation. The disruption startles them, jostles them so they fall off the parent train, forgetting that they are, in fact, the parent and the one who should be in charge, and makes them question their own ability to lead. In extreme circumstances it makes the parent forget exactly what the uncomfortable and unspoken topic of conversation was going to be, resulting in the parent's shrugging and mumbling an "oh forget it" or "it wasn't important," before quickly retreating to another room to handle something manageable like emptying the dishwasher or balancing a checkbook.

But this time the strategy doesn't work. Louis is frazzled but undeterred and proving to all of us that he's taking this guardian thing very seriously.

"I'm not comfortable letting Caleb stay here while I'm out of the house," he blurts.

It was apparent that Louis was nervous when Caleb arrived, but I thought it was because Louis had just announced he was going out on a date. This is a landmark event and Louis's first real date since Arla's mom came out of the closet wearing flannel and Birkenstocks instead of satin and Manolo Blahniks. Guess his agitated state had nothing to do with his mystery date and everything to do with my boyfriend.

"Dad, that's ridiculous," Arla scoffs, flipping a kernel of popcorn into her mouth and channel surfing with the remote.

Now that she's back to calling him Dad and not Daddy, I'm guessing the perceived threat level has dropped from high alert to normal.

"I know Mason trusted you, Caleb. He told me so himself," Louis says. "But I can't imagine he trusted you enough to leave you and Dominy alone in the house together."

I remain silent for only one reason: Louis is absolutely right.

"They won't be alone, Dad," Arla observes. "I'm playing chaperone."

Before Louis can even contemplate this offer, Arla starts talking again.

"And if you agree," she says, "I promise not to interrogate you about your new lady friend."

Since he's apparently desperate to keep his private life private, this seems to seal the deal for Louis. As long as the deal is sealed on his terms.

"You have an hour, Caleb," Louis states. "I'll have a squad car circle the area in exactly sixty minutes, and if your car isn't gone by then, he'll be instructed to haul you in for questioning."

"Wow, you're even tougher than Mr. Robineau was," Caleb declares, impressed despite being threatened.

"I'm new at this boyfriend thing," Louis replies. "So I'm looking at this as training for the inevitable."

Arla doesn't have to see her father's smirk; she knows it's there. Dropping the remote to pick up a fashion magazine, she doesn't even look up when she tosses a zinger back at her father. "What makes you think I won't turn out to be a lesbian like Mom?"

Louis sheds his responsible parent skin and reveals his inner pouty child. "You would do that just to remind me every day that your mother left me for another woman, wouldn't you?"

"It's a definite possibility," she says, lifting the magazine up to cover her face so her father doesn't see her starting to laugh.

Ignoring his insolent daughter, Louis turns back to the only boyfriend he currently has to deal with. "I trust you, Caleb," he states soberly. "And in my line of work you have to learn to trust your gut."

The second the door closes behind Louis, the three of us crack up laughing. We're laughing so hard I'm convinced he's going to come back inside to find out what the ruckus is all about.

"Trust his gut?" Arla says. Then she drops her voice to a whisper and asks, "Does he know he has a werewolf living under his roof?"

Instinctively, I run into the hallway to make sure Barnaby isn't at the top of the stairs eavesdropping. Nope, he's still presumably in his bedroom doing his homework. Still, he's been too sneaky and untrustworthy lately to take any more chances; time to steer the conversation away from my affliction and toward her father's new affection.

"So any idea who your father has a date with, Arla?" I ask, sitting on the floor facing the couch.

Tossing the magazine onto the floor dramatically, she sighs. "Not a clue, and it's not for lack of trying."

Sliding on the floor across the room from me, Caleb leans back against the couch and presses his feet into mine, a flirting tactic that's both chaste and cute. "Not that I know anything about divorced parents," he starts, "but isn't that kind of weird?"

I haven't thought about it, but it kind of is. Unless Louis is waiting until the relationship is more solid just like Essie's doing with her relationship. Hold on just one bleeping second! What if Louis's relationship *is* Essie's relationship? Could that possibility be possible? Possibly! That could explain why Essie kept mum and didn't tell me her boyfriend's name. 'Cause I'm living with her boyfriend! But Louis and Essie? They'd make a quirky couple for sure, but they're both great people, so it might just work. Until I have proof that Louis and Essie are sitting in a tree k-i-s-s-i-n-g'ing, I should probably keep my assumptions to myself.

"This is the first woman he's dated since my mother lesbified," Arla replies nonchalantly. "So I think he's making sure it'll lead to something at least semiserious before introducing her to the family."

"Makes sense," I say, hoping my smile doesn't give away

the fact that I think I know who Louis's lady friend is. "Especially since your family just got extended. Might be a little much for someone he's just casually dating."

"Exactly," Arla agrees. "Honestly, I'm just happy he's happy."

"That was happy?" Caleb asks, a surprised look on his face.

"For a cop and the sudden father of three," Arla says. "What you saw was my father in a state of bliss."

Once again laughter fills up the living room. Laughter that is Hooverized when Barnaby makes his entrance.

"I'm going over to Jody's house," he announces, bounding toward the front door.

"No, you're not," I inform him.

I'm shocked when Barnaby turns around and I see his face. Who is this person? How did I not notice the stubble growing on his chin and the long strands of hair on the sides of his face? Is this new? For a moment I'm reminded of my sudden hair growth, and I wonder if Luba's curse extended to include my brother. But no, no! It was just for my father's firstborn. When the shock of his physical appearance wears off, another shock takes its place. He's taunting me. It's as if he's been waiting for me to try and stop him from leaving.

"And why aren't I?" he asks.

"Because it's dark . . . and it's not safe outside."

And just like that I've fallen into his trap.

"Of course it's safe outside," he disagrees. "It's not like there's a *full moon* out tonight."

Chuckling to himself and unable to hide a self-satisfied grin, Barnaby leaves. It takes over a minute for any of us to speak.

"It was him."

I think that was Caleb's voice. I'm not sure because I've been repeating the same phrase over and over in my head.

"No question about it, Barnaby was the one who informed Louis of the connection to the full moon," Caleb clarifies.

While Arla and Caleb chatter about what this may or may not mean, I focus on my breathing so I don't freak out. All I can think of is how Barnaby previously threatened me and how he said that he would find out what role I played in my father's death. He's made the first connection, and he's secured an ally in Louis. Worst of all he's linked to Luba. I pray it's just an innocent friendship, a young boy fascinated by this old, odd creature, but in my heart where there's no thought and only feeling, I know their relationship is much more complicated.

Like with my brother cub in my dream, all I want to do is protect Barnaby. Jess feels the same way.

The computer in the living room suddenly turns on, even though no one is standing near it. At first we think it's just a malfunction, an electrical surge, even though the TV, the lights, and none of the other appliances in the house are affected. When the computer screen turns golden yellow, I know my friend is trying to communicate with all three of us.

"It's Jess!" I announce.

Neither of them is shocked. I've told them enough about my connection to Jess and how she sometimes shows up in the most unlikely situations to offer guidance and information, so they accept that we're being visited by our friend from some other supernatural plane. Since I'm the only one who can see Jess, she must have something to say to all of us, so she's figured out a more efficient way to communicate on a group level. Clever!

A bright light emanates from the screen, and the computer seems to throb with life. The light becomes so blinding we have to shield our eyes until it retreats back into the computer, as if that's the light's resting place. And then Jess's message becomes clear.

The computer goes back to its normal color and slowly

words start to scroll across the screen, words in bright yellow: *Keep Barnaby Away From Them.*

Them?

"Who's 'them'?" Arla asks, reading my thoughts.

"Jess," I say, "who are you talking about?"

The three of us look around the room as if another one of her signs is going to miraculously appear, but nothing in the room changes.

"Jess, c'mon!" I shout. "You have to give us something more than just that one message!"

Obeying my orders, Jess makes the word *Three* in the same color yellow start to blink on the screen.

"Which three?" Caleb shouts at the computer as if he's staring right at Jess's face.

In response, the word dissolves, only to be replaced with the phrase *All Three of Them.*

The words stay on the computer screen for a few moments and then, along with Jess's golden light, they disappear. Jess has finished her mission and has returned to her new home.

Arla and Caleb look more confused than stunned, even though they understand they've just been visited by their dead friend. They look as if they're still trying to decipher Jess's message, but I can't imagine that they don't understand it. Most likely, they don't want to believe it. Unfortunately, I've known for quite some time that my brother is in trouble and is in need of protection. I don't know if I'll be successful in saving him, but I now know more than ever before that I cannot give up trying. At least I know exactly who I have to protect my brother from.

"Jess's message is really very clear," I say.

"Well, on one level, sure it is," Arla concedes. "We have to keep Barnaby away from three people."

"But which three?" Caleb asks.

I will say the three names they're afraid to mention because of the terrifying possibilities and the complex implications. I don't know what it means or how the three of them are connected or how frightened I should actually be. All I know is that Jess has given me ammunition that I can use in the next phase of my fight.

"We all know who Jess is referring to," I say calmly.

"We do?" Arla asks, not exhibiting her usual smarts.

"Of course we do," I reply. "Luba, Nadine, and Napoleon."

They might not have made the connection immediately, but when neither Caleb nor Arla protests, I know that I'm right.

Now I just have to find out how all three of them are connected.

Chapter 12

"Tell me everything you know about Luba, and tell me right now!"

Essie stares at me in silence, and the pause allows me to take a good look at her. She's changed yet again. Cosmetically, she looks the same. Her haircut, makeup, and clothes are still stylish, but she's aged since the last time I saw her. Did her date with Louis go that badly? If she was even out on a date with him? She drums the desk with her right hand, and I'm almost distracted from my objective because her newly manicured fingernails are painted a really interesting shade that I've never seen before, kind of like a smoky purple. But while the color is pretty, her nails aren't; they're bitten. Her left hand mats down a flyaway hair, and her eyes dart to the front door. I know the reason she looks different. She's nervous.

"Essie, are you all right?" I ask.

Her forehead creases, and she smiles at the same time, as if to answer yes and no simultaneously. She reminds me of someone who has a gun to her back and is trying to give a clue about her predicament without stating the obvious and risking retaliation. And by retaliation I mean being murdered.

"Of course I'm fine dear," she replies unconvincingly. "Just been a long day."

Now I know she's lying. It's 8:00 a.m.

I remind myself to focus on the reason I cut my first class of the day to run here to The Retreat and make a mental note to broach the subject of Essie's emotional issues—which I really, really hope have nothing to do with Louis—some other time. I have a feeling that conversation will require way more time than I have at the moment, so best to keep things on topic.

"What do you know about Luba?" I repeat.

Essie purses her lips and shakes her head slightly. I can't tell if she is annoyed with me or just confused by my question. "I already told you everything I know about her," she says curtly.

Not getting anywhere. Time to switch to Little Orphan Dominy mode. Good-bye direct 'n' demanding; hello sweet 'n' charming.

"I know you have, Essie, and you've been incredibly helpful, super duper helpful, which is what you always are to me... you know, helpful and stuff." I blabber on, confident that I'm merely highlighting the fact that sweet 'n' charming doesn't come naturally to me. "But I was wondering if maybe, just maybe, there was something you forgot."

Essie doesn't even take a second to think about my question. "No, I told you everything I know," she replies, her voice as flat as her expression.

This fishing expedition is not going to go anywhere unless I start to use a very specific hook. "How has Luba been feeling lately?" I ask.

Bingo! Essie's eyes brighten and expand and come back to life. It's as if every lash of her false eyelashes is ending on an exclamation point.

"You've noticed she doesn't look so good too?" she asks in reply to my question.

"How can you *not* notice?" I ask.

Three questions and still no answer. However, I think our dialogue is finally making progress.

"Despite how terrible she looks, she still walks around here as if she's the queen of this place, like some Indian Princess," Essie blurts out. "Sorry, *Native American* Indian Princess."

"I knew what you meant," I reply, moving a few papers on her desk to the side so I can sit.

"We keep getting lectures about how we have to be politically correct, how the cultural landscape of our country is changing and our sensitivities have to change with it," Essie explains. "I tried to tell Olive... oh she's the head of PPR."

That's a new one. "PPR?"

"Patient Personnel Relationships," Essie clarifies.

"Gotcha," I say. "Go on."

"I tried to tell Olive that I'm just shortcutting, being more efficient, which is what they always want us to be, by calling Luba an Indian without the Native American," Essie says. "But Olive keeps telling me that I'm not being politically correct."

I wonder what Olive would think if she knew I called Luba Psycho Squaw? I wonder how much longer Essie is going to want to discuss cultural linguistics? I wonder if Essie is going to take a breath so I can speak? Finally she inhales!

"Like you said, Es, you only have to look at Luba to know she isn't doing so well. She looks like she might be seriously ill," I say, remembering how ravaged her body and face looked the last time I saw her. "Have her doctors said anything about her condition?"

Unexpectedly, Essie starts to laugh. A mischievous chuckle that blossoms into a full-blown belly laugh. Not the most appropriate reaction when discussing someone's extremely poor health.

"Are you kidding me? She's treated like royalty around here," Essie divulges. She smoothes out some strands of her hair that got tousled during her laughburst and manages to control herself so her laughter has subsided into hiccups of giggles. "They wouldn't dare risk talking about her in public."

They wouldn't dare? *They* as in doctors? I didn't think doctors took orders from anyone.

"Why not?" I ask. "Would they get into trouble if they did?"

All forms of laughter are now silenced, and Essie's light-hearted expression disappears completely, replaced by a blank mask. But it's a mask that has been worn so often it's threadbare and tattered and I can peek through it. Behind the mask, Essie is scared.

Enough fooling around. Clearly, Luba is an important person at The Retreat. Maybe she exerts as much power here as she does in my personal life. If that's true, then Essie knows Luba can be dangerous. I doubt very much that Essie understands the supernatural component of Luba's powers—that's not something that Essie would ever be able to keep quiet about—but I do believe she understands that Luba is special.

Since it's obvious that I'm not going to get much further talking about the big picture, it's time to whittle things down and make it personal.

"Essie, has my brother been spending more time with Luba than usual?" I whisper.

Leaning back in her chair, Essie casually looks to the right. I'm blocking her line of vision, so I guess she's trying to catch a glimpse of the front door. Right before I'm about to turn back around, I realize she's not looking at the front door; she's trying to look at the main office, which is located at the other end of the hallway, tucked away in a corner as far from the patient rooms as possible.

"He has," Essie replies.

I'm so caught up with my latest discovery that I don't know who Essie's talking about.

"Who?"

"Barnaby," she reminds me. "Barnaby's been spending a lot of time with them in Luba's room."

This time I am paying attention, and once again that word frightens me. "Them?"

"Luba and that volunteer girl," Essie answers. "Nadine."

I'm staring at Essie, and I'm watching her mouth move, but I don't hear a word she's saying. A veil has dropped over my eyes, a thin veil that's decorated with the image of Barnaby, Luba, and Nadine in the old witch's room. Under normal circumstances there would be no reason for me to be alarmed by this news. I know that Barnaby has visited Luba, and I know that as part of Nadine's job functions here she has to attend to patients. But my circumstances are not normal. And neither are Luba and Nadine, so this news is unsettling.

My primal instincts to protect my brother are on red alert; he's in danger. But from what? Exactly what are Barnaby, Luba, and Nadine doing together? The possibilities are frightening and wicked and devastating. But they could be worse.

"Does Nadine's brother Napoleon ever join them?" I ask.

I must have interrupted some very important train of thought, because it takes Essie a while to switch gears and answer my question.

"She has a brother?"

"Yes, a twin," I reply. "They're not identical, of course, but his hair is the same dark brown, and he has the same round face. He's maybe an inch or two taller."

"No, I've never seen anyone else with them," Essie confirms. "In fact the only visitors Luba ever seems to have are Barnaby and Nadine and . . ."

I wait a moment for Essie to finish her sentence, but she

doesn't; her mouth stays closed. Her painted purple-red lips purse together as if they were sewn shut.

"Who else, Essie?" I demand more than ask. "Who else has been visiting Luba?"

"That is confidential, Ms. Robineau. Would you like staff sharing private knowledge about your mother's visitor list with anyone who seeks such information?"

The voice is not readily familiar, but when I turn around I recognize the face immediately. It's The Cell Keeper. That's my nickname for the guy; everyone else refers to him as Winston Lundgarden, the hospital administrator. Although my father approved of The Retreat and always felt my mother received the best care possible here, he never trusted Lundgarden. Without any reason to doubt my father, I always shared his opinion. Now that I'm seeing Lundgarden this close for the first time in years, my thoughts about the man don't change.

From what I remember he was always well-dressed, which around here means his typical attire is a business suit as opposed to a cop uniform or a jeans and flannel shirt combo. But now he looks like more of an outsider than ever before. His suit might be store bought, but it wasn't bought at any store within a hundred-mile radius of Weeping Water; the fabric and cut and style scream imported. It's a deep shade of navy, almost, but not quite, black. His shirt is navy with white stripes, and his silk tie is burgundy with specks of gray. No, not specks, stars.

The knot in Winston's tie is thick and formidable and complete with the little dimple underneath that my father was never able to achieve the few times he wore a tie to a formal event. Winston's wrinkle-free shirt is form-fitted to his body, and the cuff of his suit pants breaks seamlessly at the top of his unscuffed brown wingtips. If I measured the length of shirt that is visible under the sleeves of his suit, I'm sure it would equal an inch and a quarter, which is considered the only acceptable length to the fashionably unchallenged.

Perfection isn't relegated only to Lundgarden's wardrobe. Although his hands are clasped in front of him, I can see enough of his fingernails to know that he, unlike Essie, understands the importance of manicure maintenance. He's smartly decided to forego the smoky purple nail polish and opted for a cleaner, more natural look. His skin is unblemished and taut and smooth; if he's had any plastic surgery done, David Copperfield held the scalpel, because Winston looks magically youthful, but completely natural. The only thing that looks fake on him is his hair. No man Lundgarden's age has or should have hair this thick or this dark.

I squint a little bit, trying hard not to look like I'm squinting, and I can't see one strand of gray. Lundgarden has got to be at least sixty years old. He should have a few strands of gray hair, no matter how well kept he is, and there isn't one on his entire head. And it's a very big head.

His hair is parted in the middle and feathers back in perfect symmetry, covering the tips of his ears slightly and greeting the collar of his suit. Not only is it a dated look, reminding me of rock stars in music videos from the eighties that MTV sometimes plays late at night when it gets all retro and nostalgic, but it's inappropriate for a man of Lundgarden's stature and especially for a man who is trying desperately hard from the forehead down to remain current. I know that I sometimes put far too much importance on superficial things like looks and clothing and appearance, but I can tell with one detailed glance that this man is hiding something.

One of the many lessons I learned from my father is that the best way to find out if someone is keeping secrets is to ask them about those secrets directly.

"What's wrong with Luba?"

Lundgarden's eyes remain focused on mine despite the fact that Essie's knocked over her pencil holder and scattered its contents onto her desk. I doubt her fumbling was accidental; it was definitely in reaction to my question. The man standing in front of Essie's desk doesn't seem to be rattled at all. He also doesn't seem to have any answers.

"Nothing's wrong with Luba," he replies, his voice strong and smooth. "She's an ideal patient."

"Because she's sick?" I ask.

This question results in a slight shift in Lundgarden's physical position. His hands unclasp and reach behind his back, presumably to connect once again.

"Luba's physical condition, Dominy, is monitored constantly," he replies, his words sliding out of a terse smile. "And I can guarantee you that, for a woman of her age, she is in exceptional health."

"Sick wasn't meant to be an adjective for her *physical* condition," I reply.

Another eruption occurs on Essie's desk, but I'm not sure what's fallen over now, because this time I copy Winston's unblinking stare and don't visually investigate. It's a wise choice. If I had turned I would've missed Winston's body shift.

My insinuation that Luba is mentally unstable has made Lundgarden's physical stability falter as well. His head leans forward, and his eyes sort of roll upward, like he wants to charge at me like a rabid bull, if those things actually get rabid. His shoulders do this weird thing by rolling inward and drooping, so they look menacing and soft at the same time. It's a contradictory shift in his appearance. Part of him looks as if I've taken a sledgehammer to him; the other part looks as if he's ready to take a sledgehammer and whack me with it.

When he speaks his voice still contains that smarmy smoothness, but it lacks the fortitude it had a few moments ago.

"Ms. Robineau, may I remind you that accusations about a resident's mental capacities are not taken lightly, and any such diagnoses should be left to the professionals," he states.

"Not lumbered about haphazardly by the children of the incapacitated."

What?! I jump off the desk so quickly that Lundgarden stumbles backward, looking like a scared boy in a big man's suit. For no other reason than added effect, I pick my backpack up off the floor and sling it over my shoulder. It works; Lundgarden flinches. He wants to get personal by bringing my mother into things? I'll up the ante by adding my brother to the equation.

"The old witch has been inappropriate with my brother," I declare.

It takes three seconds for The Cell Keeper to reclaim his composure. It's amazing how quickly he goes from coward to commander, but he does. And he does it with precise detail.

"Whatever Barnaby told you about Mrs. St. Croix," he says, "was a lie."

My mother's incapacitated, and my brother's a liar. Well, okay, he's probably right, but there's no way I'm letting him get away with such language.

"Barnaby hasn't said anything, because victims who are abused usually keep their mouths shut!" I shout. "But there's no reason for him to be in her room with the door closed, and if you don't put an end to it, I'm going to call the police."

Smiling devilishly, Winston goes in for the kill.

"Are you referring to your new guardian, newly appointed Sheriff Bergeron?" he asks rhetorically. "Louis knows all about Barnaby's, shall we say, vivid and highly entertaining imagination."

Deep inside of me I howl. No sound emerges, but I can feel the intensity of the scream nonetheless. I want to strike out with my paw and rip off a chunk of Winston's unnaturally young-looking skin and devour it while he screams out in agony.

"My brother isn't making anything up!"

I hear something else topple over onto the floor next to

Essie's desk, but I'm shaking so hard that this time I think I'm the cause.

"So you share his belief that full moons are the reason for the recent rash of killings in our quiet hamlet?" Lundgarden asks.

My backpack slips down my arm as I reach out to grip the side of Essie's desk to steady myself.

"You, like your brother, hold the Weeping Water *werewolf* responsible for our latest tragedies?"

I swallow hard, pushing back the fear and rage and hysteria that I can feel swirling inside of me. This man has gone from untrustworthy to dangerous with only a few choice words. He knows things; I don't know how he knows things, but he does. I don't know if his knowledge has led him to uncover the truth about me, but I can't stand still any longer to find out.

"I need to see my mother," I whisper pathetically, and race down the hallway to Room 19.

Shutting the door behind me I've separated myself from one dangerous person and come into direct contact with another.

"Luba!"

She lifts one finger up to her lips. "Shhhhh."

The sound extends for longer than it should, not ending, but melting into the air, like an imperceptible poison seeping into the wind. The circles under her eyes are almost as dark as her hair. I have to fight the urge to leap over my mother's bed and tackle Luba to the ground when I see the tips of her long black hair touching my mother's arms. Just being grazed by her hair could be like being injected with a dirty needle.

The thing I'm looking at is rancid. I don't care what Essie or Lundgarden or anyone says; Luba looks like she's dying right in front of me. Even her voice sounds weak. Evil, still, but weaker than the last time I heard her speak.

"Such a beauty, your mother."

"Don't talk about her!"

"Be quiet!"

I'm hit in the chest, as if someone slammed a two-by-four into me. As frail as Luba looks, there's still power within that skeletal frame. But her deep, slow breaths are signs that her power cannot be sustained for much longer.

"I was paying the woman a compliment," she hisses. "Asleep for so long, and yet she's still retained her beauty. That is quite an accomplishment."

I don't want her talking about my mother even if she is praising her. I want them separated. I want my two worlds never to collide. But if that's what I want, I need to start sounding as if I have as much power as Luba.

"Why are you here?" I ask sternly.

"To offer a warning," she whispers roughly.

Bracing myself against the wall, I prepare for a shock worse than any physical battle. I'm only slightly relieved to know that my instinct was correct.

"During the next full moon there will be an added attraction," Luba announces. "Orion's constellation will be visible in the night sky."

I can feel my knees buckle, and I try desperately to keep my fear from showing on my face.

"It will be a magnificent and revealing sight," Luba continues. "Orion, the hunter, will be taking his rightful place in the sky as predator while the soft glowing moon becomes his prey."

If her words weren't disturbing enough, her actions make it that much worse. While talking about Orion, Luba slowly spells out the name in the air, as if her skinny index finger contained invisible ink. Invisible, but leaving a permanent impression.

"I so look forward to seeing you again, Dominy," Luba taunts. "When the curse takes hold of your pretty little head once more."

After Luba leaves I allow myself to crumple to the floor.
Watching my mother sleep peacefully a few feet away, I want
to crawl in bed beside her. I want whatever disease has taken
over her body and mind and soul to afflict me too so I don't
have to be aware of the things happening around me.

Orion. The name frightens me. Correction, not the name,
but the memory connected to it. I remember Mrs. Jaffe in her
basement the night of Nadine and Napoleon's party. She
wrote the letters *O* and *R* on the bowl the same way Luba
just did in the air, and I understand that she was beginning to
spell out the name Orion. The name that was in Jess's diary.
The name of the tattoo on the twins' legs. And now the name
that Luba has just spoken as a warning.

Melinda Jaffe is part of this too? How can that be?! And
what exactly is she a part of?!

Sitting on the floor, sweat covering my forehead and my
upper lip and drenching my armpits, I'm exhausted, unable
to move. Luba, with only the smallest attempt, has smashed
the honey jar into millions of tiny pieces, and the honey is
spilling out in every direction. And no matter what direction
the honey travels, it will never know the safety of its jar
again.

Because I know that I'm about to learn something important, something that will answer all my questions and that
frightens me. And even though one nightmare is about to
come to an end, another more terrifying nightmare is getting
ready to begin.

Chapter 13

I'm still scared.

It's been weeks since I last saw Luba, and I haven't been able to shake this feeling. The feeling that my life is about to change—once again—and not for the better. How it could possibly get worse, I have no idea, but dread and anxiety and fear are all firmly clinging to the insides of my stomach, reminding me every second of every day that there's more to this curse than I originally thought. A curse within a curse. There are going to be more surprises and obstacles that I'll have to deal with and overcome and survive. It's a feeling I've kept to myself, but time's up. Tomorrow night is the full moon.

"Napoleon's in on it too."

I thought being blunt would be helpful. I thought it would be better to make my indictment direct and simple and unemotional. But when dealing with boyfriends it's impossible to be unemotional. So my direct approach has had an indirect result. Archie hates me.

"I am sick and tired of you bashing my boyfriend!"

Archie's outburst is justified. So is his anger for that matter, but neither will make me change my mind.

"I wish it weren't true, Archie," I reply. "But it is."

With just a handful of words, I've destroyed Archie's happiness. He can't press Rewind and gullibly believe that Napoleon's innocent. He can't because I won't let him. I love Archie too much to let him live under false pretenses; there's no way I'm going to let him hide from the truth that Napoleon's one of them. Archie, however, is still hoping for a loophole.

"You don't know that for certain!" he replies.

My heart breaks a little because I can already hear that Archie's voice is stronger than his conviction. He knows, but he doesn't want to understand. I wait for the final school bell to stop ringing, the one that comes fifteen minutes after the official end of the day to alert students that the school buses are set to leave. If you're not on a bus by the time the bell stops ringing, prepare to walk home. Or, in this instance, face the truth.

I've gathered most of the Wolf Pack in what's become our favorite meeting place, the small soundproof room off the music studio. I overheard Gwen say that band practice was taking place out on the field this afternoon so they could perfect their drills for some upcoming statewide competition, so I knew that if we waited a few minutes the entire marching band would be outside and we could enter the room without being detected. My plan worked perfectly. My confidence as a leader is sky-high until it's time for me to speak.

"So, Domgirl," Caleb starts. "Why the emergency meeting?"

I take a deep breath and am about to speak when I see the back of Archie's notebook. He has scribbled *A + N 4ever 2gether.* In black Sharpie. So the phrase will never fade, so the sentiment will be indelible. I wish I were like the rest of Two W, ignorant as to who N is, but I'm not. I know that Archie and Napoleon have entered blissful boyfriendom, so I can't find the words fast enough, the gentle, kind, humane words that will destroy their relationship and take all possibility of permanence out of their coupling. Arla finds her voice first and sets the meeting on a totally different and unnecessary course.

"Are we officially ousting Nadine from the inner circle?" Arla asks, noticing her absence. "Because if so my vote's a yea."

"Yea yea for a no no to the Nay Nay," Archie adds.

Crossing his arms, Caleb leans his head back against the foam-padded wall and adopts a very scholarly expression, kind of like the way he looked when he first started tutoring me. "Does a double positive negate a double negative?" he rhetoricalizes. "If so does that mean you want Nadine to remain a member of the Wolf Pack or do you suggest that we, um . . ."

"Toss the lying bitch out with yesterday's fashion trends?" Arla says, finishing Caleb's question. "Acid-wash jeans, platform flip-flops, and Nadine."

"Nicely stated, Bergeron, even though I don't understand why acid-wash jeans are offensive," he replies.

"One of the few reasons to be thankful for the Two W school uniform," she says.

"What about you, Winter?" Caleb asks. "Do you vote yea or nay to exile Nadine?"

Without hesitating, Archie answers, "The time has come to set the bee free."

But where the bee goes, the butterfly is sure to follow.

"I know Napoleon isn't a member of the Wolf Pack," I say. "But he is our enemy."

Again, Archie's response is immediate. "That's ridiculous!"

"I'm sorry, Archie," I say. "I really am."

"No, you're not!" he scoffs. "You've always hated Nap. You've tried to hide it, but now you think you've come up with a slick way to get rid of him forever! Well, I'm not going to let you get away with it!"

And I'm not going to let Napoleon get away with hoodwinking my friend, which is why I finally decide not to be gentle and kind and humane and blurt out, "Napoleon is in on it too."

I don't know why I'm surprised by the intensity of Archie's reaction, but I am. I know Barnaby is somehow involved with Luba and Nadine. He shot me for God's sake! I love him, but I'm suspicious of him; I have balance where my brother is concerned. Archie has to find the same kind of balance with his boyfriend. But his reaction is ferocious, and I have the feeling that he wishes he could borrow my wolf fangs and claws and attack me, make me take back every disagreeable word I uttered. But I guess brothers are different than boyfriends. I mean, how did I expect Archie to react? What did I expect him to say? *Sure, okay, whatever you say, Dom. I mean, my life just revolves around whatever you want, so just say the word and I'll disown my very first boyfriend.* He's in love with Napoleon. He feels like his life is just beginning, and I'm suggesting that it has to come to an abrupt and final end. His pissed-offedness shouldn't be surprising.

"I wish it added up differently," I say. "But I've been thinking about it for weeks and the only logical conclusion is that Napoleon is connected to all of this."

"Along with Luba and Nadine?" Caleb asks.

"And Mrs. Jaffe," I add.

"You think she's in on it too?" Arla asks.

I relay how Luba and Mrs. Jaffe used the same gesture to spell out the word *Orion* and how the twins' mother had been extolling the virtues of the stars and astrology the night of the party.

"So now you think the four of them are in on the curse?" Caleb says, summing up my hypothesis.

"As implausible as it sounds," I reply. "Yes."

The cushioned wall feels comforting against the back of my head, and I lean into it farther. It's soft, but firm, and beyond the embrace there's support underneath. The situation doesn't call for it, but I can feel a smile form on my lips because I'm reminded of my father; his touch and his voice were always gentle, but underneath was a foundation as strong as concrete. Before my smile reaches its full potential, it's ripped from my face, not with a fang or a claw, but with words.

"You're a spiteful idiot, Dom!"

Archie has never spoken to me like this before. Part of me understands that he's just frightened, but the other part of me acknowledges that by condemning his newly minted boyfriend to eternal residence in enemy territory, I may have unwittingly unleashed Archie's inner beast.

"Hey, Winter," Caleb scolds. "Take it easy."

Ignoring his friend, Archie keeps striking out at me. "Listen to yourself, Dom!" he barks. "You just disproved your own theory!"

Arla whips her head to the right to face Archie, the curls of her chestnut brown wig continuing to bounce even after she stops. "Theory? What are you talking about, Archie?"

In one quick move Archie repositions himself to sit on his knees and lean forward. He looks like he's kneeling around a campfire, about to tell a ghost story. A ghost story that, sadly, we're the stars of.

"Jess warned us to keep Barnaby away from *three* of them, not four," he reminds us. "We know that Jess can't tell us the whole truth, but we also know that she wouldn't lie to us or deliberately try to confuse us."

No, she would never do that.

"Which means one of them isn't our enemy!" Archie concludes.

In the silence that follows Archie's summation I can almost hear the insistent buzzing of the bee and the desperate wing-flapping of the butterfly. No matter what anyone says, no matter how long we debate, the bee and the butterfly will not leave on their own. They need to be forced out deliberately; they need to be defeated. And it sounds as if I may have to do the extermination on my own.

Sheepishly, Caleb looks at me, his teeth biting down onto his thumb. "He's right, Domgirl," Caleb says, not allowing his teeth to let go of his flesh.

"Of course I'm right!" Archie shouts triumphantly. "If Barnaby needed protection from all four of them, Jess would've said so, but she was very specific; she said three."

Arla loops her wig hair behind her ear and rubs the ends in between her fingers. It's an absentminded gesture that I've seen her do for years whenever she's taking a test, whenever she's searching for the right answer. Now, she's searching for the right way to respond so it doesn't look like she's flat leaving me to join the majority.

"Well, that is what Jess said," she adds. "Keep Barnaby away from all three of them."

If I'm destined to be alone, then so be it.

"I remember what Jess said, Arla," I reply.

Her back stiffens at the flatness of my voice. Nervously she flips the hair back over her ear and continues, "So if Mrs. Jaffe is part of this too, then most likely Napoleon isn't."

I know exactly what they're doing. I know exactly what's going on inside all three of their minds. They're looking for a way to separate Napoleon from his fate. I've been trying to do the same thing since Luba spelled out the word *Orion* in the air with her bony fingers. But no matter how hard we all try, there isn't one.

Even still, buoyed by the support Arla and Caleb have shown him, Archie allows himself a moment to embrace his cocky football player side. A moment is all I'm going to give him. He clasps his hands behind his head and leans back confidently. "So there you have it!" he exclaims. "You have absolutely no proof that my boyfriend's dangerous."

His moment is over.

"Nap has powers. I've seen them."

Slowly, Archie's arms descend down the walls until they're lying limp at his side. Little red blotches appear on his cheeks, resembling a child's attempt to apply rouge. And a teenager's attempt to conceal anger. "What do you mean he has *powers?*"

For the first time I wish this room were much larger so there would be more things for me to look at, but no, I can't look away; if I'm going to be honest with my friend, I have to look him in the eye. "I'm not sure exactly," I start, "but he and Nadine have a silver light that lives in their bodies, like the wolf spirit lives in mine."

"Are you serious, Dom?" Caleb asks.

"Yes," I answer. "I know I should've told you about it, but...I didn't understand what it meant, until now. It means they're definitely linked in some way to Luba."

Archie isn't returning my gaze. His eyes are focused on the floor, but he's listening to what I'm saying. And examining every word. "If the light lives inside of them, how can you see it?"

"The light emerges from their bodies," I reply. "Sometimes I think it's a defense mechanism, but other times...I think they use it as a weapon."

"You think, Domgirl," Caleb says. "Or you know?"

I can feel Caleb tug on our invisible string. He wants me to understand that I need to be very specific, that what I'm saying is terribly important, but most of all he wants me to know that whatever I say he will believe me.

"On separate occasions I've seen them use their silver light as a weapon against someone else."

Can't be any more specific than that. There can't be any wiggle room for interpretation. Or can there?

"To defend themselves," Archie grasps. "What's wrong with that?"

"No, Archie, not to defend," I reply. "To attack."

Archie and I don't have an invisible string connecting our two selves; all we have is friendship. And unfortunately friendships can sometimes be severed.

"I don't believe that!" he claims. "I don't believe my boyfriend would ever attack another person with some silver light, some special power that you say he has. Nadine, yes, she would do such a thing, but not Nap."

Guess it's time to get even more specific.

"I saw them!" I scream. "I saw Nadine use her light to try and control Barnaby, and I saw Napoleon use his to attack his sister."

Sometimes being specific totally backfires.

"Kind of the way you used your wolf-strength to fight against Barnaby?"

Arla's question hovers over my head and threatens to choke me the way I felt I was being choked by a plastic bag when I first started to transform. It threatens to change my world in very much the same way the curse has. Not because her words bring with them destruction, but because her words offer clarity.

She's right. After watching the way Nadine used her silver light against Barnaby, I'm convinced she was up to no good. But I don't have proof that Napoleon is evil or dangerous, only that he's a brother who's used his special power in a fight against his sister. Supernatural sibling rivalry. I'm guilty of the same crime.

"So what you're saying, Dom, is that you and Napoleon are exactly the same?"

I'll accept Archie's gloating. I deserve it. Arla's summation is a lot harder to accept.

"Maybe the whole Jaffe family is connected to Luba and they're all cursed just like you are," she proposes. "Which is really kind of a good thing when you think about it."

I am thinking about it, and I don't know how a curse can be a good thing. Or how any type of association with Luba can be a good thing.

"Because if they're under her spell, the twins are just like you, Dom," she explains.

Just like me?! Now what is she talking about? Is she suggesting they're werewolves too? No, no, that's not what she's saying at all. I can tell by the relaxed expressions on Caleb's and Archie's faces that they're getting it too. Arla's comment doesn't really change much, but we understand what she's talking about.

"Nap may not be evil," Caleb clarifies, "but he may be nothing more than an evil pawn."

"So now my boyfriend's an evil pawn?!" Archie shouts.

"Well, which would you prefer, Archie?" I ask.

"Maybe he's . . ." Archie begins.

"Nuh, uh, uh, uh," I interrupt. "Those are your only two choices."

Slowly I can see Archie age. The anger in his eyes disappears and is replaced by something that resembles, but isn't quite, acceptance. He's still innocent enough to retain hope that I could be wrong, that there could be a third choice, but he's smart enough to know that there most likely isn't. It's a constant fight. I saw it in my father's eyes when he told me about the curse. He clung to the hope that it was superstition, but knew it was fact. The way Caleb and Arla are avoiding Archie's gaze, I know they agree with me. We've accepted adulthood without any hope. Napoleon might be slightly different from his twin, he might use his powers differently, but in one way they are similar: Neither of them can be trusted any longer.

Arla swipes the air to shoo away a fly that's gotten trapped in our private sanctuary. She jerks her head to the side, and the way her hair moves I can see her scar. It reminds me that I've now wounded two of the three people in this room. How soon before I damage Caleb's life too? *Don't think about that now; concentrate on one victim at a time.*

"Look, Archie, I don't know which three out of the four Jess was referring to," I admit, "But no matter how you look at it, Napoleon is connected."

Even though he's much calmer, Archie's hands fidget once again until his right hand literally grabs the left to keep it from moving. "And no matter how you look at it, you can't prove that he's dangerous."

"No, I can't," I reply. "Not yet anyway."

The only sound in the soundproof room is the ticking of the clock on the wall over Caleb's head. Now that the room is bathed in silence, the ticking seems louder than usual, but I guess this is how the room always sounds when no one is here. In a similar way Napoleon's true nature isn't going to change just because he's now Archie's boyfriend. If he was evil before, he's going to be evil tomorrow night when the full moon returns. If he's nothing more than an innocent bystander, that won't change either. I just have to persuade Archie to promise he won't fill Nap in on what we know before then.

"You can't say anything to Nap about this," I say. I like the sound of my voice; it's hushed, but strong. "It's only for one more day. Promise."

Squirming on the floor, Archie nods his head in agreement. It's a reluctant promise, but a promise nonetheless.

"From what Luba insinuated, I'll find out the truth tomorrow night, on the anniversary of this curse," I advise, "when both Orion's constellation and the full moon will be visible."

Unable to control his anxiety any longer, Archie jumps up and starts to pace the length of the small room. "What's this constellation have to do with the curse anyway?!"

"It seems to have everything to do with it, Arch."

Caleb's voice is compassionate, but that's not why Archie stops moving. Caleb's grabbed him by the ankle, firmly, to make him stand still so he can focus. My boyfriend gets it. We're on the verge of discovering something important, and we all need to work together; we need to be unified; we do not need to start infighting.

"I'm sorry," Archie says, shaking his head. He seems so lost, as if he wouldn't know where to go even if he had the freedom to move. "It just doesn't make any sense to me."

Raising my hand to grab onto Archie, I pull him down so he sits next to me. He doesn't flinch; he grabs hold of my hand, grateful for the connection. I don't let go of him even after he's sitting cross-legged on the floor, his knee touching mine. He won't look at me, but he hasn't broken our hold. He's letting the warmth of my skin penetrate the coldness of his.

"I agree with you, but it's undeniable," I state. "The twins both have the tattoo of the constellation, and Luba and Mrs. Jaffe spelled *Orion* in the same exact way."

"And Nadine told us that she loves astronomy," Arla chimes in.

"Don't forget that Jess drew the constellation in her diary," Caleb adds.

"We may have no idea what it all means," I say. "But there's no way all of these little pieces are coincidences."

The long, worried silence that follows is broken when Arla shifts her position and her foot accidentally knocks over a box of trumpet mouthpieces. Scattered on the floor they tumble and roll and spin until, of course, three mouthpieces separate from the group and don't stop moving until they reach the other side of the room, each one connected to the other.

"Maybe it's more random than we think," Arla suggests, staring at the three pieces. "Maybe Nadine and Napoleon have nothing to do with your curse and are simply connected to Luba."

"What do you mean?" Caleb asks.

"Psycho Squaw could have cursed them in the same way she cursed Dominy," Arla explains. "Maybe Mrs. Jaffe pissed her off too, just like your father did."

Three cursed teenagers in one small town? The odds are against it, but the odds are also against finding proof that lycanthropy exists, so why can't it be possible? Thinking about it, I realize it actually does sound like a plausible explanation.

"That could explain why Jess freaked out when she saw Napoleon in church," I say.

"I would freak out too," Archie mumbles. "Napoleon doesn't go to church."

Oh really? "He must have had a spiritual crisis, because I saw him there," I reply.

Running his fingers through his hair, Archie massages his scalp for a few seconds before speaking. Interestingly, his scalp is slightly darker than the rest of his skin. "He told me he doesn't believe in organized religion," he shares. "The last time he was in a church was for Jess's wake."

"If that's what he said, then he lied," I claim. "I saw him in church months later."

This time Archie doesn't protest my accusation against his boyfriend. I'm not sure if he's accepted that Napoleon's duplicitous or if he's too tired to fight.

"When Jess appeared to me at St. Edmund's, she wouldn't

let Napoleon see her," I say. "I thought it was because he was her ex and she was still more Jess than supernatural sun goddess, but maybe it was because he's inhuman too."

"Because Jess said only humans can't see her," Caleb says, connecting the rest of my unconnected dots.

"Exactly!" I shriek. I'm not thrilled that Napoleon could also be cursed, possessed by some supernatural spirit like I am, but I am excited that we're starting to make sense of what moments earlier was indecipherable. We haven't uncovered the whole truth yet, but we're getting close. Or are we?

"Or it could've simply been Jess acting like Jess," Archie refutes. "She never explained exactly why she ducked when she saw Nap, right?"

"No, she never did," I confess.

You can practically hear the air being sucked out of the room along with the sound until Caleb, the annoying voice of reason, speaks.

"So essentially, folks," he says, "that puts us back to square one."

"Until tomorrow night when we can join Dominy after she transforms," Archie announces. "And find out exactly what's going on."

"Absolutely out of the question."

Ten seconds later, I figure out that I'm not the one who spoke. It takes me another ten to realize that Caleb shares my opinion.

"It's the only way I'm going to find out if my boyfriend's a liar, evil, a supernatural creature, or all of the above," Archie proclaims loudly, obviously getting some of his strength back. "There's no way I'm missing that."

"It's too dangerous, Arch," Caleb replies. "And we can serve a better purpose than tailgating Domgirl through the woods."

"Like throwing my father and the citizen's brigade off track," Arla concludes.

Watching my boyfriend, my best friend, and my stepsister strategize and discuss my fate, I realize they really are a well-oiled machine. They may argue and bicker and disagree, but they all share the same fundamental purpose: to protect me.

Reaching into his backpack, Caleb pulls out a small box and offers it to me. "I was going to give this to you later in private, but we really don't have any secrets from one another," Caleb says. "It's sort of a pre-birthday gift."

"I told you guys," I reply. "I don't want any gifts this year."

"And is this a *really* private gift?" Arla asks, tugging uncomfortably on her wig hair.

"Open it up, Dominy," Caleb says, his eyes twinkling. "So we can all find out."

It's not private or personal or anything that I ever really wanted for that matter. "It's a GPS," I say, staring into the box.

"Brilliant!" Archie cries.

Feigning an "I couldn't agree with you more" look, I add, "Absolutely!"

Caleb's high-pitched laughter is so loud it reverberates off of the padded walls instead of getting sucked in by the foam.

"You have no idea why I gave that to you, do you?" he asks.

I hear my gigglaughs join in with Caleb's sound and reply, "None at all."

"It has an elastic band, see?"

When he leans over to show me the wrist accessory on the GPS, his hair falls into my forehead. I can smell his shampoo and his breath and his skin, and I get a rush throughout my whole body. I adjust my position and curl my leg underneath me to conceal the shudder that just took over my body.

"I have the same one, and they're hooked up like walkie-talkies," Caleb explains. "I thought you could strap it to your ankle before you transform so we can track you and then steer Louis and company in the opposite direction."

It's the sweetest thing I've ever heard. Both Archie and Arla groan when I give Caleb a thank-you kiss. We groan louder when Arla mushes up our mushy moment and turns it into something gross.

"I'd like to put that thing on my father so I can find out who his mystery girlfriend is," she declares.

"He still hasn't told you?" Archie asks.

"Nope," Arla replies, shaking her head. "And it's getting serious."

Once again, I keep my suspicions that his new gf may be Essie to myself. There's enough mystery and speculation hanging in the air regarding Napoleon and his true nature; no need to add the mystery of Louis and his true love into the mix.

"Seriously serious?" I ask. "How can you be sure if he hasn't said anything?"

"Because I found these stashed in the vanity underneath the bathroom sink."

Staring at the condoms in her hand that she pulled out of her purse, we let out a huge, collective groan. Mine is the loudest. I will never look at Louis the same way again. Or Essie! And Gwen will never look at us the same way again either.

"Oh my God! I am so, so, soooo, so sorry!"

Standing over us, Gwen looks like a giant who just stumbled upon some very inappropriate dwarf-tivity. As she holds up her clarinet horizontally to cover her eyes, she's obviously a giant who wishes she were blind.

"I swear that I won't tell another living soul about this," she shrieks.

"It's okay, Gwen," I say. "Nothing like that is going on."

"I know," she replies, lowering her clarinet so we can see one eye. "Those things are still unopened."

Stifling a laugh in order to preserve her reputation, Arla says, "Gwen, listen to me, none of us in this room were about to have sex. None of us have ever had sex for that matter. Do you understand me?"

Ignoring Arla, Gwen pursues more practical matters. "Could someone please pass me the box of reeds?"

"Gwenevere! You can open your eyes," Archie says. "We just needed a private place to talk about some, um, personal things."

"That's good! We learned in health class that communication before intimacy makes the experience better—and safer—for both parties. Or all four parties," she asserts. "The box is to your right, Caleb."

Caleb is laughing so hard he almost drops the box when handing it to Gwen. With her eyes still closed and doubly protected by her clarinet, she grabs it and starts to leave. Just before she closes the door, she whispers, "Do you want me to stand guard until you're all finished?"

I catch Caleb's eyes, and I'm not sure who's looking at him: the girl or the wolf. Suddenly I wish my friends were gone and I could take Gwen up on her offer, allow the passion that is starting to grow within my stomach to rise and bleed out, give myself over to Caleb completely. I feel as primitive and as hungry as I do when I first transform and need to feed. Unfortunately, the girl is not going to get to be as wild as the wolf.

"Thanks, Gwen," Archie pretend-whines. "But you know something? You kind of ruined the mood."

"I'm sorry! I'm always doing stuff like that!" she exclaims. She is feeling braver now; her eyes are only half-shut. "My older sister is always complaining that I bother her and her boyfriend when they want to, you know, be alone, but I can't help that we share a room!"

We have officially reached the point of no return. This girl is not going to return to wolf-like territory, so it's time to leave. On two legs. Standing up at the same time, we surround Gwen and give her a big group hug.

"Thanks, Gwen," I say. Then I add a white lie just to make her feel important. "If it weren't for you, we probably would've made a hugomungous mistake."

I don't let her know that she's probably given us the last laugh we're all going to have for quite a long time. Stealing a glance at Caleb, Arla, and especially Archie, I know that they're thinking the exact same thing.

Chapter 14

I need a distraction. In spite of Gwen's unintentional stand-up routine, the day is not going well, and tomorrow has the potential of being even worse. Like epically worse. Thankfully, for as much as my life has changed, it's also remained the same, and whenever I need help, Jess comes to my rescue.

Halfway home I tell Arla that I have to make an unplanned visit to Jess's house, and because Arla isn't threatened by my strong connection to the Wyatt family, she doesn't ask to tag along. However, as we part ways she reminds me to be home before dinner so I don't give her father proof that I disregard his and the town's curfew for the under twenty-one set. It's hard enough as is to sneak out of the house when Louis thinks I'm a law-abiding citizen; no need to make him suspect that I'm a juvenile delinquent who needs to be watched 24/7.

Calling after Arla, I promise that I'll be home early enough to help set the table. She doesn't turn around, but merely raises her hand to wave good-bye to me as she keeps walking down the street. She isn't angry or being dismissive; she's just got someplace to go. So do I.

I've wanted to contact Mrs. Wyatt many times over the

past few months, but every time I started to dial her phone number or walk toward her house I was consumed with guilt. Today's no different, but today the guilt is mixed with something else: optimism. I'm not sure how I'll be greeted on the eve of the anniversary of Jess's death, but I have to take the chance and find out. When her mother opens the door to greet me with a warm smile and a full-bodied hug, I realize the sense of hope wasn't a result of my relationship with her; it was a result of my relationship with her daughter.

Behind Mrs. Wyatt, Jess is floating in the air, her head a few inches above her mother's, her golden sunshine filling up the entire living room. If I hadn't closed my eyes to let the tears flow, I would have had to close them to shield them from the blinding light.

"Dominy!" Mrs. Wyatt squeals. "It's so good to see you!"

She continues talking, but her mouth is nuzzled against my neck, and she's crying so hard that it's difficult to make out what she's saying.

"It's good to see you too," I say, though I doubt she hears me over her own words and her sobs.

When we both stop crying, Mrs. Wyatt and I look at each other, not just a glance, but an extendalook, to really take each other in. I notice that there are bags under her eyes, puffy and several shades darker than the rest of her skin. Her hair has grown since the last time I saw her, and sections of it have turned gray, not just at the roots, but some strands change from black to gray at the tips. Slightly unkempt, she looks like she's standing in front of a fan, gray and black wisps of her hair lifted up and gliding on the breeze coming in through the slightly open window. Age is clinging to Mrs. Wyatt, and it's all because of me, because I murdered her daughter.

That fact grabs hold of my mind and, involuntarily, I gasp for breath. I'm sure Jess's mother thinks I'm trying to prevent myself from weeping again, not that I'm trying to shake the truth from my soul, separate my current self from my past actions. But whatever she's thinking and whatever she sees when she looks at me mustn't be the truth because she smiles.

"Jess always said you were the most beautiful girl at school," she says quietly. "More beautiful than any girl in those celebrity magazines she loved so much."

The comment doesn't surprise me. Jess often told me the same thing when we would be alone in our rooms experimenting with makeup and trying out new ways to wear our hair. It was never a remark based in jealousy, but a casual observation from one friend to another.

"And I see that Vernita's magic potion has worked wonders on you," she comments.

She holds my chin in between her fingers and turns my head from left to right to inspect my skin. "Not an unsightly hair ruining your beautiful complexion," she observes.

Nope, now that the wolf has been released, the girl shows no physical signs of being a hairy beast.

"Promise me one thing though, Dominy," Mrs. Wyatt says, her fingers moving from my chin to my hair. "You'll never try to change the color of your hair the way Jess did. The color of fire suits you."

Wild flames are appropriate for a wild animal I guess.

"I won't," I promise. "I'm actually growing quite fond of my wild red mane."

"I wish Jess had been happy with her hair," Mrs. Wyatt says, sighing and smiling at the same time. "Most girls would kill to be blond, but Jess hated it. Always dyeing her hair, straightening it, trying to look like she was Japanese. Oh she never learned to be happy with how she was born."

I'm struck by this comment because it makes me realize there's something I never knew Jess and I shared. We both struggled with our birthright. My tears return and so does Mrs. Wyatt's hug or perhaps it's the other way around. Doesn't matter. I knew I came here for a reason. I thought I was coming here to comfort Mrs. Wyatt and, in some small way, for her to comfort me. But the truth is, Jess is comforting us both.

I'm sitting across the kitchen table from Mrs. Wyatt, a glass of lemon-drenched iced tea in front of me. She looks over my shoulder and out the window over the sink. Her face is bathed in a mixture of sunlight and her daughter's glow. I don't know where the natural light ends and Jess's sunshine begins, and this time specifics don't matter. It doesn't make any difference where the line is drawn that separates natural from supernatural; what matters is that Mrs. Wyatt and her daughter are still connected. Whether Mrs. Wyatt knows it or not.

"I know this is going to sound bizarre, like I'm some crazy hick," she starts. "But whenever I feel the sunshine like this, like its rays are settling right into my heart, I feel like my little girl is saying hello."

Reaching out to grab her hand, I want to tell her she's right. I want to tell her that her daughter is right next to her and that she's made up of all the sunshine a mother's heart could hold, but I can't. She'll think I'm the crazy one, and, besides, she'll never truly understand. Better to let her just imagine the impossible. And tell her something that'll remind her how wonderful her daughter truly was.

"Jess loved you so much, Mrs. Wyatt," I tell her. "That's why she agreed to share you with us."

"Share me?"

A puzzled look slides across her face that I need to wipe away by sharing a memory. I can feel Jess's glow behind me, warming my back like I'm sunbathing near Weeping Water River on a hot August day, lying facedown on the grass. She isn't saying a word, but she's communicating; she's giving me her blessing to tell her mother about our secret.

"Neither Arla nor I really know our mothers," I continue.

"Mine's been in a coma forever and Arla's... Well, when Mrs. Bergeron stopped being a wife, she also kind of stopped being a mother."

The actions of Louis's wayward ex-wife aren't news to Mrs. Wyatt, but they're still unfathomable and unsettling to someone like her who considers motherhood a lifelong commitment. Except for a slight pursing of her lips and shake of her head though, she doesn't let the complete disgust I know she's feeling for Louis's ex escape her body.

"So Jess told us years ago that whenever we wanted, we could share you," I inform her. "As sort of a substitute mom."

Upon hearing this revelation Mrs. Wyatt is unable to contain her true feelings; they're simply too overwhelming. When the rays of Jess's light hit her mother's tears, it looks like she's crying liquid gold. I've seen many wonders, many breathtaking images thanks to Jess, but this is a truly glorious sight.

"My Jess..." Mrs. Wyatt whispers. "She never ceases to amaze me."

If she only knew.

Even if she doesn't, Misutakiti does.

The moment Misu enters the room he starts barking maniacally. Not at Mrs. Wyatt or at me, but at Jess. I can tell from the direction in which he's looking and the way his tail is wagging, like a metronome on speed, that he sees his beloved Jess. She knows it too. As she kneels down to greet her pet, Jess's eyes turn a few shades brighter, but joy quickly turns to disappointment when Misu runs right through her.

"Misu!" she cries.

"Calm down, boy!" Mrs. Wyatt orders.

Unable to control his glee at seeing Jess after such a long absence, Misu turns around and tries to make contact once again. This time when he leaps through her, Jess falters a bit;

she actually stumbles, not at all like the poised goddess she's become. I guess that's because here in this house she isn't some deity; she's just a girl who misses her family very much.

Grabbing hold of Misu by the collar, I pull him close to me so I can whisper in his ear. I have no idea if he'll be able to hear me now that I'm not in wolf form, but it's worth a try to prevent Mrs. Wyatt from putting the poor thing into his crate for a few hours as obedience training.

"Misu, listen to me," I instruct. "We have to act natural in front of Jess's mommy."

Success! Instantly, Misu looks at me with eyes that contain more intelligence than most humans, and he immediately sits on his haunches and offers me his paw like a well-trained dog. He can hear me! Communicating with animals must be a carry-over trait just like enhanced vision and super speed. Sometimes this being half wolf thing actually comes in handy.

"Oh my!" Mrs. Wyatt exclaims. "Jess was the only one who could get him to quiet down like that so quickly."

She kind of still is. As I hold Misu's paw, Jess kneels next to us and looks right into her dog's eyes. She's looking at Misu the way her mother looks at pictures of Jess.

"Oh, Misu, I think I miss you most of all," Jess says.

Even though I react a split second after Misu, there's enough time for me to lean forward so it looks to Mrs. Wyatt like her dog is licking my cheek and not Jess's. I'm not sure why they're able to touch all of a sudden—perhaps the head Omikami had a pet dog too when he was human so he sprinkled some mercy into Jess's sunlight—but for a fleeting moment they are connected once more. I suspect that their bond would have remained unbroken for a bit longer if her brother, Jeremy, hadn't waltzed into the kitchen at that very moment with his latest girlfriend glued to his side.

"My brother is dating Rayna Delgado!?" Jess shrieks so loudly she startles both Misu and me. I topple over onto the floor as Misu lunges toward Rayna, stopping a few inches in front of her, his body tense, his tail rigid as a spear. Slowly, his growl fills the room, deep and gravelly and a growl that cannot be mistaken for a friendly hello.

"Misu, knock it off!" Jeremy growls back.

"Dominy!" Jess screams even louder. "Why didn't you tell me that my brother is dating that skank?!"

"I didn't know anything about this!" I scream in my defense. And of course I don't scream silently.

"I didn't know I had to get your approval," Rayna replies sarcastically.

Clutching the leg of a kitchen chair, I begin the long, somewhat embarrassing, journey to stand vertical. "Um, sorry, I . . . It's just a shock, you know, seeing the two of you as, um, well . . . the two of you."

Even if I had heard a rumor about their pairing, I would never have believed it. Jeremy is a college freshman at Big Red, reserved and studious, and, fashion-wise, very preppy. Like old-school eighties, bright-colored-polo-shirt-with-the-collar-up preppy. Rayna is a high school junior, like me, and the closest she's ever gotten to preppy and studious was dressing up like a slutty Catholic schoolgirl in freshman year for Halloween. Their coupling is definitely mix 'n' match, and even Misu is offended by the pairing.

"Jeremy, get that mutt away from me!" Rayna cries.

"He is not a mutt!" I yell back.

"Well, he is a mixed breed," Jess confesses. "But don't tell Delslutto that!"

"Misu, I said stop barking!" Jeremy shouts, pounding his foot on the floor, the toe of his penny loafer getting dangerously close to Misu's face.

"Don't you dare!!" Mrs. Wyatt shouts.

And for the moment anyway, her maternal instincts are revealed. She tenderly grabs Misu by the collar, while sternly pointing a finger at her son. I know that she loves Jeremy as much as she loves Jess, but right now if Mrs. Wyatt had to choose between parenting her dog or her son, Jeremy would need to dial 1-800-New-Mother.

The shame that takes over Jeremy's face, making his eyelids half-close, suggests he understands that he's crossed the line and enraged his mother. His silence also suggests that he's not going to push his luck. He knows that it's only because Rayna and I are in the kitchen that his mother isn't screaming, putting him in his place for trying to hurt Misu, even if he was only doing it as a way to shock him out of killer-dog mode. Rayna, however, has not taken the hint and is still in killer-girlfriend mode.

"Jeremy," she whiney-pouts. "You promised you would drive me home."

"Oh my God, her voice is worse than her dye job," Jess snips.

I have to agree with Jess on that one even though I have absolutely no idea what color Rayna's hair is supposed to be. We don't have any classes together this year, so I don't see her every day, but even from across the hallway I would have noticed a change like this. Guaranteed she did not go to Vernita, the beauty-gician, because there is no way she would've let Rayna out in public with that crime scene on her head. Could be ash blond, could be mahogany brown. Maybe outside in the natural lighting I'd be able to figure it out. What's unbelievable is that whatever the color, it's not nearly as bad as the high-pitched nasal twang she's adopted. I guess she's trying to sound cultured and sophisticated around Jeremy since he's a college boy. Instead, she sounds like a petulant hooker.

"And I will not have a boyfriend who breaks his promises," she pouty-whines.

Out of the corner of my eye, I see Jess leap into the air until she's completely horizontal, facing the floor, and lying right above Rayna's head. She shoves one golden finger down her throat and then opens her mouth wide so a stream of golden vomit pours out of her and onto her intended victim. A glob of yellowy liquid lands on top of Rayna's head, splitting perfectly to pour, in even amounts, down the sides of her body.

I open my own mouth, but I'm in such shock at the disgusting, yet mesmerizing, sight that no sound comes out, and luckily no one's paying attention to me so my jaw-dropping remains unseen. Jess and her vomit also remain unseen, although Rayna does try to wipe something off of her arm and her chin, so I'm pretty sure she feels a presence around her. It's doubtful that she knows she's showering in Jess's preternatural fluid.

And clearly Jeremy has no idea he's dating someone his sister and I consider an UGSWM—Unacceptable Girlfriend Slash Wife Material—because he's as anxious to leave with her as we are for Rayna to disappear from the premises. Scooping up the car keys from a wooden basket on the kitchen counter with one hand, Jeremy reaches out with the other to grab Rayna's elbow, and they start to leave.

"Put those back," Mrs. Wyatt says, stroking Misu's fur.

"I'm going to drive Rayna home," Jeremy replies.

"Not in my car you aren't," she replies. "Yours is right in the driveway."

Busted! Jeremy's probably more furious at being embarrassed in front of his girlfriend than he is about getting caught trying to pull a fast one right underneath his mother's eyes, but for whatever reason he slams the keys into the basket with such force that it flips over. So much for a quick getaway. Now he has to hunt and peck through the basket's overturned contents to find his own car keys. Instead of being driven home like the princess she thinks she is in a new Nissan Xterra, Rayna will have to squeeze into a ten-year-old beat-up Ford Taurus like an ugly stepsister. The latter is a much better description of her anyway.

"I hope she sits in the spot where I peed!" Jess cries just as the unhappy couple leaves the house.

"You peed in Jeremy's car?" I ask silently. *"You never told me that."*

"It was a long drive, I drank a lot of soda, and he was making me laugh," she replies.

I guess there are some more things I still don't know about Jess. Or her mother.

"Thank you, Misutakiti," Mrs. Wyatt says, kneeling down and rubbing her nose against his after Jeremy and his hopefully soon-to-be-ex-girlfriend leave. "I know I shouldn't admit it, but I can't stand that girl either."

I collapse onto the floor, and the three of us become a mass of fur and laughter and hugs. Jess watches us from a distance, golden tendrils of sunlight curling around her face and her body, and she smiles wistfully. She's nearby, but she'll never be anything more than a visitor to this world again.

In many ways, I feel exactly the same way.

Chapter 15

Today may be my birthday, but thanks to Luba, it's definitely not a day for a celebration.

Luckily, Louis and my friends agreed with me, and they all promised that they'd ignore the calendar and we'd have a little party next week. If next week we find any reason to celebrate. Jess, however, would like the party to start early.

"Happy birthday to you!" she sings. "Happy birthday to you!"

Just because Mr. Dice is also the choir director doesn't mean he approves of singing in his algebra class, and anyway I'm not in the mood for it.

"*Jess, I'm scared*," I silently confess.

"Which is normal," she replies.

Jess is floating in the air to my left and looks as if she's lounging my bed. Horizontal, hair dangling off the edge of the mattress, one leg bent, the other crossed so her left ankle is resting on top of her right knee. All she needs is nail polish or a trashy magazine to complete the picture. She looks so much more normal than I've felt in ages.

"*Even for the unnormal?*"

As she rolls her head to face me, a golden arch flies through the air and then melts away.

"This is now your normal," she says. "It's really time you get used to it so you can begin to trust your power."

I do have a lot of powers, that's true, but I would trade them all if Jess could shed her sunshiny persona and return to me as a regular human girl. But I have to stop wishing for that because it's not going to happen. It's time to wish wisely.

"*I wish that tonight reveals answers,*" I declare. "*And that I know what to do when there are no more questions.*"

What was that noise? Startled, I snap my head to the front of the room, but only see the back of Mr. Dice as he scribbles some numbers and symbols on the blackboard. Glancing around the class, I see that Gwen and the rest of them are either paying attention or frantically trying to copy down Dice's writings in their notebooks. No, the sound I heard isn't human; it's Omikami. Worse than that, it's laughter.

"*What's so funny?*" I ask.

"You so funny little grasshopper," Jess replies in her best politically incorrect Japanese accent. "Dominysan, there are never 'no more questions.' "

Great! "*I get to be stupid for the rest of my life,*" I complain.

"Stupid is thinking you have to answer every question on your own."

Jess's voice is back to normal; gone is any pretense of humor even though she's smiling.

"Remember to follow your guts. You have two sets of them now, you know," she says. "And if all else fails, just follow the light."

I follow Jess's light as it disappears from the room, and I'm amazed at how quickly my surroundings turn to darkness without her. It's as if I'm in the belly of a forest standing underneath century-old trees that act like a natural canopy through which no light can penetrate. When I look up I find my situation is even worse. Mr. Dice is standing over me, and I'm consumed by his shadow.

"Dominy," he says. "Did you do your homework?"

Did I? Think! "Yes!"

He smiles, ignoring the snorts and snickers that launch all around us.

"Excellent," he replies. "Then would you mind handing it in?"

For a moment I don't respond; all I do is stare at his hands, one of which is holding the piece of chalk that never seems to leave his fingers, as they slowly descend into his pants pockets. My gut swivels, and I feel like I'm watching a clue; his movement means something, but what? The seam of the pocket on his right pants leg is smeared with chalk. Maybe it's a letter: maybe it's actually a symbol that I'm supposed to decipher. But even with my super-enhanced vision I can't see anything. It's just a smudge.

"Homework," he nudges.

Fumbling through my notebook, I rip out the pages containing last night's assignment and hand them to him. Mildly surprised that I'm actually able to produce my homework, he pulls his chalk-less hand out of his pocket and takes the papers from me. When he turns to walk back to the front of the class, something drops onto my desk.

My gut was right; I was being given a clue. I was just focusing on the wrong pocket.

"You like Hello Kitty?!" I shout in disbelief.

This time he smiles with a hint of embarrassment instead of measured patience. Shuffling back to my desk, he grabs the Hello Kitty keychain I'm holding in my hand.

"A gift from my daughter," he replies over the catcalls and comments from the class.

It's also a gift from Jess to me, another reminder that no matter what the circumstances, deadly or dead boring, she'll always be around.

There are times, however, when I wish Jess were with me not to offer protection or guidance or wisdom, but just good old-fashioned girl-to-girl backup. Standing in the hallway that connects the gym to the school's offices, I could use it.

Mr. Lamatina had asked me to deliver a stack of flyers to the nurse's office, printed announcements reminding all students that flu shots were still available. It's so incredibly appropriate that the resident hypochondriac is spearheading the Two W wellness campaign and not the woman who gets paid to keep us healthy. Anyway, this meant I would be late for gym, so I agreed as long as he gave me a permission slip.

After dropping the flyers off to a very perturbed Nurse Nelson, I started walking toward the gym. What should have been a quiet, uneventful trip turned into the exact opposite.

"You made the wrong choice, Nap," Nadine seethes.

With or without backup and with or without Napoleon's consent, I can't keep silent. I've heard Nadine berate her brother before, and when I thought it was just commonplace sibling rivalry I kept my mouth shut; it wasn't my place to butt in. Now that I know Nadine and even Napoleon are not at all common and are potentially dangerous, I should probably run right past them as if they don't matter to me. But Nadine's words do matter. Maybe because the hateful sentiment behind them is more common than I'd like to admit.

"Being gay isn't a choice, Nadine," I snap. "Any wannabe nurse knows that."

When Nadine turns to look at me, I don't see her face right away; it's covered completely by the silver mist that usually lives deep within her soul. She looks like a medieval knight prepared to do battle, kill or be killed. When the fog lifts to reveal her face, I see that I was right. She's glaring at me with such disgust and disregard that it's clear that I'm her enemy, but such an inconsequential one that she can't even be bothered to alter her expression.

"I don't care who my brother is attracted to," she hisses.

"Then why are you always yelling at him that he's made the wrong choice?" I spit.

I'm not sure why I feel the urgent need to defend Napoleon, but I do. Maybe it's not really Nap I'm defending, but Archie and all the kids like him who are always being bullied. Or maybe I'm just stupid and have made a huge mistake.

Standing behind his sister, Napoleon shakes his head from side to side. His eyes widening, he's trying to make me understand that I've asked an inappropriate question. If I have, why isn't Nadine shocked that I know about her brother's homosexuality? Why isn't she ranting about how he's unnatural and a deviant and how he's going to burn in hell for his life choice? She's not doing any of that. She doesn't care that her brother's gay like Nap's led us to believe. All she cares about is that I've insinuated myself into her conversation.

"I would have expected you of all people to understand that there are more important things in life than having a boyfriend, Dom," she sneers.

"Exactly!" I shout. "One of those things is family support."

She sneers slowly as if it's being carved on her face.

"You see, Napoleon," she says, her voice much softer, not normal, but definitely not as vile as it just was. "Even Dominy understands the importance of family."

When Nap speaks it's with such vulnerable passion that I feel like an outsider. And yet even though he's speaking directly to his sister, I feel that his words are meant for me.

"I *love* my family, Nadine," he states. "Without you, I'm nothing."

Nadine doesn't return the sentiment; she doesn't thank her brother for such a heartfelt revelation. She merely presents a warning.

"Remember that and you'll never have to live without us."

Harsh! "Geez, Nadine, give the guy a break!" I yell.

"And there's no reason for you to worm your way into our family business."

She's right. I don't know why I'm defending Nap when I know that he's connected to my curse. Even if it's a small connection, even if he never asked to join the party, he's still a guest. I mean, really, what am I doing? I just forced Archie to admit that Napoleon is the enemy, and now I'm defending him like he's my friend! But maybe standing up for Nap is really an attempt to stand up for myself? Is the wolf that's buried deep inside of me trying to tell me something? If he is, he better work faster, because Nadine does not look happy.

"I thought you knew the world was filled with magical surprises," she says. "But I guess your brother's right; you're not as smart as you want the world to believe."

My brother?! I'm so shocked by her comment that I can't even respond. I can't stop her from leaving and disappearing around the corner. Now it's just Nap and me. I don't care if he's the enemy, my savior, or something in between; right now I need him to be my informant.

"Why is Nadine talking to my brother about me?"

"I have no idea why Nadine does any of the things she does," he replies.

I listen to his words, but more than that I listen to how they make me feel. I'm concerned. Not about me, but for Nap. He's telling the truth.

"In fact," he continues, "I have no idea why my family does any of the things they do."

I'm curious and frightened by his remark, but I need to know more.

"What do you mean?" I ask. "What kinds of things?"

Now Napoleon's frightened; I can see it in his eyes. He's said too much, and even though I can sense that he wants to say more, that he wants to purge his mind and his heart and his soul of things that shouldn't belong there, he hesitates. Not sure if it's out of loyalty or fear. When he finally speaks, he sounds calmer, as if he's articulating a thought that's lain dormant for years.

"I'm an outsider, Dominy," he states. "And I can't wait to get the hell out of this town."

An image pops into my head of a young boy throwing clothes into a bag, methodically moving around his bedroom grabbing the items he's going to need for a trip. But the boy isn't Napoleon; it's Archie.

"Nap," I say. "You're not thinking of running away, are you?"

He's not surprised that I've drawn this conclusion; he's not really even relieved. He's too lost in his own thoughts. But not too lost to have a game plan.

"It might just be the best thing for everybody in this town if I did leave and never came back."

Could I have misjudged Napoleon? Could I seriously have let this whole Orion thing and Jess's message cloud my mind? I honestly don't know what to think, and I spend all of gym class and the rest of my day trying to figure it out. The only thing that makes me turn off the Nap light that's burning a hole in my mind is seeing Louis and Barnaby plopped on the couch playing video games when I come downstairs after dinner.

Racing back upstairs I barge into the bathroom just in time to see Arla wipe her mouth with a towel. I know that look; she's wearing after-vomit face. Since the door was unlocked, I'm guessing this isn't something she typically does and rule out bulimia. She just threw up because of me. I rip off some toilet paper from the dispenser and wipe away a piece of extra-clingy vomit that refuses to let go of Arla's bottom lip. Immediately I'm reminded of when Nadine did the same thing for me, when she was pretending to be my friend. I have got to find out what's going on with her, which means I have got to get out of this house and see Luba.

"Why is your father still home?"

"Because he and Barnaby want a boys against the girls video game tournament," Arla replies. She keeps her voice quiet, but it's as frantic as I'm beginning to feel. Correction, as I already feel.

"Tonight?!" I shout. "They want to have family game night . . . *tonight?!*"

"Yes!"

"Don't they know that there's going to be a full moon out tonight?"

My question was rhetorical, but Arla responds as if I were trying to goad her into action.

"Daddy!" she screams, bounding down the steps into the living room with me hot on her trail. "Why aren't you out looking for the killer like you've done every other night that there's been a full moon?"

I know that question sounds absurd, but I accept it. I can't accept Louis's reply.

"We thought it was a good idea," he says, his voice oddly unemotional, "but we were advised that it was a wild goose chase."

"We?" Arla asks, hands on her hips in full daughter-as-wife mode.

"Me and Barnaby," Louis replies.

Now that's strange. Not only is Louis trying to make it appear as if he's more interested in battling the spaceships on the TV screen, but now he's making it sound as if Barnaby is his deputy, instead of his ward. What's really going on with him, and what's happened to make him change his mind about finding The Weeping Water Killer?

"And who advised you that you were wasting your time trying to protect the citizens you get paid to protect?" Arla asks.

"Louis's new lady friend," Barnaby replies.

So that's it! Essie doesn't want a vigilante for a boyfriend.

She's probably afraid he'll get himself killed before she gets a marriage proposal.

"Mrs. Jaffe was afraid Louis would get hurt."

My brother's words take a moment to settle into my mind. Melinda Jaffe is Louis's girlfriend? Not Essie!! I grab Arla's hand just as she grabs mine, and we hold each other tight, trying hard not to freak out any further. But why isn't Louis freaking out? Barnaby just spilled the beans about his romantic conquest, and he hasn't flinched. His expression remains calm and focused on the stupid game that he's playing. Why is he acting so nonchalant? Like he's taken a tranquilizer, or he's under a spell.

Without speaking another word we both race up the stairs to Arla's bedroom, shut the door behind us, and jump onto the bed. Kneeling, we face each other, our hands clasping so we're completely connected physically and emotionally. We have never, ever been closer.

"Your father is dating Melinda Jaffe?!"

"I could wind up related to the bee and the butterfly!"

"This is getting way too complicated."

Arla squeezes my hands even tighter. "Oh my God, do you know what this means?"

Sadly I already do. "Your father is sleeping with the enemy."

That breaks our hold. We jump off the bed, shaking our hands and arms wildly as if this will de-cling the image of Louis and Melinda getting all romantical and R-rated.

"I need air!" Arla shouts, opening up the window and gulping in the cold air.

While Arla clutches the window frame and presses her forehead into the screen, I pace the room as we continue chatting about how wrong it is that Louis and Melinda are dating, examining the relationship from every angle.

Does Louis really like Melinda, or does he suspect, as we

do, that she may also play a role in the serial killings? Does Melinda like Louis, or is she attracted to the power that the chief of police wields, or is she manipulating him to have the police on her side? Have Nadine and Napoleon known about our inter-parental relationship and kept quiet about it, or has Melinda adopted Louis's "don't ask, don't tell" policy?

We're chattering so quickly and so fervently that neither of us sees that the sky outside has changed; it now contains a full moon.

Dropping to my knees in agony, I must look to Arla as if I'm mock-praying, asking God to intervene and make her father find another woman or turn gay so he splits up with Mrs. Jaffe. She's half-right. I'm asking God to intervene, but only to protect Arla.

The transformation feels different this time. No, not different, more like the way it used to when it began. It's filled with excruciating pain and fear; it feels as if everything is starting over. My breathing has turned into quick, violent panting and the plastic bag over my head has returned; underneath my skin my blood heats up until it feels like it's boiling just below the surface. I lurch forward onto all fours just in time to bury my mouth into the carpeted floor to muffle my screams when my limbs snap in the opposite direction. Even though this feels exactly right, exactly the way it used to, I know that something is wrong. The wolf is taking over completely. It doesn't want to share my body: it wants to own it. Which means in a few seconds I won't recognize Arla standing right in front of me.

I hear the words in my head: *Get out of here!* But I have no idea if I spoke them out loud or if I changed into a wolf before I got to warn Arla.

Despite the soft breeze trickling in from outside, the moonglow feels warm on my fur. The master always makes its slave feel comfortable. Tonight the master isn't alone.

Three bright stars shine alongside it in one commanding line. Orion is keeping the moon company.

Pangs of hunger push against my stomach. I need to feast on flesh and blood and bone. Looking at the girl in front of me, her skin the color of mud, I swallow a thick mouthful of saliva in anticipation of the meal to come. I raise my lips to bare my fangs, show her there is no escape.

Lifting one paw and then another I walk toward the creature. She looks like they all do, too frightened to make a sound, too aware that soon life will be taken from them. In mid-stride I decide to show mercy on this thing. I'll steal her life slowly so she can remain alive longer than she should.

Terrified by my encroaching presence, the girl stumbles backward and falls onto the floor. Both of us are now on all fours, her face inches from my snout. Bravely, she lifts her head up, and I see her face is scarred. A wound, once deep, now almost healed, surrounds her left eye. This child is a fighter. And she's fought me.

Arla?

I try to fight through the fog the wolf spirit has cast over me to see Arla, to try and let her know that I won't hurt her. I don't know why this is happening. I thought that we had come to an understanding—the wolf and I—that we would share this body, that we would become a team, no leader, no follower, but two equals. Why the betrayal? Why the change? I look out the window at the moon, its blinding light shining on me and through me, and I know that the reason lies outside.

Before I lose control and do something that I will not be able to forgive myself for, I leap over the bed and through the window screen. I wish I could remain in midair for the rest of my life, not a threat to those I love, not in danger from those I fear, just hanging and floating and flying, a part of the world, but separated from it. Within and without at the same time. But that isn't my fate.

My paws hit the ground with more force than I expect, and I feel a sharp twinge in my front right leg. The pain shoots up into my shoulder and travels across my back until getting lost somewhere near my haunches. It doesn't disappear; it merely buries itself into my bones, taking up residence, refusing to let go. Just like the moon.

The combination of moonglow and starlight pulls me forward, and I fight to remain conscious. I know that it would be safer to give in, let the wolf take over, but I have got to remain in control because I'm not only being pulled toward danger, I'm being pulled toward my destiny.

I walk past The Weeping Lady, and I can hear the tree bark creak as she turns her head to watch me. An overwhelming sense of sadness ripples through her branches and reaches out to me. She knows my life is about to change, and she knows there is nothing anyone can do to stop it. When I see the black mist swirling in front of me, turning the peaceful night sky into a menacing sight, my body stiffens. The time has come for secrets to be revealed.

Following the mist farther into the woods, I can't see my surroundings. No trees, no moon, no Orion, just black. Like emptiness, like death, like Luba.

As the mist begins to part, I see Luba hovering above the ground in front of me. She looks more fragile and more powerful than ever before. Disgusting and soiled and ancient.

"It is time, Dominy."

Her stench rushes past me, pausing to frolic on my fur in an attempt to infest me with her evil. She's already stolen my body; now she wants my soul. She can't have it! I refuse! But the breeze begins to stir, and I realize there is power in the air, power within Luba and everything she touches.

"Look up, child," she commands. "Witness the origin of my strength."

Raising my head, I wince at the sight. The moon is gone. I don't know if it's hiding somewhere deep within the confines of the sky to rest or to seek protection. In its place is the constellation, Orion, three magnificent stars, their light blinding everything around them.

I bow my head to escape the constellation's glow, but I can't escape Luba!

"Orion, the original hunter, the original power, the origin to those of us worthy of embodying his spirit," she cries. "The hunter lives within us, and so the hunt for prey will never end!"

She's talking about me. I'm the prey.

A pathetic yelp escapes my lips, and I retreat several steps until my body will not move any farther. I know I'm not the one commanding my body to remain in place, and so I claw at the earth to try to break the spell.

Luba's thin fingers are pressed against her chapped lips, and she cackles maniacally. And then there's silence as she spreads her arms to present her cohorts. The blackness around her lifts to reveal that floating in the air on either side of her are Nadine and Napoleon. The demon has been joined by the bee and the butterfly. But why? How?! Why would these two join forces with someone so destructive, so evil? Why aren't they fighting to break free from her hold? Why do they look like they belong at her side?!

Luba answers my silent questions, and I feel the horror of her words, because now everything makes sense.

"I believe, Dominy," Luba hisses, "that you've already met my grandchildren."

Part 2

There are three above, there are three below
Starlight overshadows the moon's weak glow

Now my world will change, my fate will shift
Because of the power contained
within this trio's gift.

Chapter 16

Remember, Dominy, you are a fool!

Yes, I am. And I'm looking at the proof. Not one enemy, not two, but three! How could I have been so stupid? How could I have been so blind for so long? The clues were all there—the three stars, Orion, the tattoos, Jess's warning—all there for me to see, all there for me to ignore. Until now. Because evil has just tripled.

My howl is so loud and so ferocious, not because I'm filled with anger, not because I'm filled with a desire for vengeance, but because I'm filled with self-loathing. Cursed or not, I am a fool. I've been used by Luba, and now I've been used by her grandchildren. Her *grandchildren?!*

The concept is sickening. To think that these two people, one of whom I called my friend, whom I trusted, confided in, shared my secrets with, are nothing but sadistic liars. Blood-linked to Psycho Squaw! It makes no sense, and yet it makes perfect sense. Luba's son Thorne must be their father. The unborn child Luba was carrying when my father killed her husband grew up to marry Melinda Jaffe and had these twins.

The bee and the butterfly did not come to Weeping Water

by accident; they came here because they were summoned by the devil herself to help carry out her demented plot to destroy my family's life. I knew they had powers. I knew they were closer to wrong than they were to right, but I allowed myself to think that there was a chance they were like me: victims. Now, looking at the twins flanking their decaying grandmother, I know they are hardly innocent, definitely not unwilling; they are as sick and destructive and malevolent as their matriarch. And I swear on my father's life right here and now that I'll make each one of them pay for the role they've played in his death and my fate.

I may be outnumbered, but these three have met their match.

In response to my silent ranting, Luba raises her hand, her thumb and pinky touching so her three middle fingers are pointing at me, and three streams of black smoke materialize from her fingertips. Three ribbons of deadly black fire are racing in my direction. But I don't care what deadly power is contained within that smoke; I don't care what horrors the ribbons can inflict if they touch me; I refuse to move.

I have powers too. I can feel it in my guts.

Just as three rays of smoke are about to pierce my body, I let the wolf spirit take complete control, and I feel rage cyclone through my body. Opening my mouth I give the feeling the freedom it craves. The crash is silent, yet visible, and I can actually see the red cloudburst, the manifestation of my fury, shoot from my mouth and collide with Luba's black energy.

Black and red twist and conjoin and weave in the sky like a demonic fireworks display, good and evil combining to form something that neither wants to claim.

As quickly as the mists appeared, they evaporate, rising to become part of the sky, part of something much larger. I have no idea if I'll be able to create such magic again; it may be a part of the spirit I can't control. But Luba doesn't have that problem. She may look tired and weak, but she has backup.

Luba glances toward Nadine and the black smoke slides out of her hair to encircle her granddaughter. Slithering around and around and around her until it's created a cocoon from Nadine's head to her feet, the mist starts to pulse as if connected to her heart. I can see Nadine's face through the black, woven smoke, and it's repulsive. She looks deliriously happy, ecstatic to be engulfed by her grandmother's filth.

Next, Luba turns to Napoleon and releases her darkness to take her other grandchild prisoner. It moves toward Napoleon, but its approach is more tentative, not as confident as when it swarmed over Nadine's body. About an inch or two from Napoleon's skin, the mist stops, unable to get any closer. It surrounds him, outlining his body, but never getting any closer to his frame. The blackness is trying to penetrate, trying to connect, but it's either too weak or Napoleon is too strong. That's not it; that's not it at all. Peering at him with my spirit eyes, I can see that his are flooded with tears. Luba's essence can't touch him because he's still good.

He *is* being used . . . just like I am.

Moving closer toward the trio, I tilt my head so my fangs catch the starlight and growl ferociously. Let them see what they're dealing with. I'm not Napoleon; I'm not a confused boy, trapped with nowhere to go. I'm a wolf. I may be their creation, but I'm not their puppet.

In response to my approach, Luba raises her hands to suck back her foul smoke. No longer embraced by their grandmother's black energy, Nadine and Napoleon descend to the ground and begin to walk toward me with Luba trailing behind, still a few feet in the air.

Good, waste all your energy on showing off. You'll be drained when the time comes to fight.

And then I learn an important lesson: Never underestimate your opponent. Luba looks frail; Nadine looks ordinary;

Napoleon looks reluctant. Despite all that, together they're lethal.

Three arms rise up toward Orion's constellation, one arm for each star, and like a lit fuse, light begins to travel from the stars toward earth. I know I should run; I know I should escape, but my body is frozen, and I truly don't know if I'm immobile because of my own fascination or because I'm under their spell.

As their hands capture more and more light, their bodies melt into the glare. I can't see them any longer; the unnatural light is blinding. First Nadine is obliterated by the starlight, then Luba, and just before Napoleon's face disappears from my view I see him mouth the words, "I'm sorry." It's the last thing I see before I slam into a tree several hundred yards behind me.

Before I open my eyes, I feel the pain fusing into my back and spreading out like a cobweb on my skull. I roll slightly to one side and stretch my legs. I can move, so I must be alive. There's a burning sensation throughout my whole body so intense that I sniff deeply, convinced that I'll smell that my skin and fur and bones have turned to steaming charcoal, but I only smell the scents of the night. And then an odor pouring down on me like rancid rain.

When I open my eyes, I see the three of them standing over me, two snickering crones and their silent companion.

"Did you enjoy that, Dominy?" Nadine asks.

"We do hope you did," Luba chimes in. "That was a small taste of our power."

"Just a way for us to quench our appetite," Nadine adds.

Defiantly I growl and let the sound continue even though it feels like stones are being rubbed along the inner lining of my throat. I'm so dry; I feel brittle inside and out. The shock of the starlight feels like I've been electrocuted. I try to stir, lift my head, but my body gives out, and I fall back onto the ground. A screech rips through the air that reminds me of the call of some damned creature. When I see Luba laughing, I know that I was right.

And when I hear Arla's screams, I know that the night has gotten much, much worse.

"Children!" Luba wails. "Remove the intruder!"

Without hesitation Nadine sprints toward Arla, who's standing in a clearing about a hundred yards away. Frightened into submission and illuminated by the combination of moon and starlight, Arla's a waiting target, unable to move, unable to defend herself. The only chance she has is if she starts running. Now!

"Aarrrrgghhh!!!"

My indecipherable sound penetrates the fear gripping Arla's body, and finally she turns to run. Struggling against my own pain, I take longer than usual to stand, but when I do I see that Luba and Napoleon haven't left my side. One has remained because she considers herself too lofty to get her hands dirty, the other because he doesn't want to get his stained any further.

"Napoleon!" Luba cries. "Help your sister!"

Napoleon looks deep within my eyes for just a split second, but it's long enough for his thoughts to penetrate into mine. I know everything there is to know about him. He's frightened—for me, for Arla, and for himself. He isn't as powerful as his grandmother or his sister, but he has his own strengths. And despite his fear he isn't afraid to use them.

Watching Napoleon sprint after Nadine, I'm amazed at how fast he can move. Is his ability natural or spell-driven? I don't know, and I don't care as long as he gets to Arla before Nadine does.

I leap into the air, but the glare of the starlight makes me miss a clean landing, and my paw is punctured by a sharp twig jutting out from the base of a fallen tree trunk. The pain sears up my leg, and I have to pull back several times before I can wrench myself free. Limping and bleeding I continue on just in time to see Nadine fly into the air and land on Arla's back.

"Get off of me!" Arla screams as they both fall to the ground.

Rolling Arla onto her back, Nadine straddles her, her knees pinning Arla's arms down. "Not until I'm looking at your corpse."

"Help!"

Arla's cry is impulsive, but futile.

"Give her to me!" Napoleon orders. "Let me prove myself! Let me get rid of this one."

I watch Napoleon's actions in disbelief; I can't believe what I'm seeing. In two incredibly quick moves he's knocked Nadine to the ground and pulled Arla up off of the earth. He's holding her close to him, her back to his chest, and his forearm is wrapped around her throat. His arm is smooth and pink and strong; veins are visible underneath his skin, making it look like there are long, thin tubes running through his body. He appears stronger than I remember, and again I don't know if this is how he normally looks or if tonight's ceremony has increased his virility. And he's cunning. He isn't out to kill Arla or me; he's trying to protect us.

"Don't fight me, Arla," he whispers. "I want to help you."

Unsure, Arla claws at his arm and kicks at him.

"Trust me," Napoleon adds.

"No, brother," Nadine says. "Trust *me!*"

Either I'm not the only one with super hearing, or the twins truly are psychically connected despite the fact Nadine told me earlier that they weren't. The only thing that matters is that Nadine is now royally pissed off.

"This voyeuristic bitch is mine!"

With one hand Nadine shoots a streak of silver light at her brother, causing him to duck out of the line of fire. In doing so, he loses his grip on Arla, and instinct overtakes her and she starts to run. I count three strides before Nadine catches her, whips her around so they're facing each other, clutches her by the throat with one hand, and lifts her off the ground.

"Nadine, stop!" Arla cries, her voice desperate and distorted, her fingers frantically clawing at Nadine's arm to try and break free from her hold. "You don't want to do this."

Nadine lowers Arla so their faces are less than an inch apart. They can each see the creases in the other's skin, the freckles on the other girl's face, the scars. Nothing can be concealed, so Nadine decides to tell Arla the truth.

"No, Arla, I really don't," she admits. "But you've left me no choice."

"That's right, my child," Luba hisses. "Make your grandmother proud."

At the sight of his grandmother hanging in the sky like a limp, beat-up rag doll, Napoleon's bravado and courage flow out of his body, slowly, but certainly, like water twirling down a drain. The flow can't be stopped; it can only be watched and mourned.

Napoleon falters, but catches himself before he falls into the ground. He leans over, hunched, defeated, and grabs his head between his hands. His sobs are so loud they can be heard over Arla's screams and my growls. I look at Nadine, hoping that her brother's breakdown will distract her, but it's only made her more focused. She is definitely a girl who likes to be in control.

"Kill . . . her . . . now!" Luba bellows.

Smiling innocently, Nadine lifts Arla higher off the ground and squeezes her neck even tighter. Arla tries to dig her fingers in between Nadine's, separate Nadine's hand from her throat, but it's no use. I have to move now; I have to do something even if I don't have all my strength back.

Lunging forward as high as I possibly can, I aim for Nadine's body. If I can just rip some flesh from her body, it should be enough to make her drop Arla, give us some time to fight back. But Napoleon has other ideas.

"No!"

Two streaks of silver lightning blast through the air, one hitting me in the side, the other hitting Nadine in the back. We both tumble to the ground with Arla falling on top of us. Shaking my head, I swallow hard to try to moisten my throat, which is still parched. I nudge Arla and look her in the eye, wolf to girl, just so she knows she isn't alone. I hope my eyes say everything that's in my heart: I will die trying to protect her from this insanity.

"What the hell are you doing?!" Nadine screams.

Hands and knees pushed into the dirt, Nadine looks just like me right now, an animal on all fours, filled with primal instinct and no inhibitions.

"If we kill her it will draw attention to us," Napoleon asserts. "All we have to do is make her forget."

From the look on Nadine's face this proposition seems worse to her than actually strangling Arla to death with her bare hands.

"Are you willing to take that risk?" Luba asks.

Pausing to look at Arla, a glimmer of concern breaking through his steely gaze, Napoleon takes a moment to respond. When he does his voice and his intention are clear; he's made the decision for them. "Yes."

"Then so be it," Luba says. "I will allow you—this *once*—to override my command."

Crawling backwards, Arla has no plan to run; she's just obeying her body's refusal to be still. "What . . . what *risks?!*"

Lifting Arla off the ground without touching her, Nadine places her in between her and Napoleon. Arla twists her body violently in a valiant attempt to break free from Nadine's invisible hold on her, but Nadine's grip is mighty. "What are you doing to me?!" Arla shrieks. "What are you talking about? What *risks?!*"

"You'll live," Nadine replies.

Thank God!

And then Nadine completes her sentence. "But we may suck out your mind when we try to erase your memory."

"Noooo!!!" Arla screams.

Ignoring her protest, Nadine and Napoleon raise their hands, and two streams of silver light fly out and drill into both sides of Arla's skull. Her thrashing stops momentarily as her body lifts even higher in the sky, and her eyes whip back in her head, leaving only the whites of her eyes remaining. Then the movement resumes and her body shakes uncontrollably, four limbs moving in different rhythms. Her mouth opens wide, and I can almost hear her silent screams. There's nothing I can do but watch and jab at the earth with my paws, trying to destroy the guilt and shame and self-hatred that I'm already feeling, knowing that once again my friend is being viciously harmed because of me.

Bubbles of sweat have formed on Napoleon's brow, and several beads are dripping down the sides of his face. Nadine's legs are trembling. This ritual, this game, is taking its toll on its participants as well as its victim.

"Hold on, children!" Luba cries. "It's almost finished!" Her face shines in the starlight, a psychotic version of pride.

And then it's over. The silver beams of light retract. Arla slams into the ground face first. Nadine and Napoleon stumble, able to do nothing more than catch their breath. I run to Arla and put my snout next to her throat. I can feel her pulse; she's still alive.

With a flip of her hand, Luba makes Arla's body roll over, and Arla looks peaceful, like she's sleeping. There's no way of knowing what damage the twins have done, but because of one of them, Arla has a chance of waking up.

"Children," Luba says, "take me home."

Linking arms with her grandmother, Nadine bends her head, and her lips graze my ear when she speaks. "This is just the beginning, Dominy." And then she lets out a growl that sounds more primitive than anything I've ever heard come out of my own body. A growl that morphs into maniacal laughter.

His head slightly bowed, Napoleon grabs Luba by the other arm. Regardless of what he's feeling inside, he's acting like the dutiful grandson. Maybe it's a ploy; maybe it's the truth; I don't know. Even if he's conflicted, he's still connected to Luba and his sister. He may not be as morally corrupt as they are, but their blood flows in his veins.

When they dissolve into the night sky, I look at Arla, and I have no choice but to be thankful that he spared her life. I'm not ready to absolve him of his sins, not until Arla wakes up and I know that she's safe and not permanently damaged by their memory swipe. My fur sways before I feel the breeze, and when I notice Arla's eyelashes fluttering, I think it's because of the gentle wind. But it isn't. She's already waking up!

Whimpering, I rub my snout on her arm, a futile attempt to let her know that I'm here and I won't hurt her. But she isn't scared; she isn't terrified of my presence. She also doesn't appear to be herself.

"Please forgive me," she whispers.

Problem is, it wasn't Arla's voice that I just heard. It was Napoleon's.

Chapter 17

What happened?

I don't know if I've spoken the words or if I've thought them to myself.

"Dominy, what happened?"

They're not my words after all; they're Caleb's. What is he doing here? With Archie by his side. And why am I in human form when the full moon is still looming overhead? I look down and see that a blanket is covering me and not my glorious red fur. I'm no longer a wolf; I'm Dominy. How is that possible? Have the rules of this curse changed? Or do I have more control over this spell than I realize? That would be amazing if it were true, but I can't ponder those thoughts now. Such reflection will have to wait for later when I'm not lying on the grass naked next to Arla.

"Arla!" I gasp.

Why isn't she moving? Why does she look like she's dead? Vague images flash through my mind, and I see her screaming and running and falling to the ground. No, I refuse to believe that I could have done anything to her. I have the spirit under control, we're working together—*I, it, we* would never harm a friend. My heart stops, would we?

"Is Arla all right?" I ask, my voice shaking along with my body.

"She's fine," Archie replies. "Looks like she's sleeping."

I close my eyes and breathe deeply and roughly until my body stops shivering from the thoughts that were just racing through my head. Now that those thoughts are placated, new ones arrive.

"What are you two doing here?" I ask.

"A Wolf Pack's never too far from its leader, is it?"

Caleb's question is meant to make me smile, but it only spurs more questions. Recognizing my need for quick answers, Caleb offers me as many as he can. For some reason Arla had the GPS device around her arm, so when it stopped moving about an hour ago he and Archie followed the trail, thinking that it would lead them to me and possibly Luba. They never imagined they'd find Arla passed out next to me. Archie adds that he brought the blanket I'm clinging to in case I transformed and needed some privacy, but they never expected to find me post-conversion. They didn't think it was possible for me to change back until daybreak; I didn't either.

"I guess the rules have changed yet again," I whisper, more to myself than my unexpected company.

"We found this a few yards away," Caleb says. "Arla really came prepared."

My boyfriend hands me a plastic bag filled with sweatpants, some underwear, a sweatshirt, and sneakers. But these are Arla's clothes. Whatever. She must have brought them with her when she came looking for me. I can't remember. Unlike after recent transformations, I can't remember anything.

"My head is a total blank," I say, tying the laces of my sneaker.

"You don't remember anything?" Caleb asks.

"Zilch."

I look up at the sky, which is now a dark navy blue. It looks immense, so much bigger than we are, and I feel puny because I know that it holds so many mysteries that we'll never unlock. What's contained in the sky just beyond our vision? Will we ever find out if anyone is looking back at us? How can three stars line up so perfectly in one straight line?

"Nadine and Napoleon were here," I blurt out, finally remembering a bit of what happened.

"You saw them?" Archie asks.

"Yes," I reply. "They were here with Luba."

Archie's eyes search mine. He wants more information, and he wants me to shut up at the same time. He doesn't want proof that his boyfriend is connected to the woman who's cursed me, but that's all I have to offer. And I'm too tired and my mind is too foggy to lie, so all I can do is tell what I know.

"It's like we suspected, Caleb," I say, looking up at the stars. "They're connected to Orion."

"The constellation?" he clarifies. "But how?"

Shaking my head, I draw the blanket closer around me; unprotected by my wolf fur I feel the chill clinging to my body. "I don't know, but they are. All three of them—Luba, Nadine, and Napoleon." I see Archie wince at the mention of his boyfriend's name. "I'm sorry, Arch, but it's true."

Wordlessly he responds by simply nodding his head. What else is there to say when you find out the love of your life is connected to a source of evil?

"So the tattoos and Jess's diary and the references to Orion by Luba and Mrs. Jaffe weren't mere coincidences; they actually meant something?" Caleb asks, consolidating what we currently know.

I nod my head. "They were all clues to their connection," I confirm. "What that connection is I can't remember."

I may not remember how the twins are connected to Luba,

but I do understand their goal. They didn't kill Arla and me, but they left us here side by side as some sort of warning. A reminder that they're superior.

"But they didn't hurt you, Dom," Archie observes. "I mean you two are fine."

"Well, Domgirl's fine," Caleb corrects. "Jury's still out on Arla."

Gently, I nudge Arla's arm to try and wake her up, but she obstinately clings to sleep. At least I pray she's sleeping. I shut my eyes tight because an image of my mother pops into my head, and I can't bear the thought of Arla's becoming like her, unresponsive and silent. If that happens, I know that I'll be to blame; the only reason Arla is out here is because of me. She must've followed me after I left the house. Temptation must've been too hard to resist; she wanted to see firsthand what secrets were going to be revealed. I refuse to believe that the only revelation will be that she will suffer the same fate as my mother and never wake up again.

"Arla!" I scream. "Wake up!"

My voice is abrupt and loud and demanding, and it startles Caleb and Archie, startles them into action. Flanking Arla on either side, they lay the blanket over her to keep her body warm and start to rub her arms, let her know that she isn't alone, let her know that she has to come back to us. I kneel at her feet and grab her ankles. I can feel blood pulsing through her veins, so I know there's still hope that she'll open her eyes and everything will return to normal. But why is she taking her sweet time?

"C'mon, Arla," I say. "Wake up!"

Now the boys start to raise her arms up and down, trying to trick her into thinking that she's moving, that she's already awake. It actually works! Her eyes begin to quiver, and her arms try to break free from the boys' hold; they're no longer limp. She digs her heels into the ground as if she's stretching or walking or desperately trying to outrun whatever force has got such a hold on her. Her movements quicken and become more urgent. At the same time we all let go of her, and freedom sets her free.

"Let go of me!"

"Easy, Arla," Caleb says. "It's just us."

Wild-eyed, Arla looks around, her expression quieting only when she determines Caleb was speaking the truth. She's only surrounded by her friends, no one else.

"Are you all right?" I ask.

Sitting up, Arla looks at her body and comes to the same conclusion we've already come to: Outwardly she looks fine. Internally, maybe not.

"My head is killing me," she groans. "Are they gone?"

She remembers too! Greatly relieved, I allow myself to smile. My friend isn't hurt. I didn't give her yet another scar—physically or emotionally; she didn't suffer once more from the curse that is supposed to only affect me. She's unharmed by whatever events just transpired. But obviously not untouched.

"I'm connected to Luba," she announces.

"What?!"

That's the collective response, and it's filled with disbelief and disgust and disapproval. There is no way that Arla is connected to Psycho Squaw. Or is there?

"Dom, don't you remember?" she asks.

Obviously not. At least not as much as Arla does.

"My father is dating Melinda Jaffe!" she exclaims.

While Caleb and Archie shout and ply Arla with requests for more details, my memory returns. Barnaby casually mentioning that Mrs. Jaffe is Louis's girlfriend; Louis not getting angry that Barnaby revealed what he had been trying to keep secret; Arla and I freaking out over the disclosure of her father's love life; my sudden transformation.

"I turned into a wolf in your bedroom," I divulge. Arla nods her head in agreement. "But how did I get outside without anyone seeing me?"

"The old 'crash right through the window screen' routine," Arla replies.

The way she's holding the sides of her head, it looks like something is trying to crash through her skull, from the inside out.

"But how does your father's girlfriend connect you to Luba?" Archie asks.

"Because Melinda's kids are working with Luba," she confirms. "They were here!"

"You saw them?!" I cry.

Completely awake now, Arla stands up. She doesn't need the blanket any longer for warmth; she has enough fire in her belly, so she lets it fall to the ground at her feet.

"The three of them were floating in midair in front of you!" she shouts, unable to fathom how I can't remember such an image. "It was like something out of a horror movie! Luba in the middle, Old Lady Ringleader, and her two minions on either side. I have no idea why they've joined forces with her, but the three of them are working as a team."

"So those were the three that Jess was talking about," Caleb adds. "Luba, Nadine, and Napoleon."

"No."

Archie's voice isn't loud, but it isn't weak either. It's final. He refuses to believe his boyfriend could actually be a part of something so consciously evil.

"I don't believe you," he says.

"Archie, honey, I know this is a shock," Arla says, her voice now more like a quivering flame than a roaring fire. "But I saw him hanging in the air alongside the other two."

Fists clenched, Archie starts to pace, moving randomly to the left, then the right, hoping that he'll move toward the

truth that will disprove what the rest of us have come to believe.

"So okay, Nap was here. . . . He's somehow, *somehow* connected. That doesn't mean he's . . . like them; it just means he
was here."

He was more than here; he was participating.

"They were raising their arms in unison toward Orion and
collecting its starlight like fuel to hurl at Dominy," Arla de-
scribes. "And they weren't trying to start up a game of supernatural dodge ball. They wanted to hurt her."

Thank God there was a witness this time, because I don't
remember any of this. It's like the first transformations, like a
plastic bag is over my head and my vision is distorted. I can
only see glimpses of things, and if I want to see the whole picture I have to put all the pieces of the puzzle together. For
some reason Arla has a perfect snapshot of what happened.
Maybe because she was just an observer and not a participant, I don't know, but however it's happened, I'm grateful.
At least we have some answers. Even if we don't have the full
explanation just yet.

"If he was there," Archie says, "he was there against his
will."

Shaking her head Arla refutes his words even before she
speaks. "There's no way you can brainwash someone to act
like that," she states. "I'm sorry, Archie. Your boyfriend cannot be trusted."

The night sounds take over. The wind, the birds, the noc-
turnal animals make noise all around us because we can't.
The sounds are solemn, like the mournful chanting of a cluster of monks, the only purpose to remind us of our faults and
our need to ask forgiveness for our sins. I know the sound
well. And now, unfortunately, Archie knows it too.

"But . . . this can't be."

He says the words, but he doesn't believe them, not really.

I look up at the moon, and once again I'm filled with an incredible feeling of ambivalence; I'm in awe of its majesty, but filled with rage at its lack of mercy. I'm the one who's cursed; I'm the one who should be suffering! Instead it's as if I'm in quicksand, descending lower and lower into some unknown hell, and the quicksand isn't satisfied with only one sacrifice, so it's making me reach out and bring extra bounty with me. I'm paying back my friends' loyalty and support and love by introducing them to pain and anguish and despair.

"I love him."

Archie's words are quiet, but they bounce off of the trees and the ground like thunder in the night. I want to cover my ears; I want to run and hide, but I can't. Caleb must know that I'm fighting the urge to break free, that the pain I'm inflicting is almost too much to bear, so he sits next to me and holds my hand, but that only makes matters worse. This is all Archie's ever wanted, all he ever dreamed about: to sit on the ground in the middle of the night holding his boyfriend's hand. I've taken that away from him; I've destroyed the first dream he's ever had that came true. Restlessly, I turn my head. I don't want them to see me cry, but they can hear the sobs. Nothing I do seems to protect them. Nothing I do seems to shield them from the truth.

"Don't cry, Dom," Archie whispers.

And nothing I do seems to make my friends leave me.

"Why . . . why don't you people . . . hate me?" I ask.

My voice is barely a whisper, as if my question is almost too heavy, too impossible a thought to speak out loud. My friends find the response to be an easy one. I feel arms wrapping around me, and I try to push them away, but they're determined to grab hold of me.

"No one could ever hate you for any of this."

I have no idea who's talking, not that it matters; one voice speaks for them all. Now it's my turn to speak.

"I'm so sorry, Archie," I say, my words and my arms wrapping around him.

"Me too," he says. "I guess it was too good to be true."

"*Gone away is the bluebird.*"

Why in the world is Arla singing?

"*Here to stay is the new bird.*"

And in Napoleon's voice?

"*He sings a love song, as we go along...*"

And why in the world is Archie staring at her as if her lyrics contain the key to unlocking all the mysteries of life? Because they may not unlock all of life's mysteries, but they do unlock some of ours.

"*Walking in a winter wonderland.*"

"Napoleon?" he asks, his voice filled with wonder.

Slowly life returns to Arla's eyes. While she was singing they were vacant and lost, as if they had been removed from her body. And in a way they were, because they were being controlled by someone else, by Napoleon.

"Hey, what did I miss?" she asks, rubbing her forehead with her fingertips. "I think I spaced out for a bit."

"No, I think Napoleon was just using you as some sort of psychic conduit," I reply matter-of-factly.

"Oh is that all," Arla replies, equally nonchalant.

"That's our song," Archie stammers.

"'Winter Wonderland' is your song?" Caleb asks, incredulously.

"Nap loves that Caleb calls me Winter. He says it's perfect," Archie explains. "So he sings that Christmas carol to me when we're alone."

"And you think Nap is using Arla to communicate with you?" Caleb asks.

"It's possible," Arla claims. "I remember that they did something to me."

"What?!" Archie demands.

"They both grabbed me, Nadine and Napoleon, and then it's all a blank."

Regardless of what the twins did to Arla, she doesn't look like she's in any pain, her headache is gone, and she doesn't seem to be suffering from any other physical repercussions as a result of this telepathic connection. But this is only the beginning of their bond; who knows what this is going to do to her. Or to Archie.

Breathing deeply, his chest rising up and down underneath his jacket, Archie tries not to cry, but he can't stop the flow of tears that slide down his face. He's too overwhelmed with memory and promise.

"He said he wanted to learn how to be a good friend, like Caleb is, because he never had any friends," Archie sobs. "So he used Caleb's words to make our connection even stronger."

It's the most beautiful thing I've ever heard and also the most painful. I'm reminded that Caleb and I have our own connection, our invisible string, our playacting of Jane Eyre and Mr. Rochester. Archie and Napoleon are no different.

"This changes everything!" Archie squeals.

"Maybe," Caleb says softly. "But you still have to be careful."

Wiping away his tears and accepting a warm bear hug from Caleb, Archie agrees. "I know, I know," he says. "My boyfriend is caught up in something . . . something that could potentially be deadly. I've seen enough to know that." Archie stands back, releasing himself from Caleb's hold; he's found the strength to stand on his own. "But thanks to Arla, I've also heard enough to know that he's trying to tell me not to give up."

"I don't know what I did, Arch," Arla states. "But if it gives you hope, you hold on to it."

"But like Caleb said," I interrupt, "keep your eyes open along with your heart."

Standing here in the middle of practically nowhere, I feel like we're finally getting some direction. We know that Nadine and Napoleon are working with Luba in some capacity. There's the possibility that Nap is fighting against her hold, so that's a welcome thought—not one that we can fully embrace yet, but one that we can entertain.

I also suspect that the wolf and I are working even closer together. Ever since I woke up I've felt this new sensation—like the spirit's lingering within me. He gave up his physical dominance over me so I could be with my friends, but he didn't let go of me completely. I've always carried over some physical remnants of the wolf with me when I return to my human form—enhanced vision, pumped up athleticism—but this feels different. The only way I can describe it is that my soul has changed. It's making room for another. That must be why I was able to transform back before the full moon disappeared from the sky: Because I really didn't change; I brought the wolf spirit back with me, and we're fusing together in even more complicated ways.

Sadly, I'm not the only one in the midst of a complicated transformation.

I have a visitor when I enter my bedroom. Once again Barnaby is waiting for me, sitting on my bed.

"We meet again, Sis," he says. His mouth in full smirk alert.

"This might not be our house, Barn, but this is still my room," I reply, equally as smug. "No trespassing."

"And no sneaking out in the middle of the night for a hot rendezvous with your boyfriend," he snipes. "Or whoever else you're meeting out there."

His body isn't the only thing that's changed; his attitude has too. Barnaby's always been snippy. He's my little brother, and he's been scrawny most of his life, so he's had to compensate verbally for what he lacked size-wise. But this is beyond growing pains. His voice is ugly.

"What I do is my own business, not yours," I seethe.

"And what if I fill Louis in on your business?" he asks. "I'm sure he'd love to know that his new daughter is a tramp."

I laugh in Barnaby's face. If that's the worst Louis thinks of me, I'll take it. "There are things in this world that Louis and you don't need to know about," I admit.

My brother takes a brave step forward. He's not afraid of me. Not yet. "Like how Daddy died?" he asks.

The mention of my father makes something inside of me snap, like when my limbs break and push me toward my fate. Time to shove Barnaby closer to his.

"Daddy died for both of us!" I scream.

"No, he didn't," he replies, his voice unnervingly calm. "He died for you."

The wolf that I've brought back with me takes over, and I grab Barnaby by the throat and lift him off the ground. Looking at my brother I swear I can see a red-furred claw gripping his neck, where I can see his veins widen and push against his skin as if they want to rip open his flesh and douse me with their blood. I smile at the thought of it. Shower me with your blood, Barnaby; let me taste what's inside of you.

When I see his eyes turn black, I know that his blood will taste like poison.

Gone are his beautiful blue eyes, the same color as my father's; gone are his eyes entirely, and in their place is complete darkness. The whites are gone, the irises, everything, replaced with black the color of Luba's hair. I'm staring at my brother and my enemy at the same time.

Terrified, I release my grip and throw Barnaby out of my

room, slamming the door shut behind him. Just as Napoleon reached out through Arla to communicate with Archie, Luba is reaching out through Barnaby to communicate with me. Both sending warnings that this game is far from over. The curse was only the beginning.

And that an all-out war is about to break out.

Chapter 18

Welcome to Curse 2.0.

In one night it's as if this curse has mutated, become something new and different, something that I have to decipher and overcome yet again. I feel like I'm right back where I was a year ago, in the dark, blind, and blindsided. This time I don't have my father to look to for comfort and salvation. But I do have my mother.

If I'm completely honest, however, I'm not sure if I wound up here at The Retreat because I want to find some peace with my mother or because I want to find some chaos with Nadine. Since our last late-night meeting that I still don't fully recall, the twins haven't been in school due to a joint case of the flu. The real reason is because Luba's the one who's sick.

Nap sent Archie a cryptic message saying he and Nadine had to stay home and help his grandmother heal. Guess I was right: Psycho isn't invincible; she needs her slaves to be in attendance while she tries to recuperate. I was kind of hoping Nadine would take a break from monitoring Luba's temperature to return to work, but Essie informs me that Nadine isn't scheduled to volunteer today. Oh well, I'm sure I'll see her again soon, and hopefully by then my memory will return. In the meantime it looks like Original Essie is back.

Sitting behind her desk, Essie is uncoiffed, unmakeup-ed, and unapologetically miserable. It can mean only one thing.

"Having boyfriend trouble, Es?" I ask.

"For that I'd have to have a boyfriend," she replies, rolling her eyes dramatically.

So that's what's bothering her, romantic issues. My heart folds up a little bit upon hearing about Essie's breakup; I really was hoping that her new guy would be a keeper. I'm hardly an expert, but I get the sense that Essie doesn't have too many girlfriends, so I decide to offer my services, even if I only listen to her problems. It should make her feel less alone.

"It started out like a fairy tale," she begins. "An answer to my prayers. But I guess fairy tales aren't for old women, and before I knew it . . ."

She abruptly stops in mid-sentence, ending our "just between you and me" girl chat. That's because it's no longer just the two of us. We have company.

The front door bursts open as if thrown off its hinges by a sudden wind gust, but instead of a howling whoosh of air, the hallway is filled with laughter. It's Winston Lundgarden and what looks like a fox. My mouth waters, remembering how delicious fox meat tastes, but this isn't an animal; it's a woman wearing a floor-length red fox-fur coat. She can't be from around here, because women in this part of Nebraska opt for parkas when it's cold outside, or maybe, if they're fashionable, a shearling coat. No one around here ever looks that sophisticated. Which makes sense because the woman Winston is canoodling with isn't from around here; she's from Connecticut. Winston's lady friend is Louis's lady friend, none other than Melinda Jaffe. I wish I were telepathically connected to Arla so I could fill her in on what I'm seeing.

And what I'm learning! Seconds before Essie speaks, my wolf-girl instinct kicks in just by looking at Essie's expression, her face is one huge snarl.

"I can't believe Winston dumped me for that...that... *witch!*" she whisper-screams.

My world just got a bit more complicated. Just like Melinda Jaffe is two-timing Louis with Winston, Winston is two-timing Essie with Melinda Jaffe! Winston is Essie's boyfriend, not Louis. Well, ex-boyfriend to be exact.

The way that Mrs. Jaffe is glaring at Essie, she clearly has the same level of animosity for her rival. Or wait a second, is she looking at me? I can't really tell. Lundgarden, still annoyed by our last conversation, has his hand on Melinda's fur shoulder and is trying to get her to walk quickly into his office, but she obviously likes the scenery. Perhaps I'll give her a show that she can tell her kids about later on when she slinks back to her haunted house.

Imitating Luba, I raise my left hand, letting my thumb and pinky finger touch, and point my remaining three fingers in Melinda's direction. Her face goes pale, and she needs to lean into Winston for support as she recognizes the sign of Orion. Learning your enemy's code is always a good strategy. Pushing my luck, I wave. "Hi, Mrs. Jaffe, nice coat," I call out, my voice dripping with cheerfulness. "I have one just like it."

Involuntarily, Mrs. Jaffe runs her palm down her sleeve as if she's awakening the dead red fur, willing it to come alive. Even though I've always been against wearing fur to make a fashion statement, I have to admit she looks pretty good in the luxurious pelt. Not as sumptuous as I do when I'm wearing mine, but pretty good nonetheless.

Lundgarden, his face contorted into a malicious sneer, practically shoves his girlfriend, or whatever Melinda is to him, into his office. But just as they're about to disappear, Melinda flicks her shoulder to free herself from The Cell Keeper's clutch and reenters the hallway. She doesn't move, and Winston doesn't join her; she just stares. I think I've just won my first tiny battle with this woman. Nope, wrong again. Melinda isn't looking at me; she's staring at Essie. Have I made another mistake?

When Lundgarden's office door closes behind them, Essie lets out a very long breath.

"Dominy, honey, you shouldn't have done that," Essie admonishes.

Turning to face Lundgarden's ex, I ask, "And why not?"

As she swallows hard, Essie's fingers nervously tap dance on her desk. She squirms in her chair and pulls herself close to her desk, until the edge is pressing into her stomach. Only when she feels secure and in a familiar position does she respond.

"Wins...Mr. Lundgarden is a very...*powerful* person," she says.

Speaking slowly for maximum effect without giving too much away, I reply, "And, Essie, so am I."

Eyes darting down the hall toward the front office, Essie scoots her chair even closer to her desk as if to anchor herself so she can't be suddenly yanked away and tossed outside. She doesn't look like a scorned girlfriend any longer; she looks frightened. Could "powerful" be a euphemism for something more menacing? Could Lundgarden be linked to Luba too? Maybe, maybe not. The only definite is that Essie got off lucky.

"You're too good for him, Essie," I say. "I hope you know that."

Essie can only nod her head and force herself to smile.

"And Melinda isn't half the woman you are."

In response to this comment, Essie can't even force a smile; the nod exists on its own.

I can't think of anything else to say that Essie will want to hear, so I just give her a hug that she half-heartedly reciprocates and continue on with my real reason for being here.

As I turn the corner to enter The Hallway to Nowhere, I steal a glance at Essie. Head down she's poring over her celebrity magazine, but she's disinterested; the spark's gone out of her face, the spark that had only recently returned. I hate The Cell Keeper almost as much as I hate Psycho Squaw.

I don't know if I'm more upset than I care to admit about Essie's thwarted romance, but when I turn the doorknob to enter my mother's room, I'm anxious. I almost turn around to leave, but I can't think of a good reason, so I stick to my original plan. Exiting early would've been the better decision.

A yellow light fills the entire room, and hanging in the air is such a strong aroma of cherry blossoms, I would swear the ceiling is lined with perfume sachets of the scent. The only explanation for the appearance of these phenomena is that Jess is paying a visit. But why?

When I see the empty bed I literally gasp and stumble backward, not stopping until I crash into the wall. Unable to look away from the terrible sight, I stare at my mother's bed, its covers pulled down as if my mother just got up to go to the bathroom or take a walk to the little garden out back. I clutch at the wall for support, but its smooth surface doesn't offer any. I look like a cat trying to sharpen its claws.

"M-m-mom," I stutter. "Mom, where are you?"

Nothing breaks the silence except my panting.

Silently I pray that this doesn't mean that my mother has died and they've taken her to a holding area in The Retreat until an ambulance is ready to take her to the morgue. The words tumble out of my mouth as if I've known them my whole life, as if I recite them each night before I crawl into bed. Truth is I haven't prayed in years, even when I should have; even when my life depended upon it, I couldn't remember the words. Now I can. The sheer ability I have to speak these words aloud doesn't offer me solace; it frightens me. If I remember how to pray, I must suddenly have the need.

Our Father who art in heaven . . .

By the time I say amen I'm sitting on the floor shaking. This can't be happening; my mother can't leave me. I need her now! I need the hope that she symbolizes! She's fighting the demons surrounding her like I have to fight mine. She is not allowing the disease flowing through her veins and her mind and her soul to overtake her and possess her completely, like I'm not allowing this curse to destroy my life. But if she's gone, if she's dead, that means she didn't win. So I could lose too.

The yellow glow flickers, and I hear static electricity in the air. I gaze up and expect to see that one of the long, cylindrical fluorescent lightbulbs has burnt out, but instead I see another miracle. All the yellow light in the room has gathered to swirl like a jaundiced cloud above my mother's bed. Crouched on the floor I'm watching the sight, partially amazed and partially terrified; I have no idea if I'm watching something good or something bad.

Finally, the yellow light stretches into a thin vertical line, and I expect to see Jess appear like she usually does, but instead I see my mother. She materializes out of the glow and floats horizontally for a few seconds in the air before gently descending back to her bed. Everything is back to normal; my mother looks the same as she always does. But where the hell did she just come from?

"Someone asked to see her," Jess answers. "Someone who couldn't make the journey, so I brought your mother across the final divide."

Jess's voice whispers in my ear; I can feel her breath against my earlobe. I whip my head to the right, but she isn't there. She's speaking to me from another dimension, beyond the grave, or wherever she hangs out when she isn't near me.

"Who?"

I'm so confused and disoriented and shocked that I don't even bother to ask my question silently. Not that there's anyone else in the room who can hear me.

"Who had to see my mother?!"

Jess doesn't answer, but my mother does.

"Your father says you need to listen."

I don't see my mother's lips move. She isn't looking at me, her eyes aren't even open, but I know she spoke those words, and I know she was speaking them to me.

Instead of being grateful that Jess drove her to dead-man's land to chat with my father and bring me back some words of caution, I'm furious with her. If she can speak with my father, why the hell can't she break free from this coma?!

"Listen to *what*?!" I scream. "Wake up and tell me exactly what he said!"

Never in my entire life have I spoken this harshly to my mother. Not when I was a little girl and didn't completely grasp the meaning of respect, and not when I got older and became frustrated with the fact that my mother was never going to speak to me again. But in this past year she's opened her eyes, she's spoken to me, she's proven that she can sever the shackles that are keeping her in this horrific vegetative state, and yet she chooses, for the most part, to remain silent. And now she can actually allow Jess, a supernatural entity, to help her visit her dead husband. It's not fair! If she can do all of that, it's time that she start acting like my mother again!

"What's wrong with you?! Why are you just lying there instead of helping me?!"

At some point during my tirade, the door must have opened, because there are people standing next to me, but I don't acknowledge them; I continue yelling at my mother.

"Why are you ignoring me when I need you more than ever?!"

"Dominy!"

I can feel a hand on my shoulder, and I fling my arm up into the air with such force that whoever was trying to grab me is now rising up into the air. I watch Winston Lundgarden crash onto the floor, and he does not look like a happy man.

"Young lady!" he cries, awkwardly on all fours. "What the hell are you doing in here?"

"I could ask you the same thing!" I shout back.

He is so flummoxed, his jaw actually drops. I guess no one's ever talked to The Cell Keeper like that before, the way he deserves to be spoken to.

"I am the director of this facility," he pompously informs me, finally standing. "And I will not tolerate such inappropriate behavior from you. Despite the fact that your mother is one of our permanent residents."

Is he smiling? Is he smiling because my mother's coma has been diagnosed as irreversible and she has no chance of leaving The Retreat except to move from her bed to a coffin?

"May I remind you, Dominy," he says, "this is a hospital."

Like hell it is!

"I don't know what this place is, Lundgarden, but it's definitely not a hospital," I reply. "Essie may think you've got some power that makes you untouchable, but I don't. And I intend to find out exactly what you and your staff are doing here!"

It's not until I'm practically in front of the door that I realize Melinda Jaffe is blocking my exit.

"Tell me, Dominy, what else does that old woman think of Winston?" Mrs. Jaffe purrs. "And of us?"

Oh my God! What have I done? Why do I get the feeling that I've just sealed Essie's fate?

"Nothing," I say quickly and stupidly. "Nothing at all."

But Melinda knows I mean exactly the opposite.

"That's what I suspected," she replies.

Shaking my head erratically, I try to get the image of the woman standing in front of me out of my head. Not because I agree with Essie's declaration that she's a witch, but because in this room she looks exactly like my mother.

No! I close my eyes so the image disappears and in my

mind so does the resemblance. "Get out of my way!" I command, eyes closed tight.

Stumbling into the hallway I'm so distraught and confused and outraged that I start to walk right into the depths of The Retreat instead of to the left toward the front desk. I'm about to turn around to correct myself when I hear squeaking. Nadine is here. She's not carrying her clipboard, which is usually soldered to her hands, so this must not be a professional visit. When I see her staring at me, smiling devilishly, her hands clasped in front of her, I know that her trip here was completely personal.

"Hello, Dominy," she calls out. "I have something to tell you."

Her voice is different. It's deeper and flatter and devoid of any emotion. This is who she really is, a soulless creature, just like Luba. And this is why my father wanted to talk to my mother, to tell me to listen to whatever this freak has to say. Jess probably can't relay such messages, but there's no law stating that a mother can't talk to her own daughter.

Even if Nadine weren't leading the way, I would know that we were headed to Room 48. Once inside Luba's room, however, I would never have imagined I would find Napoleon sitting in a chair next to her. I must look shocked, but it's not for the reason Nadine thinks.

"You haven't forgotten my grandmother already, have you?" she asks.

The plastic bag is ripped off my head; globs of honey are spooned back into the jar; the truth returns to my mind like water rushing through empty streets during a flood. I couldn't stop the memories if I wanted to. Luba is Napoleon and Nadine's grandmother; Melinda is Luba's daughter-in-law; and I've officially been lured into enemy camp.

I'm quick, but Nadine proves quicker. By the time I reach the door, Nadine has telekinetically locked it, and even with my super strength I can't reopen it. I'm in human form, but I'm a wolf, trapped in a cage.

"The time has come, Dominy," Luba hisses, "for us to tell you about our heritage."

All I want to do is escape from this prison. Maybe if I can make it to the window, I can break through the glass and be free. We're only on the first floor; the fall won't be that steep. But then I remember my father's message.

"I'm listening," I reply.

Smiling like some grotesque coquette, Luba grabs her grandchildren, one emaciated hand clutching either descendant, and yanks them close to her body so three become one.

"Good," she replies. "Because it really is one helluva story."

Chapter 19

The last time someone told me a story, it was my father telling me about the origin of the curse. I have a feeling this story is going to be worse.

"It's time to go back to the beginning," Luba states.

I was right. I don't want to hear what she has to say; I already know everything I need to know. Jess warned us to keep Barnaby away from Luba, Nadine, and unfortunately for Archie, even Napoleon. He may be cringing slightly as his grandmother's bones press into his, he may not want to be an active participant among this triumvirate, but for whatever reason he cannot escape. He cannot break free, and therefore he cannot be my friend's boyfriend.

The fourth member of their troop, Melinda, must also play a part, but hers is by default. She bore Luba's grandchildren; she's not connected to her by blood though, and that must be the reason she's being left out. She's close enough to revel in their glories, close enough to convince herself she's been offered membership to their cult, but she can only bear witness; she has no power of her own. These three have the power, and I'm about to be told what it is, how they obtained it, and, perhaps, what they plan on doing with it.

Correction, I'm about to be shown.

"Ready, children?" Luba asks, her normally dull, black eyes suddenly gleaming.

"Yes, Grandmother," Nadine replies excitedly.

When Napoleon answers I can only detect obedience in his voice. "Yes."

Together they raise their hands and point them at the door, making it vanish and replacing it with a silver tunnel. Squinting, I can't see anything contained inside. It looks unfilled and unending and unreal. And yet I know that if I want answers to Luba's family's origin, answers that may help me break this curse, I have to walk inside this hollow shell. Could lead to revelation, could lead to destruction. The only thing I'm certain of is that I have no choice.

"Follow me," Nadine commands.

Standing at the threshold of the man-made—or maybe that's creature-made—tunnel, Nadine doesn't hesitate; she walks right into the silver light. Well, if she can do it, so can I. We may be on decidedly opposite sides of the moral tracks, but I'm just as strong as she appears to be.

I can feel and smell Luba's stinky breath on my neck, and I think that she'll follow me into this new space, but I'm wrong. She may love both her grandchildren, she may need both of them, but she clearly doesn't trust them both.

"Napoleon," she says. "You're next."

Quickly falling in line, I don't have to turn around to know that Napoleon is behind me; I can smell him. His scent is as strong as his grandmother's, but much more pleasant. Oddly, it smells like the incense that the priests burn at St. Edmund's, and, unless I'm deluding myself, unless I'm trying to make Nap better than he actually is, I smell the faint trace of cherry blossoms within that musky fragrance. If he has the church and Jess on his side, maybe there's hope for him after all.

When I feel his hand tugging against the sleeve of my jacket, I know there's hope for me. He's reminding me that I may be on my own for the moment, I may be plunging into unknown and evil territory, but I'm always connected to goodness.

Walking through the silver tunnel is like walking through water. I can breathe and see easily, but the air around is tangible. It doesn't prevent movement; it comes along for the ride. Whatever this substance is—natural or magical—it's clinging to me. It's not becoming part of me or trying to burrow into my skin. It just wants me to know that it exists.

Looking down past the silver light, I see nothing but blackness; Luba's hospital room is long gone. So is the earth for that matter. Somehow the four of us are walking, our feet not touching anything solid, and yet we don't fall through to be swallowed by the emptiness below. Above us, beyond the silver canopy is more blackness. It surrounds us, kept at bay, but I suspect it longs to make us a part of its massive nothingness.

When I think about exactly where I am, walking through an enclosed corridor with my enemies to witness the tale of their beginnings, I start to panic. If only I could hide within the wolf's body, disappear within the soft contours of its fur, maybe I could feel safe. As it is I feel like I'm walking through space with escorts leading me to my doom. When we land I realize we've merely walked through time.

"Welcome to my past, Dominy."

Luba is standing in a field of overgrown wildflowers and weeds. I have no idea where we are, and yet I know that we've touched ground outside Nadine's family cabin. Glancing to my right I see confirmation, one small cabin, sturdily built, the same cabin where I tried to kill Archie the night of my second transformation. The same cabin that now stands in the shadow of the larger one that was built decades later, which in the time I'm currently standing in, doesn't yet exist.

Three arms rise at the same time, emitting three beams of silver light that fuse to become one, and instantaneously we're all transported inside the cabin. Wincing, I turn away from the sight I'm shown, but I'm immediately drawn back to the young woman lying on the floor, her legs bent and spread, trying to coax out the child who refuses to be born.

"Get out of me!!"

The woman is young and beautiful and terrified. Sweat covers her face and makes her pale white skin glisten, mats down her jet-black hair. Guttural cries and anguished groans tear out of her body with such ferocity that the sounds threaten to slash open the flesh around her mouth. She is in pain; she is in labor; she is in Luba's memory.

"This is the woman your father created," Luba narrates. "This is me about to give birth to my only child, alone, without my husband, shunned by my people."

Stupidly I ask, "Where's your family?"

"When you cannot produce your husband's killer, everyone thinks he's taken his own life," Luba replies scornfully. "And if your husband will not stand by your side, neither will your tribe."

Annoyed at either my interruption or the lonely vision of herself as a younger woman, Luba angrily swipes her hand in the air, marking it with a trail of silver. She reminds me of Jess and how golden sunlight follows her wherever she goes, however she moves. I'm startled by how similar good and evil can look.

The scene within the cabin changes, and young Luba is now holding her son. But there's no sigh of relief, no beatific smile as she gazes at her newborn, who lies naked in her lifeless arms except for the slime and blood that still cling to his fresh skin. There's no joy in her eyes, only anger.

"You are fatherless," she says, her voice flat and dead. "He was taken from you by an evil man, and you are now an albatross, a thorn in my side, a reminder of how shameful my life has become and how glorious my life should have been."

My heart breaks for this child even though I know he will

grow up to become the father of the twins, because her words are more hateful than any curse Luba could inflict. These are words no child should ever hear. And they're followed by instructions no child can ever disobey.

"Together we will avenge your father's death," Luba continues. The formulation of her plan is beginning to bring life back to her, her words starting to employ the rhythm of a lullaby. "Together we will make this vile man and his own child pay for destroying our lives. Your father and my husband will not have died in vain. That is our blessing; that is our curse."

This child, this innocent baby is exactly the same as me. His only crime was being born to wickedness, having a mother as immoral as sin. My only crime was being born to a man who made a fatal mistake, who for a brief and solitary moment became wicked. We both survived only to suffer for the actions of our parents. Only one of the twins, however, seems to agree with me.

Nadine is staring at the scene of her father's first moments on this earth with indifference; the man means nothing to her, while Napoleon looks as if he is fighting every muscle in his body to stand still and not race forward to snatch the baby from Luba's disinterested arms. But he gives in to the power enslaving him and doesn't move. It doesn't matter that he probably can't break the time barrier and actually become part of the scene we're watching unfold; he doesn't even try. I know if that were my father being held by such an unmaternal mother, I would make every attempt to free him from a life filled with misery. A sense of relief floods my body. I may be a victim, but I'm not a coward. As we travel into the future, turns out that's just what Luba's son is.

"Thorne?" Luba says.

"Yes, Mother," he replies.

"She said yes?" she asks.

Now Luba's slightly older, but still looking more like the

young woman who gave birth to an unlucky boy moments ago than like the old, withering woman standing next to me.

"Yes, Mother, she did."

I know the man I'm watching is the twins' father, but how could I know that? Suddenly, my mind melds with the wolf's, and I remember that I've seen his face in a photo before! In the cabin, while stalking Archie and Nadine, I saw a photo of this man, the twins, and Melinda. I thought they were what they appeared to be—a happy family. How wrong I was.

"How surprising," Luba replies. "Obviously Melinda sees the majesty and power and magic that lie just outside your grasp."

"No, Mother, she sees the man that lies inside of me!" her son snaps. "The man you refuse to see!"

Old Luba smirks; Young Luba laughs out loud. Instinctively, I know that this is a rare occurrence, Thorne's showing courage and standing up to his mother. Even the twins sense that this is something out of the ordinary, and they begin to watch the past unfold with more interest than before. Thorne's victory, however, is over before it truly begins.

"That's because there is nothing to see," she mocks. "Only a bastard child."

"I am not a bastard!" Thorne shouts, but his voice cracks on the last syllable, voiding out all the strength he was trying to attain. "I have a father."

Slowly, Young Luba walks toward her son, and he physically cowers, growing smaller during her advance. His face is etched with a fear that is not born from surprise, but from a lifelong education.

"If your father were alive, he would disown you," she whispers through her sinister smile. "You have proven yourself over and over again to be an unfitting heir. You do not embrace his power; it is not your mission to see it fulfilled."

"Because you only want to use it for destruction," Thorne argues.

"The Hunter wants me to avenge his spirit!" Luba cries. "Your father would have discarded you with the trash and led me to our bedroom to produce another, more appropriate and satisfying and worthwhile heir. Do not fool yourself, Thorne. You are only alive because your father is dead."

Cheeks flushed, fists clenched, Thorne wants to remain silent. He knows the consequences speech will bring forth, but his mother's words cannot remain unchallenged. "If I'm so disgusting, why have you let me live?!"

A shadow drops over Luba's face—no, not a shadow, her true spirit, dark and relentless and merciless. When she speaks to her son, it's in a voice I've never heard before. "Because mankind has left me with no other legacy, so I have no other choice but to let you live." Looking forward at nothing and at her older self at the same time, Young Luba continues. "Until you have served your purpose and I can be finally be rid of you."

The silver light swirls around me, and I can feel my body being tossed in the dry liquid, like snowflakes inside a snow globe. Drifting and spiraling and falling with no control to stop or change direction until there is no more movement, until the decision to stop moving has been reached by someone else.

When Luba and her grandchildren drop their hands, I see that the decision has been made. We're in a hospital room. Melinda Jaffe is propped up in bed, exhausted from recently giving birth, attended by a doctor and a nurse, with Luba by her side. Thorne is nowhere to be seen because he doesn't matter any longer. He has done his job; he has fathered Melinda's twins.

Holding one child in each arm, Luba whispers, "Orion's prophecy is fulfilled . . . and three shall lead."

I lose my balance as the images swirl and the hospital room is gone. We're in a nursery tucked away in a part of a home. Melinda is holding Nadine, and Luba is holding

Napoleon; Thorne is holding the empty air in his hands. The way his fingers are opening and closing it seems as if the air doesn't want anything to do with him either.

"I thought I was to be part of the prophecy," he whines.

"The stars found you unworthy," Luba replies, never taking her eyes off of her grandson.

"Let me prove myself!" Thorne wails.

"It's too late," Melinda says. Nadine cries out and her infant voice sounds very much like agreement. "The children have the sign that you were never born with."

The poor man has no idea what he's up against; he never has. "What sign?" Thorne asks.

The women raise each child triumphantly and let their blankets fall to the floor, like white flags signaling the beginning of a race. In this instance, it signifies the end of Thorne's. Each child bears a mark just underneath his or her left hip bone, three stars in one line, Orion's constellation. We were wrong—they're not tattoos; they're birthmarks!

"It's the same mark your father was born with," Luba says proudly. "The same mark that never touched your skin because when you were conceived it was given to me. I should have known then that it was a sign that you were unworthy, but I was foolish."

Slowly Old Luba raises her thin, white hospital gown to reveal legs that would look paler than her face if they weren't invaded by blood-red veins and purple-gray bruises. Proudly, she lifts her gown just high enough to show me the same row of stars that are on her grandchildren's skin and presumably were on her husband's skin as well.

"They are the marks of Orion," she explains. "My husband was a descendant of the original hunter, the hunter who looms in the night sky. His light shines brighter than the moon and more powerful than the sun."

Now the connection makes sense, but it's impossible. "Orion is a myth!" I shout. "He never existed."

"And neither do werewolves," Nadine retorts. "And yet here you are."

She's got me. One impossibility means there can be others. They don't need explanation, but Nadine offers one.

"The original plan was for my grandparents and their child to be the triumvirate," she explains. "But your father ruined that and soiled my father's spirit, turning him into something that could only wilt in Orion's shadow, not prosper."

So now my father is to blame for killing Luba's husband and neutering her son?!

"Silence!" Luba cries out, obviously able to hear my private thoughts. "Our spirits had been untouched. We were living solitary lives, living off the land until your father poisoned us with man's evil."

"And in return you cursed us with yours!"

"Because that, Dominy, is the way of the hunter!" Nadine sounds as vindictive as her grandmother. She truly has inherited more than a birthmark; she's inherited Luba's vengeful spirit as well. A spirit that bypassed Luba's only child.

"Daddy didn't agree, and that's why he moved us from here," Napoleon adds, picking up the story. "He told me that he wanted to keep us from his past. He never believed in the prophecy or the powers of Orion."

"Because Orion never believed in him!" Luba scolds. "And Orion will refuse to believe in you if you continue disparaging his name."

Unable to control her disgust with her grandson, Luba flicks her head in his direction, her hair whipping around her like serpents' tongues, and Napoleon is slammed into the wall of silver light. This time, perhaps because Napoleon wasn't prepared, the light penetrates and wraps around his body, his arms, his legs, and his neck. Grasping desperately at the light around his neck, Napoleon tries to pull it away from his throat so he can breathe. The one thing he doesn't do is call out for help, because he knows neither his sister nor his grandmother will run to his side. I'm a different story.

I only succeed in running about three strides before the light I'm standing on shifts and breaks apart to wrap itself around my legs. I'm frozen in my spot, unable to do anything but watch Napoleon suffer and his relatives gloat.

"My son was a jealous fool," Luba relays. "He never understood the power that we're after because it is not a power he would ever be able to share in. Luckily his wife did."

"That's why she finally got Daddy out of the way," Nadine finishes.

My body doesn't move this time, but the images around me do. Gone is the nursery, gone are the infants. In their place is a kitchen. The twins are now about ten years old, and they're sitting around the table eating with their parents. They keep on eating even while Thorne begins to choke.

"Melinda," Thorne gasps. "What . . . have you done?"

Little Napoleon stops eating and watches his father clutch his throat in horror, much the same way Napoleon in the present is doing right now. It's an eerie double-vision, like father, like son.

"Napoleon," Melinda sweetly chastises. "Eat your food before it gets cold."

Obediently, Little Napoleon continues to eat, but his eyes never leave his father. Not while Thorne chokes, not while his face turns blue, and not even after he slumps forward onto the table, upturning his plate and spilling his glass of water. The water drips off the table in a quick, steady flow until it connects the past to the present, connecting the Jaffe kitchen with the silver light, one unbroken line of undisputed evil.

"Your mother poisoned your father?" I ask dumbfounded.

"In order to prepare us for our rightful roles in the world," Nadine replies, as if her mother's actions were completely normal and justified and sensible.

"Self-righteousness doesn't become you, child," Luba sneers. "You and your father have also killed, so there should be no room in your heart to cast blame."

An accident doesn't add up to murder and neither does killing while possessed. No! My heart and mind and soul may not be pure, but they are not blackened by the sin of premeditated murder. That's one thing I know for sure. And now that I know the truth, I am not going to let these . . . *sick, twisted* psychopaths get away with it!

"Witches!" I shout. "That's what you are! Witches who deserve nothing but payback!"

In an instant Nadine appears before me, gliding through the silver like a strong wind.

"Bring it on!" Nadine curses. "I've been dying for a real challenge ever since I came to this backwoods town!"

When her mouth opens again, words aren't hurled into the air; insults and curses and enchantments don't come. The only thing to escape her foul mouth is a stream of black smoke, exactly the kind that slithers out of Luba's pores.

Nadine thrusts her head at me like a ram knocking heads with another of its kind, and I'm terrified, not because a black ball of smoke is heading at my face, but because we are born from the same spirit. We both come from Luba's energy, which means, as disgusting as it sounds, we share the same heritage.

But if we share the same heritage, that means we share the same power.

Mustering every ounce of strength I have, I yank my feet free from the silver shackles binding me to the floor. Diving to the left, I hear the black ball fly past me, its flight filled with the sounds of terror and sorrow and fear. My own.

I escaped in time to miss the bulk of the impact, but Nadine's weapon still skimmed my arm and burned my flesh right off, leaving behind a gross wound of mutilated skin, the bone underneath jutting out. It reminds me of how Jess looked after I killed her.

"Enough!" I scream, and once again a red cloud tumbles out of my mouth and flies at Nadine's face. At the last second she jumps up, saving herself from the impact of my fury and preoccupying her long enough for Napoleon to take action.

"Leave her!" Napoleon cries as he lifts me up off the ground.

He shoves something in my pocket before hurling me into the bowels of the silver light and through the tunnel. When I open my eyes I'm in my bed. I have no idea what time it is or how I returned here, but when I feel my arm throb, I know where I've been. So does Jess.

Working quickly she takes my shirt off and lets her preternatural light drip into my wound. The pain is devoured by her sunshine, and I'm not surprised to see the gash heal itself and close up. My arm looks unmarked in a matter of seconds. There is goodness in the world, and Jess is proof of that. She points a finger at my pocket, and it's like she's pointing a flashlight at me.

"I'm not the only proof, Dom," she says, her voice uncharacteristically wistful. "There's more."

Opening the note Napoleon tucked into my pocket just before he freed me from his sister's wrath, I see that he's written "Help me."

How? How can we help him if Nap has never been able to help himself?

"All I can tell you, Dom, is that we still need to keep Archie away from him," Jess informs me. "Just because Napoleon wants to be good and do what's right, doesn't mean he's not going to hurt those who try to help him."

"So what do we do?" I ask.

"We'll do everything we can," Jess replies, the tone of her voice not changing. "But sometimes evil has to win out."

What?! Why? "That can't be a rule."

"Oh but it is," Jess replies. "There has to be balance in the world. Good and evil, life and death, hunters and the hunted. If everything were equal, there would be chaos."

I ponder her words. I know they must be wise, but I don't understand them.

"You will," Jess replies, sounding reassuring and cryptic at the same time.

The flesh above my healed wound reopens briefly, but this time there is no pain, only reassurance that a golden light shines within me. From now on, no matter what enemy I face, I'll carry a little bit of Jess around with me.

And after what I've witnessed tonight, I'm going to need as much backup as I can get.

Chapter 20

"Way to go, Domgirl. You just got Archie killed."

What?!

"He told me about Napoleon's note."

Okay, now Caleb's accusation makes a little more sense. Even though he's just accused me of being an accessory to a crime, he looks even more handsome than he usually does. His hair is tucked underneath a Two W ski hat, and except for a few rebellious wet curls peeking out and resting on his forehead his face is uninterrupted, touched by nothing more than the crisp afternoon air. He must've taken a shower after football practice, which is when Archie probably filled him in on what I told him earlier.

"I told Archie not to tell anyone," I say.

The words sound foolish to me too. I mean really, what did I expect Archie to do? I couldn't keep this amazing discovery to myself; why should he? And that's exactly what Caleb is trying to make me realize, that by sharing Napoleon's information I've put my friend's life in jeopardy. Again!

"Napoleon is Archie's *boyfriend*, and you've told him that

Nap's being held captive inside some paranormal prison!" Caleb rants. "Any of that sound familiar?"

If I can't make the correlation that Caleb is setting up, comparing my plight with Napoleon's, then I'm an idiot. And now that I think about what I've really set in motion by sharing Nap's plea for help with Archie, that might be exactly what I am.

Archie's got natural hero sensibilities. For so many years and for so many different reasons he's played the victim, the one who had to be rescued from fights, both physical and verbal. So now that he's stronger and more confident and self-assured, he almost feels as if it's his duty to come to the aid of the less fortunate, the bullied, and the powerless. Since his boyfriend definitely falls into that category, Archie is going to do whatever is necessary to save him. Have I unwittingly led Archie right into a death trap? I thought I was doing the right thing, but did I just make another huge mistake? But as the British would say, wait one bloody second! If Napoleon is just like me, then isn't Archie just like Caleb?

"Would you prefer not to know about my secret?" I ask.

Caleb tilts his head toward me so the stray strands of hair dangle in the air. "What do you mean?"

"I didn't want you to know about my curse, I wanted to shield you from the truth, but you found out anyway," I explain. "And didn't that make you feel better? Didn't it bring us closer together?" I don't wait for his reply; I continue my assault. "And wouldn't you have resented it if you found out years later that I shut you out from knowing about the most important, life-changing thing that's ever happened to me?"

His smirk tells me everything I need to know. He agrees with me. He knows that while my disclosure about Napoleon's letter may have put Archie in danger, it was the right thing to do. Let's face it, just being my friend means he's in danger anyway. Luba and Nadine are not just loose cannons; they're loose nuclear missiles. Their actions are unpredictable, and we don't really even know what they're fully capable of doing. Their power might be like Jess's, otherworldly yet limited, or they could hold the fate of not only our lives at their evil fingertips, but the lives of the entire world as well. Two words scribbled on a piece of paper from a desperate friend really aren't going to change Archie's fate. It was sealed the day he decided to be a member of my Wolf Pack.

"You know, you're a lot more insightful ever since you became part wolf," Caleb quips.

He's being flippant, but he's right.

"The curse is a blessing in some ways," I reply. "It's kind of forced me to grow up and look at the world through a new set of eyes. Literally."

"Still the most beautiful eyes I've ever looked into," he whispers.

His fingernails feel smooth rubbing down the side of my cheek, and my body fills up with warmth when he tugs on my earlobe, softly, just letting his skin connect with mine. Resting my forehead against his chin, I cover his hand with mine to embrace the warmth, collect and contain it, because the days are getting colder and I'm going to need Caleb's spirit for protection, just as I'm going to need the wolf's spirit for strength.

I shiver, and Caleb wraps his arms around me, drawing me close to his body. His heart is beating normally; adrenalin isn't racing through his veins; he's acting like a prince should, stalwart and calm and ready to do battle. But he's so calm that I wonder if he understands a battle is brewing, a new fight is underway. When he speaks, I know that he understands this, probably understood it before I did.

"You have to promise me from now on you'll think things through and not just react without understanding the consequences," he whispers.

"You forget that I'm part animal now," I say. My words bury themselves into his chest before they can be whisked away by the wind so they stay just between the two of us. "We react; that's how we survive."

"No," he corrects. "You survive by how you react."

I push away from Caleb so I can look him in the eyes. "Now who's being insightful?"

Before Caleb replies, he leads us to sit on a patch of grass, frosty, but not snow-covered. Both of us are cross-legged, facing each other, holding hands, like we're doing some joint meditation.

"You need to be cunning and clever," he instructs. "You have to listen to the wolf spirit speaking to you, guiding you, but then you have to act upon that guidance wisely."

His voice is so solid, so tangible, so strong, that I can almost see our invisible string materialize between us and become one unbreakable line from Caleb's lips to my heart. I tug on his hands so he knows that I'm tugging on our string, so he knows that I understand what he's trying to teach me. For as much as I've grown and for as powerful as I've become, I still need a tutor. Even if I don't always want to listen to what he has to say.

"I don't want to hear you speak at another one of our friend's funerals," Caleb says, his tone of voice much less blunt than his words.

"Caleb!" I shout.

I try to break free from his grip, sever our invisible string, but Caleb is too determined to maintain our connection. He isn't letting me go.

"I'm not trying to frighten you or piss you off, but you have to understand that everything has changed," he says, his gaze never leaving my eyes. His stare is almost hypnotic, and I want nothing more than to look at the grass or his knee or the part of the sky that exists far, far away from where we're sitting, but I can't because I know that he's speaking the truth and I know that I need to hear the words come from someone other than myself.

"Now that we know Luba isn't acting alone and her curse wasn't a one-time-only effort, but the beginning of some larger plot," he says, "we have to reexamine everything, and you have to accept the fact that even though you're the center, this is no longer just about you."

I know that, Caleb. I may be the bull's-eye, but the target's gotten a whole lot wider.

"I do understand, I really do," I confess. "And I've never been more frightened in all my life. I thought that the scariest thing that could ever happen to me was the start of the transformation, because I know there's absolutely nothing I can do to reverse it; I can't stop the pain or the inevitable change that's about to happen. But at least I know what's on the other side; I know that when the transformation is complete, I'm going to be this . . . thing."

Caleb scootches closer to me, uncrossing his legs so they wrap around me, and he leans his forehead into mine. I'm so flustered by the beauty and the intimacy of the moment, I can't tell if his skin is cool or damp or warm, but it doesn't matter, as long as it's touching mine, as long as we have a connection and there's no separation.

"I don't ever want to hear you say that again," he sighs.

"It's what I am."

"No, it isn't."

"Yes, I'm this . . ."

"You, Dominy, are this amazingly special creature," he pronounces. "Beautiful and wild and special."

His eyes are so close to me that I can see them for what they truly are, brown patches of earth, unwavering and secure and reliable. And they're mine. I don't move; I can hardly breathe I'm so filled with emotion, but I can feel our string pull us even closer together when Caleb speaks practically the same words that I've just spoken in my mind.

"And you're mine."

Once again I can feel passion stir inside of my stomach

and rise up and down and throughout my body. I don't blush despite the fact that I want Caleb to make love to me right here on the grass. I want him to push me down onto the dirt, and I want to experience what it's like to be physically connected to another human being, no separation, no beginning and no end. But then I look into his eyes. He's not crying, but they're moist, and I realize I already know what that feels like. Our consummation can wait; the pleasure I've heard about will be ours one day, I know it will, but for now we don't need to do anything further to know that our commitment to one another is real. No matter what Napoleon's fate is I hope that he and Archie experience this. Everyone deserves to know that there's another person on earth who will sacrifice everything for them.

I'm so blessed that I've had two.

My father's tombstone looks like all the others, and yet it stands out among the rows of rectangular stones. His name—Mason Barnard Robineau—is carved into the slab of concrete or whatever the material is that's used to create your final nametag, and it always surprises me. I never knew him by that name, just Daddy, so it's almost like I'm looking at the gravestone of a foreigner instead of my father. In some ways I am.

In the last few months of his life he fully exposed himself to me and shared his secrets and regrets and shame with me, but that was only because he felt he had no other choice, only because he knew his time on earth was coming to an end and he had to arm me with as much ammunition and information as possible so I could live after he was gone. Kneeling on top of the dirt that covers his coffin, I wonder what other secrets he took with him. What stories didn't he share with me, what parts of him will I never know? Who is this man who called himself my father?

"If only we knew then what we know now," I say out loud. "Maybe things would have turned out differently."

I can't bring myself to speak the rest of my thought out loud. Maybe you would still be alive.

When Luba told me the only way to break the curse was for me to kill my father, it sounded like an insane proposition. But time not only heals, it makes the unfathomable palatable. We thought we were doing the right thing, but we didn't know what we were really dealing with; we didn't know how easily we could be duped and betrayed and oppressed. That's what Caleb was trying to tell me before: We need to learn from our mistakes, learn that if we want to overcome this unknown evil, we need to acquire as much information as possible before reacting. Or else this cemetery will be littered with the tombstones of more of our loved ones.

Inhaling deeply I hold the cold air in my lungs for as long as I can and then let my breath rush out of my body, taking along with it the fear that lives deep inside of me. I know that like honey in a jar, not all the fear will leave me, some will cling to my soul, determined and resilient, but enough of it will be gone so I can speak the words out loud.

"If only you had told me all of your secrets, Daddy, maybe we wouldn't have been so scared and confused, maybe we would've done things differently," I say. "And maybe you'd still be alive."

"I doubt that."

Nadine's presence next to my father's headstone doesn't surprise me as much as it disgusts me. I can almost see the silvery slime drip off of her flesh and contaminate my father's grave. I imagine her spirit burrowing through the ground, drilling through the exterior of my father's casket, and latching onto his body, whatever's left of it, and infecting his remains with her malicious energy. Not that it matters. Pieces of his body may still linger, but his soul, the most important part, is long gone, and it's gone to a place that Nadine will never be able to enter.

"Get away from my father's grave," I growl.

Smiling, Nadine plops onto his tombstone like she's sitting on a barstool, one foot pressed into the dirt, the other dangling in the air.

"Why?" she asks. "I have just as much right to be here as you do."

"You have no rights when it comes to my father!" I scream. "He's dead because of your grandmother."

"No, you idiot," Nadine replies. "He's dead . . . because of me."

A serpent shoots out of Nadine's hand, no, not a snake but a silver lasso that curls around my wrist, cutting into my flesh, bringing me on another journey into the past, another flash of history that will now be a part of my memory. Before the scene even begins I know that it will be an unwanted piece.

We're in Nadine's cabin, and I'm watching myself as a wolf stare at my father. If I focus only on the eyes of this majestic animal, I see it's as if I'm looking in a mirror; the color and the expression of the eyes are the same. The only sound in the room is from my breathing, quick pants that remind me of the sound I heard when I transformed in Arla's bedroom and the first time I transformed unexpectedly when I was with Jess. The sound is no longer frightening, but oddly comforting because it links me with the wolf. It's what I see that is unbelievably frightening.

My father looks at me for the last time, his eyes peering deep within the wolf's eyes in search of his daughter. It breaks my heart when he shuts his eyes tight, because I know that he thinks he's lost her forever; I know that he thinks she can't possibly see him from underneath the fur and fangs and claws, but she's there, she's looking right at him, she'll never leave him! Until the black lightning strikes her in the back.

Looking into the past as an observer, I can see what I never saw before; I can see Luba attack me from behind. Her energy, black and twisted and cruel, knocked me out so my father was left alone with unexpected company. My father's eyes remained shut, so he never saw Luba intervene and alter our history once more, and he never saw Nadine's face contort like that of a rabid animal and her body hurl forward and attack him.

"Grandma wanted your daddy dead, so I killed him," Nadine tells me. "I understood the need because the curse had only just begun; it would've been such a sin to see it end so soon."

She's speaking to me in this sing-song, childlike voice, like a higher-pitched version of Luba's gravelly tone, and I'm amazed that someone who looks so normal could be so demented. Nadine wears her sanity like a costume, and now she's decided to take it off so her true self can breathe.

"Look at how I make my fingers sharpen into claws so, when they rip into your father's face, he thinks you're attacking him," Nadine squeals, pointing at herself from the past. "He's so convinced it's you, he never once opened his eyes."

She's right. All during the pain that Nadine inflicts upon my father, he keeps his eyes closed. Despite my being held up by the silver light my knees buckle, and I fall to the floor of the cabin. I don't feel the wood underneath my knees, but I don't fall through the floorboards either. I'm being suspended between two worlds at once, one more devastating than the other.

If only my father hadn't been so afraid of seeing what he thought was happening! If only he hadn't tried to protect whatever remnant of his daughter he felt still existed within the body of the wolf, he would've seen that someone else was trying to kill him. If he had just for one second, one moment, opened his eyes, he would've seen that someone else was trying to keep the curse in full force and not reverse it! Before I realize it my screams are filling the cabin alongside my father's. Despite his most valiant efforts, he can't conceal the pain that he's feeling; he has to give it a voice. He has to allow his screams the chance to live, even while his life is being taken away from him. The sound of my father's howls is unbearable.

"Stop!!!" I scream. "Stop it!!!"

I can't stop what this witch has already done, but I can stop her from gloating. I can stop her from using my father's death as a source of pride.

"Enough!"

The word roars out of my throat, but quickly turns into something indecipherable, a growl, a sound that doesn't belong to a girl. Startled by the sudden ferocity ripping through time and space, both Nadines—the killer from the past and the tour guide from the present—are startled. My father's lifeless and bloodied and desecrated body falls to the floor with a thud, and while one Nadine callously wipes his blood off her lips with the back of her hand, the other stares at me with a confusion that causes the silver rope to disentangle from me. Our connection is destroyed and so is our link to the past. Not that it matters. I've seen everything I need to see. Luba didn't kill my father. She was too much of a coward to do the deed herself; she enlisted her granddaughter to do the dirty work for her. And Nadine didn't disappoint; she carried out the deed with gusto.

Ignoring Caleb's instruction, I react without thinking.

"I'll make sure you're locked up for what you've done!"

Laughing hysterically, Nadine jumps off of the tombstone and lands on top of the bouquet of flowers that adorns my father's grave, a crushed clump of yellow and pink and red petals lying helplessly underneath her boots.

"Oh really?" she asks. "If you tattle on me, I'll tell everyone that you killed your BFF, and to prove it I'll tie you up in the town square during the next full moon so everyone can witness firsthand that you're nothing but a disgusting killing machine!"

We're at a stalemate. Neither one of us can really harm the other without exposing our own secret and unleashing it onto an unsuspecting and, most likely, unforgiving world. Neither one of us knows what move to make next, but then inspiration strikes. Unfortunately, it strikes Nadine and not me.

"I take that back, Dominy," she seethes. "Caleb was right. You really are such an amazingly special creature."

That's no coincidence. She didn't randomly choose the same words Caleb just spoke to me. She must've overheard him; she must have been watching our private moment. Or something much worse than that happened.

"How did you know he said that?" I snap.

Floating, rather than taking a few steps toward me, Nadine smiles. "Your boyfriend and I are very close you know."

That isn't true, it can't be true, and neither can this! Why am I transforming in the middle of the day, under the blinding light of the sun? It isn't possible!

The burn ignites underneath my skin like someone poured gasoline into my veins and struck a match. Heat engulfs and envelops my body, and the wolf growl that ripped through the air moments earlier is long gone; in its place is the scream of a terrified girl. What is happening to me?!

Looking down at my body, I see I look the same. The outside remains untouched, but internally I can feel the wolf trying to take control, trying to break free, but why? Are the rules changing again or am I simply losing my mind?

Frantically I swipe at the air in front of my face because I can't see. The world around me is fading away, not replaced with darkness, but with a shadow, an undeniable presence separating me from the rest of the world. Like the plastic bag has been lowered over my head and the world is distorted.

I stupidly clutch at my throat and try to rip the plastic bag off of my face even though I know that there's nothing there; there's nothing tangible that I can grab onto. I'm fighting against an unseen enemy. But why isn't the enemy taking complete control of me? Why do I still feel skin on my hands and neck and not fur? Why haven't my limbs snapped in the wrong direction and why am I still standing upright? Shouldn't I be on all fours, clawing at the dirt, growling at the unseen moon? Why am I still a girl and not a wolf?

Because this is just a game, a game that Nadine wants to play and one that she's going to lose.

Since she's part of Luba, she must be connected to the curse and its power, which means, in some way, she must be able to control it. That's what she's trying to do now; she's trying to force me into a transformation even though the sun is occupying the sky and not the full moon. Nice try, Nadine, but even you're not that powerful. You are, however, that stupid if you think I'm going to let you win.

Now that I understand what's going on, I can react, but not instinctively. I need to heed Caleb's lesson; I need to think, and act only when I've weighed my options. Being strong isn't enough; I also need to be smart.

Although I'm no longer having difficulty breathing or seeing, I claw at my throat and flail my arms in front of me to let Nadine think I'm still under her control. Slowly I can feel my strength begin to pulse through my veins where seconds earlier I thought they were being burned by my boiling blood. Panting wildly I must look like I'm gasping for air when I'm simply pumping up my body, letting the adrenalin take over, letting it consume me until I see that Nadine has let down her guard, smugly confident that I'm lost within the shadows of her power. Wrong.

Striking out I easily hit my target: Nadine's throat.

The choking sound she makes means she was as stunned by my actions as I wanted her to be. The crashing sound she makes when she flies into the tombstone and splits it in half means my action was way more powerful and destructive than I had intended.

Lying on the ground, the two symmetrical pieces of stone on either side of her, Nadine starts to laugh. Not like an amused teenager, but like the vindictive granddaughter of a witch. She's reveling in the damage she's helped create, and I can tell she can't wait to share this story with her family. I can see her sitting at her dinner table regaling them with the tale of how she pushed Dominy into defiling her father's gravesite.

Why not help her out so she can tell an even more interesting story?

While Nadine is sprawled out on the ground, her fingers pressed to her lips, sick laughter spilling out of her like pus from a wound, I silently apologize to my father and bang my fist onto one of the two pieces of stone to shatter it. A part of me understands that what I'm about to do next is wrong; it's violent and unethical and immoral. But I ignore that part of my mind. I'll deal with the consequences later. I know what they'll be, I've thought about them, and now I'm ready to act.

Grabbing a piece of stone, one with a sharpened edge, I lift it over my head and throw it down onto Nadine, aiming straight for her head. My movements are quick, but so are hers. She doesn't move; she doesn't roll out of the way; she doesn't do anything; she allows the spirit within her to offer protection. I'm disgusted when I realize she's mastered the same technique that I'm working on. She has learned how to coexist with the spirit that possesses her soul, so they each can act independently from each other as well as in sync. It's something I've yet to discover.

Just as the stone is about to impale the space between

Nadine's eyes, her body disappears, giving way to a silver cloud. Parts of the cloud look like satin, others like fog, and I assume this spirit is like a human being who has many different sides. When the cloud parts I see Nadine's truth that can no longer be buried.

A burst of black darkness erupts and rises up out of the silver shimmer. It sways in the breeze for a few seconds before the silver rises up to join it, and then both colors intertwine and spin around each other until their coil is so tight they have no choice but to unravel. When they're done spinning, Nadine is standing in place of the black and silver light.

"Missed me," she says.

Unable to think of a way to fight back, unable to think of anything that can satisfy the rage filling up my body, I lash out at Nadine with words.

"Damn you!" I cry.

"Correction, Domgirl," Nadine lashes back. "You're the one who's damned."

Chapter 21

Thank you, Nadine.

As much as she's taken from me, my former friend has also given me something quite unexpected: freedom. I've been living with the guilt that I literally killed my father when that guilt was never mine to own. Yes, I still know that he died in a futile attempt to release me from the curse, so he died *for* me, but he didn't die by my hand. My French ancestors call that *le différence humungo*.

And yet how can I hate her? I mean how can I really blame Nadine for doing something I was going to do myself? We both had our selfish motives: I wanted to break the curse; she wanted to maintain its hold on me. I'm no better than she is. So while I despise Nadine more than ever, I owe her.

Not that I'll ever send her a thank-you card. My gratitude will remain unspoken. Even if I wanted to express my thanks, it would be difficult, because I haven't seen much of her since her gravesite visit. None of us have.

Fleeting glimpses of her in the hallway, usually snickering with Rayna Delgado of all people, or turning a corner at The Retreat, but no more confrontations, no more journeys to the past. It's as if she's biding her time, waiting for the right moment to make her next move.

Napoleon's been acting the same way, keeping his distance from me. It's as if he never stuck that *Help me* note in my pocket. Honestly, I'm not sure what's better—their silence or their actions. Because within any silence is a voice that can't be ignored.

Archie's told me that every time he tries to discuss the Jaffe clan, Nap changes the subject, saying that he'd rather concentrate on his very own Winter Wonderland. Borderline TMI, very sweet, but also very scary. Nap can remain silent about his family, but that doesn't mean his family will remain silent. Their voices screech like animals sound right before they kill. And whoever hears that sound cannot be considered lucky.

But so far Archie has been. He and Nap were able to spend the pre-holiday season together, collect memories and private moments, before Nap and the shrews left town. He told Archie they were going to spend Christmas in Connecticut, but we wouldn't be shocked to find out they really went to some Club Med for homicidal witches.

Even if that turned out to be true, the biggest Christmas shocker would still belong to my brother. When Barnaby handed me a beautifully wrapped present on Christmas morning, I thought for sure he had uncovered my secret and was giving me a book on werewolves or had partnered with Lars Svenson to put my face on the cover of the *Three W* with the headline "Weeping Water Serial Killer Finally Caught." But underneath all of that shiny gold paper, it was a real Christmas gift. And not just any Christmas gift, a thoughtful one: a copy of *Jane Eyre* with a funky Japanese anime cover.

In one fell swoop he managed to include Caleb and Jess in his gift. I remember looking into my brother's eyes for the follow-up, the gotcha moment when he reveals the true meaning of his gift, that he's going to end my relationship with Caleb and expose me as Jess's killer, but I only saw my little brother looking back at me. Correction, my little brother all grown up. I got the impression that for the past few months he's been under some sort of a spell. Just like Louis.

Speaking of my guardian, I hate that Louis is going to become collateral damage, but even if Mrs. Jaffe weren't cheating on him, we'd still have to break up their relationship. She's not like Napoleon; she's not fighting against Luba; she's part of the horror. Plus, she killed her husband! We can't risk the two of them getting any closer and Louis's suffering the same fate. No, our New Year's resolution is to expose Melinda Jaffe for the maniacal fibber she is. At least that's my resolution.

"I don't know if I can do it, Dom," Arla says.

She's sitting on her bed combing out the newest wig her father got her for Christmas, a strawberry-blond shag that's about three shades lighter than my own hair color and about six inches shorter. I'm plopped into her beanbag chair. If anyone saw us they'd think we were trying to figure out how to spend the weekend and not how to destroy her father's love life.

"You have to," I reply.

"I know I have to. We've let this relationship fester way too long," she replies. "But for the first time in years my dad's actually happy."

"Would you prefer he be a happy corpse?" I blurt out.

Arla almost drops her wig. "Dominy!"

"Sorry, but the time of the year for soft and fuzzy thoughts has passed," I declare. "It's resolution time, and we have to resolve to separate the cop from the lady-killer. Or would that be the husband killer?"

"Could be either," Arla replies. "Depends upon if you want the phrase to include an adjective or a hyphen."

At least Arla's taking grammar seriously, if not the situation.

"Well, if the constant in the equation is *killer*, we have no choice but to break your father's heart," I say. "And I have the perfect solution."

Clutching the wig close to her, Arla pleads. "Please tell me your plan is convoluted and surreptitious and doesn't involve me speaking to my father to confess Mrs. Jaffe's true nature along with all our other secrets?"

I cock my head to the side and make that annoying, adult tsk-tsk sound. "Don't you know me better than that?" I ask. "It's time we resurrect our detective team, like when we uncovered Nadine's tattoo."

"Which is really some icky supernatural birthmark," Arla grimaces.

"Exactly," I reply. "But if you, me, and Archie work together, I have a way that we can help Louis learn the truth without ever having to say a word."

"If I didn't always have a headache," Arla says, "the sound of that would give me one."

"Sorry about the headaches," I reply.

Shaking her head, but furrowing her brow at the same time, Arla says, "It isn't always so bad, and it's better than the alternative. And my only alternative if I want to help my father see the light about his girlfriend is to join in, so you can count on me."

Excellent! That was easier than I thought. Or was it?

"On one condition," Arla adds.

"And that would be?" I ask.

"As long as my father doesn't find out I played any part in his emotional devastation."

Not a problem. "Your role in our mission will remain secret."

And once Archie finds out what the plan is and that he can't tell Napoleon in order to protect him from his mother's possible wrath after she's dumped, he's also on board. In fact, he's giddy at the prospect.

"We haven't even celebrated our six-month anniversary, and I'm already lying to my boyfriend!" he squeals. "I feel downright heterosexual!"

Admittedly we're all way more excited than we should be. A man's emotional fragility is at stake, and since Melinda has proven to be an MWM—Most Wanted Mom—we should not feel cavalier while crouched in the bushes in front of the Jaffe house. We should be serious and dour and nervous, but we're not. Jaded or justified, we're acting as if we're about to watch a movie and not a middle-aged man get his heart shredded into tiny little pieces and bleed all over whatever remains of his self-confidence.

"That's his car," Arla whispers.

Through a small hole in the thick bush, I can see Louis's car pull up in front of the house. When he gets out, Arla grabs my hand, because she notices that he's wearing the new sports jacket she bought him for Christmas, the one with the chocolate-brown suede elbow patches, the one he told her he'd only wear on special occasions. Tonight definitely counts as one, but not in the way that Louis imagines.

When Melinda opens the door, it's evident by her wardrobe that she has no idea tonight was supposed to be special. She's wearing a long, fluffy pink bathrobe. It's actually really cute and something Jess would covet, but not appropriate attire for a woman on a date. However, it is appropriate attire for a woman with the flu.

"Oh, Louis," Melinda says, her voice rough and nasally. "Didn't you get my text?"

Awkwardly, Louis steps back when Melinda doesn't immediately allow him entry into her home. The light from the half-moon is strong, and it shines on Louis, creating a soft halo around his head, not perfectly angelic, but as close as a man can get.

"No . . . I . . . " he stammers. "Are you sick?"

Physically? Probably not. *Mentally?* Absolutely!

"I have the flu," she says. "Came over me this morning. I'm so sorry, but I have to cancel our date."

Ever the gentleman, Louis has a substitute option for whatever out-on-the-town plans he had for them.

"That's all right. I can stay and make you my world-famous chicken soup," he says. "Well, it's Weeping Water famous anyway, a local favorite. I haven't posted the recipe online, though Arla keeps telling me I should make videos of me cooking and put them on the Internet. She thinks I could be 'Cop Chef' and have a huge following."

Arla pokes me in the arm and mouths the words "I really do," giving testimony to her father's rambling.

Unfortunately, Melinda isn't a foodie.

"I'm sorry, I'm not up for any company," she says, clutching the collar of her bathrobe.

Even though he doesn't have much experience dating, Louis is perceptive enough to deduce by her body language that there is no way he is getting lucky or anywhere near her tonight. The bad news is that we aren't either.

Our plan was to sneak into the house before they left for their date, swipe Melinda's cell phone, and text Winston to rush over for a rendezvous. When he showed up and saw Louis with her, we assumed nature would take its course, and Louis would discover that Melinda was two-timing him. Her sudden sickness hasn't just ruined Louis's evening; it's ruined ours too.

Then again, maybe not.

After Louis drives away I feel a flutter in my stomach; could be optimism, could be a premonition. Whatever it is it's enough to convince me the night will not be a total loss.

Stepping onto the front lawn, I look up and see that, despite the January chill, one of the upstairs windows is partially open. I walk closer to the curb, and the glow of the half-moon is strong enough for me to see into the room, just as Melinda enters. Naked and carrying two glasses and a bottle of wine. Why not let the cold in when Winston Lundgarden is already lying on your bed waiting to warm you up? The evening has become gross and fortuitous at the same time.

"This is perfect!" I whisper-shout to Arla and Archie after rejoining them in the bushes. When I tell them what I just saw, they don't share my opinion that I've witnessed perfection.

"How can this be perfect?" Archie asks. "The plan is ruined."

"And those two are going to have old people sex right above us," Arla adds.

Sometimes my Wolf Pack is as sharp as a flock of lost sheep.

"If we're grossed out by just thinking about it," I say, "how do you think Louis is going to feel when he sees the two of them in action?"

Arla's jaw drops, and her head shakes. "Dominy, you are a brilliant werewolf."

A truer compliment was never spoken.

"Archie," I say.

"Yes, ma'am."

Okay, so my Wolf Pack isn't always shrewd, but they are snarky, which is sometimes a lot more fun.

"Did you bring your lock-picking apparatus like I asked you to?"

"No, ma'am."

Now my Wolf Pack is just plain disobedient.

"Why not?"

"Because we don't need to break into their house when my boyfriend gave me a key."

Arla's jaw drops again. "Archie! Have you snuck in before to, you know, have your own private meetings?"

"I do not kiss and tell, Arla," Archie says, which actually makes us both sigh with relief. "But since we did a lot more than kiss . . ."

"Quiet!" I shout more than whisper. "Our time is limited, and we need to spend it exposing the truth behind Mrs. Jaffe's sex life and not Archie's."

Following Archie up to the front door, Arla whispers in his ear. "I want to hear every single detail about your Napolerendezvous when this is all over. Deal?"

"Deal." Archie grins.

Once inside the Jaffe living room, we keep the front door slightly ajar in case we have to make a quick escape, but we're not greeted by anyone, and the rest of the house is silent. I look at my fellow break-in artists and bring my finger up to my lips so they keep quiet. I'm reminded of the many times my father used this signal on me, but instead of feeling depressed, the reminder energizes me. I'm following in his footsteps and being proactive just like he always tried to be.

Using my enhanced hearing I can hear sounds coming from the basement. It's only the TV, but that means someone is down there. Upstairs I hear soft classical music, strings of some sort, maybe violins, but since I know very little about classical music that's as specific as I can get.

When I see a cell phone amid a pile of magazines on the coffee table, I'm certain it's Melinda's. Nadine and Napoleon are witches, but they're also teenagers, so I'm pretty certain they have their phones on them or nearby at all times. When I notice that the phone isn't password protected I'm certain; it has got to belong to an adult.

Deftly scrolling through her contacts, I find Louis's name and type in a text, then press Send. As expected, he immediately responds, and I reply. I place the phone down on the mountain of magazines and turn to Arla and Archie.

"Our work here is done."

"What did you tell him?" Arla asks.

Shaking my head, I motion toward the door just as I hear creaks in the house; sounds like someone's coming up from the basement. Whoever was walking up the stairs changed his or her mind, but our situation hasn't changed—this conversation needs to be held outside and pronto before we're caught.

Scrambling quietly outside, I make sure that the door is kept unlocked, and then we resume our hiding spots in the dense bushes lining the front of the house. The space is small and a bit more claustrophobic now that our adrenalin rush has shifted from excited to nervous, but we have no other choice; we have to stay. We set this plan into motion; we have to watch it unfold. And Arla wants to know exactly what my text is unfolding.

"Tell me, Dom," she demands. "What text did you send to my father?"

"Just three little words, actually three little numbers," I clarify. "911."

"You *are* a brilliant werewolf, Dom!" Archie whispers loudly. "Using cop-speak to lure a cop to the scene of a crime."

Louis is lured faster than we thought. This time when he pulls up in front of the house, he's followed by two squad cars. Oops, I hadn't expected that. I had thought his devastation would be private, known only by him, Melinda, and Winston; I never thought he'd have to share it with his entire squad. The way the color is peeling off of Arla's brown skin, I can tell she's thinking the same thing. I clasp her hand and hope that she understands public humiliation is a much better fate than what happened to the first Mr. Melinda Jaffe.

We huddle close together so we're not seen when Louis and several police officers race up the front steps, their heels hushed by the light coating of snow on the ground. After a slight hesitation during which Louis checked to see if the door was unlocked, they then disappear into the house.

Maybe we should leave now. Maybe this isn't something that we should witness. Maybe it's too late.

"Awkward!"

I don't recognize the voice floating down from the upstairs window. Must be one of the newer members of the police force. But a few seconds later I hear a more familiar voice on the front steps.

"I said can it, Gallegos!"

It's Detective Owenski. My father said he was one of the most loyal men on the force, too gruff and unmotivated to want to be anything more than the excellent cop he is. Seems like he's transferred the loyalty he once had for my father onto the new chief of police.

"But, O, come on," Gallegos retorts. "Catching his girl-friend in bed with another guy with his backup as an audience?! Can't get any more awkward than that."

"And if you say another word about it in front of the chief or behind his back," Owenski replies, "you'll be transferred so far away from this town, you'll need a map to get back. Understood?!"

From where I'm hiding I can see Gallegos's feet shuffle from side to side on the sidewalk; his body is fighting the urge to say more. Luckily for him, his good sense wins out, and he answers his superior the way his superior wants him to answer.

"Yes, sir."

"Good," Owenski grunts. "Now let's get out of here and give the chief some space."

Underneath the roar of their cars speeding away, I hear Arla mutter, "What have we done?"

Archie answers before I can speak the words. "We ruined your dad's reputation, but we just saved his life."

Actually, Louis might have needed some help securing his mortality, but he has no problem defending and upholding

his reputation. The more I get to know him, the more I realize what a good man he is.

"Save it, Melinda," he says.

I can't see his face—he's standing with his back to us—but
I can hear his voice clearly. It's like a slab of concrete with
only a slight crack in its exterior, wounded, but still strong.

"But, Louis," she replies, her throaty voice making the
most out of the foreign pronunciation of the name. "You
know how I feel about you, and I know how I make you feel.
Let's forget this ever happened and move on. I promise you
won't regret it."

I don't know why I'm disgusted; I don't know why I expected her to have more shame and not try once more to seduce Louis. I guess I thought she'd have a little more respect
for herself and her ex-boyfriend and be honest. Louis's self-
respect might have taken a hit tonight, but not enough for
him to misplace it altogether.

"I was already betrayed by a woman," he asserts. "I swore
to myself it would never happen again."

And then Louis proves he knows how to twist a knife as
easily as Melinda has proven she knows how to stab a man in
the back.

"Have fun with the old man," he shouts at her, just before
jumping into his car and driving off.

Melinda's about to have fun, but not at all the kind Louis
had imagined. "How's the view from the bushes?" she asks.

Snagged! Dammit, we didn't include getting caught as part
of our plan. Or an escape route. Listening to my instinct, I
come up with a plan that isn't necessarily original, but hopefully will work. "Run!" I scream.

Following my orders, Archie and Arla start to sprint away
from the house, but Arla stops short when she sees Luba appear out of what she thought was the night. A foot behind
her, Archie stops only when he crashes into Arla, causing

them both to fall onto the grass. Being so close to ugliness would make the bravest souls cower, so I understand when Archie and Arla grab onto each other to combine their strength. If I were alone, caught between evil and her daughter-in-law, I would fight back, confident that I would survive, come out scathed, but alive. However, standing behind my two friends, I'm not willing to take that chance. I can't risk their lives, so we'll just have to deal with the consequences of being caught behind enemy lines and think of another plan that will set us free before Luba and Melinda decide to teach us a permanent lesson for trespassing.

"Would you three come inside?" Melinda asks. "I hate giving the neighbors a free show."

I don't know what's more gross, staring at Luba's emaciated body or watching Winston wiggle back into his pants. The phrase "the clothes make the man" has never been truer. Beneath the fashionable exterior lies a body that's pasty and hairy and wobbly. I don't have a crush on Louis like Jess and Arla had on my dad, but I've seen him without his shirt on at pool parties and the annual Policeman's Picnic near the lake, and his body is superior to Winston's in every way. Even Louis's face, though bruised and banged up a bit, has charm and kindness and character; all Winston's face has going for it is that it's wrinkle-free. And it's not smooth enough to make a person forget the bumpy and overgrown landscape below his neck. How Melinda can look at him without his clothes on is beyond me.

When he's finally dressed, as if on cue, Nadine enters the room from the basement. I didn't hear her walk up the stairs, so she was either waiting patiently for Winston to finish dressing or she floated up the stairs. Now that I know a bit more about her personality, I'm sure it was the former. The girl's a sneak, not a showoff.

"I thought I overheard more masculine voices," she says. "Was there a man here?"

"Winston is as close to a man as we're going to get in this house," her mother scoffs. "But you should be kinder. He serves us very well."

He may serve, but he's not happy about it. His mask-like face morphs into an undeniable scowl that no restraint could hide. If Melinda and her daughter notice, they don't respond. Most likely scenario is that they do notice; they simply don't care. Winston, like Louis, is nothing more than a pawn, a plaything.

"Sorry, Mother," Nadine replies, without a trace of sorry in her voice. "But you know what I think of him and that old cadaver receptionist at The Retreat."

"Essie's done nothing to you!" I shout. I know I should keep my mouth shut, but I have to defend my friend. I never expect Winston to piggyback onto my defense.

"If it weren't for my special relationship with Essie," Winston brags, "there's no way we could have kept Luba's presence at The Retreat quiet."

"Calm down, Winston," Melinda says, stroking his cheek with her fingernail. "Essie has played an important role in keeping Mother's whereabouts secret."

"Yes, she has," Winston replies, shivering slightly.

"She has, however, outlived her purpose," Melinda adds.

"No!" Both Winston and I scream at the same time. He because Melinda's drawn blood and me because I can't believe I have more regard for human life when I'm covered in fur and devouring dead rabbits than these people have while walking upright. How could they have become this way? How could they have become so apathetic and malicious and bloodthirsty? And how can one man be so narcissistic?

"My face!" Winston cries. "I'm going to need stitches."

"Seriously, Winston," Melinda sighs. "Be a man."

"Enough tittle-tattle," Luba hisses. "How shall we handle the intruders?"

Walking past us, her rancid smell now overwhelming, Nadine acts as if we're not even there. She grabs one of the magazines from the pile and flops down onto the couch, whipping past page after page, not even taking in the pictures. Correction, she is a show-off; she wants us to think that she isn't interested in what just happened here.

"So did these three buffoons bust up your relationship with Scarface?" Nadine inquires.

"Shut up!"

I grab Arla's arm and roughly pull her back before she can back up her comment with a punch. Standing up for your parent is one thing; getting yourself killed over it is another.

The left side of Nadine's mouth rises just slightly, the only physical indication that she's heard Arla's order. However, the girl knows way more than she's indicating.

"Let me guess," she begins. "Wolf Pack channeled their inner Scooby Gang and played teen detectives to let Scarface know Mommie Dearest is cheating on him with Winnie the Pasty Pooh, and they did it by picking the lock to the front door so they could get in here—the same way they picked the lock to my locker to hide my clothes and get a peek at my birthmark."

"You knew we staged that?" I ask, honestly surprised.

Tossing the magazine onto the cushion next to her, Nadine crosses her legs and looks at me. Her smirk turns into a full-blown smile. "You people must be as dumb as Caleb to think I'm actually that stupid."

This time Arla has to hold me back so I don't attack Nadine. I don't utter a word, but just the fact that Nadine has once again insinuated that she and Caleb are close infuriates me. It's all I can do to restrain myself and not teach her a lesson in keeping her hands off of my boyfriend. As crazy as it sounds, sometimes I wish I could become a wolf at will!

"Jokes on you, Witchipoo!" Archie shouts. "We didn't pick the lock; Napoleon gave me the key!"

Love is not only blind; it's dumb too. How could Archie

possibly think offering up that tidbit would be a good thing? It's not good for us, and it's definitely not good for his boyfriend.

"Oh really," Melinda says. She raises her chin so the lamp-light catches her profile. It doesn't create a halo around her like the moonglow did to Louis, but instead it accentuates all her features. Unfortunately for me, it highlights her nose, the one characteristic she shares with my mother. It's delicate and soft and sophisticated, nothing like the voice that erupts from her throat. "Napoleon!!!"

"Yes, mother."

I don't know if Nap was watching us from the hallway, but he instantly appears. When I look at him, his guarded expression drops long enough for me to see his true nature. He might have been born with the mark of the devil, but he's not like the rest of his family. We might need to protect Archie from him, but it's not because of what he would do to Archie; it's because of what his family would do if they knew Nap would prefer to live a life with Archie, away from this witchcraft and this vile energy and the immoral actions, separate from this so-called triumvirate as they do the bidding of Orion, the hunter. Napoleon's only fault is that he's weak, and weakness in the presence of black magic is a fatal flaw.

"The pretty albino that you seem so enamored with has just told us a secret," his mother starts. "Did you give him the key to our home?"

Archie's back is like a sheet of metal, tense and flat and strong; he's willing his body to help Napoleon, hoping that his courage will somehow fly out of his body and latch onto his boyfriend's. But the silver mist that surrounds Nap's body deflects as well as it protects, and no matter how strong his attempt is, Archie can't reach him. Nap is on his own.

"Yes," Napoleon replies.

"Fool!!!"

Luba's voice is like that of the banshees I read about. It

penetrates the air and the earth and the skin and turns into something tangible. In response, Napoleon's hands shake so violently that the book he was holding falls to the ground. I shudder when I see it's the book about New York that Archie gave to him for Christmas. Archie told me that his dream was for him and Nap to escape to New York and live their lives there, lost in the crowded city, away from Nap's family's control. The only way Napoleon is going to escape his family's hold is if he fights back, and, looking at him quiver at the sound of his grandmother's voice, there's no way that's happening anytime soon.

"How many times do you expect to be forgiven?" Luba asks, breathing heavily. "How many times do you expect to be given another chance before you suffer the consequences of your stupidity?"

Still shaking, Napoleon manages a reply. "I'm sorry, Grandmother."

"Sorry isn't good enough any longer!" she bellows, holding on to the back of the couch for support. "I granted mercy once, but now you must help me make these . . . idiots . . . pay for thinking they are untouchable!"

Without uttering another word, Luba extends her hands, and they are immediately grabbed by Nadine and Napoleon. Knowing her place, Melinda steps back to observe. She has no preternatural power of her own, but she enjoys watching it put on display.

Quietly, the three of them start moving their lips in unison, and I'm reminded of the many times I saw Nadine and Napoleon do this in the past. How stupid could I have been? They weren't praying or stuttering nervously or even psychically communicating with one another; they were chanting, casting a spell, onto me or onto my surroundings. Like they're about to do right now.

Arla lets out a gasp, and Archie and I both turn to look out the window, at the mesmerizing, unnatural sight she's staring at. Somehow these three beings are controlling the moon, turning it from what it is into something new.

Inch by inch the first quarter moon spreads like the second hand of a clock, until its face is entirely covered in a shining silver light. They haven't shrouded the moon with the mist that emanates from the twins's bodies; they've altered the course of nature and transformed the first quarter moon into a full moon. And everybody in the room knows what happens to me when the full moon hangs in the sky.

"Get out!" I shriek as I begin to feel the burning sensation course throughout my body.

Arla's been in this situation before, and I don't blame her for not wanting to be this close to me again when I change shape. She grabs Archie's arm and yanks him with such force that he's airborne for a few seconds. But just as her hand grips the doorknob, I see Melinda knock them to the floor and lock the door shut. She isn't supernatural, but she is strong.

"Napoleon, help us!" Archie cries.

The desperation in his voice is met by silence. There's nothing Napoleon can do to protect him or Arla or me; all he can do is watch as the spirit that was supposed to remain buried within me for a little while longer rise to the surface to reclaim my body. Through my wolf eyes the room looks different; it's not like there's a plastic bag wrapped around my head, but my vision is distorted. I blink my eyes when I look at Luba, because she doesn't look real; she looks more like me than she does herself. She's crouched on all fours, her head twisting back and forth, her hands digging into the ground. I blink my eyes again and realize I must be hallucinating. The old woman must have fallen to the ground, exhausted from exerting such grand power.

With tears in his eyes, tears of shame and regret and fear, Archie grabs a lamp and flings it out the front window. Not even wasting time to clear the broken glass out of the way,

Arla scurries outside, followed closely by Archie. Nadine takes a step forward, but I get in front of her and growl loudly. I don't know if she sees something new in my eyes, perhaps the desire to rip her body to shreds at any cost, or if she too is exhausted from the exertion she's just made, but she backs off and lets my friends escape. Which doesn't make her mother happy.

"Get them!" Melinda shrieks. No one responds to her command, not her family or Winston, who's crouched in the corner of the room shaking.

"P-please d-don't hurt m-me," he stutters pathetically.

"Listen to yourself!" Nadine yells. "You sound like an old woman."

The comment makes her mother smile. Melinda's right eyebrow rises; she's thought of something, an idea that fills her with a great deal of joy.

"I know what will prevent this night from being a total failure," she says. "Someone needs to take care of Essie. Don't you agree, Mother?"

My growl is so loud it obliterates Luba's response. Not that anything they say will matter. All that matters is that I protect my friend. It's the only thought in my brain as I jump through the front window, barely avoiding the jagged pieces of glass still wedged into the window sill.

I don't know if Essie is still at The Retreat, but it's the only place I can think of to look. Not that I have any other choice, because I don't know where she lives. While racing over to the building I've visited so often as a girl, I realize this transformation is different. Perhaps it's because it's man-made, but I feel completely aware; it's as if the fur and claws and fangs are a costume that I'm wearing. The wolf spirit is with me, absolutely, but it's living inside my brain like it does when there isn't a full moon out. Maybe that's why my voice sounds more like a girl's scream when I see Essie's body on the ground next to her car.

The snow next to her fallen body is pink with her blood, and the stain is growing as her blood continues to flow out from her many wounds. Her head falls to the side, and her eyes meet mine. She isn't frightened; she isn't perplexed. She seems happy to see me.

"Dominy," she whispers.

She recognizes me; even like this, she knows who I am! I don't know if that's because the girl is so close to the wolf or because Essie is so close to death. It doesn't matter; at least Essie knows she isn't alone. And neither am I.

In the distance I see another wolf, nothing at all like me. This one is mangy with matted black fur, thick clumps of foam spilling out of its mouth, and bloodstained paws. This wolf, whether real or supernaturally created like me, is the thing that's killed Essie. The thing that doesn't want me anywhere near her.

"Melinda . . . she's your . . ."

"I know," I reply silently. "Melinda's my enemy."

A rough growl spews out of the other wolf's mouth, disturbing the cluster of foam and making some of it spit into the air. Droplets of spittle litter the ground at its restless paws. It wants to attack; it wants to kill again; it wants to let me know who's dominant. When I look into its eyes, I learn something else. They're not only black; they're lifeless and empty and bottomless. The darkness connects to its soul, so body and spirit are joined as one malicious entity. The wolf's eyes are just like Luba's.

Has she hijacked this animal? Has she taken control of this creature and made it do her bidding? Has she commanded it to kill Essie to procure a double victory? Because not only has Luba silenced Essie so she can't tell anyone about her or her twisted connection to Melinda and Winston, but Luba has also made it appear as if the town's serial killer has struck again.

Slowly the disgusting and malnourished beast walks toward me, one paw, then another, its gait not hesitant, but wary. It may not know exactly what I am, but it knows we're on opposing sides. There is absolutely no way this thing is violating Essie's body any further.

The black wolf stops suddenly and shakes its head, whipping it back and forth, left to right. Saliva flies out of its mouth and onto its dirty fur, its body reacting with shivers and spasms as if its own bodily fluid scorches its skin. The animal is definitely under duress and fighting Luba's control, but there's nothing I can do to save it; it's going to have to save itself.

A series of grunts lands on my ears like an axe slamming into a tree trunk. Bam, bam, bam! It's the sound of destruction, the kind of destruction that can only end in death. The wolf is heroically trying to escape, trying to break free, but when I see the black irises of its eyes grow until the white parts of the eyes are hidden, I know all attempts are futile. Luba has won.

One powerful lunge, and the black wolf is on top of me. Snout to snout I can smell her; I can smell Luba's dank odor, and I have to turn my face to the side because I don't want my body to be polluted. At the same time I push against the wolf's chest with my front paws, and I easily sever our bond. It's clear why Luba's chosen this animal to possess; it isn't strong. I don't know if it's diseased, but it's weak and therefore it was easy prey. For both Luba and for me.

Snarling viciously, but not moving, the black wolf thinks it can intimidate me without having to engage in any more physical contact. Think again!

Even though I can't switch places with the wolf spirit because the full moon isn't real and the wolf spirit is still resting, hiding deep within me, I have enough of its power and instinct and primitive behavior to act on my own. I make no sound as I leap through the air, and, before the black wolf can move, my paw has slashed through its left shoulder, ripping deep into its flesh, my nails scraping against brittle bone.

Its howl is pitiable. And when it peters out there is silence. The animals that live under the dark canopy of night have no response to such a pathetic display. There's no place for such a creature in their world, and so its cry is ignored.

Unlike Essie's death. Her spirit, clean and shiny and free, rises up from her battered body and floats higher and higher until it moves beyond my vision. My silent prayer sounds like a whimper as I beg God to allow Essie the chance to be greeted by her loved ones in heaven. Ashamed, I bow my head and poke at the ground with my snout, because I'm fully aware that my spiritual awareness is much stronger as a wolf than it ever was as a human. Perhaps man isn't the only creature to be molded in God's image.

When I look up, I see that the parking lot is empty. The rabid wolf is gone. And why not? It's done Luba's bidding, and it knows it's no match for me, so why hang around any longer?

I sit next to Essie's body for quite some time, my tears falling into the puddle of her blood. As I lie underneath the glow of the artificial moon, I cling to the blissful image of her spirit as it began the next phase of its journey. It was calm and focused and accepting of its fate.

But now, as the scent of Essie's rotting body poisons the air, all I can think of is that because of me someone else has been brutally murdered.

Chapter 22

Essie's dead face is everywhere. In my mind, in my memory, in this week's edition of the *Three W*.

Louis throws the paper onto the kitchen table, and I see that my friend has made the front page. I suppress a satisfied smile because looking at her photo I know that she has finally achieved the kind of notoriety she always admired in others. Our local newspaper might not be as famous as Essie's beloved national tabloids, the ones she would read incessantly while she was supposed to be working, but the *Three W* has made Essie a celebrity to at least one small community. And while it's obvious that Essie didn't have photo approval, she would have been pleased with the image Lars Svenson chose to use; she looks beautiful.

Despite looking dowdy and rundown and depressed for so many years, Essie was a good person. When we first began our family outings to The Retreat, she went out of her way to be kind to me and to Barnaby. She kept a stash of candy for us in the bottom drawer of her desk, and she would stockpile small gifts like activity books and Colorforms that she would give to us, her way of softening the blow so our visit wasn't only about spending time with our comatose mother. It was also about spending time with Aunt Essie.

I'm not sure when things changed, but at some point Aunt Essie became the crotchety old lady sitting behind the front desk. The evolution, like most, was probably a slow one, but then again, maybe her life altered as quickly and as drastically as mine did. Maybe it was the death of her husband that changed her. Or it could've been something else equally tragic and devastating. The sad truth is I'll never know, because I didn't pay attention when I was younger and I didn't care enough to ask when I got older.

What I do know is that certain events and people in Essie's life transformed her from an engaged, empathetic woman into a detached and apathetic person. A person who didn't care very much about anything or anyone, especially not herself. It was only recently that she decided to peek out from behind her magazines to take the first tentative steps and start living again. Only to be struck down as if she had violated some cosmic rule. It's as if the stars had gotten together to have a celestial powwow and decided to teach Essie a lesson, make her pay for daring to want more out of life. Well, maybe not all the stars, just the three that make up the constellation Orion.

The entire Jaffe clan caused Essie's death. Luba, Melinda, and Nadine wanted her out of the way because she knew too much about them, and Napoleon didn't do anything to protect her. Exactly how much damaging info Essie had, I can't be sure. For certain Essie knew Winston was breaking the rules to keep Luba a resident of The Retreat and that he was two-timing Essie by dating Melinda. There's the possibility that Essie could have stumbled upon more of their secrets, and, even if she didn't fully grasp them, even if she didn't understand how deadly these people were, Essie had become an inconvenient woman. And the best way to make an inconvenient woman convenient is to silence her. Which is exactly what Luba did.

As much as it pains me, I have to hand it to her; Psycho Squaw chose the best way to kill Essie, a way that bends the spotlight of suspicion away from her and her troop and at the same time feeds into the fears of the townspeople. She's made it appear as if the serial killer has struck again to commit murder number four. And playing right into her plan, Lars Svenson and even Louis have taken the bait.

In bold block letters right above Essie's smiling photo, in all caps for maximum emphasis, is the headline: Full Moon Killer Strikes Again. It's eye-catching and frightening and sure to make this issue a sellout. Unfortunately, only a select few know that it's wrong.

"Cool name!" Barnaby squeals. "Did you come up with it?"

"No."

Louis's one-word answer speaks volumes about his current mental state. It's filled with anger and determination and courage. The reappearance of this alleged serial killer has forced him to remember who he is in this town and what role he plays. He's no longer second fiddle; he's no longer the fool behind the king's badge. It's time for him to step out from behind the blinding light of my father's shadow and prove to everyone, including himself, that he deserves to be the policeman in charge.

"Starting tonight I'm revising the town curfew to include everyone. No one's allowed out after dark," he announces. "These killings have got to stop!"

Staring at Essie's picture, Louis looks almost invulnerable. Standing next to the kitchen counter, he's caught directly inside a beam of sunlight that's streaming through the window; it's ignoring the rest of us and focusing solely on him. The sunlight softens his face like natural airbrushing, so he looks younger and stronger and braver. The sunlight has revealed his true essence like the photo in the *Three W* has captured

Essie's true nature. Despite Luba's machinations it's as if small pieces of the town are wresting free from her magic. But it seems there are others who are still spellbound.

"Guess the full moon really does have the power to kill," Barnaby proclaims.

"There wasn't a full moon last night," Louis replies.

"According to Lars's article the police station received twenty-three phone calls last night from people saying that they had just witnessed a first quarter moon suddenly turn into a full moon," Barnaby conveys.

Flipping through pages of the *Three W* to continue reading the cover story, Arla adds, "An hour-long full moon? Impossible."

I'm adding actress to Arla's already impressive resume, because she makes her comment with such natural conviction, I almost believe that it's true. Even though I know otherwise. Even though I saw with my own eyes how Luba and Nadine and Napoleon joined forces to thwart Mother Nature and create an unnatural phenomenon.

"Eyewitnesses are notoriously untrustworthy," Louis states. "I'm sure it was just an illusion."

"That's a lot of untrustworthy eyewitnesses," Barnaby retorts.

Tossing the paper onto the kitchen table with much less force than her father did earlier, Arla shrugs her shoulders and crosses her arms; it's her best impersonation of an unconvinced reader. "Just because it's in print doesn't make it true," she says. "Lars is more interested in selling papers than he is in telling the truth."

Surprisingly, Barnaby agrees with her.

"Which is why he didn't print the whole story?" he relays.

"What do you mean?" Louis demands.

"There was another incident," my brother replies. "Involving Luba."

Louis pulls the kitchen chair out from underneath the

table so roughly that the metal legs of the chair squeak loudly against the linoleum floor. He sits down, leans forward, and places his hand on top of Barnaby's. It's more a gesture of power than compassion; he wants to know what information Barnaby has, and he wants Barnaby to know he isn't leaving this table until he gets it. My brother turns out to be a cooperative witness and immediately confesses all that he knows.

"Essie wasn't the only victim last night," he says. "Luba was attacked too."

"Melinda's mother-in-law?" Louis asks. "How do you know her?"

Luckily the two of them are so focused on each other and their conversation that they don't see me and Arla desperately trying not to freak out at the mention of Psycho Squaw's birth name inside our house.

"She's the lady at The Retreat," Barnaby begins to explain. "The one I visit as part of the school's volunteer program."

I can't remain quiet any longer; I have to know what Barnaby's talking about, even more so than Louis does. "Where was she attacked?" I ask. "At The Retreat, where Essie was found?"

Slowly Barnaby turns to face me, as if he's just now realizing I'm in the room. His eyes are cold, and his lips form the hint of a smile. He looks nothing like he did at Christmas. He's back to the way he was after my father's death, and I have absolutely no idea what's going on inside my brother's head. When he speaks, I realize I have absolutely no idea what happened last night either.

"She was outside The Retreat looking at the stars like she always does. She's sort of an amateur astrologist; she can tell you anything about yourself by looking at the constellations." He beams. "She can even predict the future by how the stars are aligned and their positions in the sky."

Louis's hand presses down a bit harder onto Barnaby's,

not enough to cause pain, but to remind him that our questions still remain unanswered.

"What happened to this Luba last night, Barnaby?" Louis asks.

"It was dark so she couldn't tell if she was attacked by somebody with a knife," he replies. "Or by a wolf."

Did Barnaby just look at me? I'm so flustered I can't speak. So Arla does.

"If she really was attacked, why didn't she report it to the police?" she inquires.

A gray cloud falls over my brother's face, and his blue eyes lose their likeness to my father's and suddenly become darker. I don't know if I should reach out and slap my brother across the face or wrap my arms around him and hold him tight. Sadly, I fear that either action will cause my brother to slip even farther away from me.

"Luba doesn't trust the police, not the white man police anyway," he says. His voice is cold and harsh and unrecognizable. The words he's speaking have been told to him. They're not his own; they're Luba's. "No offense, Louis, but remember she's Native American Indian and, well, the white man has done certain things to them that don't necessarily warrant their trust."

"Yeah, we've encountered that problem for years," Louis replies in standard cop-talk. "But if she was attacked, she should've at least gone to the hospital."

"Um, she kinda lives in a hospital," Barnaby snarkily replies.

As quickly as the darkness overtook him, it's gone. Am I imagining things? Am I giving Luba too much credit? I mean, Barnaby is fifteen. Mood swings and nasty comebacks come with the territory. All of that is forgotten when Barnaby offers more details about Luba's attack. What he says changes everything.

"She'll be fine," he announces. "Just has a huge gash in her arm."

I see my red paw strike the air and slice open the black wolf's left shoulder.

"Which arm?" I demand.

Scrunching up his face, now more preoccupied with playing a game on his cell phone than offering details, Barnaby mumbles, "Dunno, what's it matter anyway?"

"Tell me!"

I know I shouldn't be shouting. I know I shouldn't be making a scene or causing Louis to look at me the way he's looking at me right now, like he doesn't understand who I am or a single word I'm saying, but I have to know. I have to know if my suspicion is correct.

"It was her left arm, just underneath her shoulder, satisfied?" Barnaby replies.

Luba was the black wolf! She killed Essie! But how is that possible? She cannot be a werewolf too; we cannot be the same! Unable to stop my body from shaking, I get up from the table, fully aware that I'm making an idiot out of myself.

"Dominy, are you all right?"

Louis's voice is kind, but concerned. He isn't stupid—he's a detective for God's sake; he knows when people are lying; he's been trained for these types of situations. *Get it together, Dominy, or else you're going to have to confess to the whole truth, and that will definitely get you thrown into a padded cell or the electric chair.* I take a deep breath and do what I always do when trapped—sprinkle the truth with a little lie.

"Sorry, Louis. I don't like Luba," I reply. "I don't trust her, and I don't approve of her being Barnaby's buddy."

Actually that's the complete truth without any lie-sprinkling whatsoever.

"You don't get to approve my life," Barnaby snipes, not even bothering to look up from his phone. Until Louis rips it out of his hands.

"No, but I do," he declares.

The gray cloud returns, turning Barnaby's face and voice to stone. "Give me back my phone," he demands.

"No," Louis snaps back. "And don't talk to me in that tone of voice either."

Watching my brother fidget in his chair, I can tell that he wants to answer back. He wants to make some snotty, sarcastic comment, but he's got enough sense to keep quiet. He's pushed Louis, and he knows it. Our guardian will stand for a lot. He understands that all three of us—Barnaby, Arla, and I—are going through a transition. Sometimes it's fluid: other times it's difficult. Today is definitely a difficult day. But before it becomes memorable, out-of-hand difficult, Louis does what he rarely has done before; he reminds us who is the parent.

"You're living under my roof now, so I'm not asking for your respect; I'm demanding it," he says, his voice quiet, but firm. "Do you understand me?"

The cloud hasn't lifted entirely, but Barnaby knows when he's beaten. "Yes."

"You watch your mouth when you speak to me, and I don't want you doing any more volunteering if it involves Luba," Louis adds. "You understand that too?"

Barnaby nods his head briskly. "I understand."

I don't know if he's agreeing because he knows that's what Louis wants to hear, because he knows he was wrong, or because he's trying to break free from Luba's grip. How powerful is that woman? I mean she looks so frail and feeble, and yet she continues to amaze me. Can she really have my brother under some hypnotic hold?

And maybe the curse wasn't random after all; maybe the reason Luba turned me into a werewolf is because she didn't want to be one of a kind and was craving company? The more I learn about this woman, the more complicated she becomes. Same goes for her granddaughter.

"I don't know which photo I prefer," Nadine says. "Essie before or Essie after."

Time spent in study hall is not meant to be used for 'show and tell', but that's exactly what Nadine is doing. When she holds up the two images, she actually makes me flinch. I've seen Essie's face on the cover of the *Three W*; that's old news so to speak. But I have not seen the picture from her autopsy report. I don't even ask Nadine how she got the report. It doesn't matter; it isn't going to change the data. Or the photo.

Yes, I was at Essie's side when she died, but I wasn't myself; I was a wolf, and my vision was being filtered. Now the image is crystal clear, and I can see exactly what Essie's body looked like moments before she left this earth. She looks just like Jess did and my father, and I have to swallow hard to avoid throwing up my lunch on the table.

So much of Essie's face is covered in streaks of dried blood. Her nose is hanging loose to one side, her left earlobe is missing, and there's a deep gouge over her left eye. No wonder her spirit left her body so easily; who would want to remain in such a useless host?

"Which one do you like, Dom?" Nadine asks. "Intact or mutilated?"

Sitting across from me, Nadine lifts one picture and then the other as if she has to get ready for a date and she's asking me to decide between two dresses. I'm surrounded by chatter, nonsensical murmurings, and I wish I could switch places with anyone else in this room. But that would make me as vile as Nadine, because I would be forcing someone to live my life and deal with all the pain and insanity and heartache that's been thrown at me like a downpour, making me feel like I'm drowning and I'm never, ever going to get dry.

In the corner of the room I see Gwen half-studying, half-chatting with The Worm. She catches me looking at her, and her face lights up. She waves at me, all smiles, and when I lift my arm to wave back it feels like a cement block. Why is it getting so hard to be normal? Why is it becoming so hard to do the things I used to do?

"C'mon, Dom, which one?"

Ignore her, Dominy. No need to get detention over a stupid comment.

No! It's more than just a comment; it's more than just a stupid joke. It's someone's life. It's my friend's life! And Nadine has absolutely no remorse over what her grandmother has done, over what she helped her do.

"Why are you doing this, Nadine?" I ask.

Most of the students in study hall are doing anything other than studying, so while the conversation isn't as loud and as animated as it is during lunch, it's noisy enough that we can't be easily overheard. And even if we are, who's going to believe the real story, that a werewolf is chatting with a witch, trying to find out her motivation. Nadine doesn't answer; she doesn't reveal her intentions. She just tilts her head a bit so her face looks lopsided.

"And don't tell me it's because your grandmother's forced you to do all these things," I say.

Nadine straightens her head and juts out her chin; it's the picture of defiance. "My grandmother hasn't forced me to do anything," she replies. "I feel blessed to have been born with such power. I wouldn't change it for anything."

"You could change how you use it," I remind her.

Slowly, Nadine looks at me as if I still can't comprehend first-grade English. "You still have no idea who you're dealing with, do you?" Nadine asks. "We are descendants of Orion . . . the *Hunter*. To us, the rest of the world is prey, waiting to be captured or destroyed. The more we conquer, the more powerful we become. And you've been my prey for longer than you can imagine."

I can feel my nails digging into the palms of my hands. I'm forcing my body to remain rigid and my voice to remain calm. "I know what you've done to me," I say.

"Not everything," she says, like a mischievous imp.

She killed my father! What else could she possibly have done?

"Remember the Lorazepam I gave you in the syringe to knock you out?" she asks. "It was really a placebo, completely harmless."

As despicable as Nadine sounds, she's fascinating. "You let me transform in front of my friends when you knew I could easily kill them?" I ask, stunned by her callous nature.

"Of course I did," she replies, nodding her head, all smiles. "We had to test the limits of the wolf's strength. He's a strong one, I have to say, and I'm surprised no one died that night. Though Arla did get one heckuva scar."

She's barren and hollow and hateful. Maybe she has been brainwashed since she was a little girl; maybe she was born that way. Whatever the reason, I honestly don't think there's any hope for her. Or her artistic talent.

"Your drawing sucks."

Confused, Nadine turns the newspaper around so she can peer at the front page. It takes her a moment to see the drawings along the border of the article; she probably doodled them absentmindedly and forgot about them. I can't.

"You got the color of the full moon right," I say. "But the wolf is all wrong."

Looking at the drawing more closely, as if it were a piece of fine art, Nadine purses her lips and shakes her head. "I disagree," she replies. "That's what you look like when you're killing people."

I remember Caleb's instruction—act thoughtfully. Placing my arms on the desk in one horizontal line, one hand on top of the other, I lean forward and face Nadine, my red hair, unruly and a mass of curls, hanging in the space between us.

She doesn't move back; she allows her personal space to be violated, but I can tell that the close proximity to me is making her uncomfortable. Good.

"The wolf shouldn't be a pretty redhead," I whisper. "It should be black and rotting and old. Like your grandma."

Involuntarily, Nadine starts to crumple up the paper in her fist. Obviously, I wasn't supposed to know about Luba's involvement or her ability to become a wolf. Ah well, two more secrets that are no longer secret.

"How did you find that out?" Nadine asks.

Her voice is so fragile she almost stutters. She sounds almost human.

"Just how stupid do you think *I* am?"

Sometimes people react mysteriously. I truthfully didn't think that what I said was so terrible, but before I know it Nadine leans across the table, grabs my throat, and starts choking me.

Immediately, my hands fly up to my neck, and I easily pry her off of me. She must be so angry with me that she forgot to use her magic, so when she is flung back in her chair and has to grasp at the desk to stop from toppling over, she's nothing but a girl trying not to fall on the floor. When I look at her, however, I don't see a girl. I see an enemy.

Leaping over the desk I feel like a wolf in flight, my body extended, and I can see the flash of fear take over Nadine's eyes. It only lasts a second, but it lasts long enough for me to know that despite all her bravado, despite her lack of morals, I can defeat her.

"Get off of me!" she wails.

I know there's a crowd around us; I can sense them and smell them and hear them, but it doesn't make me stop. Watch me if you want, watch what I can do!

My lips hiss into her ear when I speak, and I can feel saliva growing in my throat and dripping out of the sides of my mouth.

"You will *not* defeat me!"

Underneath me, Nadine's clawing and pushing and pulling become more frantic. On her own, without her brother and her grandmother, she's nothing; she's useless. Against one opponent she might have some success, but against two—the wolf and me—she's bound to fail. Until she gets reinforcement.

"Get off of her, you crazy bi...!"

The element of surprise on her side, Rayna Delgado is able to push me off of Nadine with one unexpected shove. By the time I get up, Mr. Dice, the study hall monitor, is already standing in between Nadine and me. There's nothing else I can do unless I want to start an all-out brawl with the shoo-in for teacher of the year. Willing myself to calm down, suppressing both my own anger and the wolf's primal instinct, I finally feel in control. Just in time to hear Mr. Dice sentence both of us to detention.

"I think you should rethink that, Mr. Dice."

Although he's a new teacher, he's not accustomed to being contradicted so openly by a student. Especially one as unstudious as Rayna.

"Would you care to explain that comment, Miss Delgado?"

"Look at her," she says, waving her arm up and down like she's one of those vapid spokesmodels on a game show and Nadine is the grand prize. "She's hurt. She needs to see Nurse Nelson."

She isn't hurt. If I had wanted to hurt her I could have. She's just out of shape, so she's winded. Can't he see that?

"Take her directly to the nurse," he replies. "I'll check in on you in a few minutes."

Okay, he either can't see it or he's just taking the cautious route.

It's odd that Rayna came to Nadine's defense. I know that they've been hanging out together, but I didn't think they were friends. Maybe it's the result of magic, or maybe Rayna has just been looking for an opportunity to strike out against me ever since our awkward moment at the Wyatt house. I don't have time to dwell on it, because Mr. Dice grabs me by the arm, my own private escort to Dumbleavy's office.

We walk down the hall silently, the students parting like they're the Red Sea and Mr. Dice is playing Moses in some Japanese production of the Bible story, but when we get to the end of the hall we make a right instead of a left. In other words, we're walking in the opposite direction of the principal's office.

"Uh, Mr. Dice, where are we going?" I ask.

When he doesn't respond I'm not sure if I should be concerned or curious.

"Mr. Dice . . ."

"Keep walking."

The last classroom on the left is not actually a classroom; it's the rehearsal space for the drama club. During the school day it's usually not in use unless kids are rehearsing for *Grease*, this year's musical, and the cast needs to run lines or go over some choreography in private. Why is Mr. Dice taking me to an isolated part of the school? Why did he lie to me and to everyone in study hall when he said he was taking me to the principal's office? And why am I not running away from him?

Because I see a yellow light spilling out from underneath the door. Jess is waiting for me. Turns out she's waiting for us both.

Before the door closes behind us, I notice something different. Jess isn't floating in the air; she isn't sitting cross-legged and hovering a few inches above a desk; she's kneeling on the floor, and when we enter she bows.

"Hello, Masutā," she says.

I cover my eyes because the golden light is brighter and more glorious than ever before, because the light has been doubled. The light isn't just coming from Jess; it's coming from Mr. Dice as well.

"Jess, haven't I told you before that you don't have to bow in my presence?" Mr. Dice asks this in the same tone of voice he would use if he were asking a student to stop chewing gum in class.

"Yes, Masutā," Jess replies, though she remains kneeling and bent over so her forehead touches the floor.

"So you can get up," he informs her.

"Yes, Masutā."

Finally Jess stands up, and she looks even more beautiful than the last time I saw her if that's possible. Her light is radiant.

"And please stop calling me master," Mr. Dice asks, a trace of weariness creeping into his voice.

"Yes, Masutā," Jess replies. "I mean, sir."

Daisuke Takamoto, the man we call Mr. Dice, Two W's newest teacher, isn't a teacher or a mister after all. If he isn't either of those things, what exactly is he?

"How many times do I have to tell you, Jess," Mr. Dice says, circles of golden sunshine pouring out of his mouth. "I am not your master; I'm your mentor."

And the blank is filled in.

"Oh my God!" I cry. "So the Hello Kitty keychain wasn't your daughter's; it was a clue!"

"Dom!" Jess cries back. "Show some respect when you're in the presence of a Sarutahiko Okami and use your gentle voice!"

"Excuse me! Would that yelling be *your* gentle voice?!" I snipe. "A Saru-what?"

It looks like Mr. Dice is smiling, but I'm squinting from the sunshine overload so I can't really be sure.

"Dominy," Mr. Dice or whatever his name is replies, "I'm Jess's guardian."

Guardian, mentor, master, whatever he is, I'm glad to

know for certain that Jess isn't alone in her realm. Now Mr. Dice looks just like Jess, dripping in honey gold, sunlight pouring out of every pore, but there seems to be something else mixed in, a serenity, a calmness that Jess doesn't yet possess.

"Is an Okami like an Omikami?" I ask, trying to make sense of this new knowledge.

"The simple answer is that yes, they're related," Dice explains. "My spirit is more earthbound, while Jess is part of the celestial universe."

"That was the simple answer?" I ask incredulously.

Maybe it is that simple because I can see them both clearly now without squinting. Jess is a bit more relaxed and standing in the middle of the black box stage where she spent many hours going over her lines and practicing scenes as president of Broadway Bound. The glare of the light is still strong, so it's hard to see her expression, but I'm guessing that there's a part of her that wishes she were still human so she could put on another show for an actual audience, unlike the show she's putting on right now.

A few feet away Mr. Dice is leaning against the wall, watching her with what I can only describe as fatherly pride. I guess just because you're a supernatural deity doesn't mean you know everything; there's always more to learn.

"So you came here to help Jess find her way?" I ask.

"I'm here to help both of you," he replies.

Hope and excitement race through my body, intertwining to create a new feeling. Could this be the answer I've been looking for? Could this be the key to unlocking this curse?

"No."

I'm not sure who answered, Jess or Mr. Dice, but I know what *no* means.

"Then how are you going to help me if you can't break this curse?"

There's way more attitude in my voice then I intended, but

I can't help myself. Essie's death is still weighing on me. She's the latest person to die because of me, because she got caught in the crossfire of this feud between Luba and me, so I'm a little testy.

"The world is filled with so much mystery, Dominy," Mr. Dice explains. "Most of it's good, but some of it's bad."

"Yeah, tell me about it," I reply.

Mr. Dice smiles at my sarcasm; Jess doesn't.

"You've been handed more bad than good lately," he says. "So I'm here to balance out the scales."

Taking a deep breath I realize that it would be foolish not to accept such otherworldly help or to piss off a sun god. "Thank you."

"So while I'm here trying to show this one the ropes . . ."

"*This one* would be me," Jess interjects.

"Yeah, I got that, Jess," I say.

"I'll try to help you as best I can," Mr. Dice replies.

"But you can't break this curse, can you?" I ask.

"No, I can't," he answers. "But I know someone who can."

What?! When will these super-powerful beings realize that the best way to get our attention is to give us the information we crave immediately?! Enough with the hocus pocus and the fancy light show, I mean, that looks spectacular, but I want facts. If he knows who can break this curse, if he knows where I can find this great and powerful Oz, then tell me.

"Who?!" I cry. "Who can break it?"

"You can."

Chapter 23

"Me? That's what you expect me to believe?"

I don't care if I'm being disrespectful to an elder and in this case probably an elder to the zillionth power, but does Mr. Dice—or is it Okamidice?—really expect me to believe that I have the power to break this curse? He might be like an almighty, all-powerful wizard, but this *isn't* Oz and I'm not Dorothy and I can't just click the heels of my stolen ruby-reds to travel through time and space to break free of the werewolf's clutches. It's like Arla's interpretation of the fairy tale is coming true. Is this wizard as passive-aggressive as Glinda? No, I refuse to believe that it's always been that easy, and I also refuse to allow him to drop a bombshell of Okamian proportions and let him get away with it.

"If I can break this curse, then break it down for me," I demand. "Show me how I can do it, and don't slip into teacher mode and make it as complicated as all those algebra equations you teach us."

"I can't show you," he replies.

"Because you're a liar!"

"Dominy!" Jess cries. "You're like standing at the corner

of Blasphemy Boulevard and Sacrilege Street. Whichever way you turn you're still about to enter the danger zone."

"Where the hell do you think I've been living for the past year, Jess?" I scream, at full volume, not even caring if I attract a crowd including Dumbleavy. Let him see who he's hired to teach his impressionable students. "I've been forced to relocate to the danger zone, so if Dice here can help me move out, I'd like to know about it now and in full detail!"

"I understand your frustration, Dominy," Mr. Dice says, his voice a stark contrast to my yelling. "But as Jess has already explained to you, beings such as ourselves are limited."

Again! How many times do I have to hear about the limitations of the Omikami?! "What's the purpose of such great power if you can't use it?!" I bellow.

"Our power may be great, Dom," Jess says. "But there's a higher power above us and another power above that and probably some more layers that I don't even know about yet, and each power has incredible abilities that you can't even imagine. They're the ones who call all the shots, not us. Did I not already explain to you about balance?"

Why is she asking me questions? Why isn't she answering mine?

"Remember?" Jess asks.

Think, think back. . . . Yes, yes, I remember what Jess said about balance. The world needs to be filled with opposites; it needs to be filled with both good and evil, or else it'll tilt or freefall or career out of the solar system into some other galaxy, and we'll all crash and burn. Like that would be any worse than what I'm going through!

"Yeah, balance must be maintained," I spit.

"That's right," Mr. Dice replies. "So if a higher power gives all of its knowledge and secrets to a student, then how will that student learn? How will that student complete his or her own journey?"

"If the *her* you're referring to is me," I say, "then it means

I'll be able to complete my journey a whole lot faster than I'm doing right now."

"And you will have learned nothing!" Jess screams, clearly forgetting her mandate about speaking in a gentle voice. "And you will bring nothing with you to the next level, the higher level, except your same bad attitude!"

"I've *earned* the right to have a bad attitude, Jess!"

"AND SO HAVE I!!!"

When Jess screams I stumble backward and don't stop until my back hits the wall. Her cry is filled with such passion and intensity and anger that her words turn into flames that shoot out of her, making her look like a sun-drenched dragon. The flames—a multitude of yellows doused with a hint of orange and even red—flicker wildly until they disappear. They look so real I wasn't taking the chance that they were just an illusion, just the typical byproduct, the expected trail of sunshine when Jess speaks or waves her arms or floats around. This display of power wasn't benign; it was meant to warn. And remind me that I've been acting like a selfish child. The one big difference between me and Jess is that I'm the one who's still alive.

"I'm sorry," I say. "To both of you. I know none of the questions I'm asking come with easy answers, it's just that . . ."

"The easy way out can also be the most attractive," Mr. Dice says.

"Exactly."

"Well, Dominy, trust me when I tell you," he says, "attractive isn't always best."

One glance at Jess and I know her anger is gone. And I know that she doesn't agree with Mr. Dice. Extraterrestrial Guidance Counselor or not, there is no way that she will believe what he just said is a universal truth. I may be separated from Jess by some giant dimensional divide, she may be physically altered, but some things never change. Jess will always be just a little bit superficial.

"Sometimes he can get carried away," Jess whispers.

The small room is suddenly filled with Mr. Dice's laughter, which spreads out like a cool breeze, each note dancing in the air like a golden snowflake. I was wrong; there isn't an ounce of darkness on him or in him. He meant what he said: He's here to help. And he's a man of his word.

"There are some amazing things that we can do," he says. "Things that I'm teaching Jess."

When an Okami uses a word like *amazing* to describe his talents, I take notice; he must have quite an impressive list of tricks up his sleeve. "Like what?"

"Shall we, Jess?"

Mr. Dice holds out his hand, and Jess floats toward him, resting only when her hand is firmly in his. "Of course," she replies. "C'mon, Dom. Don't be afraid."

But I am. I've been in this position before. I've given up my power to allow others free rein to make me travel to the past and bear witness to memories that should have remained unseen. I can't go through that again.

"I don't want to take a trip to the past," I state.

"No, we're not taking you on a journey to the past," Mr. Dice says. "Or the future."

"Then where are we going?" I ask.

"Inside your brain."

The moment I felt Jess's and Mr. Dice's hands in mine we were transported through a tunnel of sunshine. The trip took only a few seconds, but I wished it had lasted longer. I felt like I was flying in the sunlit sky, not surrounded by thick globs of silver fluid, and most important I felt like I was leading the way. I wasn't being pulled someplace I didn't want to go, someplace from which I knew I would only have to make the return trip with an even more damaged mind. Now that we've landed, I'm not sure the destination is any different than it was during the trip I took with the Psycho Family, despite the improved travel accommodations.

I'm standing in between Jess and Mr. Dice behind a high row of thick bushes, which is the only thing that separates us from an open field. I hear a rustling in the trees on the other side of the clearing that stops only when the noisemaker makes itself visible. It's a deer.

She walks calmly into the center of the field, knowing full well that she's on display, knowing full well that she's walking onto a sacrificial altar, walking to her death. But she isn't scared; she knows her fate is to die within the next few seconds, when my father pulls the trigger.

"Daddy!"

Jess and Mr. Dice are now gone and in their place, my father is standing next to me, looking like the adult he was when he died, but carrying the gun he used to kill as a teenager.

"Watch this," he says.

Raising his rifle he places the long, thin barrel in between some branches and rests the butt on his shoulder. He tilts his head slightly so his cheek presses against the rifle's body, and without looking he inserts his finger into the trigger hole. He slides his thumb alongside the trigger guard as he waits for just the right moment to pull his finger back and set into motion my destiny.

Why are they showing me this? I thought they said we weren't going to the past but inside my brain? This is not my memory; it was an unwanted gift! I don't want to remember this. I don't want to see any of this!

"Patience, Dominy."

My father's voice is soft, and he's peering at me from over the belly of the rifle like he's looking at me from the other side of my crib. Why would he want me to see this? Why would he want me to see him kill? Well, I don't care what he wants. I'm not looking!

When I hear the rifle explode, I close my eyes. Just to make sure I can't see anything at all, I cover my eyes with my hands. They want to play games; well, I can play games too!

The only problem is that they're more skilled than I am when it comes to game playing.

I wait for as long as I can, until I know for sure that the deer has been killed, and then I open my eyes. I was wrong. The deer is still standing stoically as the bullet continues to split the air in slow motion. Before I can turn away, the bullet returns to maximum speed and rips through the deer's chest. I can see the bullet travel through her body like a wave, the skin rippling up and down and up and down until the bullet reaches the poor animal's leg and flies out of its body, bringing with it a spray of blood. Like someone filled a sprinkler with red paint.

"No!"

My scream is useless; it can't change anything. It's also pointless. The deer is unharmed. Unharmed? I saw her get shot.

"Keep watching," Jess instructs.

"And remember, Dominy, every curse has many layers," Mr. Dice says.

"Like one of those Russian dolls," Jess adds. "Open up one and there's another underneath."

"Exactly," he replies. "You might be able to break one curse, but not all of them."

"What's the good in that then?!"

Mr. Dice smiles, but there's no joy in his eyes. "You have to figure out which curse you can live with."

This time the deer's body doesn't vibrate; it doesn't give any warning. One second she is standing there looking straight ahead, and the next she bursts open. But this time there's no blood spray. Her flesh and bones don't clutter the air and fall onto us like shrapnel. This time the deer doesn't die; she simply changes shape. She's like a piñata that explodes, leaving behind nothing but millions of insects.

"Run!"

I don't know who screamed, but I listen to the command.

Someone grabs my hand to pull me along, make me run even faster. It's my father. He's not saying a word, but I can see terror on his face. I know I shouldn't turn around, I know I shouldn't waste the time, but I have to see what's chasing us. I have to see what's so terrible that we have to flee as if our lives depended upon it. One glance and I know.

A swarm of bees and butterflies is chasing us, huddled so closely together they look like a large black cloud zipping through the sky. The buzzing and the flapping are deafening. Their flight is creating wind at my back, and I know that they're gaining on us. Soon we're going to be covered and bitten and stung.

"Jess!"

I don't know where she and Mr. Dice are, I don't know if this is real, but I know I have to get out of here.

"Make this stop!"

"You can," she replies.

Why is everyone telling me that I can stop all of this madness? Do they think I want to live my life like this?! Do they think this is how I want to spend my days? Is everyone completely certifiable!?

"We just want you to see what's right in front of you," Mr. Dice says.

The only thing I see right in front of me is a bed. A bed? With thick covers that could be used as a shield to protect us from the bees that are already starting to sting the back of my neck and from the butterflies whose wings are already slamming against my ears.

Tugging on my father's hand, I pull him toward the bed. We get in between the covers and hold down the fabric before any of the insects can join us. Inside our flimsy asylum all I can hear is our breathing, all I can smell is our sweat, all I can see is my mother looking over at us.

"Welcome home," she says.

Her voice is warm. Her smile is bright. Her eyes are filled

with love. She reaches out her hands, and I latch onto one while my father tenderly grabs the other. Once again we're a family; once again we're safe. But wait, we're not a family; we're missing one person.

"Where's Barnaby?!" I scream.

"He isn't welcome," my mother says.

How could she say such a thing? No, wait, she isn't talking. This is my brain; these are my thoughts. Why am I making her say something so horrible? Barnaby is my brother, and no matter what he does or what he's done, I have to protect him and keep him safe. There's no way my mother would disagree with that; there's no way she wouldn't welcome him back into our family. What could he possibly do that would make her want to abandon him?

"He's chosen another family," she says.

"No!"

My scream causes the covers to billow, and I can hear the bees and the butterflies on the other side of the cloth buzz and flap louder as they try to hold on to the material in search of a worn piece that they can rip apart to squeeze through and attack.

"He's confused. . . . He's scared," I cry. "He doesn't know what he's doing!"

My words fall on deaf ears. They don't want to hear anything I have to say about Barnaby. They've already made their decision; they've already disowned him.

I let go of their hands; I don't want to touch them any longer. I don't want to feel my parents' skin on mine. They're cruel and ugly and unforgiving. They're like Luba, and if they don't want any part of Barnaby, I don't want any part of them.

"Why did you make me see this, Jess? Why?!"

"Because you wanted to know how to break the curse!" she replies. Her yellow light slips into the makeshift tent, but she doesn't fully appear; neither does Mr. Dice. They're both gone, and I'm alone. Alone inside my own mind with my hateful parents and still no answers.

"And how can I do that?!" I shout. "Tell me."

"One of the curses can be broken by taking your mother's advice," she replies.

Her voice swarms around me like the insects outside. I feel fear growing in the pit of my stomach, and it makes it almost impossible for me to speak.

"I should abandon Barnaby?" I finally ask.

"No," Jess answers. "You should kill him."

Chapter 24

Kill Barnaby? That's insane. I want out; I want to be out of my brain and out of here. Now!

In a flash we're back at school. My parents are gone, and I'm alone with Jess and Mr. Dice. As far as I can see a bit of their sunshine has faded. They're not as bright, they're not as magical, not when they tell me that I have to kill my brother. Then I remember the last person who told me that I had to kill a family member: Luba told me to kill my father.

"Jess, is that really you?" I ask.

"Of course it's me," she replies. "Why would you ask such a thing?"

"Because you just told me to kill Barnaby, that's why!" I scream. "After you told me that I had to protect him. What's going on?"

"Be careful, Jess," Mr. Dice instructs.

"No, be honest," I interrupt.

Jess bows her head, and the motion causes a few drops of gold to fall to the ground. When she looks up so I can see her face, I see that she's crying. "Things have changed, Dominy," she admits. "Barnaby isn't who you think he is."

I can feel my head begin to swirl. Slowly and then quickly

the room starts to spin around me; it's like I'm trapped within the eye of a tornado. I know that Barnaby's different. The change was set into motion the night I killed Jess, the night he suspected that I had something to do with her murder. It got worse when my father died, and ever since we moved in with Louis and Arla he's only become more distant and erratic and hostile. Palling around with Luba and Nadine definitely has not helped. But can Barnaby really be under their spell and lost to me? Forever? If that happened I truly don't think I could follow Jess's instructions and kill him; I'm not that strong. But I'm also not strong enough to survive watching Luba and her family destroy my brother's life. I'd rather die trying to free him from their clutches.

"Dominy, are you all right?"

The voice sounds like it's right inside my ear, and yet it's so far away. I don't know if I should hold on to it or cover my ears with my hands to block it out. My brother is changing; my brother has to be protected; my brother is standing right in front of me.

"Barnaby?"

"None other," he replies. "What the ef's wrong with you? You look like you've seen a ghost."

Well, the Japanese version of a ghost. Two actually. One of whom told me I have to kill you. So should I do it now in the school hallway? I could grab the side of your head and bash it into the metal lockers, three times should do it, and watch a trickle of blood form on your temple and drip into your eye, slide down your cheek and your chin until it drops onto the floor at my feet. Or I could strangle you like I tried to do once before, press my fingers against your neck and watch your skin turn blue. Your neck is thicker now, but I'm stronger, so you're still no match for me. I will always be your big sister, and I will always be able to kill you.

What the hell am I thinking? And why in the world did Jess plant these thoughts in my head? Or, more accurately, why did she split my head open so I could see the thoughts that were already there? I can't believe that she would do such a thing; she's never been cruel or violent. Even when I was those things to her, she never responded in kind; she always saw the good, the light, the hope. But maybe there's no more hope for Barnaby? Maybe Luba's gotten to him and infected him and turned him into her slave.

Looking at my brother I wonder how long he's known Luba and been in her company. She could have been brainwashing his mind and possessing his soul for much longer than I suspect. The only reason I found out about their connection is because I stumbled upon her at The Retreat. Barnaby never mentioned her before; their relationship could've been going on for years. If that's the case, maybe I have no other recourse but to kill him. This could even be like with my father—if I don't kill him, someone else will.

"Freak girl, you haven't listened to a word I said, have you?"

Barnaby's staring at me, his head slanted downward slightly because now he's almost two inches taller than I am. He's growing up and growing away from me unless I do something about it, unless I reach out and try to make him understand that he needs to be careful, that he needs to listen to me, that he needs to know there are dangers out in the world that he cannot fight against alone.

I almost laugh out loud when I realize if I said any of those things to my brother he would laugh his head off and think that I was crazy. He's fifteen. He doesn't want to be told what to do. He doesn't want to be reminded that he isn't invincible, especially not by his sister who he considers an enemy more often than he considers a friend. No, I need to lighten things up, act as normal as I can. If I even know what normal is anymore.

"I heard some of your blabbering," I reply sarcastically. "Bottom line it for me."

"Nadine's having a party."

Should I check my e-mail for an invite? "That, um, sounds like fun," I lie.

"Not for those of us who didn't get an invitation," he barks.

Consider yourself lucky! So I was right; I wasn't just imagining a connection between my brother and the witch. Hopefully, it's just a harmless crush like the one he had on Arla when they first became track teammates. But, unfortunately, harmless is not an adjective that I can pin on Nadine.

"Maybe it's just for juniors," I surmise. "Or it could be for the business club she's in, Future Losers of America? The one that's made up of all the kids who are too homely to make a living based on their looks alone, so they're going to have to apply themselves and choose a boring career to collect a paycheck."

Barnaby doesn't find my humor humorous. Should I tell him the truth? That Nadine only sent invites to the members of her grandmother's demonic cult? That's the most likely scenario, and knowing that Barnaby was kept off the guest list fills me with more joy than I can describe. It's actually hard to maintain my snarky face when I'm so happy.

"I don't know who else got invited, but I didn't," he whines. "I mean Luba said . . ."

Happiness is officially destroyed.

"Luba said what?" I ask, desperately trying to sound bored and not intrigued.

Barnaby's eyes are like two blue spotlights. They're bright and shiny, and they're trying to see through me; they're trying to see if my question is covering my real motive. Well, try as hard as you like, Barn, but I've become a master at hiding.

Shaking his head nervously, he replies, "Nothing."

"Dude, the old lady said something," I reply. "What was it?"

Sometimes you have to be careful what you ask for, because you might actually be given the truth.

"She said . . . she said that Nadine and I would make a nice couple."

I press down so hard on the top of my locker door I can feel the metal edge cut into my fingers. *Concentrate on the pain and, in fact, squeeze harder so there's more pain to focus on.* Anything has got to be better than what I was just told. Nadine and Barnaby! A couple! That's sick, and no, I cannot let that happen. I'll tell Barnaby the entire truth about me and my father and being a werewolf and the curse right here and now in the middle of the hallway before I ever let him go on a date with the girl who murdered our father. That's not going to happen, not on my watch.

"At first I didn't like Nadine, but now, you know, she's really cool," he says. "Not that it matters 'cause she isn't interested."

My brother is hurt and deflated, and I couldn't be happier. Time to spread some big sister cheer.

"Barn, nothing I can say will make you feel better," I begin. "But isn't it better to know now that she isn't into you than to waste time trying to turn her into your girlfriend? I'm sure there are tons of girls who would love the chance to snag a track star as their boyfriend."

The way Barnaby looks at me almost makes me want to cry, and I have to resist the urge to hug him. It's like someone has unscrewed the mask that's been welded to his face, and he looks sweet and hopeful and innocent, everything a little brother should be and everything that Barnaby once was. Please God, let this be a turning point; don't tease me with just a fleeting moment; let Barnaby be free. Let him be the person he is right now. I promise that I'll do whatever you want me to do to make sure that happens. One member of this wretched family deserves the chance to be happy.

"Thanks, Dom," he mumbles.

I watch him walk away, his shoulders hunched over a bit. He's still not standing as tall as he should be, but he didn't run from me; he didn't tell me to go to hell or that every bad thing that has happened to him and the entire world was my fault, so this is definitely a start. I don't know what Jess and Mr. Dice were talking about. There is no need for me to kill my brother.

My gigglaugh mingles with the clang of my locker when I slam it shut. My brain would be such a fertile playground for a psychiatrist. Seriously, they would have a field day if they could ever get inside and analyze my innermost thoughts. And when they're finished with me, they can examine Napoleon.

"Nadine's invited Rayna to our cabin tonight."

"I know. Barnaby just told me about your sister's soirée," I say. "But no worries, Nap, I really didn't expect an invite."

I turn to leave, but in a flash Nap is on my other side blocking my exit. His body is shaking like he had to run outside and forgot his parka. Or like he's sick. I think he's come down with Nadinitis.

"You didn't get an invite because she isn't having a party," he explains.

"Then why does she want Rayna to go to your cabin?" I ask.

"She won't tell me," he replies. "And whenever my sister won't tell me something, it means she's up to trouble."

"Does your sister want you to join her?"

Napoleon's embarrassed, but at least he doesn't evade my question. "Yes."

Nadine might not have told Napoleon about her motive, but she needs him as much as she needs Luba. The three of them have to work together if they're going to create any mischief. Which means only one thing.

"Rayna is in serious trouble," I say.

A few beads of sweat appear on Nap's forehead, and he presses his hand against a locker for support, knuckles against metal. When he opens his mouth to speak, no words come out. He tries again, but nothing. He swallows hard, and finally he can speak.

"Will you . . . please . . . help me?"

This is the second time Napoleon's asked me to help him. I don't know what he's really asking me to do, but instinctively I know that I have to agree. I also know that he could be luring me into a trap, so I have to wave my own bait in front of his nose to see if he grabs it.

"I'll meet you at the cabin tonight," I confirm. "And I'll bring Archie with me."

"No!"

The sound of his hand clanging against the locker echoes down the hallway. A few people take notice, but everyone's so caught up in their own drama that they're immediately bored; we're just two kids having a mini-fight. They have no idea that I've just had a major revelation. Napoleon cares for Archie enough to protect him. He may not be able to protect or defend himself from his family, but at least he loves Archie enough to try to keep him safe.

"You cannot tell Archie," Napoleon insists. "You'll only be putting him in danger. He's already doing everything he can to protect me and . . . and, well, just don't tell him anything."

"I won't," I reply.

"Thank you," Nap says. "Come to the cabin at seven tonight. That's when she told Rayna to show up."

"I'll be there."

I grab Napoleon's arm before he runs off. "Truce."

"What?"

"I want you to agree to a truce with me right here and now," I demand. "I don't know what you really are, and I don't really like you, not a hundred percent anyway, but you love Archie and so do I, so I want us to be on the same team, you know, formally and everything."

There's strength behind Napoleon's eyes, way, way behind the fear. The grip of his handshake is a bit flimsy, a bit weak at first, but once he gets used to feeling my flesh press against his, it gets stronger.

"Archie is the only thing I have in my life worth living for right now," he declares.

Now his grip is solid. As solid as his voice. "Truce."

The cabin looks so much different now that I know what's taken place inside of it. It's no longer a safe haven or a rustic retreat; it's a death house. I can almost see the wooden exterior buckle and bulge as it gasps for breath in anticipation of the next life it's going to take. I look up into the sky and see that the moon is only three quarters and not full. I won't be doing any killing tonight. Now that I know I can trust Napoleon, I doubt very much that he's going to help Luba and Nadine manipulate nature to force another full moon. The first time the trick was impressive. If they try it again, it'll only be redundant. I've learned that, when it comes to Luba, she always has some new stunt to unveil.

When I see her sitting on the couch in between her grandchildren, she looks so old and so frail; the only new thing she's going to unveil is her casket. She literally looks like she's standing on death's door. The only thing stopping her from dying is the fact that Death probably is hesitating and not sure if it wants her company.

"Welcome back," Luba says.

Her voice is hardly audible, a rough whisper, like the sound the hooves of a deer might make as it scratches the earth just before it drops dead from a gunshot to the stomach.

"You know me," I reply. "I love a party."

"Then you've come to the right place," Nadine remarks. "I thought my brother might extend an invitation."

So much for making a surprise entrance.

"Kinda low attendance," I say, looking around the cabin. "Sucks having no friends."

"We're only expecting one more," Nadine says, smiling. "And here she is now."

Jumping off the couch, Nadine rushes to the door, as excited as if this were a real party, and practically drags Rayna into the cabin.

"Hi, Rayna," she beams. "I'm so glad you could come."

Once Rayna gets an eyeful of what she's walked into, she definitely doesn't share the sentiment. Coming to a remote cabin without her boyfriend probably sounded like the recipe for some no-strings fun, but now that she's here, Rayna doesn't look happy. Guess she never imagined she'd be splitting the six-pack she's holding in her arms with a grandmother.

"You never said this was going to be a family party," she groans.

"Sorry, Ray," Nadine replies. "I didn't think you'd mind."

Luckily Rayna Delgado is not a shrinking violet. She's one of those girls who loves to play dress-up and look pretty, but underneath she's as tough as any of the guys in school.

"Well, I do mind," she barks. "I'm outta here."

Rayna hasn't even turned completely around and Nadine is standing in front of the door. She looks relaxed, but there's no way that she's letting Rayna leave. She has plans.

"What did I tell you, Rayna?" Nadine asks rhetorically. "Didn't I tell you that we have a lot in common and if you just gave it a chance we could be really good friends? And aren't we?"

Even watching Rayna from behind I can see that she's uncomfortable, head bowed to avoid Nadine's gaze, standing with one hip jutted out, just waiting for a chance to get out of here.

"Yeah, sure, you know, despite what I first thought of you, you're not bad," Rayna stutters, "but..."

"Then trust me, we are going to have a super memorable night tonight!"

And I don't even have to see Nadine's face, but I know that she's moving her lips and casting a spell on Rayna to make the girl agree to stay. Napoleon's lips are clamped tight; he's not even opening his mouth to breathe. Nadine is on her own, but I guess there are some things she can do by herself.

"Fine!" Rayna gasps. "I'll stay for like a half hour."

"That's all the time we'll need," Nadine says.

What is she planning? And why has she invited Rayna here by herself? I know the two of them have gotten chummy, but I figured it was just two rotten eggs getting together to compare notes and see which one smelled worse. I had no idea that they had actually developed a friendship.

"I'd like you to meet my grandmother," Nadine says with too much sweetness in her voice. "This is Luba."

Rayna's body language is as unsubtle as her vocabulary; she actually flinches when Luba shakes her hand. I'm a little surprised that she doesn't wipe her hand on her thigh to get rid of the elder cooties.

"So very nice to meet you, Rayna," Luba murmurs. "You were right, Nadine. She is lovely."

I have absolutely no idea what's going on or why Nadine has arranged this little get-together, but it seems that Rayna's figured it all out. And it appears that there has been a huge misunderstanding.

"Whoa, Nellie!" Rayna shouts, raising her free hand like it's a stop sign. "Sorry to disappoint you, Nay, but I'm not like *that*. I didn't think that sort of thing ran in the family, but you being twins and all must mean the gay gene just got divided between you and Nap."

"I am not a lesbian!"

I want to slap the disgusted expression right off of Nadine's face. Being a lesbian would be a huge improvement over being what she really is.

"Don't freak out, Nay; there's nothing wrong with it. I think your brother and Archie make a really cute couple," Rayna replies, gaining some respect from me at least. "It's just that I have a boyfriend, and I'm not in the market for a new one, let alone a girlfriend. Sorry if I led you on or anything and, you know, I'd be lying if I said I wasn't flattered, but I'm so not curious about how the other half lives."

Rayna catches my eye, but she doesn't catch my meaning. I'm trying to urge her to leave, to stop talking and just dash out the door before it's too late. But she thinks I need her help.

"Dom, you want to hitch a ride with me?" she asks.

Of all the times to start being polite! No, I do not want a ride. I just want you to leave here before Nadine reveals why you're here in the first place.

"No one is leaving," Nadine says.

"Watch me."

Once again Nadine is too quick for Rayna. Before she can even take a step closer to the door, Nadine raises her arm, and the doorknob bursts into flames.

"What the hell?!"

"I told you!" Nadine declares. "No one is leaving."

I know exactly what's going on inside Rayna's mind; she's trying to give reason to the unexplainable. She's trying to logically understand how a doorknob can burst into flames, but she can't. So now she's eyeing all of us suspiciously, wondering which one of us is going to crack, tell her that it's a dumb parlor joke that Nadine's been performing since she was a little girl. When the silence threatens to choke her, Rayna starts to look around the room for an escape. Maybe she can jump through the window, or if she can make it to the back room, maybe there's a window there that she'll be able to open and crawl out of. I can't be a hypocrite and say that I like Rayna; I don't. But I feel sorry for her right now because I know exactly how she feels. Luckily, I know exactly what to do. Divert the attention away from the innocent bystander and onto me.

"Great trick, Nadine," I say. "Now why don't you let Rayna go so you and I can finally have it out."

"I don't know what you're talking about, Dominy," Nadine replies. "I don't want to have anything out with you."

As she shakes her head disapprovingly, Luba's face is practically covered by her long, straggly hair. "Some girls are so egotistical," she says, each word an effort. "They think every moment is about them."

"Everything you people do is about me!" I shriek.

Luba looks up at me, her two black eyes surrounded by bloodshot red veins.

"Not tonight, dear."

Clutching the six-pack tightly with one hand, Rayna starts to flail her other arm in the air. She's trying to come off as forceful, but she merely looks frightened. "You people are all seriously in trouble!" she rants. "I told Jeremy I was coming out here to a party, and he's . . . he's meeting me here in like ten minutes so you better . . ."

Nadine's harsh laughter silences Rayna. "You didn't tell Jeremy anything because you're a whore and you were hoping to have some fun here tonight without him," Nadine correctly surmises. "You're bored silly with college boy because all he wants to do is wait until marriage, and you're so slutty you can't wait until lunchtime to have some fun. Isn't that right?"

It's obvious by Rayna's shocked expression that Nadine hit the nail on the skank's head.

"Oh my God, how do you know that?" Rayna asks. She's so amazed by Nadine's knowledge, she's not even trying to defend her own morals. "Did you read my mind?"

"No," Nadine replies. "But Grandma did, and she likes what's locked inside that pretty little head of yours and your pretty little body."

"Dom . . . Dominy, do you know what's going on?"

"I have no idea," I reply honestly. "But stay by me. I'm going to help you."

Once again Nadine's laughter, loud and guttural and un-natural, spills out of her body and into the room. "How are you going to help her from up there?"

"What are you talking about?" I ask.

Nadine doesn't answer. Instead she raises both hands as if she wants to wrap them around my neck, and, although she's several feet from me, I feel pressure around my throat, but nothing like the impact when my back rams into the ceiling.

"Dominy!" Rayna screams.

Her scream is so loud I hardly hear the beer bottles break into little pieces when they crash onto the floor. I try to move my arms and legs, but it's like they're super-glued to the ceiling. The second I sense that the connection is loosening, I see tiny silver ropes break through the ceiling and wrap around my wrists, my ankles, my waist, and my throat before disappearing once again into the wooden slats above me. I'm chained up tight, and I have a perfect view for what they're planning to do next. If I had any sense I'd bang my head against the ceiling until I blacked out or stretch my arm through the silver rope so I can gouge out my eyes and go blind. But curiosity makes peo-ple stupid, and I'm about to become a fool.

"Dominy!!" Rayna shrieks. "What's going on?!"

The poor girl tries to twist the doorknob that is no longer engulfed in flames, but as expected it's locked. She rams her fist into the window, but the glass merely bends as if it's rub-ber and not glass.

"Let me out!" she cries.

"Oh we'll let you out, Rayna," Nadine says. "In our own special way."

Terrified, Rayna starts to run around the circumference of

the room but doesn't get any farther than the corner. She whips around to face her three captors. Her mind understands that something horrific is going to happen, but her body refuses to give in so easily. She's twitching; her fingernails are clawing at the walls; her jaw is shaking, but nothing other than unidentifiable sounds are coming out of her mouth.

"Leave her alone!" I scream. But when I see Nadine and Luba join hands, I know there's nothing else I can do. Wait! If I can just reach Napoleon, if I can prevent him from holding his grandmother's hand, maybe I can stop them; maybe I can save a life instead of watching one end.

"Napoleon, don't!"

Nadine looks at me, and I can see the silver light surrounding her become tinged with black. She doesn't want any competition when it comes to controlling her brother's spirit.

"Don't listen to that animal!"

"Napoleon! I know you don't want to do this!" I cry. "Think of Archie!"

And sometimes the most obvious thing to say is also the most idiotic.

Nadine's sneer turns into a smile. I haven't prevented disaster. I haven't convinced Napoleon to stop helping his family. I've given Nadine all the ammunition she needs to ensure that Napoleon will do exactly as she wants him to.

"That's right, Napoleon. Please do think of Archie," she whispers. "Think how beautiful his white skin will look lying inside a red velvet coffin. It can be easily arranged. Just make a choice. You're either with your family or you're against us."

I can hear every heart in the cabin beating. It's like thunderous drums banging and banging and banging, only relenting when Napoleon's sobs become too loud. And when a bloodcurdling scream erupts from Rayna's body as she sees him grab hold of his grandmother's hand.

Immediately, three pieces of silver light fly out of Nadine's, Luba's, and Napoleon's bodies, traveling through the air in quick, jagged spurts until they connect, and then like a rocket the single stream of light pierces Rayna's heart.

She begins to convulse, her body slamming against the wall, her eyes rolling back into her head, so all I can see are two white orbs staring at me blindly. She is too consumed by pain and fear to even beg for help. And then the change begins.

Slowly another silver thread starts to fly out of her mouth. As it exits, her body begins to shrivel, the smooth skin on her face wrinkling like a dried leaf; her luxurious black hair turns brittle and gray, and her back curves as if the bones underneath her skin are no longer strong enough to keep her upright. They're sucking the life out of Rayna and transferring it right into Luba.

The silver thread moves through the air and enters Luba's open and eager mouth. Just as Rayna aged before my eyes, Luba becomes younger. Her skin color turns from ash to alabaster, her hair regains shine and returns to the beautiful ebony color it had when she was a younger woman, and her body grows strong and vital. By the time she's swallowed all of the silver light, she is no longer frail and breakable and old, but healthy and sturdy and, as disgusted as I am to think it, beautiful. This is the woman who cursed my father; this is the woman who started all this agony.

Seconds after I watch Rayna collapse to the floor, a mass of wrinkled flesh barely covering a skeletal frame, I feel the ropes retract, and I fall. Luckily, my wolf-like instincts prevail, and I hardly feel the impact when I land. I almost give in to my primitive nature, the part of me that wants to devour Nadine and attack Luba and even rattle Napoleon by the shoulders for his part, but there's another person in the room who needs my help. Rayna.

It doesn't matter that I don't like her. It doesn't matter that she isn't my friend. What matters is that she needs my help, and she needs it desperately.

Racing to her side, I kneel next to her and tenderly lift her body until I'm cradling her in my arms. I gasp because she feels so lightweight, it's as if she's made out of paper. Her eyes are dull and unfocused, like they used to hold meaning until someone erased them with a dirty eraser, leaving behind dark blotches. She has no idea why they've done this to her, but she understands that all hope, along with her youth, has left her body.

"Finish . . . this," she whispers.

What? No . . . no! I can't do that. I don't say a word, but my head is shaking so Rayna will understand I can't be of help. But she insists.

"Please, Dominy . . . help me."

I look up at the three souls who destroyed the one that I'm holding, and I can't believe what I'm witnessing. Napoleon is so lost in his own grief and guilt that he can't even look at me. Luba is so lost in her own newly acquired beauty that she's actually staring at herself in the mirror, admiring her renewed looks. Only Nadine is watching me; only Nadine cares what I'll do next.

"Well, Dominy," she says. "Are you going to grant the poor girl her last request?"

There's absolutely no reaching Nadine; there isn't a shred of humanity or decency or morality inside her body. How did she ever turn into something so vile? And how can I ever do what Rayna is asking of me?"

"With my help."

Jess's light appears before me. Its glow is soft, not the blinding, show-offy light I've grown accustomed to, but more like the spark of a night-light, just enough to let me know that I'm not alone and that I have nothing to be afraid of.

"Please, Dominy . . ." Rayna says, gasping for breath. "I can't stand . . . the pain."

"Jess, I . . . I can't do this," I say, the tears flowing down my cheeks and stinging my flesh.

The golden light grows large enough to wrap around me, reminding me that Jess is nearby; she's with me like she's always promised.

"I can't do this for you," Jess says. "But I will take Rayna with me and bring her to the other side."

I know that I've killed before; I know that I've taken life, but it was always as a wolf. It was always when I was buried underneath an uncontrollable spirit. This will be the first time I'll take a life as a human being, with forethought and not in self-defense. But looking at Rayna's misshapen, broken body and the pain slithering out of her eyes, I know that it's the only humane thing to do.

"Please, God, forgive me."

Slowly I place my shaking hand on top of Rayna's mouth, and at first her tiny body struggles. The will to live is such an incredible force; it's built into all of us and stays with us no matter how much we plead for death. All I can hear is my own crying, so I have no idea if Rayna is making any sounds when I press down just a little bit harder. I keep my hand there until her body stops moving, until I see, for the second time, a soul release itself from its bodily host.

This time is different than when Essie died; this time Rayna has Jess waiting to take her on the next phase of her journey. I don't know where she'll wind up, but I know that it has to be better than here. Holding Rayna's lifeless body in my arms, I take solace in knowing that I helped in some small way to make her afterlife more bearable than her death.

"Well done, Dominy," Nadine comments. "A bit on the sentimental side, but really, well done."

I don't have the strength to answer or argue with or attack Nadine; I have to use every ounce of strength I have left to bury Rayna's body. Let her family and Jeremy think she ran away or was kidnapped. I can't allow them to see her body like this; such a sight would be incomprehensible to them. No, I have to reserve my strength to dig a hole in the ground somewhere deep in the woods and cover Rayna's body with dirt so she'll never be found.

And save just enough strength so I can cry myself to sleep tonight.

Chapter 25

The graves are piling up.

Everywhere I turn I see another tombstone belonging to someone who died because of me. Some of them I killed, some of them I watched die, and one died thinking he was doing me a favor. Jess, my father, that vagrant Elliot, Essie, and now Rayna. Five for one. The odds really suck if you come into contact with me.

Each day since Rayna's death—correction, since I killed Rayna—has been worse than the one before. Each day since then I've carried with me those five lives, the people who are no longer living and wondered what they'd be doing if they hadn't known me, if they'd never met me. They could be celebrating each day of their lives, enjoying the simplest pleasures or ignoring the gift that they'd been given. It doesn't matter; at least they'd still be alive.

Sitting in my classes, working through cheerleading practice, hanging out at home, all I can see are five mutilated and defiled and half-eaten corpses, piled one on top of the other to form a teetering death tower, a symbol of the horror I've unleashed onto this town. That's my gift to the world. And all I can think is that the world would be a better place if only I had never been born.

It doesn't matter that my father was the catalyst or that Luba was the origin or that Nadine is the disciple. If it weren't for me, none of this would have happened. It's that simple.

"No, it isn't, Dominy, and you know that."

The ramifications of my being born and turning sixteen might be complicated, Mr. Dice, but break it down and every death has a common denominator: me.

"I'm really not in the mood for any more Omikami advice," I say. "Protect my brother, kill my brother, don't trust Napoleon, no wait he can be trusted, kill Rayna it'll all be okay, listen to my gut, you're never alone. I'm tired of it, Mr. Dice, and I don't know how much more of this I can take!"

"You've been dealt a difficult hand of cards; that's true," he replies. "But you can't cut a new deck."

I hear someone in the study hall laugh, and I assume it's me. "Sounds like you're getting your spiritual guidance from an old detective movie."

"Sorry, sometimes things do get lost in translation," he adds. "How about *kishi kaisei?*"

Wake from death and return to life. The words Archie spoke at Jess's funeral.

"What if I don't want to?"

"Well, in the end the choice is yours, Dominy," he says. "You can make whatever decision you wish. But remember . . ."

"Oh my God," I interrupt. "Please do not tell me that I'm blessed."

"No," he says. "Remember that with every choice there are consequences."

When I turn to the right to face Mr. Dice, he's no longer there. His words cling to me as I walk out into the hall, I think I understand their meaning, but my mind is so cluttered and anxious, I'm not a hundred percent sure that I know what he meant. Maybe one of these days someone will actually say exactly what's on their mind instead of just being cryptic.

"I love you, Dominy."

My boyfriend has the most perfect timing. Let's see if he can follow up his words with action. Right here in the hallway.

"If that's true," I whisper, "then . . . make love to me."

If Caleb is startled by my brazen request he doesn't show it, not in his expression or his body language. His beautiful brown eyes don't blink; they don't glance around to focus on something other than me; they gaze right into my eyes as if they're connected to me by some silly imaginary thread. Obviously, the connection isn't as strong as I thought.

"No," he replies softly.

No? Doesn't every guy fantasize that his girlfriend is going to ask him to sleep with her? Isn't that why they ask a girl out in the first place, in the hopes that it's going to lead to her bedroom or the backseat of their car? Why does my boyfriend have to be different? And why is he leading me into an empty classroom and closing the door behind us? Hmm, has he changed his mind?

"I dream about making love to you, Dominy, which is not something I ever thought I'd admit to you," Caleb says, blushing slightly. "And one day I hope to make that dream come true, but I want it to come true because we both want it."

Someone hasn't been listening.

"I just told you what I wanted," I snap.

"And I want to have sex with the girl, not the wolf."

Caleb's hand reaches out to grab mine. I know his touch will be soft and welcoming and warm, but I don't want that right now. I want rough and unkind and painful. I want to be hurt; I want to be blamed; I want to be punished for the things that I've done!

"That's ridiculous!" I shout.

"You don't want to have sex with me because you love me or even because you just want to get it over with and I happen to be around," he says. "You want a distraction so you can forget about everything that's going on."

No, Caleb, I don't love you. Right now I hate you. For being right.

"So I'll forget, and you'll finally get laid," I reply, wincing a bit at how crude I sound. "Don't guys consider that a win-win?"

Caleb gazes at me with such intensity that I'm the one who has to turn away.

"You really have no idea how I feel about you, do you?"

Wiping away my tears, I have to cover my face for a minute until I stop shaking and before I can speak again. "I do know how you feel. That's the problem."

"Because you don't feel the same way?"

This time I reach out to Caleb, awkwardly grabbing his wrist and his forearm, any part of his body, just to have an anchor to something good. His blond curls are pushed back, no longer falling against his forehead. I wonder for a second if this is the way his hair fell today or if it's a new hairstyle that I'm just noticing. Why don't I know these things?

"Before all this started I wasn't sure how I felt about you, Caleb," I say, rubbing my fingers along his knuckles. "I mean, there's no one else I want as my boyfriend, never has been, but was I in love with you? I wasn't sure."

"What about now?" he asks, placing his hand on top of mine. The calluses underneath his fingertips feel good against my soft skin. Too good.

Pulling my hands away from his abruptly, I cross my arms and lean against the door. "It doesn't matter how I feel, Caleb, because I'm not worthy of your love. I'm not worthy of anybody's!"

"Oh will you shut up with that!"

His voice hits me like a cannonball, and I'm stunned; Caleb's never spoken to me like that before. And he's never looked so pissed off either. Throwing his books onto an empty desk, Caleb starts to pace the room, and for the first time I notice that his muscular body could be more than sexy and alluring; it could also be dangerous. The way that he's snarling at me and clenching his fists, I'm not sure what he's going to do to me. I wanted to be hurt; well, maybe Caleb's going to do just that.

"I . . . I'm sorry," I stutter.

"So am I!" he yells. "Because obviously I can't do anything right! I stand by you; you push me away. I try to uncover the truth about Nadine; you yell at me! I tell you that I love you, and it's not good enough. What do you want from me, Dominy?! I mean seriously, what do you want from me?!"

Instinctively, Caleb knows I don't have an answer, so he doesn't wait for me to respond.

"Do you want me to go away and leave you alone? Do you want me to forget everything about you, everything that we've been through? Because if that's what you want, just let me know and I'll do it!"

"Is that what you want, Caleb?" I ask. "Would you like to forget you ever met me?"

I'm terrified to hear his reply. But thrilled when I hear him scream.

"No!! That's not what I want, and you know it! What I want is my girlfriend back! The one who wasn't afraid to share things with me no matter how ugly they got. I mean for God's sake, Dominy, I know that you're a werewolf and I've stood by you! What more proof do you want that I love you and I'm not going to leave you?"

You might if you found out that I killed when I wasn't a wolf, that I'm actually capable of taking a life when I'm not covered in fur.

"I'm sorry, Caleb," I mumble. "I just don't know how much more of this I can take."

He stares at me for a moment before picking up his books. His voice is quiet, but I can hear what he says just before he leaves the room. "Neither do I."

Nice going, Robineau; push away the only boyfriend you'll probably ever have. Well, if I'm not going to have sex, I might as well feed.

A few hours later I'm standing within a thicket of trees, the radiance of the full moon above slicing through the branches and bouncing off the snow-covered ground to create a prism of light that sprinkles me with its power. Bending to the moon's will, I feel the burning and then the breaking and then I'm gone, replaced by something stronger, something that never questions what it is: the werewolf. And tonight I'm going to allow it to be as violent as it wants to be.

I see a cluster of tiny footprints in the snow and bury my snout in them. The scent is fresh. A rabbit family is nearby, but that's not what we want to feed on tonight. Through the darkness I see a fox, its fur the same deep shade of red as mine, and when it sees me it becomes paralyzed, unable to flee to safety. I could devour it and imagine that it's really Melinda Jaffe wearing her fur coat. Growling deeply, I thrust my head forward, and finally the fox races into the brush; it scurries away never knowing that I had no intention of chasing after it. No, tonight is going to be a special kill, and I'm prepared to wait until dawn to find it.

An hour later my search is over. Slowly I move toward my prey, pressing each paw down lightly onto the snow so I don't make a sound, letting my body sway naturally with each step. If only the deer would turn its head, it would see that I look like the hunter that I am.

My fangs pierce the deer's neck while it's still chewing on some grass. The impact causes it to topple over; its legs furiously try to regain contact with the ground, but do nothing but stir the night air. I rip my mouth away from its neck and take with it a chunk of flesh that I quickly devour. The taste is pungent and fresh and bloody, and I can feel my saliva growing in my mouth. I need more.

Just as the deer is about to stand up, its bent, quivering legs almost vertical, I attack again, this time with my claws as well as my fangs. Ripping deep into its flesh until I scrape bone, burrowing my snout inside the deer's stomach to expose its organs, biting through skin to swallow the fresh meat just underneath. This is more than just a feeding; this is a ritual. This curse began with the death of a deer, and that's how it will continue. Unleash my savage lust onto the animal that started this horror.

When I'm finished, when my own belly is bloated and my white fangs stained red with the blood of my prey, I step back and look at the ravaged animal with pride. Then I clamp down hard on its neck, the part that's left of it, and I drag the animal away from the bushes and trees and rocks onto a flat, untouched piece of ground, the corpse's blood smearing the ground, creating a red rainbow so my kill can be visible. Some dead bodies were never meant to be buried.

And others were never meant to be found. Which doesn't mean they won't be missed. When Rayna didn't show up for class there were a few whispers among the student body. When she missed the first practice for the upcoming regional cheerleading competition, speculation about her whereabouts grew. And this morning when her face appears on the cover of the *Three W* as the suspected latest victim of the Full Moon Killer, the school is whipped into a frenzy.

I don't know how I survive listening to Dumbleavy's latest speech about how we can't assume the worst has befallen our friend and how we can't give in to fear. Oh really? Crawl inside my head, and I'll show you something to be afraid of. He urges us to continue to hope and pray and tell the police anything that Rayna might have said or that we might know about her that could provide a clue as to her whereabouts. I feel like raising my hand and asking Dumbleavy if he'd like to know where Rayna's spirit or her body is because I could lead him to both. The first is within Psycho Squaw; the second is in an unmarked grave in the middle of the low hills. I wonder if he'll label me a hero or the murderer that I am.

I have the same question for my friends.

My sanctuary becomes cramped when Caleb, Archie, and Arla ignore my requests to leave me alone and they barge into the small music closet. I was having such a wonderful time sitting in the corner, reliving the moment when I killed Rayna, banging my fists into the foam soundproof walls, screaming until my lungs ached. Such good times ruined by such good friends.

Well, let's see how good.

"Dominy, you have to stop avoiding us," Archie declares.

"It's been like living with the Invisible Girl instead of a werewolf these past few days," Arla says.

Oh to be invisible! Now *that* would be a curse I could handle. Never have to see anyone again, never have to worry if they can see the death that clings to my face, that I can't shake off no matter how many times I try to smile or laugh or cry. *Why couldn't you have cursed me with invisibility instead, Psycho?!*

"Domgirl, I am going to tell you one more time you are not alone," Caleb whispers. "So knock it the hell off and stop acting as if you are."

The three of them have joined me on the floor, Caleb sitting next to me, his arm around me, and Archie and Arla kneeling in front of me. I stare at them for a moment and take them in, making sure I remember what they look like because I've been missing so many important details lately. Archie's cut his hair again, the left side anyway, buzzed it short while the right side has retained its length. He looks handsome as always, his violet eyes twinkling against the white backdrop that is his face.

The scar over Arla's eye has settled into her skin, made permanent residence on her face, but in the compromised light of the closet it's hardly noticeable. She's wearing her short black wig, the one cut in a severe bob, which makes her nontraditional features look even more exotic.

And Caleb looks just as handsome as ever. His blond hair is slicked back again with a little gel, so I guess this is the new clean-cut look he's going for. It makes his face appear stronger and more inviting than ever.

My boyfriend and my friends are all so beautiful inside and out. I feel ashamed to be contaminating their space. I start to cry when I think of all the ugliness that I've brought to their world, stains and scars and blemishes that can never be washed away or hidden with makeup because they cut too deep.

"Domgirl, c'mon, you have to stop this."

I love how Caleb smells; I always have. A little bit of cologne, a little bit of sweat. He smells just like my father used to when he would hold me close to him, when he would whisper in my ear that I was his little girl and he would always keep me safe and nothing would ever harm me. My father was such a liar.

"I killed Rayna," I say through my sobs.

The silence my comment provokes weighs down on us as if the ceiling has just caved in. When the ceiling lifts and they can breathe again, Archie is the first to speak.

"During the last full moon?" he asks.

I shake my head, my forehead rubbing against Caleb's chest.

"Okay . . . okay, Luba and Nadine . . ." Caleb starts.

"They must've done something to you again, controlled

you in some way so you turned into a wolf," Arla rationalizes. "You would never . . ."

"I wasn't a wolf," I say quietly.

Caleb doesn't let go of me, but I can feel his body begin to tense up. His transformation is a bit more subtle than mine.

"But . . . but that doesn't make sense," Archie says, sitting back on his haunches, the impact of my words making it difficult not to topple over.

"I wasn't a wolf," I repeat. "I was human when I killed her."

Grabbing me roughly by the shoulders, Caleb twists me around so we're facing one another. There's a flicker of light in his brown eyes, enough to light up the whole room. He believes in my goodness so much, he almost convinces me that I'm anything but terrible.

"Tell us exactly what happened," he demands.

The anger and sorrow and guilt that I've been feeling these past few days bursts to the surface like a geyser, spilling into the room and drenching Caleb and my friends with my filth.

"It doesn't matter what happened!" I scream. "I killed Rayna! I have no excuse. I can't blame this one on the wolf or the curse! I did it! I killed her with my own hand!"

"Dominy, why?" Arla's voice hits me somewhere on my left.

"Why would you do such a thing?" Archie's voice slashes on my right.

"Because she's brave, and I'm a coward."

A silhouette of light surrounds Napoleon's body as he stands in the doorway. For an instant I think Jess has brought him to me, but when he closes the door the light disappears. The only thing that's brought him here is his own conscience.

"Nap," Archie says, standing up to grab his boyfriend's hand. "What are you doing here?"

"I listened to our connection."

When Nap speaks again Archie's impish smile is quickly wiped away.

"My connection to Arla."

"Me?" Arla asks.

"Nadine may be my biological twin," Napoleon states, "but Arla's my psychic twin. Isn't that right, Arla?"

"Well, um, it looks like that could explain a few things," she mumbles. "My headaches for one."

"Your psychic twin?" Archie exclaims. "I thought that was a one-time thing."

"It was actually a failed attempt to try and suck Arla's memory out of her mind," Nap explains. "I guess when my sister and I work together we aren't always successful."

"Well, Nap, your tag-team effort could've been a lot worse," Arla adds, "than just, you know, opening up some sort of psychic tunnel with me on one end and you on the other."

By Caleb and Archie's confused expressions, it looks like they could use a little more information, but now's not the time.

"I'll explain it all later," Napoleon says. "Right now you need to know the truth about your friend. What Dominy did to Rayna was selfless and heroic, and if I weren't such a coward Rayna would still be alive."

Away from his sister and his grandmother, Napoleon looks so capable, nothing like the wilting little boy he becomes in their presence. They really are slowly killing him. The way Caleb jumps up and presses a finger into Nap's chest it looks like he may want to quicken the pace.

"You know something, Jaffe," Caleb barks. "I've had it with you and your sicko family. I know Dominy is innocent, and I don't buy your mea culpa act, so spell it out so we can understand it. What the hell happened to Rayna?"

"My sister, my grandmother, and I sucked the life out of her and left her a hollow shell," Napoleon replies calmly.

"Rayna would've died a slow, agonizing death if Dominy hadn't honored her request to kill her."

Caleb's knees buckle, and he stumbles a bit, his foot barely missing my fingers on the floor. He shakes his head from side to side, but keeps his eyes focused, staring right at Nap. "You . . . you destroyed Rayna, and because you're such a douchebag you forced Dominy to clean up your mess!"

Napoleon's gaze is as intense and unyielding as Caleb's. "Yes, that's exactly what I am and that's exactly what I did."

Archie tries to intervene, but he isn't strong enough or fast enough to prevent Caleb from punching Nap. In his nose, in his ear, in his chest. He ignores Arla's and my cries to stop. Archie's the only one with the good sense to know that Caleb isn't going to respond to voices, only actions—so there's a momentary pause in the pummeling when Archie grabs Caleb in one of those wrestler's holds, his arms scooping up under Caleb's armpits and then interlocking his fingers behind Caleb's neck.

"Let go of me, Arch!" Caleb pants.

"Not until you promise to stop," Archie says, his voice equally winded.

"Not after what he made Dominy do!" Caleb screams. "He needs to pay!"

"He *is* paying for it!"

Arla's voice brings everyone to a halt. It's urgent and strong and commanding. When we turn to look at her, we see that her face looks as anguished as Napoleon feels. It's incredible; they really are connected.

"Arla," I say, "do you know how Napoleon feels?"

She nods her head slightly, and from the look in her eyes I think she's experiencing the worst emotional pain she ever has since she realized her mother didn't only run from her father but abandoned her as well.

"I don't understand it," she explains. "Ever since that

night I've felt weird, moody, and I've heard snippets of voices and thoughts. Images keep popping up in my head that don't belong to me, but I thought it was the headaches and stress—you know we've all been under a lot of stress lately." She covers her face with her hands, laughing and crying at the same time. "But that isn't it. My brain isn't only mine anymore; it's yours too. Isn't it, Nap?"

"I think so," he replies.

"Can you feel what I'm feeling?" she asks. "Or know what I'm thinking?"

"I've been able to block it out, but lately it's gotten stronger," he adds. "It's almost the way I used to be with Nadine when we were very young, before we knew what was expected of us . . . or at least before I knew. I think Nadine understood my grandmother's plan before she could speak."

"You've sensed a link to Arla ever since that night Luba revealed to me that you and Nadine were her grandchildren?" I ask.

"Yes," Nap replies. "But since you didn't say anything, Arla, I thought it was best to keep it to myself."

"Once again you were too scared to take action," Caleb fumes.

Napoleon's mouth opens to speak, but except for a weak sigh, no sound comes out. He tries again, but fails the second time as well. He almost looks like he did when he and Nadine would chant together to cast a spell, but alone he looks like what he is, an ashamed young man trying to find the words to explain his actions and his emotions.

"I'm not like you, Caleb," he admits. "I've never . . . I've never had any friends who I could count on. I've never known any way to live other than the way my family's taught me."

I finally understand what Jess originally saw in him: Napoleon's a damaged spirit who needs guidance if not salvation.

"Well, you have friends now," I say.

Looking at the floor, at his feet, at his tears falling on top of his sneakers, Napoleon can't speak; he's doing everything he can not to break down in front of us. But even if he did, we'd all reach out to help him stand up again. Even Caleb.

"I'm sorry," Caleb declares.

His words are almost as destructive as his punches. Nap waves his hands in front of him as if unable to accept Caleb's kindness, and his tears flow even more freely down his face.

"No . . . don't . . ." Nap says. "I . . . I don't deserve that."

"Oh yes you do, and don't you ever forget that."

Archie is grabbing Napoleon by the shoulders forcefully in the exact same way that Caleb grabbed me just a little while ago. They may not have known each other as long as Caleb and I have, but their bond is just as strong. Their invisible thread just as unbreakable.

"You're under a spell, like Dominy," Archie explains. "And like we're helping her, we're going to help you."

Nap doesn't try to break free from Archie's hold with his body, only his words. "You don't understand," he says. "My family will never let me go."

"That's because you've never had any other place to go to," Archie beams. "And now you do. You have me."

Nap swoons a bit, and Archie has to press tighter into his shoulders to keep him standing; his emotion is so overflowing that it threatens to consume Arla, and she collapses into my arms. Because Napoleon and Arla are so close to each other physically, their mental connection is stronger than it's ever been before, and she's feeling things with the same intensity that Nap is. I feel Caleb wrap his arms around both Arla and me, and he buries his face in my neck, my hair obstructing his vision. Napoleon's raw response is almost too painful to watch, and I'm about to look away, until I see Archie, emboldened instead of frightened, take Napoleon's face gently in his hands and look him directly in his eyes.

"I know I'm not old, but sometimes I feel like I've lived several lifetimes, and I've waited my whole life for someone to share it with," he declares, his voice shameless. He doesn't care if we overhear his innermost thoughts, as long as Napoleon understands what he's telling him. He does.

"I feel the same way about you," Nap replies. His voice isn't as confident as Archie's, but the shame that overwhelmed him moments ago is definitely starting to fade. "Without you I literally don't have anything else to live for."

Archie kisses Nap. It's gentle and strong at the same time. When Archie pulls away, his grip on Napoleon is still powerful, and when he speaks his words are passionate. "Then live with me, or we'll run away together," he says. "Together we can break this hold your family has on you."

But will passionate words and heartfelt intentions wilt in the presence of evil?

"She's coming."

Arla announces what Napoleon can feel in his soul.

"It's Nadine," Nap confirms. "Oh my God, she must be able to tap into my mind."

Thanks to my super hearing the sound of her applause arrives before she does. "Bravo, people!" she cheers. "This is a terrific hiding spot. If my brother weren't so weak, I would never have found it."

And if the closet were any smaller, she wouldn't fit in here. Have I not noticed how fat she's gotten, or is this a recent transformation?

"Seriously, Nadine, don't you witches have a spell to lose weight?" I ask.

Smirking, Nadine seems amused by my comment, rather than aggravated. "Not all of us are preoccupied with our looks, Dominy," she replies. "Some of us are more concerned about inner beauty."

"Honey, you're as ugly on the inside as you are on the outside," Archie snipes.

"Says the albino," she snipes back. "As much as I'd love to keep chatting with all of you, I merely came to amend a piece of advice I once shared with my brother."

Holding Archie's hand, Napoleon seems to have some extra strength to stand up to his sister. "Really? I thought you never changed your mind about anything, sis."

"Oh I don't," she replies. "I once told you that you had to make a choice, but since you're so incredibly indecisive, I wanted to let you know that the choice has been made for you."

"What choice?" I ask.

Even though the floor is carpeted, I can still hear Nadine's footsteps when she walks toward me. "That, Dominy, is a family matter," she replies. "And you of all people should understand the importance of keeping family secrets."

Just before she leaves she turns to add, "But don't worry. You'll all find out about this one soon enough."

The second she leaves, the air in the closet becomes fresher and easier to breathe. Her comment, however, is not as easy to decipher. The only thing we can all agree on is that whatever she was talking about, it cannot possibly be good.

Chapter 26

The more I get to know people, the more everyone seems to be like The Weeping Lady. We're all stuck in between two worlds at the same time.

I'm the perfect example of someone who possesses dual citizenship in both the real world and Freakville, but there are so many others. Jess is my best friend and a Japanese sun goddess. Mr. Dice is teacher by day, Omikami mentor by night. Napoleon desperately wants to be a normal teenager, but his family refuses to allow it. And then there's my mother.

I've avoided going to The Retreat since Essie's death because the thought of seeing someone else behind the receptionist's desk, someone who I know is Essie's permanent replacement, will be confirmation that Essie is not returning to her post. I'd have to accept that there really has been a changing of the guards. I know that Essie is in that proverbial better place and away from all this madness, but I miss her. She was a constant in a sea of change. When I enter The Retreat I see that rough waters indeed lie ahead.

"Looks like somebody's been demoted," I say.

Nadine waves her hand over the book she's reading, and

the text on the front cover disappears before I can read it. Probably some ancient tome on witchcraft or astrology or both so she can hone her skills.

"And it looks like somebody needs her mommy," she replies, handing me an index card with the number 19 written on it in black ink.

I hesitate a moment, not out of fear, but strategy. Once Nadine relaxes, I grab the card and rip it out of her hands so forcefully that I hear the edge of the card slice into Nadine's finger. I'm as surprised to see that her blood is red as she is to see that she's bleeding.

Grimacing slightly, Nadine points the index finger of her uncut hand at the open wound, and a thin, silver light emerges. It acts like a laser to seal up the cut, and she's unwounded in seconds. Still I consider it a small victory.

"Do you think mommy's going to speak to you today?" Nadine asks, back to snarky form.

I don't answer, but simply smile at her instead. It works.

"Or do you think her pathetic soul has finally given up and decided to call it quits?"

Once again my father's tactic proves its mettle. Keep quiet and your opponent will fill up the silence with ammunition so you can bury him. Or her.

"You believe in the existence of the soul, Nadine?"

"Of course I do," she replies. "Just because it can't be seen doesn't mean it doesn't exist."

"So how does it make you feel to know that yours is going to burn in hell for all eternity?"

Her blood, which just ran so freely from her finger, drains from her face. What do you know? Nadine is more human than I ever imagined. Might as well test her limits. "But it must be some relief to know that you're going to burn to a crisp alongside the rest of the women in your family," I add.

"Only the women?" she asks. "Have you now made yourself my brother's personal savior?"

As I lean over her desk, my hair—kind of wild and curly today—falls forward and swings in the space between us. "Your brother may not have as much power as you do," I whisper. "But he has something you'll never have."

Taking the bait, Nadine replies. "And what would that be?"

"Friends."

Nadine's face contorts into such a mask of hate and disgust and jealousy, it's obvious that her feelings are so out of control that she can't even use her powers to attack me. You might be able to take the witch out of the teenage girl, but you can't take the teenage girl out of the witch.

Just before I turn the corner to The Hallway to Nowhere, I add, "I hope you enjoy your mother's company as much as I enjoy mine. You two are going to be together for a long, long time."

Asleep, my mother possesses more maternal instinct than Melinda Jaffe could hope to acquire in a hundred lifetimes. You're either born with it or you're not. And even though my mother has been basically silent for the past decade, I know what's in her heart. Because it's in mine too.

I reach into my bag to find my mother's Guerlinade, but it's an unnecessary gesture; the scent is already floating through the air. It's almost as if with each shallow breath my mother takes, the smell of lilacs and powder fills up the room. Like the memory has strength on its own.

"Hi, Mom. How are you?"

My usual question latches onto the fragrance and glides along with it in the air. There is no verbal response this time, nor do my mother's eyes open wide to look at me, but there is a change in the room. We have a visitor. Make that visitors.

"What are you two doing here?" I holler.

Arla and Archie stare at me as if they want to ask the same question. "We thought you needed backup," Arla claims.

"To visit my mother?" I ask.

"To get past the gargirl at the front desk," Archie states.

I'm impressed. "How'd you know the role of the receptionist was now being played by Nadine?" I lift my mother's hand and place it on her stomach so I have room to sit on her bed.

"I overheard Napoleon discussing it with Luba," Arla explains. "Via our psychic hotline."

"Can you hear all of Nap's conversations now?" I wonder aloud.

"No," Arla replies, sitting on the foot of my mother's bed. "I think I can only hear things he wants me to hear. Like advising me that you might need help to get past his sister."

"And just how'd you two get past?" I inquire.

"Archie picked the lock to the back entrance." Arla beams.

Glad to know The Retreat has taken advanced security measures to thwart any break-ins.

"Um, ladies," Archie interrupts.

"Yes, ma'am," I joke.

"Did no one hear my new nickname for Nadine?"

"Oh sure," I reply. "The gargirl."

"Good one, Arch," Arla adds.

"Good one?" he replies, borderline apoplectic. "That was beyond good; that was *odorokubeki*—amazing!"

"What do you think, Arl?" I ask. "Should we give it to him?"

Arla leans over my mother's legs and places her hand on the other side of the bed to mull over my request. We look like we're in one of our bedrooms and not my mother's hospital room. She nods, then finally replies. "Sure, 'gargirl' is pretty odoroky."

"*Odorokubeki!*" Archie corrects.

He slaps Arla's hand away so he can sit on the opposite side of the bed. I smile because this image is so wrong and so right at the same time. The three of us should not be sharing a bed with my comatose mother, but I know she would absolutely welcome the company. And she wouldn't even mind if a fourth joined our party.

"Jess!" I exclaim.

Her golden light wafts into the room and elongates until she materializes. When her entrance is complete, she sits on my mother's left, next to her pillow.

"I hope you don't mind my crashing without an invite," she jokes.

"You know you never need an invitation," I say. "You're always welcome."

Even if she can't be seen.

"Jess is here!?" Archie screams, his eyes peering around the room, looking for something that to him is invisible.

"Right in front of you," I instruct.

His eyes widen and brighten in her sunshine. He may not be able to see her, but he can definitely feel her presence.

"*Subarashi!*" he cries. "Oh, Jess, I miss you so much."

"And so does Nap!" Arla blurts out.

Uh-oh.

The prevailing silence is interrupted by the clumsy sound of the radiator clicking on. It's cold outside, and, despite Jess's sun-colored light, it's also cold inside. But that's what you'd expect when two exes are sharing the same bed, figuratively speaking at least.

Jess must be very confused, because her golden tendrils are flailing like roots being plucked from the earth; they want to remain in a familiar place, but are being yanked to a foreign locale. I think Jess's journey to the spiritual world might have been less painful than where she's headed now: to Maturityville.

"Tell Archie that I forgive him for stealing my boyfriend," Jess finally says, her face a golden pout.

"He did not steal Nap from you," I retort.

"She thinks I stole Nap from her?" Archie asks, first looking at me then at the empty space where Jess is sitting.

"She knows you didn't," I lie.

"I know no such thing," Jess says, still sulking.

"Jess, we've been through this already," I shout. "Nap is gay; you're not a guy; it never would've worked out."

"We could've tried!" she counters. "I love fashion and theater and dance music, and those things are all gay!"

"Jess, you're insane!" I scream.

"Jess is here too?"

Another guest? This party's starting to get a bit crowded.

"Caleb?" I ask. "What are you doing here?"

"I got a text," he answers.

"Sorry, I forgot to tell you," Arla peeps. "Thought your backup might need some backup, so I texted Caleb."

Rubbing my neck, Caleb replies, "Well, I'm glad you didn't have any trouble with the gargirl at the front desk."

It's the girls versus the guys when Jess, Arla, and I crack up laughing, and Caleb and Archie remain silent. My bf because he's confused, my BFF because he's cranky. The only sound louder than our group laughter is Arla's cell phone ring.

"Incoming!" Arla announces.

"From who?" I ask.

"Ooh, the U.K.," she replies.

"Who do you know in England?" Caleb asks.

We three girls and Archie shriek at the same time. "Nakano!"

My poor heterosexual boyfriend is still confused. "Naka-who?"

"Saoirse's Japanese sidekick," Arla replies.

Caleb looks even more confused. "And who's Saoirse?"

"You know, she's the MAC cosmetic girl from across the pond," Archie reminds him. "And Nakano's her gay guy Friday."

Caleb nods patronizingly. "I think I'm just going to sit here quietly and observe."

Which is in complete contrast to Jess. Thrilled to be a few clicks away from a person of true Japanese heritage, Jess is unable to control herself. She wraps Arla's phone in yellow light like a lasso and pulls it to her so she can read the text. The result being that the phone looks as if it's floating in the air.

The four of us scramble to one side of my mother's bed and group-read the e-convo between Jess and Nakano. The people at Apple have no idea that one of their products is in the process of documenting the very first cross-dimensional, otherworldly, supernatural dialogue. While Nakano's texts appear in the usual black font, Jess's words are bright yellow.

"This is amazing, Jess!!!" Nakano writes. "I've found a kindred spirit."

"You know what I am?" Jess writes back.

"Don't know what you call yourself," he replies. "But I can sense you're not entirely human either."

When Jess shouts in my ear, I'm glad I'm the only one who can hear her, because she's so excited she's screaming loud enough to wake my mother.

"Japanese, gay, *and* not human!" she shrieks. "Dom, I think I found my soul mate!"

"Trolling after another queer?" Nadine asks. "You really are a glutton for punishment."

By the time the door slams behind Nadine, Jess's yellow light disappears into the phone. I don't know if she's trying to follow the fiber optics to visit Nakano wherever he is in England or if she just can't stand the sight of Nadine, but she's gone. The rest of us don't have any choice but to face the enemy. But we do it as a united front.

Caleb is the first of us to speak. "Get out, Nadine. Nobody wants you here."

Fake-frowning, Nadine purrs. "But, Caleb, you said we were such good friends."

"I already told you," I interrupt. "You don't have any friends."

Stung by being ridiculed in public, Nadine turns her attention to Arla's phone, which has fallen onto my mother's bed. She opens up her hand, palm up, and telekinetically drags the phone through the air until it lands safely in her grasp.

"Let's see what type of supernatural creature Jess was chatting with," Nadine says, scrolling through texts. When her eyebrows rise an extra inch, it's obvious that she's figured it out. *"Subarashi,"* she mocks.

"You know what Nakano is too?" I ask, hoping to trick Nadine into revealing the truth behind the latest member of Camp Inhuman.

"Nice try," Nadine replies, tossing the phone into the air so Arla has to lunge forward in order to catch it. "But if you want to know what Nakano is, you'll have to do it the old-fashioned way and ask him yourself."

She places her hand on the doorknob, but stops from turning it to turn around and toss another barb. "Or you could ask Jess. Just be sure you do it before the full moon rises tonight. It's hard to talk with a mouthful of rabbit carcass."

Super gross and super wrong.

"There was already a full moon this month," I correct.

Cackling, Nadine replies, "Guess you're having so much fun with your friends that you forgot to check the lunar calendar. Tonight's a blue moon."

This time the silence is ominous because it contains truth. I'm an idiot. I've not been paying attention, and I've overlooked something vitally important.

"A blue moon?" Caleb starts.

"The second full moon to appear in the same month," Arla finishes.

"Why don't we celebrate the event by meeting at my cabin tonight?" Nadine proposes.

I remember how the evening turned out the last time I was invited to the Jaffe cabin, but Archie accepts the invitation before I can decline. "We'll be there," Archie replies first.

I don't correct him because I can tell by the tone of his

voice that nothing I say will deter him from joining me later on tonight. Nor will I be able to stop Arla.

"And I have the perfect wig for a showdown."

Another moment of real human emotion creeps into Nadine's face. It's unwanted, but unstoppable. I look directly into her eyes—werewolf to witch.

"My friends and I will be there."

Chapter 27

"A blue moon!"

"I thought it was just a phrase, you know, once in a blue moon. Never knew it actually stood for something real," Caleb whispers to me outside the police station. "Sorry, Domgirl. I should've been paying more attention to the full moon chart."

"It's my fault," I say, squeezing his hand. "I've gotten so good at predicting when a full moon will occur by monitoring the sky that I haven't been checking either."

"But now we have a plan," he says. "I just hope it works."

He really is beautiful. Once again I'm overwhelmed by incredibly private feelings, physical and emotional, and I wish Caleb and I were alone. I want to know what he'd look like against the glow of a roaring fire; I want to know how the heat will change the feel and the color of his skin. I want to know him as a girl, not a wolf. So I make my move.

I grab Caleb by the back of his neck and pull him down so I can kiss him. His lips and his tongue feel good against mine, and when he closes his eyes I keep staring at his impossibly long eyelashes. Breaking the kiss I startle him again, but it's a good startle, and it makes him laugh a little.

"Wow," he sighs.

"For now," I flirt.

There's so much more that we both want to say, but time is running out. Holding my boyfriend's hand, I lead him into the police station so we can set our plan into motion.

"Mr. Bergeron, you have to call off the curfew tonight," Caleb implores per my instruction.

"I appreciate your enthusiasm and your interest in our town's affairs, Caleb," Louis replies, "but I'm not changing my mind."

It's weird seeing Louis sitting behind my father's desk even though it's his desk now. The way he's leaning forward, his butt only sitting on a portion of the chair, leads me to believe that Louis shares my opinion. It's been almost a year, and he still hasn't grown accustomed to the fit. Maybe it's because of all the recent deaths during his tenure or the fact that Melinda was distracting him and Luba probably had him under some sort of a spell. But even though it's been a tough adjustment for Louis, he has got to listen to Caleb. My entire plan depends upon it.

"But tonight is a blue moon!" Caleb protests.

"A what?" Louis replies.

Clearly no one pays attention to the astrological charts they way they used to. Well, almost no one.

"He's right, Chief."

Detective Owenski has one of those influential voices. I suspect that he doesn't speak very often, so when he does, people take notice.

"Another full moon this month?" Louis mutters. "Tonight?"

"Yes."

That's all Owenski has to say to make Louis change his mind.

"Call off the curfew and reach out to the vigi . . ." Louis starts.

"The vigilant citizens who helped us search for this killer the last time?" Owenski adds, substituting the innocuous *vigilant* for the more controversial *vigilante.*

"Y-yes," Louis replies, his voice more thankful than commanding. Melinda really did a number on his self-confidence. Now that he's been deJaffe-ized, I hope he can get it together to lead the townspeople tonight in the direction I want him to—far away from Nadine's cabin.

"How did we all miss this blue moon thing?" Detective Gallegos asks.

Owenski's response is snide, but accurate. "When you become a really good detective, you'll realize the most obvious answers are usually the ones that are most overlooked."

Don't get too cocky, Owenski. The wolf that started this whole panic is standing right next to you. Driving home in the Sequinox, I feel as if the wolf is back. I feel primitive and aggressive, and I can't keep my eyes off of Caleb.

"You know you do have some pictures of me on your phone in case you forget what I look like," he says, smiling and staring straight ahead at the road.

"Sorry," I say, blushing a little. "I'm really proud of you."

"Well, if it weren't for Old Cop, I don't think I would've persuaded Mr. Bergeron to reinstate the witch hunt," he replies. "Which is kind of funny because it's no longer a metaphorical name, but super literal."

I remember what Jess said to me about Caleb and realize she's right; I do take my boyfriend for granted.

"Don't underestimate your power, Mr. Bettany," I say, kissing Caleb's cheek. "When this is all over tonight, you're going to get your reward."

Stopping at a red traffic light, Caleb looks at me. He never loses his smile, but the rest of his face adopts a more serious expression. "Listen to me, Domgirl," he says. "No matter what happens tonight or tomorrow or the next day, I can wait. I'm not in any rush." Serious cannot survive amid his high-pitched laugh. "Well, that's a total lie! But I don't want to rush you into anything."

I want to tug on our string with such force that I'll feel his spirit move right through me.

"You haven't rushed me at all," I reply. "For the first time in a long while, I feel like I'm in complete control."

Caleb kisses me softly a few times and then a few more until I stop counting. "Promise me you won't let go of that feeling tonight," he says, his lips never leaving mine.

Right now I'd promise him anything. "I promise."

And then he kisses me deeper than ever before, and I moan and howl at the same time. "Because when this is all over," Caleb whispers, "you and I have some celebrating to do."

How quickly I come back to reality. I force myself to keep kissing him, but I know that before I can celebrate I'm going to have to survive the night.

"I've thought it over, and there's no way that you two are coming with me tonight," I declare.

The wolf has spoken.

"And there's no way that you're telling us what to do," Archie insists.

The girl has been put in her place.

He's sitting next to Arla on her bed, and they both look like they're going to give each other a makeover, like they did last week, instead of telling me that they're going to stand behind me when I march into enemy camp tonight. Correction, not behind me, but alongside of me.

"We aren't doing this because of you, Dominy," Arla states.

Oh really? "Then why are you doing it?!"

"Because it's the right thing to do!" she replies as if I'm a few x's short of the desired amount of chromosomes. "Sure, you're at the center of this whole thing, but it's grown; it's bigger than just you now."

"So you can't be a one-girl army," Archie adds. "Or a one-wolf army, whatever the case may be."

My friends, who started out as my protectors and my defenders, have now become warriors just like me. And they have good reason.

"Luba and her family killed my friend too, Dom," Arla reminds me. "And because of her curse I was almost blinded."

"And I know Napoleon is my first, I know our romance probably won't last a lifetime," Archie asserts, "but I love him, and he's in major trouble and needs my help, so I'm going to give it to him."

"Homance?" I ask.

Tossing his head back, white bangs flailing, he replies, "Oh come on, linguistagirl! Homo meets romance equals homance."

"It's perfect!" And so are they.

I'm about to launch into a speech about how they need to be extra careful tonight, how Luba and Nadine are formidable opponents who when they team up seem to have really extra-powerful powers, but I realize they already know that. They've been paying attention; they're taking responsibility for their own actions and their own lives. It's time I did the same thing.

After Louis leaves with Barnaby and Caleb to meet the others in the center of town and lead them on a wild-goose chase far from the Jaffe cabin, I hop into Louis's car. Arla is already in the driver's seat, and Archie is riding shotgun.

"Wolf Pack ready?" Archie asks, holding out his non-trembling hand.

Arla lays her hand on top of his, and I cover them both with mine. She and I reply at the same time. "Wolf Pack ready!"

Just as we turn onto the dirt road that leads up to the cabin, Arla reaches underneath her seat and pulls out a gun.

"You stole your father's gun?!" I ask, shocked that she would do such a thing.

"No!" Arla scoffs. "Just his Taser."

Oh, well, that makes all the difference in the world. And actually it does.

"I figured it could come in handy if things get too crazy," she explains.

After a pause, Archie replies, "If?"

There's an eerie silence when Arla pulls the key out of the ignition. Nothing, no sounds come from outside or inside the car; it's as if the world is suspended. I want to say something, but I can't think of anything that would inspire courage or hope or even get them to retreat. My mind is a blank, probably because I'm trying to forget exactly what could happen when the night takes over. Still shrouded in dusk, we're safe; our lives are unchanged and not moving forward. But in a few minutes when the moonglow obliterates all sunlight, fate will take over. And, honestly, fate and I don't have the best relationship.

Walking toward the main cabin, I catch glimpses of Arla and Archie. Their strides are unbroken; they aren't hesitating a bit, and I can see in their faces nothing but determination. If I were alone, I'd look and feel the same way, but I'm not. After all this time of complaining and moaning that this curse has only affected me and that I'm the only one to have to go through this and that I have to go through it on my own, I see how wrong I was. I've dragged my friends on this ride with me. They would never have had to get on if it weren't for me.

Enough! Enough with the guilt-talk and the thinking and the self-pity. It's time for action, to see if we can end this nightmare and reclaim our lives. It's time to stop living in fear and confront our demons. In other words, it's time to say hello to the Jaffes.

"Welcome," Nadine says.

She's sitting on the couch next to Luba and Napoleon. If their mother is present, she's in the back room. Not that it matters; she doesn't appear to have inherited the witch gene either by birth or by marriage. Nope, the triumvirate hasn't added a fourth.

"You were right, Grandmother," Nadine adds. "Dominy's brought ebony and ivory with her."

"I knew she would," Luba says. "The girl can't resist an audience."

Psycho Squaw looks unbelievably young now that Rayna's blood and spirit and energy are living within her body. She looks like she could be Nadine's older sister instead of her grandmother. Problem is, I'm sure that along with her new-found youth she's also acquired increased strength and power; she's going to be harder to conquer than before. My plan has got to work. I have to goad her into showing her true self so we can simply fight wolf to wolf; that way I may have a chance to kill her, and the *Three W* will have another head-line tomorrow morning. Until then I have to let them think that we're here to fight them on their terms, not ours.

"As much as your crew should be applauded for their loy-alty and their bravery in walking into our lair," Nadine starts, "the time has come for your little posse to go kaput."

"What?!" Napoleon shouts. Sounds like he wasn't privy to his sister's plan.

"They know too much, and they're in the way of Orion's plan," she replies, not even deigning to look at her brother, but keeping her gaze focused on us. "They need to be elimi-nated."

Luba slowly runs her long, thin fingers through her now sleek black hair, probably amazed at how soft it must feel. "Starting with Dominy," she says.

Napoleon says something, but I'm distracted by the burning sensation that suddenly grips me. Whipping my head to the side to look out the window, I see the full moon hanging in the black sky, fierce and majestic. Just like me.

"Guess again!" I scream. "I have not come this far to be killed by some sick witch who needs her grandchildren to carry out her deeds!"

Luba's eyes turn completely black, and her hand stops moving in mid-fawn. Guess she didn't like being called out for what she is.

"You are nothing but a vindictive, vengeful, and *ugly* woman!" I cry. "You say you cursed me to avenge your husband's death? That you doomed me because my father took away the man you loved?! You know *nothing* of love!"

"Silence!" Luba hisses.

No way! Not until I'm finished.

"You're filled with hate and loathing and evil," I say. "You want to destroy your grandchildren, go right ahead, but we will *not* be your next victims!"

Flying off of the couch, her feet never touching the ground, Luba doesn't stop moving until she's an inch from my face. When she stops, her hair swings forward and scratches my cheek; it's like small knives jutting into my skin. The sensation isn't as sharp as her voice.

"I said *silence!!*"

A howl spills out of my mouth that matches Luba's roar in volume and intensity until her voice cannot be heard and she's the one who's been silenced. My sound grows louder and more anguished when my bones break and invert. When the needles of fur begin to cover my body, I can't stand vertical any longer, so my body lurches forward and slams into the wooden floor.

I twist my head to the left and to the right as the muscles in my neck elongate and thicken to carry the heavy weight of my snout. I snarl and growl as the pain intensifies; my fangs sever my gums, and I taste my own blood. Swallowing greedily I want more; I'm thirsty and hungry and desperate to feed, but it's not time for that. Not yet.

My voice and my howl swirl and merge until they become one new sound that human and witch and wolf can hear. "Fight me like the animal you are!"

Luba proves that while she may be shrewd, she's also proud, and she can't refuse an invitation. To my left I hear Arla scream as Luba transforms into the black wolf that killed Essie. Despite how refreshed and youthful Luba now looks, her wolf-state is the same as it was before, mangy and foul and disgusting, the personification of her soul.

Her hand shaking, Arla fumbles with her coat to pull out her Taser gun, but Nadine gets to the weapon first—with her mind. It flies out of Arla's pocket and lands gracefully in Nadine's hand. "Nice try," she smirks. "But we prefer to fight the natural way." As she tosses the gun in the air, Archie jerks forward to grab it, but it dematerializes before he can wrap his hands around the metal. The only thing that remains is Nadine's laughter. Staring at the wolf Luba has become, it's my turn to show off.

Our bodies bang into each other as we both lunge forward at the same time. I feel Luba's claws piercing my arms and her fangs try to grab hold of my neck. Quickly I sense that I'm at an advantage; I've been in this body longer than she's been in hers, so I know how to use mine more efficiently and to the best of its capabilities. Snarling viciously, I swipe at her face with my paw, and when I let go, part of her cheek dangles in the air. The black wolf cries out in agony.

In retaliation, Nadine jumps off the couch, raises her hand and points it at me. She wants revenge. Napoleon wants mercy. "Nadine, stop!" I don't know what's keeping Nadine from taking action, Napoleon's command or her conscience, but she's abiding by her brother's wishes. For the moment.

"We don't have to destroy," he continues. "We have all of

Orion's power. We can honor our grandfather's legacy, but we can do it without leaving behind us a trail of destruction."

The bee and the butterfly are staring at one another as if there is one lone flower in a patch of shriveled, sun-baked dirt. There's only enough food for one. And there's only enough room in their world for one to survive. Briefly, it looks as if Nadine may acquiesce, that she may relinquish some of the hold she wants on her brother's life, but when she speaks, it's clear whatever moment of reason she had is gone.

"A hunter needs to destroy," she declares. "That is Orion's legacy, that is what he has taught us. Instill fear in our prey so they know who is the most powerful, and then we can have anything we desire."

"We already have more power than anyone!" Nap shouts, his arms outstretched, grappling the empty air. "Look at us! We can do things people only dream about!"

"Thanks to Orion!" Nadine replies, her voice sounding like that of a vainglorious and brainwashed disciple.

"Yes!" Nap screams. "Let's prove to him that we can hunt with mercy, not for vengeance!"

Nadine takes a step forward and stumbles to the side. For a moment I can see her face completely; it's bathed by the silver starlight, and she looks more like a girl than a fiend. But she quickly steadies herself, and when she speaks, I don't hear a trace of the girl. "We have a mission," she reminds him.

"To unleash Orion's spirit," Napoleon cries. "Not to unleash his wrath!"

"And that's why you'll never be a true descendant of Orion!" Nadine says. "You don't understand that his spirit and his wrath are one and the same."

Just as Napoleon is about to respond, he's distracted, we all are, as Luba shifts back from wolf to witch. She is crouched on the ground like a grotesque demon. Her long black hair thankfully covers her naked body as she looks at her favorite spawn.

"Nadine," Luba whispers. "Don't you think it's time to show your brother and his friends which one of my grandchildren has inherited the real power of our ancestor?"

I scour Nadine's face in search of a hint of remorse or fear or sorrow, but can't find any. She raises her arm and points three fingers at her brother. I don't know if she's doing it because she truly wants to show her brother that she is stronger or if she's doing it merely because she cannot disobey Luba and Orion. But her target isn't her brother.

"Finish it, child!" Luba screeches. "Finish what I started."

No, Nadine isn't aiming for her brother. She's aiming for me.

I don't see Nadine move, but I see the blast of silver-black smoke race toward me, and I know whatever's contained in that mist is vicious and hateful and deadly. Acting quickly, I spring to the left and let my body roll into the wall. I'm safe, but Archie isn't. I whip my head around just in time to see him take the full blast into his chest, the blast that was meant for me.

A silent pause is followed by the most horrific screams I've ever heard. Archie's voice is unrecognizable, but I know he's the one who made the sound. He's the only one who was propelled into the air, and he's the only one who crashed onto the floor face-first. The only reason he turns onto his back is because his body is writhing so violently. When I see his face, I howl; I don't know where the terror ends and the agony begins. And no wonder. Nadine's black energy is burrowing holes into his body, drilling her foul stench deep inside of him, embalming him with her evil.

"*Archie!!*"

Napoleon's voice thunders through the room with such authority that everyone except Archie freezes; his body continues to pulsate. Only when Nap embraces his boyfriend does Archie's body begin to quiet. But there's nothing that Nap can do to help Archie now; all he can do is seek vengeance.

Standing in the middle of the room, Nap turns to face his sister, his voice almost sounds as wild as his eyes appear.

"Now . . . you . . . pay!"

If Nadine is frightened by her brother's maniacal proclamation, she hides it well. She actually looks amused. "Looks like you chose the wrong side to play on, brother," she says.

"You don't know how right you are, sister!" Napoleon seethes. "I've spent my entire life obeying you and that evil witch, and all of that ends right here and now!"

He raises his hand, and a pure silver light streaks out of Napoleon's flesh, piercing the air like a steel arrow, and hits Nadine right in the stomach. Shock overtakes her face and then terror when she looks down to see that her midsection has been ripped apart. There's no blood, no organs pouring out of her, just blackness. Looks like Napoleon hit her soul.

But her soul is starting to change. Within the black two silver lights begin to twinkle and pulse. I have no idea what they represent, but Nadine is horrified by the sight.

"No!!!" Nadine wails, falling to her knees.

She then turns to the only other being in the room who she knows will help her: Luba.

"Help me!" she cries, covering the hole that used to house her stomach. "Help us!!"

Us? What is she talking about? Oh yes, of course, if Nadine dies, Luba loses one-third of her power. And without Nadine it will be even more difficult to keep Napoleon under control.

Psycho Squaw understands the urgency and races to her granddaughter's side. She places her hand on the hole that used to be Nadine's stomach and begins to chant. Like before when I've heard her doing her imitation of a holy prayer, I can only pick up certain words, not entire phrases, so I don't know exactly what she's saying. Now, however, I know exactly which god she's praying to: Orion.

Luba's lips are moving frantically, and she's filling up the hole with her own black energy. *Orion, child, three, preserve.* These are the words I hear. I can string them together to figure out their meaning; she's begging Orion to preserve the life of her granddaughter. She leaves out the part about how she couldn't care less if Nadine lives or dies, how her request is completely self-serving. Which is interesting, because the more I learn about this Orion person, the more I think the sicko would help her more if he knew the truth.

But even with Luba's lies, it seems that Orion is helping his minions. Slowly the gash begins to heal. Flesh grows out of the emptiness, and soon Nadine's body is fully repaired. She's exhausted, but whole.

While Luba attends to Nadine to help her regain her strength, Napoleon and Arla try to revive Archie. Like the hunter I am, I spot an easy prey, and my body twitches as my eyes zero in on Luba. One jump, one slice into her flesh with my claws and I could kill her; but no, sometimes a hunter needs to protect his pack and not just give in to his cravings. Somewhere up in the distance, Orion, the original hunter, must be looking down at me with pride.

Or perhaps with disappointment.

Revived, Nadine has risen, her eyes filled with rage and the desire for revenge and retaliation. But that's not all. Her body is bathed in silver sweat that clings to her like a steel body shield. Obviously, Orion rewards taking action against your enemy, more than he does showing loyalty for your supporters.

"Now it's time for you to pay, brother!" she howls. "You and your chosen one."

Without thinking, Napoleon stands in front of Archie's still-limp body to defend him from his sister's wrath. He's fully prepared and willing to die to protect Archie. I know exactly how he feels, but still, I can't let that happen. Unfortunately, I've learned enough to know that I can't keep him safe on my own.

"*Jess!*"

The room remains lit only by the glow of the moon; there's no blinding sunlight to destroy the shadows, turn the darkness into something different, something good.

"*JESS!!!*"

This time my voice is louder, more desperate. I need my friend; I need her to fight alongside me, to protect me and keep my friends and me safe. Where is she?! I scream her name one more time, and finally I'm successful. Just as Nadine raises her hand at Napoleon, the room is filled with Jess's golden light, so intense it makes Luba cry out in panic as if it's scalding her skin.

"Hurry!" Luba instructs.

Luba waves her hand, and it takes me a moment to realize what she's done—she's put Arla and me under a spell; we can't move from our spots. Jess is Napoleon and Archie's only hope against Nadine.

This time the light that rockets out of Nadine's fingers isn't silver, but pure black. In the middle of the room the black stream splits in two, one heading for Napoleon and one for Archie. She's not taking any chances this time; she's aiming to kill, and she wants two for one.

"*Jess, do something!*" I scream.

But Jess doesn't act; she seems as frozen as I am. It's because she has to make a horrible choice. "I can only save one of them," she confesses.

Her words echo in my ears, creating an intense pain, but it can't be nearly as unbearable as what Jess is feeling right now. Save her ex-boyfriend or one of her best friends—that's her choice. I don't know how she'll ever decide, but she has to. And right now!

The two streams of Nadine's black energy hit Napoleon

and Archie at the same time. Both separately fly into the air. Both tremble as if they're being electrocuted. Both disappear into mists of black smoke. Only one cries out in sheer horror.

Archie's voice makes me shudder. It sounds like the cries I make when I transform, when it feels like my body is being ripped apart from its limbs, which is exactly what it looks like is happening. Hanging in the air, Archie's body shakes like a rag doll as ribbons of black and yellow light infuse it. Arms outstretched, he looks like a martyr nailed to a crucifix, but instead of bleeding blood, he's bleeding sunshine.

Somehow, Jess has made her choice—she's chosen to save Archie. In spite of that, Nadine is fighting hard to make Jess regret her decision to interfere with Nadine's devilish plans.

"Get . . . away . . . from . . . my . . . prize!"

Nadine is dripping with sweat, the constant exertion draining her, and her legs are starting to shake almost as wildly as Archie and her brother. I turn my head from Napoleon; I can't bear to watch his lifeless body thrash in the air any longer. Howling, I call out to anyone listening, to anyone who can hear me, for mercy. Miraculously, my cry is heard. By Luba.

Aware that she's already lost one grandchild, she doesn't want to risk losing another, so she grabs Nadine by the shoulder and commands her to stop.

"Enough, child," Luba says.

But Nadine is far from ready to give in. She flicks her shoulders and breaks free from Luba's hold in the same exact way Melinda broke free from Winston. Like mother, like daughter. But Luba is through playing. She doesn't care if Nadine wants to continue.

"You've done all you can!"

"And so have I," Jess tells me, her voice uncharacteristically weary and resigned.

Finally, Nadine lowers her hands, and the energy flow is broken. Napoleon and Archie hang suspended in the air for a few seconds more, and then both crash to the floor, lying next to one another. The two look so peaceful now, like they're sleeping, but only one is destined to wake up.

No one speaks as Luba scoops up Nadine in her arms and Arla crawls behind me for protection. There's no need to speak; there's no need to comment or say a word. The battle is over. For now.

"You've merely been granted a reprieve, Dominy," Luba hisses. "Use your time wisely."

Psycho Squaw and her granddaughter leave the cabin without glancing back to see if Nap is alive or dead, not out of compassion or out of curiosity. I guess they made their choice too.

Looking over at Nap I have no idea if he's alive or dead—he still isn't moving—but when Archie opens his eyes, I hear Arla and Jess breathe sighs of relief. Nadine hasn't succeeded; she hasn't taken Archie from us; she hasn't taken yet another life! But when we look at our friend closer, we see we might be wrong.

Lying on the floor looking up at us, Archie has been healed; there isn't a scratch on his body or on his face. But his eyes tell a different story. Gone is the beautiful and rare violet color, and in its place is something unique and frightening. No longer violet, one eye is completely black, while the other has turned a shimmering shade of gold. He's survived the battle for his soul, but it looks like Jess and Nadine can both claim victory. Archie's now a mixture of both good and evil.

"Hi, Jess," Archie says. "Been a long time."

And now he's no longer human.

Chapter 28

"I'm sorry," Jess says.

I want to disagree with her, but I can't because I feel the same way. Not that I blame Jess, not for a second. She's *saved* our friend's life. But if Archie can see her, that means she's also *changed* our friend's life. I just wish we knew to what extent. How much of Jess's light does he have within his body and how much of Nadine's darkness? His body goes limp, but defiantly, his eyes remain open, one black, one golden, staring straight ahead. Which side is stronger, Archie? The darkness or the light? The only response is silence. We'll just have to wait to find out, but time isn't on our side. And more enemies are approaching.

"Domgirl!"

Even as a wolf that voice makes me smile. I don't know why Caleb has come here, but I'm grateful to know he's close.

"We're in here," Arla shouts. She's clearly in duress, clutching her head with one hand and grabbing the archway of the open door with the other to steady herself. I don't think it's her own pain that's attacking her body; it's Napoleon's.

"Are you all right?" Caleb asks, entering the cabin.

"I'm fine," she lies.

"Oh my God!" he cries out once he sees our two unconscious friends. "Archie!!"

Caleb kneels next to Archie and lifts his head, cradling it on his knees, and places his fingers on Archie's wrist. I rush next to Caleb and nuzzle my head against his legs. I need to feel him; I need contact. Caleb wants answers.

"What happened?" he asks.

"There was a fight.... Nadine hit them both...." Arla conveys, her voice weary and distracted.

"Are they..."

Prince Caleb is so sweet he can't even say the word "dead."

"We don't know," Arla admits. "Jess did her best."

"Jess is here?" Caleb asks, whipping his head around as if he'll be able to see her.

"Somewhere," Arla replies. "She saved Archie's life."

"His pulse is strong," Caleb announces. "He's...he's going to be okay."

Even though my boyfriend has come face-to-face with unexplained phenomena, he's still incredibly naïve. He believes what he wants to believe, that good will always win out and evil will always be defeated. He doesn't understand about balance. Until it's staring him in the face.

"Arla..." Caleb says. "What's wrong with his eyes?"

I rub the crown of my head on his hand to comfort him. He's so cold. His bravery is giving way to fear.

"We don't know yet," Arla explains. "But, Caleb, why are you here? You're supposed to be leading my father and his gang to the other side of town. Why'd you bring them to ground zero?"

"I tried for as long as I could," he explains. "But a group of them are on their way here. There was nothing I could do to stop them, so I got free from the pack and ran ahead so I could warn you."

Bending over and clutching her head, Arla shouts. "Get them out of here!"

Like before, she isn't speaking in her own voice, but Napoleon's.

Profoundly startled, Caleb falls backward onto the floor. "Nap?!"

"They're coming!" Arla as Nap shouts. "Go . . . now!"

I push my snout hard into Caleb's knee to get him to move. I'm not sure if Caleb sees the girl or the wolf, but his lips form a smile and he nods; he understands what my action is trying to tell him, that he needs to take Archie and Arla away from here so they'll be safe. Outside, danger is approaching, and it'll be here any second.

"We have to go, Caleb," Arla says, finally in command of her own voice. "Now!"

Impulsively, Caleb grabs my head and presses my cheek next to his. I can feel the warmth of his flesh through my fur, and it lights a fire deep inside of me that burns even brighter when he speaks. "Thank God you're all right," he whispers into my ear.

He scoops Archie up into his arms and runs outside, followed closely by Arla. Just before she leaves the cabin, she calls out to the empty air.

"Jess! Take care of Dominy!"

Even though I don't see Jess, I know that she'll do just that. I sense that she's nearby, but I can't wait for her to appear. I need to get Napoleon outside so he'll be seen by Louis and his army. If I can't rely on Jess to help me do it, I'll rely on the wolf.

Opening wide, I grab Nap's ankle in my mouth, but I bite down too hard and taste blood. Hunger rushes into my stomach and my brain and my mouth like water racing into a river after a dam is lifted. Fight! I must fight the insatiable need to feast on this flesh and do what's right. I must keep my paws from crossing over the line, keep them safely on the side my father and mother and Jess would want me to stay on. No, the side that I've chosen to remain on! I may be half animal, but I don't have to act like one.

Suppressing the insane hunger rocking my body, I loosen my grip on Napoleon's leg. I drag him from the cabin, trying to avoid any sharp rocks in our path, and into the clearing so he'll be found by the vigilantes and brought back to safety.

About a mile away I smell fire, not the rage of an inferno, but the whiff of a flame, and I know that torches are close by. Howling madly, I disturb the peaceful silence until I hear voices in the distance.

"Over here!"

I had planned on Louis and his mob finding Luba in her state as the feral black wolf so they would turn predator into prey and kill her, confident that they had finally captured and defeated the Full Moon Killer. I never thought I had a plan B, but I had forgotten that sometimes fate makes plans for us. Instead of finding a killer, Louis's civilian army will find another victim. Fine! Let Luba and Nadine go free for now. If it means that Napoleon can be brought to a hospital and his broken body mended, it will be worth it.

But I don't know if there's enough time to save him. Blood has started to pour out from the huge gash in his chest, racing out from deep within his body and spilling across his pale flesh like red-hued seaweed that washes up, entangled and wet, on a sandy beach. His body is no longer twitching, no longer moving at all except for a slight up-and-down movement near his stomach. His breath is shallow and tired, and he seems ready to give in. Fight, Napoleon! Fight for your life! Don't let Nadine and Luba become victorious yet again.

Another howl spills out of my mouth, louder and clearer than before, ripping through the night and landing right where I want it to.

"It's the wolf!"

No one is behind Louis yet; it's just the two of us staring at each other, the hunter and the hunted. But underneath the sounds of the crackling flame of the torch he's holding, I can hear frantic voices and shuffling footsteps; his army is getting closer. I have to act quickly before Louis uses the gun that he's holding in his other hand, because I know for certain that he's not like my father; he didn't make a pact with God never to pull the trigger of a loaded gun. If Louis aims, he may very well shoot me. His gun may not be loaded with a silver bullet to kill me, but it'll be enough to wound me so he can claim me as his trophy. A trophy that will change shape at dawn.

Louis raises his arm, the one holding his gun, and we lock eyes.

His face is clearly visible, washed in the firelight, and I can see every crevice and mark and wrinkle on his face. It's a marred landscape, but it's still the face of a good man. A man who has squandered most of his life, avoided responsibility, and done the least amount that he had to do in order to survive. He's always allowed others to shape his life for him, his ex-wife, his ex-boss; he went along with whatever decisions they made, regardless of how those decisions affected him. Well, now he has to make his own decision: Kill the beast before him or let it survive to kill another day—that's what must be going through his mind. It's a simple decision, but for some reason he's hesitating.

Could he possibly recognize me? Does he know that beneath this costume of fur and fangs is the daughter of his best friend? Perhaps, but how could he? Whatever he's thinking, whatever emotions are creating a conflicted mass of confusion within his heart, they're making him waver, stopping him from pulling the trigger. Then again, maybe it isn't that complicated; maybe he's just waiting for me to make the first move.

My paws scratch at the dirt, but which way should I

move? Run into the brush to escape or leap forward? I could end this curse right now, free myself from these invisible chains. Maybe without me alive Nadine and Luba will move on, terrorize another girl, another community. But no! How can someone who has been so blessed allow such cursed souls free rein to hunt?

It seems that Louis and I are at a stalemate. Neither of us willing to make the first move. Until our reinforcements arrive: Barnaby and Jess.

"Where is it?!"

My brother's voice startles Louis, and the finger that's pressed against the trigger reacts. It pulls back to release a bullet in my direction, a bullet I see speeding toward my unmoving body. A bullet absorbed by a wall of golden light. Jess's simple yet effective way of saving my life. And Napoleon's.

"It got away," Louis replies. I swear I hear relief in his voice mixed in with astonishment.

"How?!" Barnaby cries. "You said it was right here!"

"I said it got away!" Louis bellows.

From deep within my hiding spot in the brush alongside the cabin, I see Louis thrust his torch into my brother's hand, and in two quick strides run to Napoleon's side. He doesn't flinch when he sees Nap's ghastly wound. The hesitation he was feeling just seconds ago has released its grip on him so he can act quickly and lift Nap's body up in his arms. But before he runs off, Louis pauses, not because he's questioning his actions, but because he's questioning what he sees.

Looking into the bushes where I'm hiding, he stops when he sees my eyes, the blue-gray standing out against a mane of red fur. His eyes widen with something, recognition or wonder or horror, I don't know, but he remains silent; he doesn't alert Barnaby or the other men and women gathering around him of my whereabouts. This confrontation will be our secret. Instead he convinces them that life and not death is the night's priority.

"Forget about the wolf," he commands, rising and turning to face the group. "We have to get this kid to the hospital."

"Oh my God, it's my son!"

I fight the urge to leap out from my shelter and pounce on Melinda Jaffe's body, rip a hole in her chest that would make the one in Napoleon's look like a pinhole, but there's still a flicker of golden light dancing in front of my eyes.

"Don't move."

I can't see Jess, but I hear her voice. She's still protecting me.

"Napoleon!"

Melinda's shriek sounds incredibly real, and if I didn't know better I'd actually think that she was grieving her son's condition. But I do know the truth. She doesn't care about him; she's just like the other Jaffe women. She only cares about following Orion's mission and reaping all the benefits his power can bring. If her son has to die, like his father before him, in order for that power to grow, then so be it.

She's a very good actress, however, and I can tell from the look in Louis's eyes that despite her infidelity with Winston, despite her betrayal, he wishes he could wrap his arms around Melinda and calm her. But his arms are full. He's holding her son, the son that she hopes will soon die. Not if Louis has anything to say about it.

"Get me to the hospital!" he roars.

I wait until I no longer hear any sounds other than the wind before I start to venture out from my hiding spot. But Jess has other ideas.

"What part of 'I'm trying to save your life' do you not understand?" she asks. She's sitting cross-legged and cross-armed, floating in front of me, an expression of disbelief on her face.

"I have to get to Archie and the others!" I silently cry.

"Prince Caleb has everything under control," she sighs. "Why do you constantly underestimate him?"

"I don't underestimate him," I protest.

"*Nanite koto!*" she cries.

"Why are you arguing with me?" I ask. "Napoleon is dying, and I have no idea what's going on with Archie."

Jess repositions herself to stand in front of me like a golden barricade. She lifts up her arms, and her hands begin to stretch out to her sides to create a sphere of sunshine all around me. I'm not going anywhere no matter how badly I want to. Or how loudly I howl.

"Oh will you shut up!" Jess cries. "There is nothing that you can do for Napoleon and Archie that you haven't already done. And what do you think you're going to do, enter the hospital as a wolf and just waltz on into the emergency room?"

She has a point.

"You have to start thinking logically, Dom," she berates. "And not like some wild beast. If I didn't stop Louis's bullet . . . Without you this town would be at the mercy of Psycho Squaw and twinemy!" she declares. "You have to protect the town like I have to protect you."

Jess's touch feels so wonderful, warm and loving and honest. Just like her words.

"You didn't mention Napoleon," I say.

Ignoring me, Jess continues to run her fingers through my fur.

"Jess, is he going to die?"

"Mr. Dice allowed me to, um, circumvent our limitations so I could intervene and save one soul," Jess replies. "I had to make a choice."

"And you chose to save Archie?"

I don't know why I'm surprised by her actions, but I am. Yes, she loves Archie, but as a friend. She was *in love* with Napoleon. If she could only choose one, why would she choose her friend over the guy she was in love with?

"For a preternatural being, you can be incredibly stupid,

you know that?" Jess states. "Friendship is just another form of love, the kind that comes first in your life and the kind that lasts much longer than whatever feelings I had for Napoleon."

I nuzzle my snout into Jess's knee so I can be covered in her warmth and her friendship. I know that she's talking about our bond, our undying connection, and it fills me with a happiness that is as rapturous as what Nadine felt when she was consumed by Orion's spirit. Right after she killed her brother.

"So this means that Napoleon is dead?" I ask meekly.

She shrugs her shoulders and sends little flares of sunlight into the dark sky. "I don't know," she admits. "There is a chance he can be saved. I just can't do anything to tip the cards in his favor."

"So we have to wait to see what the morning brings," I say.

"You're starting to learn the ways of the world, Dominy-san," Jess replies. "First thing in the morning you can go to the hospital after you transform. For now you have to stay here, and I'll keep you company. I'll even turn my head so you can have your privacy while you feed on that raccoon over there."

Jess knows me too well. I might have muffled my hunger, restrained it for a while, but it's still growing inside me, and it needs to be quenched.

Some rules can't be broken.

Chapter 29

Two of my friends. Two different hospital rooms. Hopefully, there won't be two different outcomes.

This morning when I transformed back, when the wolf spirit and I switched places, Jess shielded me with her light so I could make it from the woods to my home without anyone noticing the naked girl running through the streets. There was so much commotion at the hospital last night with both Archie and Napoleon rushed to the emergency room and hours later each admitted to separate rooms, that no one noticed I was missing. Arla told me that Louis and Barnaby asked for me, but she made up a few excuses for my absence: I was in the bathroom, the chapel, and once I had fainted and was being treated by a nurse. This almost started Louis on a quest for his wayward ward, but several hours ago Officer Gallegos burst into the hospital shouting something about a predawn bank robbery, and when you're the chief of police, crime fighting trumps stepdaughter searching, so my absence wasn't uncovered. Who says crime doesn't have its benefits?

Definitely not Luba.

Sitting in the waiting room, I see Luba walk in, and for the first time she isn't wearing her white hospital gown. She's not wearing anything fancy and definitely not anything fashion-able, but her clothes don't have the official name of The Re-treat stamped on them, so the black pants and shoes and red V-neck sweater look startling on her. As startling as the only piece of jewelry she's wearing, a silver necklace with three stars in a row that sits just below the apex of her neckline, so it looks like starlight lives on a bed of blood. Perfect.

Luba is moving slowly and dabbing a tissue at the corners of her dry eyes. The hospital staff must think she looks com-pletely normal; in fact, they must think she looks downright amazing for a grief-stricken grandmother. Only those of us who know what she really is and the part she played in her grandson's so-called accident can see past the disguise. And I'm probably the only one who can see the faintest scar on her cheek where I tore off her flesh when she was temporar-ily in wolf's clothing last night.

Flanked on either side by Nadine and Melinda, Luba doesn't sit in one of the empty chairs; she doesn't suddenly burst into fake tears to garner even more sympathy from the crowd; she walks right up to Louis Bergeron, who's returned to check in on the situation, and slaps him across the face.

"I hold you responsible," she announces.

I have to grab Arla by the wrist and use all my wolf-strength to keep her seated. We cannot do battle, not in here, not in such close quarters. Luckily, Louis is no stranger to the antics of crazy women, so he handles the situation deftly.

"And as chief of police, I take full responsibility," he replies, resisting the urge to rub his reddened cheek. "For the lives of both boys."

"You and this irresponsible witch hunt for the Full Moon Killer," she seethes.

"I am doing whatever is necessary to protect this town," he replies, his voice just as steady.

"By giving in to folklore and superstition?" Luba asks.

Louis might have dealt with crazy townsfolk, but most of

the time I'm sure it's in the confines of his office or in the middle of the night without an audience; he isn't used to being stared at while defending his actions.

"We were following the facts of the case, ma'am," he says.

"If you were following the facts of the case, you wouldn't have been running around with a bunch of *idiots* carrying torches in the middle of the night!" she scoffs. Then without even lowering her voice, she adds, "I told Melinda you were a fool."

Now she's made it personal. I'm tempted to let go of Arla and see what damage she can do to the old lady. But I know that even if Arla gets in a good punch or two, maybe even one of those Bruce Lee-style roundhouse kicks, Luba will rebound with something far more destructive, regardless of how many people are watching. *No, keep still; let someone else rescue Louis and put Luba in her place.* I would never have guessed that person would be my brother.

"Luba," he says. "Why don't you sit over here?"

Barnaby's voice is quiet, but stern. He's clearly incensed by Luba's callous treatment of Louis, but he's also surprised. This is not the woman he's come to know. Let me introduce you to the real Luba, Barnaby, and if you think this is bad, I pray for your sake that she never reveals her true self to you.

My brother takes Luba by the elbow and leads her to an empty seat in a corner of the room. She doesn't resist; there's no need for her to. She's accomplished what she set out to do: She's painted a picture of herself as an angry, yet rational woman, not a psychopath who prays at a celestial altar.

Not only that, but she's also made Louis look like, well, an idiot. And, unfortunately, I'm partially responsible. I'm the one who made Caleb convince him to lift the town curfew and reinstate the vigilante coalition. Sure, Louis succumbed to peer pressure and his own desire to catch the town's elusive serial killer, but he had let go of such foolishness. If I hadn't pushed Caleb, he wouldn't have pushed Louis. In the heat of the night, a mob mentality seems like the logical course of action, but in the harsh light of day it looks like exactly what it is: stupid.

Luckily, the murmuring of the crowd is hushed when the doctor walks into the waiting room. The good people of Weeping Water can bad-mouth Louis later; right now we need to find out if Lars Svenson is going to put another citizen's face on the front page of the *Three W*.

"How is my son, doctor?"

I want to grab Melinda Jaffe by her blond hair and bash her face into the wall. I want to break her nose so she'll need to have it fixed and her physical resemblance to my mother will cease. If I break something else besides her nose, then so be it. The woman deserves it.

"Napoleon is very strong," the doctor announces. "And so far he's also very lucky."

Not exactly the news the ladies Jaffe were hoping for, but they put on a good show of making everyone believe this is exactly what they wanted to hear from the good doctor.

"He isn't out of the woods yet. The next twenty-four hours are crucial," the doctor warns. "But it looks like he's going to pull through."

"Thank you, doctor. That's good news," Napoleon's lying mother says. "May I see him now?"

"Yes, but don't be long," the doctor replies. "He needs his rest."

"Of course, I just want to see ..."

"Doctor," I say, interrupting Melinda. "What about Archie?"

Both the doctor and Mrs. Jaffe turn to face me. The doctor smiles; Melinda doesn't.

"Mr. Angevene is doing just fine," he says. "Looks like he merely passed out from exhaustion. His parents are filling out some paperwork, but he's going to be released shortly."

"What about ..."

"Yes?" the doctor asks.

"What about his eyes?" I finish.

The doctor looks at me with a puzzled expression, and I can't breathe. "The most extraordinary shade of violet," he says. "Common among albinos."

So his eyes are back to normal. It may not be a permanent condition, but that's more good news.

"Can we see him?" Caleb asks.

"Absolutely," the doctor replies. "I'm sure he'd love the company."

After the doctor leaves, Louis finds himself face-to-face with his ex-girlfriend. Ever the gentleman, Louis offers his condolences.

"I'm glad Napoleon is going to be okay," he says.

"Thank you," Melinda replies. And then she moves an inch closer to Louis and drops her voice to a tone that I'm sure she thinks is seductive. "Unlike my mother-in-law, I don't hold you responsible, Louis," she says, flicking away a piece of imaginary dust from his shirt collar. "In fact, I know that he's only alive because of you."

Ain't that the truth!

Louis swallows hard and stares at the floor for a few seconds before replying. "Only doing my job, Melin... ma'am."

"When this all blows over, I'm going to have to find a way to repay you for your kindness," she whispers.

Oh my God! Her son almost died, she's surrounded by her daughter and Louis's kids, and she's flirting? Seriously, the woman has no self-control. Thankfully, Louis has self-respect.

"You already did that," Louis says. "When you chose to be with Winston Lundgarden."

Touché! Arla and I can only silence our giggles until Louis leaves the room; once he's gone, they're unleashed. Right in Melinda's ear. Her look of utter disdain only makes us laugh harder until Caleb grabs the two of us by the backs of our necks and pushes us into the hallway and directly into Archie's room.

"Seriously?" Caleb asks. "You had to antagonize the woman who just happens to be the mother and daughter-in-law of a pair of witches?"

Still laughing, I throw my arm around Caleb's waist. "Sorry, Cay, but seeing her reaction was worth the risk."

Wrapping her arm around Caleb from the opposite side, Arla agrees. "Plus, I think my father really took the wind out of her sails. I don't think we'll be hearing too much from her anytime soon."

"Good," Caleb declares. "Because I for one could use a rest from all this mayhem."

"Me too," I reply.

"Me three," Arla adds.

"Me four," Archie chimes in. "What am I agreeing to?"

"A breather from all the magic and craziness going on lately," Caleb announces.

If only that were possible.

"Winter, you look amazing!"

"Thanks, Bells, but I'm still not going to go out with you."

"Boys," Arla starts. "One of these days I'm going to force the two of you to make out to see if this bromance has legs."

"Sorry, I'm taken," Archie says.

When Caleb doesn't reply, I slap him on his butt. "And so are you!"

Caleb's high-pitched laughter fills the room. "Just making sure you're paying attention," he says.

He squeezes me closer to him, and he smells so clean I close my eyes and breathe it in. I'm not exactly sure what's happening to me, if it's wolf-lust or girl-love, but whatever it is, I've never found Caleb more attractive than I do right now. Very soon, I'm going to have to show him how much he means to me. Right after I make sure Archie knows.

"So, have you had any side effects?" I ask, sitting on the foot of his bed.

Shaking his head slowly, Archie replies, "Nope, just antsy to get out of here and see how Napoleon's doing."

"Do you, um, remember anything about last night?" I ask slowly.

Picking at a thread on his blanket, Archie seems to be stalling, though he could simply be trying to remember the details that brought him here. "I know there was a fight," he says. "And I took a bit of a beating."

I look over at Arla, and she's thinking what I'm thinking, that Archie doesn't remember what happened to him. He doesn't remember seeing Jess, nor does he understand that he isn't completely human any longer. He was saved, but he's been turned into something new, something that at the moment doesn't have a name. For the time being, I think it's best to keep this information from him. Let him concentrate on his recovery and his boyfriend.

"The doc said Nap's going to pull through," Caleb shares. "But it'll be a while before you two can get, um, you know, all physical and stuff."

"You're such an a-hole!" Archie jokes. "The 'and stuff' part can wait. Nap and I don't have to put the *lay* in re*lay*-tionship."

"Ooh good one, Winter!" Caleb shouts.

Watching my boyfriend and Archie high-five each other, I smile. But it isn't genuine. I'm thrilled that Archie has fully recovered from the attack on his life and that he and Napoleon seem to have a sweet relationship, but the facts remain—Napoleon is still part of Them. Just because he survived his sister's assault, doesn't mean she won't try to kill him again. Why, I have no idea, since there need to be three of them to realize Orion's power. Could be that she now has enough power without him or that she just wants to get rid of Napoleon before he finds a way to get rid of her. Whatever the reason, their family feud is far from over. But Archie and Napoleon's love affair might be.

"Something's wrong."

Arla is pressing her fingers into her forehead. I know she isn't referring to herself, but to her psychonjoined twin.

"Napoleon?" I ask.

She nods her head furiously. The pain seems to be escalating; it's a struggle for her to form words. "I love you."

What? What is Arla talking about?

"I love you . . . Archie."

She wasn't making sense because she wasn't the one talking; Napoleon was. Why does Nap's sentiment sound dangerously close to a good-bye?

"Nap!" Archie cries out. "Arla, where is he?"

We follow Arla as she runs out of the room and down the corridor in the opposite direction of the waiting room. She turns left at the end of the hallway, then she stops at Room 48, the same number as Luba's room at The Retreat. This cannot be a good omen.

Inside the room, Napoleon is hooked up to a bunch of important-looking machines, but he's sleeping. I can hear his breathing, much stronger than it was last night when he was near death. Nadine is sitting next to the bed holding Nap's hand, while Luba is standing on the other side of the bed next to one of the machines, and Melinda is sitting on a chair next to the door. They look exactly like a worried family—their silence, their expressions, their posture—it's totally perfect. And totally unbelievable.

"Archie, no matter what happens you have to remember one thing."

Arla's voice is a combination of her own and Napoleon's, as if it's being stretched between two dimensions.

"You made my life worth living."

"Nap!" Archie cries out, first looking at the boy lying in the hospital bed and when he doesn't respond, at Arla. "What's going on? What are you talking about?!"

"He's trying to tell you good-bye."

Before Archie can respond to Nadine's comment, she holds up her hand, and the door slams shut. She's lured us here, I'm not sure why, but whatever she has planned, she wants witnesses. Smirking, she waves her hand in a semicircle and stops time. Everyone in the room freezes; everyone in the room resembles a storefront mannequin; everyone except me. She wanted an audience all right, but an audience of one.

"How did you do it, Dominy?" Nadine asks.

I have no idea what she's talking about. And I don't want to waste time trying to figure it out. I want to get out of this room. The problem is, I may not be stuck in time, but once again I'm stuck to the floor. I can't move.

"How did I do what?" I reluctantly ask.

"Kill Rayna," Nadine says sweetly.

I try to yank my foot off of the floor with such force that I almost topple over. I grab onto Caleb's arm and gasp; he feels like stone. Please don't let this spell she's cast be irreversible. "I didn't kill Rayna," I protest. "You did."

Laughing heartily, Nadine replies, "Oh no, don't you remember? I sucked her youth out of her, but you were the one who actually killed her."

"Because she begged me to after what you did to her!"

"I remember now," she says, ignoring my accusation. "Didn't you just put your hand over her mouth, like this?"

Mesmerized, I watch Nadine press her hand over her brother's mouth. I was right; she is going to try and kill her brother again. I just had no idea she would make another attempt so soon.

"No!" I scream. Lunging forward I grasp at the air, but Nadine is out of my reach, and I only succeed in falling over onto the ground. Looking up I see Napoleon's body start to shake; he's trying to fight back, but he's so weak from last night's battle; there's no way he has enough strength to prevent Nadine from succeeding. If only I could break free from this spell, if only I could tear her hand away from her brother's mouth. But maybe I can fight back another way.

"Don't you need three of you to fully realize Orion's power?" I ask, struggling to finally stand up.

"You're very perceptive," Nadine replies sarcastically. "Yes, we do."

"Then stop this!" I beg. "Without Napoleon you can never reach your potential! You need him."

"Not any longer," she replies.

What? How can that be? I didn't think her mother had any power; she wasn't born with it like the twins were, and I'm guessing that their grandfather was only able to bestow his power onto Luba because he was the original recipient. If there were a way for Melinda to acquire Orion's legacy, she would've already done it.

"Nadine, you can't do this!" I cry. "Please don't! You can't kill your own brother!"

"He made his choice," she replies calmly. "He doesn't want to be part of this family, so I'm simply granting his wish."

"But you're only going to screw yourself!" I shout. "Without him, you and Luba are nothing."

Nadine doesn't care about her brother; it doesn't even appear as if she cares about her grandmother, which is odd because I thought she worshipped the woman. No, it looks as if Nadine wants all the power for herself. And she's about to eliminate one member of the competition.

Pressing down harder onto Napoleon's mouth, Nadine clutches her stomach. "We don't need my brother any longer," she declares. "Not now that I'm pregnant."

What?! *Pregnant?!* All this time we thought Nadine was getting fat, but she was just gaining weight because she's pregnant. Stunned, I feel my legs falter, and despite how in-human Caleb feels I grab onto his arm again to steady myself. Caleb? No. *No!* Did she seduce my boyfriend and turn him into her child's father? "Not Caleb!" I scream.

"I *could* be carrying Prince Caleb's child," she says. "Or . . . maybe not."

"Tell me!"

"I don't have to tell you anything," Nadine replies, chuckling softly.

"Nadine, I swear to God if you've done anything to Caleb to make him father your child, I will . . ."

"What, Dominy?!" Nadine interrupts. "What exactly are you going to do? Haven't you already learned that there's nothing you can do to stop me?"

Do not take the bait, Dominy! Do not let her change the subject!

"Have you noticed I'm not always the best student?" I crack. "Now, tell me, is Caleb the father?!"

"There are so many eligible bachelors in this little town. It really could be anyone," she says, smiling not only because she likes taunting me, but also because she knows she holds my future in her hands. "But don't ask me again, because you know how I like to keep my secrets."

When Napoleon flatlines, my first thought is how lucky he is to have finally escaped this madness. My second thought is to scream.

"Why?! Why are you doing this?!"

"Haven't you figured it out yet?" Nadine asks. "For the hunter to be truly powerful, there must be the hunted—you. That's why we came back here just before your sixteenth birthday when the curse began. You gave us reason and purpose and power."

I can just as easily take it away.

"And if I refuse to play along with your sick game?"

"You won't because Grandmother chose well," Nadine

replies. "The wolf is a hunter too, and as long as the wolf spirit lives within you, you won't be able to resist. You won't be able to stop trying to turn the tables and right the wrongs. You will hunt with as much passion and energy and guile as we will. But in the end, Dominy, we will win."

"You really think so?" I ask.

"Unlike you, Dominy, I understand that to be a true hunter you must be able to kill. It's the only way to maintain balance in the world," Nadine rationalizes. "And it's a lesson you'll never learn."

She has absolutely no idea that I'm becoming an excellent student. "Don't be so sure of that."

Napoleon's funeral was the exact opposite of Jess's, quick and quiet. No one spoke other than Father Charles who, since he didn't really know Nap very well, had a difficult time personalizing the sermon. Luba, Melinda, and Nadine, the three generations of evil, sat in the front row wearing respectful black outfits and claimed that they were too distraught due to their loss to have a repast. They thanked everyone for coming to the abridged church service, then slinked into a waiting black limousine, and probably drove off somewhere to celebrate in private.

Caleb and I sat on either side of Archie, who remained stoic throughout the brief ceremony. But when they lowered Nap's casket into the ground, he finally broke down and cried in Caleb's arms. I watched them with such pride. My friend and my boyfriend, two guys consoling one another, acting exactly how two friends should.

I wish I knew how to act. I don't know if I'll ever tell Archie exactly how Napoleon died, because I know that he'd want revenge. No, some things are better kept secret. Even if that secret can change a person's life.

"Are you okay, Barn?"

Ever since I broke the news to him that Napoleon died, my

brother has been acting strangely. Even he's noticed it. "Ever feel like you've been sleepwalking?" he asks. Before I can say yes, he continues. "I feel like this whole year has been a fog."

That's because when you haven't been furious with me about Daddy's death, you've been under a spell cast by Luba and Nadine.

"And how do you feel now?" I ask, looking up into his eyes that remind me so much of my father.

"Like the fog's lifting," he replies. His words are followed by a hopeful smile. "That's a good thing, right?"

Depends upon what's on the other side of the mist. "Yes," I say instead. "That's a very good thing."

And who knows, maybe it is. Maybe this is a sign that Barnaby is finding his way home; perhaps someday I'll have my brother back. Until then at least I have my friends.

The five of us are standing in a silent line in front of Napoleon's grave. Caleb, Archie, Arla, Jess, and me. We're thinking about the body of the boy trapped within the mahogany casket poised in its final resting place, but not yet covered with dirt. He started out as an outsider, someone we weren't sure we could trust, but once we got to know him, we knew that he was our friend. A friend who had the misfortune of having Nadine as his sister.

Just as we're about to leave, we hear a rumbling underneath our feet. The world is starting to shake, not enough to cause damage, but enough to capture our attention. Suddenly from the depths of the earth, from somewhere unseen, a swarm of butterflies rises up from the open grave and hovers over Napoleon's casket. It's a gorgeous sight, a cluster of bright, happy colors, reminding us of what was lying deep within our friend's soul.

I watch as one single butterfly, its wings a vibrant shade of violet, breaks from the crowd and lands on Archie's waiting finger. They stare at each other long enough for Archie to understand what's happening to him; he's being given a sign that his boyfriend is going to be okay. Tears slide down Archie's cheeks, but they're joined by a beaming smile. Then the butterfly lets go of Archie's finger to return to the group that's still waiting for him, and together we watch them as they fly upward into the pale blue sky.

If I didn't know it already, I know it now: The bee didn't kill the butterfly; she just gave him the freedom to live his life in a place where there's peace and joy and love. A place without a moon or stars. A place where the wolf and the girl could be free to roam without being hunted.

Maybe someday I'll find a place like that too.

Epilogue

The Weeping Lady is staring down at me. The leaves on her body are lush and deep green and vibrant. The warm early-summer breeze is making them tremble, so it looks like she's growing restless of her confinement. But it's just an illusion; she's not trying to escape, not just yet. For now, she knows this is where she belongs. She and I are very much the same.

"Freedom is coming," she says.

I know. I can feel it in my gut. "I'm not in any rush to leave," I reply.

The grass I'm lying on feels as soft as my fur. I spread my arms out and move them up and down, trying to create angel wings. But grass isn't like snow; it doesn't move; it can't be easily manipulated to create something new. Each blade of grass bends, but only briefly, then it stands up again as straight as a soldier. Like the honey that clings to the side of a jar refusing to let go, refusing to leave its body, refusing to leave everything that it calls home.

That's how I feel right now. Even though I have every reason to want to run away from here and never look back, I know this is where I must stay. For now at least.

This is where my life started, and this is where my life changed. And not only my life. Archie and Arla have both been damaged in ways we don't yet fully understand, thanks to Luba's vendetta. Pieces of my brother's life have been stolen by Luba. I don't know what they've done to him, what anti-Dominy seeds they've planted in his mind, but for now he seems more like his normal self. And worst of all, Nadine is pregnant with a son or daughter who has the potential to be born with a whole new kind of evil. But who knows? Maybe this child will represent hope; maybe he or she will inherit some of Napoleon's goodness and refuse to carry on her mother's legacy of black magic.

For some of us the journey is over. For Essie and Rayna and Napoleon, this is where their lives ended. But for others the journey is just starting. Caleb starts college next year. He hasn't decided where he wants to go, and as much as I'd like to be selfish and keep him close to me, I will not let him base his decision on what school to attend by its proximity to me. It's his life, his choice. I've finally realized that our invisible string is really, really long, so it doesn't matter if he goes to Timbuktu University halfway around the world; I know that we'll still remain connected.

It's crazy, despite all the heartache and doubt and sadness, the light of day really brings with it new hope. And an old friend.

Wrapping my finger around the sunlight dancing near Jess's body, I begin to draw the outline of a yellow Hello Kitty in the air. "Do you really think things are going to get worse?"

"I know they are, Dom," she replies. "This town of ours is about to become a war zone, and we're going to need all the help we can get." When she sees my air drawing, she squeals. "*Subarashi!* You made Yellow Kitty!"

For someone who just declared war, Jess seems very distracted.

"There's nothing we can do about it right now," she says. "So we might as well enjoy ourselves, embrace the calm before the storm."

"Or the sunlight before the darkness."

When I look up into the sky, the light is so strong I have to close my eyes. I can feel the warmth spread onto my face like armor; the sunshine clamps down onto my skin, and a burning sensation spreads out all over my body. It's like my transformations, but painless. When I open my eyes, the sun is no longer blinding. I can see through the sunshine; I can see past the light; I can see that beyond the glare and the pain and the despair there is something on the other side. I don't know what it is, but I know that it's waiting for me. Could be a curse, could be a blessing, but whatever it is, it gives me purpose.

I reach out, and Jess's hand is right where I expect it to be, right where she's always said it would be, waiting for mine. I don't want to move just yet. I want to lie here on the grass and bask in the sunglow for a while longer. But when I do get up, when I'm ready to continue my journey, I will remember what everyone—but especially Jess—has been trying to make me understand.

I'll remember that the wolf and I are inseparable. That no matter how lonely and scared and anxious we each may feel, we can never be alone. So even though I may not always feel blessed, I have to admit that this curse, with all the new and amazing and wonderful things it's shown and taught me, may actually turn out to be a blessing after all.